About the author

Gilbert Leslie is a first-time novelist who hopes his work will be well received.

DILLARD'S PROMISE

Gilbert Leslie

DILLARD'S PROMISE

Vanguard Press

VANGUARD PAPERBACK

© Copyright 2024
Gilbert Leslie
Cover art by Michelle Stadt.

The right of Gilbert Leslie to be identified as author of
this work has been asserted by him in accordance with the
Copyright, Designs and Patents Act 1988.

All Rights Reserved

No reproduction, copy or transmission of this publication
may be made without written permission.
No paragraph of this publication may be reproduced,
copied or transmitted save with the written permission of the publisher, or in accordance
with the provisions
of the Copyright Act 1956 (as amended).

Any person who commits any unauthorised act in relation to this publication may be liable
to criminal prosecution and civil claims for damages.

A CIP catalogue record for this title is available from the British Library.

ISBN 978-1-83794-160-5

This is a work of fiction. Names, characters, businesses, places, events and incidents are either the
products of the author's imagination or are used in a fictitious manner. Any resemblance to actual
persons, living or dead, or actual events is purely coincidental.

Vanguard Press is an imprint of
Pegasus Elliot Mackenzie Publishers Ltd.
www.pegasuspublishers.com

First Published in 2024

Vanguard Press
Sheraton House Castle Park
Cambridge England

Printed & Bound in Great Britain

Dedication

To my lovely wife and muse, Bunny, who started me on the journey to do what I've always wanted to do. My daughter, Jennifer, who has always inspired me. My son, Dillard, who helped me recognize the power of what makes a promise. My grandchildren, Sophie and Gabe, who always have love and time for me. And to the memory of my parents, Dillard and Doris Leslie, the ultimate inspirations for my life.

Acknowledgements

I want to acknowledge my editor, Juliet Brooks, whose insight and direction was immeasurable. My brothers Michael and Matthew Leslie, and my cousin Philip James, whose initial reactions and critiques helped shape my thoughts into expression.

Prologue

Ladera Heights, California

Friday, July 16, 2010
2.:18 p.m.

The heat from the afternoon sun broke through the lingering grip of the morning haze, as the cool as damp air slowly dissipated, allowing the rising heat and humidity to claim the day its unusual humidity began to wane. The lawn covering the hillside wilted in the direct sunlight, but a slight breeze graced the mourners atop the small hill aptly named Hillside Cemetery. Houston Jenkins and his wife Sabrina sat at the end of the receiving line next to his Aunt Ethel and Uncle Milton. Houston loosened the knot of his black-and-gray- patterned tie, which Sabrina had chosen for him. He smiled at her when she patted his knee and instinctively handed him a soft white kerchief for the sweat beading his forehead. He dabbed his face and dried his eyes under his dark sunglasses.

Guests embraced Ethel and Milton, expressing their condolences, before they moved on to Houston and Sabrina. Houston suddenly decided he should stand, balancing himself awkwardly along the slanted hillside as approaching guests reached out to take his hand and embrace him. He accepted their well wishes and feigned recognition of many of the older guests who recalled his rambunctious days as a small boy climbing over and under the church pews. "Your mother was always so proud of you," most would say, while others proclaimed, "Florence would brag about you all the time...." Listening to them revisit the joy his mother had given them brought comfort to Houston's ears.

Houston peered down the line to see the familiar faces of his work colleagues among the few remaining guests. His best friend, Israel Tate, greeted him and took his place just beyond Houston's shoulder, offering support and quietly ushering the few that lingered too long. Israel leaned forward and spoke just loud enough for both Houston and Sabrina to hear, "Just a few more people.... You doin' all right, Hou?" Houston just nodded as Sabrina returned their friend's concerns with a warm smile.

As the sun climbed to its apex, the few remaining guests waited patiently – —save for the one person no one in the receiving line appeared to recognize. The man walked briskly pasts everyone, directly to Houston. Uncertain of how to accept the abrupt encounter, Houston quickly took in the outline of his guest's face, searching for something recognizable. As the assertive guest grasped Houston's hand in a firm, calloused grip, Houston glanced over the wisps of grey in the short Afro and a small keloid scar extending from the left eyebrow. He glanced to his aunt and uncle, who seemed as surprised as he was, while the man leaned forward to bring himself closer to Houston's ear. A gravelly voice whispered with sincere regret and uncertain pauses.

"I, uh ... I was a good friend of your mom's," he said. "And I'm

sorry ... sorry I didn't ... I didn't follow up with Mrs. Jenkins when I heard the news about her. Mrs. Jenkins was a good woman ... I'm ..." He hesitated, then appeared to receive a renewed sense of purpose. "I'm Clee Jack."

But the confidence left as soon as it had come; the man's eyes darted and he suddenly cut his introduction short. Houston turned to see what caused the man to restrain himself. The calloused hand in Houston's scratched his palm as it pulled away quickly and the man turned and hastily departed into the throng of mourners.

Sabrina grabbed Houston's arm as Israel pushed past him, intending to follow the man just before he disappeared. Israel frowned. "What was that about?"

"I have no idea," Houston responded. "He started to say something. Then his eyes got big. Like he'd seen a ghost."

But it was by far not the most confusing thing he'd experienced since his mother's passing.

Later at the repast, held at the modest home of his in-laws, Houston changed into a comfortable shirt and jeans and pushed his anguish aside. As he made the rounds to guests, showing his appreciation, Sabrina's mother, Inez Sanchez, insisted he sit and eat. He brandished his second bottle of beer and left his plate of food untouched.

By the time the repast ended, Houston was numb to the phrase, "*You are in our thoughts and prayers ...*" The sound of it garbled in his head until it no longer sounded real or true. His thoughts drifted. He'd lost his mother. He'd been confronted by a mysterious guest. "*A good friend of your mom's ...*" The words bounced about in his head like a basketball walked up the court, slowly, methodically. He couldn't let it go. Each attempt to ask questions about who the man had been was interrupted with well wishes and stories of his mother and his youth. No one seemed too concerned about the encounter, and Houston began to believe it didn't matter.

Houston's Aunt Ethel had left him her car to use, and suddenly he wanted to leave. He slipped out without telling anyone, figuring he could use returning the car as an excuse to get out of the Sanchez home for a while. He needed to be alone with them and question them privately.

On the drive to Ethel's home, a few dozen questions vied to be the first. He wanted to ask all of them. Only one clear thought remained: whoever the gentleman was, he'd seemed to know something that Aunt Ethel and Uncle Milton knew, too.

A small space opened up within Houston's chest, a pinhole that would grow deeper and wider as he did his best to abate the realization that he knew nothing with certainty about his family history – —or the woman he'd called "'Mama'" for nearly forty years.

Chapter 1

Lafayette, Virginia

Thursday, July 17, 1975
10.:03 p.m.

It was a hot and sticky night in Lafayette, Virginia, and barely two hours since the summer sun had resigned its position over the city, departing with the heat and humidity it spawned and allowing the world to flourish in its absence. Dark clouds threatening rain moved westward, revealing a clear sky as those below basked in the light of a full moon. The songs of crickets and katydids competed in the distance, responding to the somber tick of the click beetle. The dimly lit streets produced elongated shadows, and an occasional gust of wind rustled through the treetops, dispersing the scent of decaying magnolia blossoms overcome by the heat.

Loretta Lynn's "'Country Bumpkin'" could be heard above the shouts and laughter emanating from Ray's Tavern. Don Stiles stepped out into the stuffy night air. His unbuttoned shirt revealed a thin concave chest with a small pot belly, and his rolled-up shirt-sleeves showed off tattoos and sunburnt skin. He stretched, taking in a deep breath before fumes of alcohol and tobacco escaped.

"I was only tryin' ta scare ''em inta thinkin' what could happen, if he didn't pay up," Don had told his cohort, Gary Pierce, earlier in the day. "I was just funnin'." It had been a pitiful explanation, and even he couldn't convince himself of its sincerity. It had been a long day of collection protection fees from small shop owners and harassing the occasional female clerk. Sometimes, he and Gary would get creative with their methods when a patron appeared reluctant; Don wouldn't hesitate to threaten the virginity of the owner's budding adolescent daughter or the sanctity of their marriage. It got results, inspired compliance. Gary wasn't above making similar threats of his own, either, which made Don feel particularly betrayed when Gary had snatched him by the collar, ripping the buttons off his shirt, pulling him off of that sweet girl. He'd thought about it all night.

Earning extra compensation was rare, but it was always split evenly between Don and Gary. However, this time, Don chose to retain both shares.

His resentment fueled his greed and helped him rationalize that he'd earned both shares; it had been his actions that led to the owner paying four months in advance. Don, having turned down Gary's offer of a ride home, felt once more for the small wad of bills in his back pocket and said he'd opt for the long walk.

A warm breeze cooled Don's sweating skin. He sauntered down the gravel street, kicking small rocks, allowing the buzz of alcohol to embolden him. Eyeing a special shortcut he'd created through backyards and alleys, he unwittingly began to move with urgency. His unfulfilled urges from the day's encounter began to stir inside him, and his fondness for the secret route encouraged his pace, because it afforded him a peeping tom's view into the bedroom of the blossoming Berlson girls.

Don leapt awkwardly over picket fences, stumbled into garbage cans, and quickened his pace after making more noise than he intended. The noise caught the attention of a German shepherd that was only too happy to make him pay for disturbing its slumber and property. It was either luck or providence that allowed Don to escape. Undeterred, Don made his way to the large sweet-bay magnolia tree, which grew in the alley directly across from the Berlson home.

Don's heart raced, ignited by the vicious chase from the shepherd and kept alive by the sight of a set of two bedroom windows at the back of the house. The lights were still on. He stopped his hurried breaths to listen for any sign that the girls were up and about, but he witnessed them bounce on their beds and throw pillows at one another.

The alcohol confirmed two of his immediate thoughts: one, he was undetectable behind the branches and blossoming magnolia; and two, that he believed the older one liked him watching. *I knows she seen me*, he thought to himself. *She jus' keep on dancin'. This time, I'mma wait till they sleepin'... Then I'mma collect my due.*

The sickly sweet smell of stale magnolias, spoiled meat, and rotting trash swirled in the humidity and would make anyone else reconsider their location. But Don closed his eyes for a brief moment, picturing the Berlson girl. He unbuckled his belt and lowered his jeans. The rush of excitement made him forget where he was. The stillness of the night air echoed his heavy panting. Dead leaves crinkled behind him, and if it wasn't for the sudden gush of warm blood streaming down his leg and soaking into his jeans, he would have finished.

Don never felt the blade that slid across his exposed thigh. He reached for the source of the sudden wet warmth with his free hand and felt the exposed blood flow. Dizzy and confused, he panicked, sticking his fingers into the lacerated flesh and seeing his blood-soaked hand glitter in the dense moonlight. Black blood dripped from his fingers and ran down his wrist. His knees buckled and he tried to fall but couldn't — something, or someone, was holding him upright. The last thing Don saw was his own bloody hand as someone forced it into his face.

He made little noise as the hand was used to muffle his screams. A latex-gloved hand kept Don's firmly in place over his nose and mouth. Don tried in vain to turn his head, see his attacker, the one who had crept up behind him without a sound. Don tasted his own blood and the last bit of bile as a serrated blade sliced through his gagging throat.

***

Deputy Abel Grimes had seen a crime scene before, but there was a difference between empirical knowledge and applied knowledge – —and Grimes had just found out the hard way. Photos in class could not hope to compare to the real thing. He returned to the alley, after surrendering his breakfast to the street twenty feet away, to fisted snickers and piercing stares.

Sheriff Beauregard '"Bo"' Clayton approached Grimes. "Betcha never seen that in them fancy schools o' yours, eh, college boy?" he said. "Now, just come 'round ova here and have a look, and tell me whatcha think." He looked back at the scene and whistled. "Shee-it! Betcha ain't gonna forget this, no matter how long it takes."

Sheriff Clayton was a large, barrel-chested man with a booming voice and a propensity to spit and swear. Though his methods were questionable, he upheld a reputation of law and order and kept the peace. The citizens relied upon his authoritarian application of the law. His particularly provincial way of dealing with people seemed to endear him to the townspeople, and it was something Grimes wanted to emulate. Grimes liked his style and believed he could cherrypick Clayton's good, influential behavior as he overlooked his other attributes.

Abel Grimes was actually studying to become a lawyer, but he

hoped to do a few years on a rural police force in the meantime. He had aspirations for political office and believed he could build a résumé through backwoods policing and glad-handing voters. As a realist, Grimes knew politics in the South weren't always as genteel as they appeared. If he was every going to become governor, he might as well start learning how to form alliances now.

Grimes cleared his throat and spat out the last bit of sour taste, which he quickly tried to wash out with a stick of gum. "Was he like that

... um ... when they found him?" he asked, voice cracking.

But Clayton was already bellowing at two other deputies. "Dawson, if I gotta say one mo' time to clear them goddamn dogs outta here, I will personally tie you to that tree myself! Ernest! Get me ... Who was it saw the body first? Jacob?"

No words came from the deputies, but a slight, wiry man named Jacob Woods stepped up. Jacob Woods was one of two garbage men who worked the southern side of town. He had a reputation for digging through whatever he could get his tobacco-stained hands on, scrummaging for something of value. He explained to the sheriff how he found the body lying behind trashcans just before seven that morning, and he'd let his dog Rusty go to investigate.

The sheriff gave Jacob a once-over, following the smeared bloody paw prints running down from Jacob's shirt to his pant legs. "It don't look like he put up much of a fight. See here ..." He pointed to the victim's right hand. "Ya can't fight back with one hand holdin' your pecker like that. Looks to me Don was eyeballin' them girls again." He turned to his deputies. "Ernest, go ahead an' cover up the body. Won't get any evidence if we don't stop them flies makin' a home in it. Dawson, go on over to the Berlson house, tell 'em I'mma stop by."

Deputy Dawson spoke out the side of his mouth through muffled snickers. "Looks like he got kill't chokin' his chicken." The sheriff shot him a look, and Dawson quickly ended his laughter and headed for the Berlson home.

Sheriff Clayton pulled Grimes to the side, away from eavesdroppers.

"How long you think he's been there like this?" Grimes asked.

"I don't rightly know. I ain't no expert," Clayton said. "But, knowin' Don was prob'ly watchin' them Berlson girls again, could be since last night." Then, changing the subject, he motioned for Grimes to come closer. He stared straight into the deputy's eyes, as if he were weighing a confession. He spoke in a soft yet determined voice. "I don't want this to get out."

"What's that, Sheriff?"

"Jacob had a note he took from Don's top pocket. Now, there ain't a lot of blood on it, so my guess is, it was put there after he was dead."

"What does it say?"

Clayton handed it over. "Take a look and lemme know whatcha think." As Deputy Grimes unfolded the note, Clayton whispered, "Here's where yer edge-ya-cation betta come in handy."

Abel Grimes saw three numbers, two words, and two symbols he couldn't identify. His stomach turned as he realized the intended threat — that this wasn't over.

11 down 32 go.

Chapter 2

Beverly Hills, California

Friday, July 16, 2010
10.:47 p.m.

As Houston drove westbound on Wilshire Boulevard, he vacillated between whether or not he should even stop by his aunt's place, as planned. As much as he tried to quell the rising anxiety in his chest, teetering between his will and his emotions, he was determined not to let it get the better of him.

Houston had left his in-laws' home in Miracle Mile, explaining that he needed to return his aunt's car, but he immediately regretted lying to his wife. What he hoped for was to be alone, to clear his mind. But now, sitting in the car, he wanted to talk to his wife. Sabrina had the uncanny ability to reach into his heart and help him express himself without the need to protect his vulnerability.

He sat at a Beverly Hills intersection, waiting for the light to change. A sudden burst of honking horns shocked him into reacting to the green light, and when he pressed harder on the gas than necessary, he shot across the intersection. Bright lights and the whoop of a police siren sent a chill through him. Unsettled, Houston pulled over to the curb, cursing himself for his momentary relapse.

Houston checked his breath against his palm. He'd had a couple of beers at his in-laws' before leaving, but he was certain he was below the limit. He popped a mint, just to be safe – —not wanting to give the officers any additional reasons to fuck with him.

The patrol car stopped and two policemen stepped out and flanked either side of Houston's vehicle as they approached. He watched them in his rearview and sideview mirrors. Passing cars slowed to witness his personal debacle, and it was all made worse by the officers keeping their high beams and red-and-blue diestress lights on, which lit Houston's face for passersby. Embarrassed, Houston kept his head down. With a glance in the mirror, he saw one officer approaching more slowly, while the other had removed his revolver from his holster.

Houston began a practiced routine. He lLowered both the driver and passenger windows, sat erect, put both hands on the steering wheel. This wasn't the first time he'd been stopped while driving. Trying to appear relaxed and calm, Houston smiled and leaned to the window, admitting to the officer that he'd inadvertently accelerated due to a nervous twitch in his right foot. One of them, Officer Reynolds, chuckled and asked him for his license and papers. He shot a knowing glance to the armed officer, who holstered his weapon as Reynolds lifted his own hand from his own weapon.

Houston announced he was going into his wallet. "Oh, uh," he

started, remembering. "This isn't my car. It belongs to my aunt, so I don't know where she keeps the registration. I'm going to look in the glove compar—"

"What do you mean, this isn't your car?" Reynolds interrupted. His hand returned to his revolver. "You have a habit of speeding off in other people's cars?"

"I don't have a habit of doing anything," Houston responded, pausing. His hand shook ever so slightly as he offered up his driver's license.

The second policeman, Officer Edwards, pulled up the license plate and corresponding registration. He made a gesture at Reynolds, and they talked behind Aunt Ethel's Lexus. While they were occupied, Houston took the chance to look for the registration. Instead, in the glove compartment, he found the notes he'd put together for his mother's eulogy.

The last thing Houston wanted was to cry in front of the policemen. He buried his head into his hands as if he could push any tears back in. He lifted his head and gazed out onto the boulevard. Her last words played over and over in his mind – —the words that had changed everything, left him in turmoil, turned his stomach.

She'd been coughing, attempting to clear her throat, but between every few words she wheezed with shallow breath. She seemed to want to say something, tell Houston a deathbed secret, but talking proved painful for her. As she'd coughed blood into a tissue and took the deepest breaths she could manage, Houston tried to make her comfortable and urged her not to talk.

"There are things about the past that are probably better left unsaid

... but I think you should know," his mother coughed.

"Save your strength," Houston said. "We can talk about this later, Mama."

"I'm not your mother," she said. "I'm your grandmother."

Even as he'd been seeking to comfort his dying mother, Houston would later ridicule himself for not listening to what she had to say. He checked her vitals, her blood pressure indicator and heart monitor, as they began to decline. Though the source of his pain, they were also a distraction. He wasn't certain whether the fluorescent lighting had changed or his mother's color had taken on an ashy pallor.

"Let's get a doctor in here," Houston offered, pressing the distress button. His heart rate spiked as he was engulfed by fear, and the antiseptic smell of chlorine bleach made him feel sick.

"Listen, baby," she managed. "I just want you to know the truth.

I'm so sorry I didn't tell you this before ... but I wasn't sure you could handle it."

"Don't worry about me, Mama," Houston said. "I can handle ...

We'll talk later." He tried to remain calm as the words left his mouth, but his heart was sinking. Only once had he allowed himself to think about her passing, but he'd always imagined it would be in her sleep, and not in bed awaiting death as she gave one last confession. When he finally had a chance to look back on it all, he realized he'd been in a state of shock. For the first time in a long while, he thought about his life without a father. His peripheral picked up movement through the small door window, causing him to turn quickly in desperation for help.

"I know you can, baby." She stopped to catch her breath. The door flung open as a phalanx of doctors and nurses rushed a crash cart into the room.

"She can't cough and she's spitting up blood, please!" Houston told them quickly, fear rising in his throat. He wiped his cheeks dry, not having realized they were wet. He held onto her hand.

Mustering the last bit of her strength, Florence Jenkins reached beyond the nurse checking her pulse. "Baby, listen," she said. "Your mother died while you were born." Florence turned her head, as if the mere thought of her daughter provided her with some small reprieve. "She and her ..." She tried to continue, but the attending physician forced an oxygen mask over her mouth and nose.

The doctor said they could only offer her comfort now. Florence struggled to speak as her eyes rolled back into her head. Carefully, Houston let go of her hand so the nurses had full access. When another distress call echoed throughout the hospital, pulling some of the nursing team away, one doctor and one nurse remained to call the time of death. Houston, now free to take her hand again, felt her last faint squeeze.

"Out of the car, please."

Officer Edwards opened the driver's side door, brandishing a canister of pepper spray. Houston, brutally ripped out of his thoughts, raised his head to take in his surroundings.

"I'm going to tell you one more time to step out of the car, sir."

Houston, now seeing two additional squad cars and a police motorcycle had been added to the mix, responded nervously, "I'm sorry, I didn't hear you. Why do I have to get out of the car. What did you pull me over for? Just give me the ticket and let me go!"

"Step out of the car, sir, now!" Edwards moved the pepper spray closer to Houston's face.

Houston jumped out of the car, meeting the policeman's glare.

Something in him was determined to regain control of his feelings. Reaching six foot two and tipping the scale at a svelte two hundred pounds, Houston stood a full five inches over Officer Edwards and spread his shoulders. Sensing trepidation, Officer Riley signaled to the other officers and moved in.

"Have you been drinking tonight, sir?"

"What?!"

"Have you consumed any alcohol this evening?"

"I had a couple of beers earlier, but I'm not even close to drunk."

Officer Riley frowned. "Sir, would you mind stepping over here up on the sidewalk to take a test?"

"Yes, I would mind," Houston replied. "I didn't have that much to drink."

"Step over here, sir. I will not ask you again." The other six officers closed in on Houston.

"No, I will not!" Houston shouted. "I'm not drunk!"

The Friday night party crowds were in full swing, but slowed to watch the spectacle. Realizing he was the focus of unwanted attention, he decided to take another approach by lowering his voice.

"I'm sorry, my mother died, and I was ..."

But the officers were past any type of conciliatory offering Houston had, and they went to restrain him.

"Hey! Get your hands offa me!"

"Sir, you know that if you fail to take a sobriety test, you leave me no choice but to place you under arrest?"

"Arrest?!" Houston protested. "For what? For accidentally pressing the gas pedal a little too hard? You can't arrest me for that. You can give me a ticket, but you can't arrest me!"

Ignoring him completely, Officer Edwards took a firm grip of Houston's arm as he pulled out his handcuffs and read him his rights and the reason for his arrest. His behavior behind the wheel at a stoplight, his apparent mental lapses, and his admission of alcohol consumption presented reasonable cause for arrest.

As he was placed into the back of a squad car, Houston's pleas fell on deaf ears. Cursing to himself, Houston wondered what his in-laws would say to his wife – —when she came to bail him out of jail on the night of his mother's funeral.

Chapter 3

Lafayette, Virginia

Saturday, August 5, 1944
7.:38 a.m.

As the morning sun crept into the bedroom window, Dillard Houston Jenkins awoke missing the warmth of his wife's body but catching the sound of grease popping and the aroma of grits, eggs, bacon, and biscuits wafting in from the kitchen. He still reached out, hoping to pull her next to him.

Dillard tried not to let the thoughts of being away from Florence ruin the few moments they had left to share. He couldn't bear the thought of her being alone, being without him. They had been married four years, but he had been gone once before – —married less than six months before he'd had to report to Shreveport, Louisiana, for induction and boot camp. In his heart, he knew Florence was a strong and independent woman who wouldn't ask for help. He'd asked his sister Ethel to stay with her while he was gone, and, to himself, he added a quick prayer for his own safe return.

In just a few months, Dillard was to be shipped out to the European theater in the 761st Tank Division of the US Army as a member of the Black Panthers. A gunnery sergeant, he was well built, six feet tall, with broad shoulders carved from granite – —and anxious to prove to his country that the Negro soldier was fit, ready, and able to defend the freedoms he'd been taught in practice but denied in reality. They'd been running circles around the white divisions in maneuvers, and now they were getting the chance to show their stuff.

He didn't get a chance to finish his thoughts before Florence bounded into the room and tackled him back into bed, with a smile as wide as Dillard's shoulders. He welcomed her with kisses. No words needed to be spoken.

Eating breakfast at the table, laughing and smiling at one another, they felt like newlyweds, giddy and hopeful. The bond of their love was unbreakable, and each day felt as exciting as the very first.

Dillard finally spoke, ending their blissful silence. "When I get back, we're gonna get a bigger place with a garden. A place where you can raise kids and won't have to worry about cleanin' someone else's house no more."

Florence stared into his eyes and smiled. "You just come back in one piece and I'll do whatever you want."

"You do that now," he laughed.

The thought of Dillard not coming back hovered over the house like a promise waiting to be broken. Neither of them would allow the other's thoughts to linger on any negativity. It was as if they could sense the impending doom, but thought their love and devotion to each other would keep it at bay.

War is hell, and the promises of the dead reside in purgatory, well after the last bullet has been fired.

Tuesday, March 13, 1945
2.:41 p.m.

My love,

You would be so proud of us, baby. General Patton himself gave a speech that got us all inspired. He said he asked for us, because he heard we were the best there is, and that he only works with the best. I am extra proud to be a soldier today!

Of course, reading about how big you're getting and the baby moving inside you has my head and heart doing flips. I just can't get over the fact that I'm going to be a father. That just means we'll have to whup them Nazis even faster so I can get home to my babies.

We've been fighting every day now for four months and we're pushing back hard. We've lost only a few of our men and the general continues to encourage us. It won't be too long now, baby.

Your adoring husband

Florence's heart swelled with pride even as worry gnawed at her heart. "Oh, Dillard," she murmured to herself. "Please be careful...."

"Girl, you gotta stop torturin' yourself." Ethel stepped into the living room with a glass of milk and a sandwich. "You been readin' that letter over and over for hours now. You need to eat somethin' to keep that lil' baby strong. You know you don't want Dillard comin' back to see how you were so worried about him that somethin' happened to the baby."

"Uh huh, yeah, you're right," Florence replied, only half listening. When Ethel brought her the sandwich, she finally looked up. "I can't thank you enough, Ethel. ForTo delayin' your trip to California to be here with me until the baby comes."

"Well," she said, "I know neither one of you would expect anythin' less of me.... And since Dillard and his two best friends are all in the Army, we're all we got."

Slender and strong, with uncommon grace and deliberate beauty, Ethel Jenkins was Dillard's older sister. She and Dillard had been instilled with the values of family and taught to always look out for one another, and that extended to Dillard's wife. When both of Florence's parents had been killed in a tragic automobile crash – —an "'accident'" never investigated further – —she had been welcomed by her neighbors, Henry Dillard and Mabel May Jenkins. They embraced and raised her as if she were their own, and had been thrilled when she and Dillard, showing the kind of love and mutual respect for one another, developed the foundations of a lasting relationship.

Florence would blossom into the strong, beautiful woman her parents had hoped for, five foot eight with the figure of a Stradivarius and the deep, even, skin tone of chocolate. She was blessed with guile, wit, intelligence, and charm, and a clear understanding of her physical beauty.

"Remember," Ethel continued, "we look after each other. No matter what."

"Yeah, I know," Florence sighed. A grateful smile crept across her glowing face. "You all have been there for me in ways I can't come close to payin' back."

"Girl, who's askin' you to pay somethin' back? You know I don't do *anything* because I have to ..." She pushed the sandwich closer. "Now, no more fussin'. Eat this, then we both need to get some sleep. You're eatin' and sleepin' for two now, you got to be respectful of what's goin' on in there."

Florence began to eat, but when tears welled up in her eyes, Ethel returned her look. "What is it, baby?"

Florence smiled broadly, trying to hold back the rush of emotions beginning to erupt. "I know I should have said this before, but after my parents died, I never felt the loss of a family," she said. "I know that sounds bad, but Mama, Pa, Dillard, you, you're the only family I've needed. You were all so good to me and I couldn't imagine my life without you all. I guess it's bein' pregnant without havin' ..." Her appreciation suddenly developed into worry. "I'm afraid Dillard's not going to make it back, and I just don't know what I'd do...."

Ethel closed the distance between them and embraced Florence, kissing her softly on the forehead. "Florence, you finally called them Mama and Pa!" she chided, as she brushed aside Florence's tears. "Come on, you know you're the little sister I've always wanted and the girl of Dillard's dreams. We got a combination in you that we never could've hoped for. I am so happy for the two of you. I only wish Mama and Pa were here to see their grandbaby bein' born. And since they ain't, we're not gonna talk 'bout it no more." She rubbed Florence's shoulders. "We're lookin' ahead with this baby. And his Auntie Ethel is gonna to be so proud to have him come all the way out to California to visit. I might even let him bring his parents." She smiled as she looked deep into Florence's eyes, hoping to abate the fear of Dillard not returning. Finally, she gave Florence a look. "Hell, why are we so sure it's a he? T— that could be a girl you carryin'."

"Oh, don't say that," Florence said. "I promised Dillard he'd be a
boy. Besides, if it's a girl, she's gonna be pretty big. Look at all hthis stomach;, a girl couldn''t do that. Could she?"

"What are you askin' me for? I'm just the auntie. You the mama!"

Both of them started to laugh, and the sadness that had crept into Florence's heart was contained by the hopes and dreams she now carried for her baby.

***

In the spacious, antebellum Dunning home, Jasper and Evelyn shared the customary drink after dinner. He stared intensely at his glass of scotch, rattling the ice every so often to drown out her words.

"It was the very least I could do for her," Evelyn went on. "After all, her mother did work for my family for several years before she died. What else could I have done?"

The question lingered in the air, and Jasper considered a response. He studied his older wife of five years and said, as sincerely as he could muster, "I think you handled that as well as anyone would expect you to. I'm sure that, uh ... *colored* girl was very grateful for your intervention."

"'Colored'" had not been the first adjective that came to mind, but he knew better than to use a racial slur in front of Evelyn. She thought she was so much better than he was because she came from money, yet still tried to treat coloreds like they were equal to everyone else. The thought made him sick, and as she continued to gab and he continued to drink, he tuned her out and wondered when the conversation would be over.

As an aspiring Southern gentleman, blessed with his father's
conniving and charming ways, yet lacking his enterprising spirit, Jasper had decided early on in life that he would get rich the old-fashioned

way – –he'd marry into it. But only after their marriage did Jasper learn that Evelyn's father, Benjamin Cartwright, had cleverly left his fortune in an irrevocable trust only to be passed down through the Cartwright bloodline. Since Evelyn was Cartwright's only offspring, if Jasper wanted the gravy train to last for the foreseeable future, he was going to have to impregnate her, and soon. But Evelyn was closing in on thirty- five and it wasn't safe for a woman to have her first child at that age. Jasper figured he'd have at least two more years of trying, and if that didn't work, he'd have to pray she outlived him.

Jasper had used his good looks and gift of the gab to forge his way into the hearts of many young ladies, but Evelyn, a few years older than he and a less attractive woman than he was a man, was wealthy enough to provide. Though not entirely unattractive, she never felt comfortable putting up a fuss when she was aware she had never been the kind of woman to turn a man's head. Evelyn, he knew, would never admit to herself that Jasper had married her for her wealth and position.

Jasper tuned in again. Evelyn was telling some story about helping out two coloreds at the department store. *The cashier should've called the sheriff,* he stopped himself from blurting out, but he contained his remark as a murmur to himself.

Evelyn stopped. "Did you say something, Jasper?" She glanced at his glass. "Are you still drinking? It's almost bedtime." She then continued, not bothering to wait for his response. "So I stood there and told the manager that if he wanted to continue to have my business, he had better do right by these ladies."

A forced smile stiffened Jasper's lips, which he swiftly relieved with a drink. Concentrating once more on the scotch, he let more of Evelyn's words slip by as easily as the liquor slipping across his tongue and down his throat. He crossed to the mobile wet bar to pour more and offered to make her another martini. She refused and kept talking.

"Her mother used to work for my family before she died in a tragic accident," Evelyn sighed. "Leaving the poor thing an orphan. And now she's pregnant and her husband's away fighting in the war. Can you believe that, Jasper?"

The last thing this country needs is niggers in the Army. I don't mind them bein' the ones gettin' killed, but heaven forbid they get used to shootin' and killin' whites. We're gonna have a helluva time gettin' them back in their place ...

"Is that so?" he said instead. "The Army, eh."

"Yes, and her sister-in-law is here for only a short time, then moving on to California."

"Well, then she should go with her."

"She just might," Evelyn said. "But when her husband comes back from the war, he's going to finish getting his engineering degree from some Negro college –, I didn't get the name. And they'll go somewhere they can get a job. I suspect they'll have better opportunities in California to get work and raise a family."

"Just what this country needs," Jasper muttered under his breath.

"More uppity jigaboos."

"What was that, Jasper?"

"No," he said, louder. "I'm just decidin' whether or not to have another drink."

"Well, don't drink too much. You don't want to upset your stomach. Don't you think it's time we get to bed?" Evelyn let the words ruminate as the silence grew deafening. She raised her hand to rest on the string of pearls adorning her neck as she continued, unabated. "Anyway, it was good to see her. She is a remarkably beautiful woman… for a colored girl, I mean. Her mother was such a nice, quiet woman. And my parents just loved her. They were so disappointed when she left our employ. I've asked her to bring her baby by once she's delivered. I swear it'll be a big baby. She's a little over seven months and her belly is so large."

Evelyn fell quiet for a moment in pensive thought. Her eyes followed Jasper across the room as she allowed her hand to drop slowly beneath her neckline towards her breast, directing her index finger to outline her cleavage under her dress.

She quickly raised her fingers to her lips and admitted, "Oh, Jasper, I do want a child of my own. I do."

Jasper took a full swig, emptying his glass. Then, more out of self-preservation than anything else, he found the will within him to turn on his empathetic charm as he embraced his wife with forced warmth. "We will, my darlin'," he said. "We will."

***

Monday, April 23, 1945
6.:57 p.m.

Ethel was busy cleaning the kitchen after breakfast and was starting to wonder what was taking Florence so long at the door. They had both been sitting at the kitchen table when the neighbor and landowner, Sundae Eldridge, came walking across the front yard to the porch. Earlier, she'd stopped by the Jenkins home to check in on Florence. And while the three of them shared a cup of coffee, she offered to pick up any letters from Dillard at the post office, after recruiting Dr. Foster to pay a home visit to address her husband's illness. Now, both Florence and Ethel perked up to see her carrying what appeared to be a few letters in her hands as she walked up to the door.

When Florence didn''t immediately return, Ethel thought she had been dragged into a long conversation with the nosy elderly woman. But Sundae Eldridge was in a hurry and had no time for conversation, as Dr. Foster had arrived. Sundae told Florence she didn't notice any letters from Dillard, just a few bills and just one letter from a Private Andrew Walker.

Florence, just nodded and took the envelopes from her as dread enfolded her heart and tightened its grasp. She turned away in silence and had barely closed the door when she slowly and uneasily opened the letter from Andrew Walker, Dillard's childhood friend and fellow soldier. She pulled out the seven-page letter and quickly glanced over it to get a gist of what was in it, hoping beyond the despair swelling in her chest that it was good news.

Andrew Walker had always lived in the shadow of Dillard Jenkins.

Andrew looked up to Dillard, and Dillard looked after Andrew. They grew up together and found their third musketeer in Benson Harris, and the three were practically inseparable. Spending their summers picking peaches on Mr. Sutter's farm, then swimming in the creek that ran along the back of his property. The boys stood up for Dillard and Florence at their wedding. The three of them went to college together and later on were drafted together.

She concentrated on the letter's neatly scripted words. Time seemed to come to a complete stop. Silence enveloped her, she felt her temperature start to rise, then it all went black. The next thing she saw was Dr. Foster leaning over her, telling her she was about to give birth.

April 23, 1945, was a day Florence Jenkins would always

remember. It was the day she gave birth to beautiful, healthy twins: Leeland and Leesa Jenkins. They came into the world with all the hopes and expectations a loving and adoring mother could ask for – —with one heartbreaking, tragic exception.

Chapter 4

Lafayette, Virginia

Friday, July 18, 1975
2.:47 a.m.

Gary Pierce dragged himself and his aching head to the front door of his rundown one-bedroom apartment at the disrespectful sound of insistent knocking. "The fuck is it now?" he muttered under his breath. A thirty-three-year-old man with no prospects, Gary could add up the total number of his friends on two fingers, and both of them knew not to cast their shadow on his doorstep without a prior invitation.

Brazen and cocky and wearing nothing but a pair of two-day-old boxers, Gary reached the front door somewhat heated. "What is it?" he called through the door. "Whad-dya want?" The knocking only continued, growing more intense.

Was it the police? Had Don done something stupid? Worse – —had Don ratted him out for something? Gary mused, and figured the police would have announced themselves.

Ruling out the police, Gary stepped back to turn on the kitchen light, prompting roaches to scurry to and from the places he'd never thought to clean. He grabbed a large, dull, rusty kitchen knife, the one he used to scale fish. He approached the door and yelled, "What the fuck do you want? Yer at the wrong door, so git, b'fore I git you!"

The knocking stopped as abruptly as it had started. Gary assumed whoever it was had realized they were knocking on the wrong door and run away. Gary shut off the kitchen light and went back to bed, taking the rusty blade with him.

Not twenty minutes later, just as Gary had been falling back into a deep sleep, the knocking started up again – —harder and louder. Gary jumped out of bed with a worse headache and an attitude to match, head and heart pounding in unison. "I'mma kick the shit outta you!" he yelled on his way to the door.

Gary raised the knife. It clearly wasn't the police. But then it occurred to him that it could be his one friend crazy enough to willingly incur his anger – ––Don. Don must've pissed somebody off and run scared, all talk and no bite, deferring to Gary as his backup.

The knocking stopped, but Gary was sure it was Don. Don could use a scare for daring to knock on his door so late in the night for no good reason. He swung open the door and took a swipe with his knife, thrusting himself out into the dim darkness. "Don, you a shit!" he yelled. At least he'd get a laugh out of this.

But nothing happened. No one was there.

Gary, wielding his knife in the most menacing manner he could muster, stepped outside and turned right and left, which made him dizzy. He'd had a few too many drinks at Ray's with Don, and his head was reeling. Though Don had had no shares to split and Gary had spent most of the night sulking, Don had offered free drinks, and turning down free drinks from Don was like turning down a handshake from the president.

A cool breeze made him realize he was more than half- naked outside and in the dark. Momentary fear engulfed him once again, and he tried to recall his swagger. Slowly but assuredly, he stepped back into his dank apartment and quickly shut the door.

Gary laid his arm across the door and let his head lean against his forearm. He took a deep sigh of relief and let his heartbeat slow down while he eased his grip on the handle of his knife. His head continued to pound. The night was cooling off and he wanted desperately to go back to sleep. The knocking must've been some bratty kids playing a mean prank, but hopefully he'd scared them off. An aspirin and a gulp of water from the tap would do him good.

Gary turned towards the kitchen just as a clean blade quickly sliced his neck from right to left. He coughed up blood and reached for his throat, dropping his own rusty blade and all pretense of bravery. He tried to get a look around, but saw nothing but the glistening reflection of the blade as it came around for another swipe across his leg. His screams only gurgled up blood as the last few seconds of his life passed into the dismal darkness of his musty apartment.

It wasn't the odor emanating from Gary's apartment late that afternoon that caused the landlord, Mr. Sturgeon, to venture in. It was the complaints from his neighbors that Gary had once again parked his car in the wrong spot, blocking access to the other assigned parking spots. Two complaints too many this time made it impossible for the landlord to ignore Mr. Pierce any longer. Always-late-on-his-rent Gary Pierce was getting an eviction notice nailed to his door that evening, when it fell open, letting out the smell of unwashed dishes, rancid alcohol, and blood from the sickening, mutilated body of his murdered tenant, and causing Mr. Sturgeon to have apoplexy on the spot.

***

The call came in around six thirty6:30 p.m. from a hysterical Stanley Sturgeon. In all his years of cheating tenants out of every nickel and dime he could think of, he had never been a witness to anything this horrendous. When word got out of a note pinned to the body, Clayton wanted to contain as much of it as he could. He radioed a couple of deputies himself, then made a beeline over to the Standard Arms apartment complex, putting himself actively in charge and getting things moving along fairly quickly. Soon, a photographer and a coroner were already in place, the body was being bagged, and additional deputies outside were keeping the gathering crowd at a distance.

But the sheriff was eventually wrangled aside by a reporter for the *Lafayette Gazette*, Percy Hawkins – —an overly aggressive and slimy journalist who wanted to make the national news before he turned thirty. He had the looks for television and the drive to get there, and he knew an opportunity when he saw one. He'd do anything to get words on the record, and was always willing to pass out a few bills if necessary. When news of a note found on the scene leaked out, he wasted no time heading to the Standard Arms.

But what Sheriff Clayton didn't want was national attention. He couldn't have the state police or the FBI nosing around in his case, undermining and challenging his authority. He'd had Deputy Dawson on the lookout for Hawkins, warning him not to release any information else he put the fear of God into them. But the God of Money was working overtime behind his back, and Deputy Dawson, a sniveling coward who propped up his grit and authority behind his badge and gun, was not to be trusted with anything. A five-dollar bill was all Hawkins needed to open up the floodgates, so it wasn't a big surprise to Sheriff Clayton when Hawkins asked him about the note.

"What note you talkin' 'bout, Percy?" Bo asked, shooting a look towards Dawson.

"Sheriff," Percy stated with a timid façade. "I have it on good authority that we have a serial killer out there, and it's my responsibility to notify the public."

"The only person you betta notify is your boss," Clayton retorted. "Tell him I will arrest the two of ya if you go writin' anythin' 'bout some serial killer. Ya hear?"

"Now, Sheriff," Hawkins cautioned,. "Let's not get ahead of ourselves. here. I'm hoping for an exclusive. I want to tell this in a way that everyone knows you're in charge of things here in Lafayette. Nothing like this has ever happened here before. This ain't the big city, and we don't harbor any weirdos. So," he said, unfolding his notepad and applying pen to paper, "what do you make of this, Sheriff Clayton?" Caught up in the uniqueness of the situation, Bo reluctantly succumbed to his fears. "Honestly, I'm just tryin' to figure this one out myself. Hell, no whites been kill't here in over ten years. Now we got
two dead within twenty-four hours, an' a threat for more."

"Ah, so there *is* a note?" Percy chimed in, catching Clayton off guard.

"I nevva said so. I tell you what, though. I'll get you all the details if you can tell me what you find with that famous snoopin' you do. You work with me, an' I just might work wit-chu."

"Gonna deputize me, Sheriff?"

"Hail no, son!. I'm just tryin' to get ahold o' this b'fore Abel gets the FB of I involved and I lose catchin' the sumbitch myself."

"All right, Sheriff. I'll come by your office tomorrow and we'll discuss our strategy. But don't hold anything out on me. The press can be like a woman scorned if we feel we're being lied to."

"Boy, you threatenin' me? Cause if you are, I will lock yer ass up an' throw away the goddamn key!" Clayton fired back.

"No! No, Sheriff, no such thing," Percy said quickly. "I was just tryin' to convey that I can be a vital part of this investigation if we're both upfront with what we have."

Clayton lifted his hand menacingly, cutting the reporter off. "If I says I'll do somethin', ya betta believe I damn sho' will." He leaned in closer to Percy, looking him up and down, and whispered, "I hope I'm conveyin' my meanin'." He gave a wry smile as he steered the reporter down the hallway.

It was almost eight thirty8:30 p.m. by the time Abel Grimes showed up, at which point Sheriff Clayton, pissed with Hawkins, was ready to leave it.

Grimes had been following up on some leads regarding the note
left in Don Stiles's pocket. He saw the case as a potential springboard for notoriety, anticipating assistance from the FBI in an all-out manhunt. Sheriff Clayton, of course, had told Grimes he'd been watching too much TV and reminded him that he, the sheriff, was still in charge of this investigation—if and when he wanted the federal government involved, ol' Bo would be the one to make the call. "Just try to find out what them scribbles mean," he'd commanded.

This had taken up most of his day in and out of the library, running down newspaper articles and studying microfiche, trying to find any connection he could to the squiggles and swirls at the bottom of the note. He knew he would eventually have to get the FBI's help, and he would find a way to do it, even if the sheriff refused to ask for it himself.

When Clayton saw Grimes approach just then, Clayton motioned for the deputy to join him outside the victim's cramped apartment. The sheriff spoke in an emphatic, strained whisper, not wanting to be heard by any spectators.

"We're doin' this by the book of Bo," he told Grimes. "I can't have shit like this goin' on in *my* town. I know neither one o' these boys was what you'd call model citizens.... Prob'ly pissed somebody off real good. But goddammit, this is *my* fuckin' town, an' I won't have it!"

But the next morning, Bo and Abel read the front-page *Lafayette Gazette* headline: 'TWO DOWN, TWO TO GO.' Clayton paced the floor behind his desk, livid. "I'mma string Dawson up by his balls! You believe this shit?"

"No, I can't," was all Grimes could bring himself to say. Sheriff Clayton gave him a look as if to say his question had been rhetorical.

Clayton knew now the extent of Percy's knowledge about the case, and the damage Dawson had done. Clayton stormed his way out of his office, leaving Abel behind, then abruptly turned around and shouted, "Get your ass in gear, Grimes!" Grimes jumped out of his seat and quickly fell in behind the sheriff.

Deputy Clyde Dawson leaned against the wall outside the makeshift kitchen, clasping his favorite mug as he took a bite out of a glazed donut. He didn't get a chance to pull the remaining piece from his mouth when Clayton shoved it back in. Dawson gagged and turned to see Clayton's beet-red, steaming face. Dawson dropped his mug, spilling hot coffee down his leg and yelping as his pants were drenched and his mug shattered on the floor. Any witnesses to this display of Dawson shrinking away in his lack of courage would tell you his pants were wet before the spill; Dawson would vehemently deny it. Deputies Grimes and Ernest were able to hold the sheriff back from any further aggression.

"Sheriff Clayton!" a voice called from the end of the hall. The

station operator, Clare Miles, a frumpy woman in her fifties, came running down and yelling at the top of her lungs. "Sheriff Clayton! There's a gal on the phone who says she's got information about the murders! She's a nurse an' said she worked with them two boys who got themselves kill't!"

Silence fell over the room as Dawson picked himself up and Clayton and Grimes ran to pick up the call. Bo picked up the line, which was now disconnected, and yelled at Clare to get the nurse back on.

Chastised by a beleaguered hunch, Grimes grabbed the paper again to satisfy his intuition. He picked up the second note, now in a plastic envelope on the sheriff's desk. There was a difference in the way Percy had written the note in the paper. And now, in the second note, there was a new word next to the block letters of DEATH: "'makes'," in small letters beside a series of hieroglyphs. Grimes pored over the new clues and pointed them out to Clayton, who watched Grimes write some notes on a notepad.

"One down, three to go. Death," he said of the first note. "Now two down, two *two* go. Death makes."

Just as Clayton was about to yell at Clare to find out her progress on getting the nurse back on the phone, she stuck her head in. "Sorry, Sheriff," she said, "but the line went dead!"

Chapter 5

Los Angeles, California

Sunday, July 18, 2010
1.:53 p.m.

Houston Jenkins kept himself busy cleaning the apartment and listening to the radio, distracting himself from his turmoil. For now, with everything going on, he felt it best to separate himself from his grief. He could pretend it didn't exist and worry himself with mundane, meaningless tasks, taking time to override the temptation to sink into mourning by focusing on what was most practical. When the phone rang, he picked up with a reluctant "Hello?", as he already felt rising dread at the thought of confronting someone possibly calling to give him best wishes, unintentionally throwing him into his grief once more.

"Hey, what's up?"

Immediately, Houston recognized the voice of his best friend, Izzy. "Nothin' much. I'm just trying to give my head some room."

Best friends since the first grade, Houston Jenkins and Israel "'Izzy'" Tate shared a relationship as close as brothers. It was no wonder most people thought they were related, but apart from their similar caramel brown hues, the two shared no real resemblance. Growing up with Houston, Izzy had been small for his age, while Houston, large at the time, had to look out for him until Israel's growth spurt late in high school brought him up to six foot two. He could now meet Houston's gaze eye to eye. Izzy, a real charmer in spite of his best intentions, quick with a humorous quip and an icebreaker, was the kind of guy whose mouth could get him into trouble almost as fast as he could get himself out of it.

(The two of them had only been at odds once, close enough to consider fisticuffs, during their sophomore year of high school. Neither of them could explain how or why it had started, but one thing led to another, resulting in led to them pushing and shoving each other around the schoolyard as a gathering crowd grew impatient, goading them on to hit each other, demanding blood.

All but one: Alvin '"AC"' Cooper, definitely '"the wrong nigga to fuck with'." AC maneuvered his six-foot-four, 225two hundred and twenty-five pounds between Houston and Izzy with a soft yet commanding, "Stop!" As a hush fell over the crowd, he leaned in close to them. "Just what in the fuck's up with you two?. Y'all like brothas. You don't treat your brotha like that. Go an' make the fuck up or I'll kick both your asses!"

As Houston and Izzy reluctantly shook hands, any intensity that remained dissipated as the crowd trickled away, and AC gave his final warning to the two of them. "I don't ever want to see shit like that again. Not between you two." They felt as though they'd been scolded by a parent rather than a peer, and stranger than their reaction was AC's involvement in the first place. He'd rarely spoken to either of them. Yet no one questioned AC, and Houston and Izzy's bond was even more deeply cemented by AC's edict.)

On the phone, Izzy got right to the point, infusing energy into the conversation. "I heard your ass got pinched by the coppers? What the fuck is up with that?"

"Nothin', man. I'm not feelin' that right now."

"Yeah, well, if you didn't do nothin' wrong, they wouldn't've grabbed you."

Houston returned with vigor, "Those assholes tried to get me for drunk driving. I wasn't even close to being drunk. So I refused the sobriety test and they took me in."

Israel chuckled on the other end. "What did you expect them to do? Let you keep driving while *black* and *drunk* in *Beverly Hills*? I know you're sad, but you ain't crazy now, too."

Houston rolled his eyes. "But get this. My in-laws came down to get me."

"You shittin' me?"

"Seriously! And they're being nice to me. Not just because-my- mom-died nice. I mean, you're-our-son-now nice."

"What'd you do, promise to divorce Sabrina?"

"Dickhead."

"You might wanna talk to your wife, then."

"I keep meaning to talk to her about it," Houston replied, "but she probably put them up to it in the first place. I don't want to get on her case."

"So, where is she?" Israel asked. "You were so down when I called, I'm guessin' she's not there.?"

"She's at her parents';, home later today." That reminded Houston.

"Hey, I need a favor. I've gotta stop by Alvin's place later and I was hoping you could give me a ride."

"A ride? Why can't you drive?"

"My license got suspended."

"Suspended? Didn't you get it back?"

Houston sighed. "They took my ass to the station, tested my blood, and took my license. I've gotta wait to appeal to the DMV tomorrow."

"Ain't your wife an attorney?" Israel asked. "I think if they test your blood and it doesn't exceed the limit, they have to drop all charges and give back your license. Right? I bet your in-laws have it."

"They wouldn't do that to me," Houston said, pausing. "Would they? They would've told me that last night."

"Check with Sabrina;, I'll bet they've got it. Police probably gave it to them so that your black ass wouldn't drive amok in the streets. Goddamn, man!" Izzy exclaimed. "Why didn't you just walk the fuckin' line and be done with it?. Shit, I don't feel like drivin' to the 'hood to see AC's crazy ass. Muthafucka scares me. He's always pullin' some crazy shit."

"Izzy, seriously?" Houston groaned. "Come on, man. Alvin ain't gonna do shit to you. He likes you. I just need to see him for a bit."

"Did I tell you that crazy bastard pulled a gun on me?"

"About a thousand fuckin' times," Houston laughed.

"Well, here's a thousand and one – —that crazy nigga was high as a fuckin' kite and I was givin' him a ride home and he wanted to stop at the liquor store and get himself a beer."

"Yeah, I remember."

"Well, that muthafucka takes out this big-ass gun and tells me to get him a beer or he'd—"

"He was only kidding!" Houston interrupted. "He was too fucked up to do anything. Fell asleep when you got back in the car." He laughed and shook his head. "Listen, are you gonna take me or what?"

After a long pause, Israel relented. "Yeah, I'll take you."

"I need to run by the store to pick up a few things, too," Houston said. "It's my night to cook."

"'It's my night to cook and I want to run by the store,'" Izzy mimicked. "I swear, ever since you got married you've become Mr. Perfect Fuckin' Husband. Get a job and you'll be husband of the year."

"I got a job, jackass. I'm working in Sabrina's old law office downtown. Rebuilding their network."

"How long'll that last without a certification?" Izzy said. "I keep tellin' you, you can get certified in less than two years. Then I could get you a permanent job with my company instead of that contracting shit you do. C'mon, man."

Houston began to feel exasperated as Izzy steered the conversation towards his career complacency. "I was in school three nights a week and working a law office during the day, and I only dropped out last quarter because my mom got sick. The fuck are you talking about? I've got one year left and then I'll get my degree and study for the bar."

"If you had your CNA you could still go to school and make even more money than your wife does," Izzy said. "You've got your BA and a ton of IT experience."

"So it's about the money."

"It's *always* about the money, you know that. You know, I'll bet this is why her parents don't like you. Your jobs don't last and you're damn near forty and still in school. They see their daughter supporting you, and she even got you this job! Her dad's old school;, you know he don't like his daughter supporting El Negro."

"I'm a late bloomer."

"Late bloomer my ass," Israel responded. "You were too comfortable working for your auntie, thinking you were gonna take over her business. You got complacent and it caught up with you."

"Okay, okay," Houston insisted, "I heard enough of that from my mom;, I don't need to hear that shit from you. The fuck you call me for anyway? To harass me?"

"Matter of fact, I did. Who better than me to help you get your ass in gear?"

"I know you still love me," Houston said. "Come on, take me to AC's and I'll let you buy me dinner."

***

At the well-kept home of Roberto and Inez Sanchez, Sabrina filled her parents' cups with coffee in their remodeled kitchen.

"So, *mija*, when are you going to tell him?" her mother asked, bubbling over with enthusiasm. "This is so exciting!"

Her father, on the other hand, was more reserved. "What are you going to do when he shows his true colors and leaves you on your own?"

"Come on, Dad, do you really think he would do that?"

"I do," he said. "I think he's one of those who's afraid of hard work and won't rise up to the challenge a marriage and family will bring."

"Roberto!" Inez called out, raising her voice in disapproval. "You know he's not like that;, don't say that. He's a good man who loved his mama and worked hard to take care of her for the last years of her life. To put up with something like that takes determination and patience." She returned to Sabrina with support. "Don't worry about what your father says, *mija*."

"I know Dad never really warmed up to Houston," Sabrina conceded. "He's not Dad's kind of guy. But I know in my heart he'll come to see Houston the way I do." She sidled up to her father and put her arms around him. "*Yo se mi oso de peluche*. I know he's not exactly the man you would have chosen for me, but I love him and he loves me. We're committed. And like I told you before, I'd like to have it, but I don't *need* your approval."

Roberto would never let on that the remark stung, that she could wound him if she wanted. He was proud that she was a strong and determined Chicana who would speak her mind and choose her own way – —even if it was against his wishes. "Well, *mija*, we shall see," he said. "I will be there for you, but I'm keeping an eye on him. I just don't want to have to get him out of jail again in the middle of—"

"Oh, Daddy, you know it wasn't his fault," Sabrina said. "He wasn't drunk. He was mourning his mother. Those officers overreacted. I bet they wouldn't have arrested him if he wasn't black."

"I don't want to hear that," her father said. "Those officers were doing their jobs. Houston should know better than to mouth off to the police in Beverly Hills. Even I wouldn't do that!"

"That's because you know how they'd treat you, and you just don't want to fight it anymore."

"I don't want to fight *you*," Roberto said. "So I will finish my coffee and not say anything else about it."

"That's not what I want," Sabrina retorted. "I want you to give us advice and tell us what you think. I just don't want you to disparage Houston. He already thinks you and Mom don't like him."

"Me?" Inez spoke up. "Why me? I've never been mean to him. Why does he think I don't like him?"

"You both know you two haven't warmed up to him. He calls you Mr. and Mrs. Sanchez and you haven't even corrected him to your first names, let alone Mom and Dad. It's been four years."

Inez shot Roberto a plea for help. "We just thought the marriage was a little ... sudden, *mija*."

"We thought he got you pregnant," Roberto admitted.

"Are you kidding?" Sabrina shot back. "What kind of daughter do you think you raised?"

"We know exactly what kind of daughter we raised," Roberto corrected. "And we are very proud of you."

"Yes," Inez chimed in, "very proud of you."

"And we trust in your judgment, even if we don't always agree. But do know that we'll be there for you, one hundred percent."

Sabrina sighed. "But can you be there for Houston, too? He's part of me, now. I'm the only family he has left. I need you to make him feel like family."

"He has his *tia* and *tio* and they are very good people," Roberto insisted, defensive. "I get along very well with Milton and Ethel."

Sabrina's eyes began to well up with tears. "I'm not talking about them. I'm talking about us, and I want my husband to know that he doesn't just have me, but that he has you, too. That he can rely on you. Just like when you picked him up last night – —that made me feel so good. It made Houston feel like you do really care for him."

Inez closed the distance between them, wiping away her own tears and tossing Roberto a look of warning. Taking her cue, Roberto seized the emotional moment.

"Of course we'll be there for the both of you." He then forced a change of subject. "This is not a time for tears! We are celebrating!"

"So, *mija*," Inez added. "When are you going to tell him?"

Sabrina collected her thoughts. "Well, tonight is his night to make dinner, so ..."

"You mean he makes dinner for you some nights?" Inez interrupted, sardonic. "How did you get him to do that? It would take an act of Congress to get your father to cook dinner for me."

"If I ever cooked for you, you would have stopped cooking for me altogether. I would have ruined you for anyone else's cooking, even your own. And I couldn't do that to you, *mi amor verdadero*."

"I'll tell him tonight," Sabrina resolved. On the inside, though, she was still having second thoughts.

"Good!" Roberto exclaimed. "Then if he is the man you say he is, we won't have any more of this drunk driving mess."

***

While driving home to their midtown apartment, Sabrina considered the best way to give Houston the news. He was still torn up about his mother's passing, but she wondered if this could be just the thing to cheer him up. She imagined sitting at dinner with him, fork in hand as she told him. They'd talk and think about names together. It would bring them closer.

Sabrina knew her first child would be a strong, beautiful boy. It had to be – —everything felt right. And if it were a girl, then they would be blessed just the same. She left her thoughts drift for a moment, dreaming of brushing the curls of her daughter's hair. She stopped herself – —it would be a boy, and that was it.

She heard voices as she approached the door and announced she was home. She found Houston in the kitchen and greeted him with a warm hug and a kiss, holding on to him for a while, hoping he would get the hint that she wanted a moment alone with it. He caught on, but quickly turned her towards their guest.

"Izzy bought us dinner from the Mandarin Inn!"

"You didn't have to do that, Israel," she said, surprised. "That's so sweet of you!" But she gritted her teeth and cut her husband a look. She tugged on his shirt, hoping to communicate that she wanted a private word.

She headed into the bedroom, and Israel watched her go. When he found Houston staring at him, Izzy sputtered, "What? Go on, she wants to be alone with you."

"You don't know what you're talkin' about."

"Hey, if my woman came home and hugged and kissed me like that, I'd want to be alone with her."

"If you had a woman, you would know that you always get greeted like that," Houston said. Slight lie.

"Not like *that*," Israel said. "Better get your ass in there."

Houston finally followed her to the bedroom, opening the door and catching a glimpse of his wife as she stood by the closet, changing her clothes and now down to her undergarments.

Even though they had been together for a few years, at times Houston still felt guilty sneaking peeks at her in undress. Sabrina was everything he could have wished for, if he had really known what he wanted. Her black hair fell into soft ringlets that bounced whenever she moved, adding emphasis to her every word, and the color nicely complemented her sun-kissed skin and soft features, her soulful brown eyes and a set of lashes Maybelline would die for. Her curves did not disappoint.

"Sweetheart," Sabrina said finally,. "I was really hoping we could have the evening to ourselves tonight."

"I'm sorry, baby." Houston sidled up behind her, wrapping his arms around her. "I was running late and didn't think I'd be able to cook in time. Israel offered to buy us dinner. More like buy you dinner and let me have the crumbs, but you get it."

Sabrina giggled. "That's sweet," she offered. "I don't know, I'm just tired and don't feel like entertaining. I was at my parents' all day and I was looking forward to just having you." She pressed closer to him with a firm amount of pressure.

Realizing his options, Houston made one of the quickest decisions he could possibly make. "I'll send him packin'."

"No, don't do that," Sabrina said. "He bought us dinner. That would be rude of us. We can have our night later, right?"

Houston softly kissed her neck. "I have absolutely no qualms about being as rude as I can be right now."

Sabrina pushed him away with a playful smile. "We both know which head of yours is doing the thinking. Go out there and set the table so we can eat."

"Izzy would understand," Houston implored. "Believe me!"

"It's not right, love. You know you wouldn't like that if you were in his shoes."

"You see, that's where men and women differ. A guy, a best friend, would never get in the way of you gettin' good with your girl, unless he was a punk. And Izzy ain't no punk."

"Go on!" Sabrina said. "Better get out there before he thinks we're doing something else, and I don't want it to be awkward when I come out."

She pushed him out and slammed the door. When Houston finally returned to the kitchen, Israel grinned. "Sounds like somebody's in trouble," he sang. When Houston didn't reply, Izzy backtracked. "I can go home and leave you two. Don't want to cause any problems."

"Hey, man, don't go. We're good."

Sabrina entered the kitchen in sweatpants and one of Houston's T-shirts. Houston brought over three beers and opened them all just as Sabrina interrupted, "I'm gonna skip the beer tonight, honey. I'll just have water, if you don't mind."

"But I already opened it."

"Sorry, sweetheart, I should've told you earlier."

Houston's irritation was palpable. "Yeah, okay."

The conversation got going as they chowed down. Sabrina entertained the thought of Houston guessing she was pregnant, but she also wanted to steer him and Izzy away from the idea. Now wasn't the right time; she wanted to be alone with him when she did it. Eventually, Houston relaxed and even started to tease.

"Izzy was so busy doing close to nothing," Houston explained. "He practically begged me to hang out."

Israel laughed dryly. "You better thank your wife," he commented.

Sabrina shot him a look of *Please, don't*. Israel shrugged, but Houston caught on.

"What?" he asked. "What's going on with you two?"

"Nothing, sweetheart," Sabrina said. "I just may have mentioned to Izzy that you were still kind of down and asked if he wouldn't mind checking up on you. That's all."

Taking the opportunity to jab at Houston, Israel responded, "Yeah, nigga, she said your ass got pulled over and couldn't handle everything comin' down on you."

"That's not what I said," Sabrina interjected. But Houston seemed to grow irritated, so Israel pedaled back.

"Hou, look, Sabrina just asked me to check up on you. She was worried, what with you being stopped by the police, on top of dealing with your mom." He tried to smile. "I was just fuckin' with you, because you were bein' kind of a dick to her about the beer."

"I wasn't being a dick," Houston said defensively. "Was I?" He tossed a look to Sabrina for support. She shrugged.

"Yes, you were," Izzy said. "But that's between you two. I just thought it was uncool. She just cares about you. But you're still doin' that solitary shit that used to piss me off all the time, thinkin' you can keep all that shit inside and not tell anyone. Well, nigga, if there's anyone to tell, it's her!"

Sabrina tried to defend herself and her husband at the same time, but Israel didn't buy it until Houston calmed down and admitted they were both right. "I know it's been tough on you," Houston said. "I guess I didn't think about it."

"You get deep into your own world," Israel added.

"Yeah, okay, I can admit that," Houston said. "It's just that I've got a lot going on, and I ..."

"That's just it, Hou," Israel said. "Your whole fuckin' life, you've had a lot going on. You wouldn't tell me, but your mom just died. You can't keep that in forever. You *need* to at least tell *her*."

Sabrina, in the middle of a conversation about her that didn't include her, still marveled at the way Israel was able to be truthful and speak without recrimination, dissipating the tension. She admired their friendship. She knew Houston had a tendency to bottle himself up – —but she also knew she wouldn't stop trying to uncork that bottle.

After a while, Sabrina excused herself, feeling queasy. This did not escape Israel's notice, and he nudged Houston. "You should go join Sabrina. I'm gonna take off anyway. It's getting late and I've got somewhere to be."

"Where are you going?"

"Why?" Israel paused. "Oh, you must really think I don't have any women in my life."

"Other than your mom? No," Houston snickered. "If you've got a woman, confess."

"What I've got is nunya business. Besides, the only woman you'd better be worried about is probably upchucking in the bathroom. Better get in there and have a talk." Israel made his way to the door and turned to Houston as he followed. "Tell Sabrina I hope she feels better. I'll check up with you later."

"Cool," was the only response Houston wanted to give. But his heart, and Israel's earlier words, urged him to continue. "Thanks." Israel just smiled and nodded as he walked out the door.

Houston joined Sabrina just as she had come out of the bathroom and was now entering the bedroom to change into pajamas. She caught Houston staring. "What?"

"I'm a lucky man," he said. "And ... I just wanted to say thank you for trying to understand me."

"Honey, I know you're going through a tough time," Sabrina offered. "*We're* going through a tough time.... We're all we have, and I know you'll open up to me when you're ready. I won't force you to."

Houston made his way across the room and wrapped her up in his arms. Sabrina, internally, wanted to direct his attention elsewhere, but his intention was adamant. Their intimacy had taken a back seat to Houston's emotional turmoil, and though she wanted his attention and hoped to direct it elsewhere, she wouldn't want to be selfish. Everyone had their own way of grieving, and coping with loss. Still, she welcomed the renewed attention.

"Is Israel still here?" she managed to say before he tried to kiss her.

"No," Houston said, muffled as he then buried his face into her neck. "He's gone."

Accepting that the moment was upon them, Sabrina placed her palm between his legs, making circular motions. A long, low hum was all he could muster. His blood stiffened him as he pulled her closer. Houston knew they were beyond words at the moment. He kissed her softly on her neck and shoulders, and his hands slowly massaged her welcoming body as she lifted his shirt over his head. He picked her up and carried her over to the bed and laid her gently on the comforter. He eased himself on top of her, gently caressing her skin as he removed her pajama bottoms and underwear, slowly moving himself up between her thighs and kissing them gingerly. Sabrina started to tingle all over.

Houston took his time and Sabrina enjoyed the moment. Houston reveled at her firmness before he slowly moved his hands over the unfamiliar plump of her belly. He cautioned himself before moving further, staying there to kiss at her navel while he took in a deep breath of her, exhaling in soundless tears, as he allowed some of his grief to escape, slowly, carefully uncorking the bottle.

Sabrina raised his mouth to hers and kissed him passionately, acknowledging his silent tears. He embraced her and entered her, returning her passion. Their eyes met in a soulful, transfixing gaze as they moved in unison. Sabrina clasped his face and wiped away his tears as he let his arms go limp and their bodies merged together. She forced his eyes to meet hers and peered deeply into his soul, mouthing, "*I love you.*" Houston sank his head into her neck and once again breathed her in. He felt comfort in her smell.

Houston rolled over to his side and pulled her close. She slid her leg onto his and he gently massaged her belly. Sabrina smiled and wondered if this was the moment for her own truth. But she resisted. Houston was happy right now.

He turned his head to kiss her forehead and told her, "You are the reason and the love of my life. I love you."

She pressed her face into the side of his chest and took a deep breath to take in his aroma, and she knew – *—This is what I've always wanted.* She smiled to herself and relaxed. They held each other and fell asleep there, in each other's arms.

Chapter 6

Lafayette, Virginia

Monday, May 17, 1954
10.:45 a.mm.

A portable transistor

A small box-sized General Electric radio became the focal point during a break in a morning conversation between Florence Jenkins and Gladys Taylor. Florence tried to push the conversation forward, but Gladys shushed her as a doting parent would shush their favorite child, placing her hand gently on Florence's exposed forearm. Gladys was anxious to hear the announcement of the Supreme Court's decision in the case of *Brown Brown v. Board of Education*. The radio announcer proclaimed they were interrupting their usual morning programming to plug into the CBS national radio feed for details on a decision. The morning sun gleamed across the white walls in the antiseptic kitchen as the radio crackled with static. Anticipation mingled with the fear of continued segregation, and both women fell silent.

The monumental announcement did not fall on deaf ears as Gladys quickly turned down the raspy sound and searched for a reaction from Florence, who was sitting across from her at the small kitchen table where their half-finished cups of coffee had now grown cold. Florence returned Gladys's gaze with a half- smile, one more of fear than celebration, and Gladys tried to cheer her up. "Flo, you know what this mean?" she said. "This mean your kids get to go to that fancy white school where you take Ashley. You don't hafta go 'cross town to them colored schools no more."

Florence left the table and headed towards the kitchen sink, where she stared out the large window into the yard lined with red osier dogwoods. She couldn't put her finger on it, but she could sense that things wouldn't be resolved as easily as enrolling her kids in the same school Ashley Dunning attended. She could feel a shift in the air around her, and for a moment she held her breath. The gravity of the decision weighed heavily on her shoulders. It wouldn't just be hope that escalated— —fear would rise, through both colored and white communities. *Lord, please let my babies be safe.*

Not getting the reaction she wanted, Gladys spoke again. "Chile, you know what this mean?"

Florence didn't want to give voice to her fears, however, so she pushed them deep into her heart and forced a smile, feigning agreement. "I'm sure that once everything works out, they might all be in the same school at the same time."

Gladys picked up on Florence's apprehension and beckoned her to come back to the table. "Now don't you worry none," she said. "Mrs. Dunning has taken to your two almost as if they was her own. If she got anything to say, she will make sure your kids be fine."

"Things will be just fine," Florence lied to reassure herself. "After all, it's the Supreme Court that voted unanimously. The Supreme Court!"

Gladys held Florence's hand and offered a comforting smile. "You'll see, baby. Your children will be betta 'cause of this." Sensing a need to redirect the conversation, she returned to the topic before they'd turned the radio on. "You know how's I knows she knew, 'cause I hear her tell Mrs. Parker she was so embarrassed. She knows she was bein' laughed at. Mrs. Parker tells her to give him an ultimatum. An' since he got nothin' of his own, he took that lil' girl to that doctor they got."

Thankfully distracted, Florence followed along. "So what happened to the girl and her baby? Did they just disappear?"

Gladys hesitated. "All I knows is, she was taken to the club an' never came back."

Uncomfortably, Florence started to ask more questions, but Gladys cut her off to offer her opinion of the doctor – —with a look of disgust and the taste of bile on her tongue. "The doctor come by one evenin' lookin' for Mr. Parker. But Mr. Parker was real mad, called him greasy an' told him he betta keep what he knows to hisself."

Florence felt a chill creep up her spine. She lifted her head up, scanning the dull whiteness of the room, glancing across the white-laced tabletop past Gladys's shoulder into Courtland and Genevieve Parker's living room.

Gladys Taylor took care of the Parkers' plantation-style home just south of the Dunnings. Gladys and her husband, Homer, had originally been in the service of Genevieve's family, the Lakes. The Taylors were a wedding gift from Genevieve's father. Neither of them could remember a time they weren't servicing a member of the Lake/Parker family. A small, wiry woman, Gladys could often be found wearing her husband's dungarees, pulling up weeds and pruning the flowers. Homer, similarly small, had been a stable hand before working for the Parkers. A quiet and religious man, Homer believed deeply in the promise Heaven held for those who suffered in this life.

Gladys liked to remind Florence of how she and Florence's mother, Ernestine, would share a cup of coffee most mornings when things slowed down between breakfast and lunch; how fondly Ernestine made it her duty to teach Gladys how to read and write; how taken she was with her mother and indebted to her for her kindness and strength. She had been doing this kind of recollection more often than before, and Florence guessed this was a sign of Gladys resigning herself to having lived a life she would not have chosen for herself, rather than a sign of her age. The Supreme Court's decision to end segregation in schools seemed to have rewarded her hopes for change.

Ready to open up about what she was feeling, Florence finally

began to voice her concerns about the ruling just as Genevieve Parker entered the kitchen. She walked with urgency, then slowed when she noticed Florence at the kitchen stove.

"Oh, hello, Florence," she issued with a slight lilt of annoyance. "I didn't realize you were still here." She quickly turned to Gladys without waiting for a response. "Gladys, I need you to fix some food for Courtland and three of the council members for supper, and have Homer run it over there right away. I don't know if you heard about that awful

decision this morning, but I'm certain the men of the Council will need to discuss the ..." She trailed off, then turned to Florence. "Doesn't Evelyn have something for you to busy yourself with?"

Her message was clear, and Florence didn't need to hear it twice. She started towards the kitchen door and met Gladys's half- smile from the pantry. She shared the embarrassment Gladys felt, but wasn't sure who she was more embarrassed for. They exchanged pleasantries and Florence quickly left through the servants' entrance in the back. She walked down the long driveway, through the gate, and headed back to the Dunning mansion.

Florence was preparing a dinner of meatloaf with mashed potatoes and carrots when Evelyn Dunning made a hastened appearance into the kitchen from the study. "Florence! How are you, dear?" she asked with genuine affection and interest.

"I'm fine, Missus Dunning," Florence replied warmly.

Evelyn was a godsend to Florence. The relationship they shared with Florence's mother, Ernestine Davis, was one Evelyn cherished and tried to emulate with Florence. Ernestine had been Evelyn's confidante and counselor, the wise elder to the shy and earnest young Evelyn, guiding her through her awkward years. Evelyn's mother would never have approved of the depth of their relationship, the closeness shared between a Negro maid and a child of Benjamin Franklin Cartwright; and when news of the deaths of Sam and Ernestine Davis reached the Cartwright home, Evelyn's mother's announcement carried a pinch of delight that didn't go unnoticed.

Florence now saw Evelyn attempt to hide the nearly empty tumbler in her hands. Evelyn had begun the habit of drinking earlier in the day, now regularly sipping a small glass of brandy before lunch. There were no doubt problems in the Dunnings' marriage, but Florence couldn't bring herself to pry. The complete care of Ashley had fallen into her lap within a few months of Florence beginning work as their maid. It was obvious that Evelyn had let go of her responsibilities as not only a parent, but a wife as well; Jasper Dunning moving out of the master bedroom made that even clearer.

"Are you all right?" Florence asked, gesturing to the tumbler.

Evelyn did her best to appear in the moment. "I'm fine, dear," she said. "When you pick up the children this afternoon, would you be a dear and stop by the five-and-dime for me for some antacid?"

Florence wanted to warn her about the effects of her drinking, but she pushed her feelings down. "I'd be happy to," she said. "Is there anything else I can do for you while I'm out?"

"No, dear. Just make sure ..." She drifted off. She seemed to peer deeply into Florence's eyes, then smiled and cleared her throat. "Just make sure you tell the store manager that I will settle our account for last month in the next week."

"I will."

"Oh, and Florence? Be careful driving home with the kids," Evelyn added. "I have a strange feeling about this Supreme Court decision, and I just want you to be extra careful. Ya hear?"

Florence felt a tinge of relief knowing that she wasn't the only one unnerved with the news of the day. With Evelyn's drinking, she would have thought Evelyn wouldn't concern herself with much of what was happening beyond her bedroom.

As she sat behind the large steering wheel of a '51 Packard Mayfair, Florence suddenly wondered how Dillard would feel about all of this. But he wasn't here.

She vividly remembered Andrew Walker's details of the way Dillard had died, as if she had been there, next to Dillard as he crawled on his belly in the mud under the wheel base of the tank. As if her heart rate increased with his own with each shot he took. As if the sweat on his brow was hers, sweeping across her forehead, as if she could see the blood spilling from the German soldier's chest. As if Florence could make him shoot again to make sure he was truly down. Dillard had always been a crack shot and took it for granted that a kill shot would only need one to work.

After shooting the five soldiers he'd encountered, he rolled out from the Sherman tank to check on his brothers-in-arms, when a single shot ricocheted off the turret and pierced his neck. Florence desperately wished she could have been there to stem the flow of blood, apply pressure, but she would have had to feel the blood under her palms and

would have had to see the panic on Dillard's face. Florence could feel her heart scream for help as his fellow soldiers struggled to save his life. She could feel the warmth of Dillard's life spill through her fingers. She felt Dillard's body collapse into her arms as he fell against the tank, before hitting the ground. The last German to die had aimed in a desperate attempt and missed the mark but hit the side of the tank, not living long enough to see how his lucky shot had turned out, yet breaking Dillard's promise to return to his wife.

A knock on her windshield interrupted her reverie. Florence looked up to see the ruddy, lean face of Deputy Beauregard Clayton.

Florence could not hide the initial repulsion and fear that changed her expression from plaintive sadness to anger to powerless fear. The tears in her eyes began to wane; she'd felt a sense of peace and acceptance until Clayton had abruptly destroyed her passive calm. All memories of her humiliation and fear of the lack of control in her life rushed back into her body, ripping apart the melancholy lull she'd managed to descend into.

Deputy Clayton knew he struck fear into the hearts of many

coloreds, and that suited him just fine. Clayton believed fear was respect. He didn't hold back a smile when he saw Florence's reaction, but he didn't seem to recognize her as much as she recognized him.

Just as suddenly as Clayton had interrupted Florence, Evelyn Dunning interrupted him as she stormed down the driveway in her evening robe and slippers. "Get away from her, you hear?" she demanded, her screams only discernible as she got within earshot. "Your business is with only one Dunning, and that is at the Council Hall and nowhere near my home. If you need any further reminders, you can discuss that directly with the sheriff, and Mr. Parker, and Mr. Dunning!"

Florence relaxed somewhat. Deputy Clayton was genuinely afraid

of Evelyn Dunning, and she made her dislike of him quite obvious. He obliged to her shouting and turned away, his determined countenance suggesting his time would come.

Florence stepped out of the car and ran to Evelyn's side, urging her to go back home. She started to speak, but her words were imperceptible under her coughing. Evelyn reached for her, and Florence did not resist,

taking Evelyn's feeble frame and urging her inside.

After she brought Evelyn back inside and then collected herself, Florence drove to the all-white school Ashley attended. It was a breeding school for Lafayette's éelite from gradtes one to twelve. Those who attended were the children of trust funds of tobacco and cotton mill dynasties – —family names that had been in and led Lafayette since it was founded in 1802. Florence wasn't allowed to enter the school grounds; she had to wait at the gate for Ashley to come out as other parents and guardians shoved and bumped into her as if she didn't exist. Florence had learned quickly to avoid eye contact.

When Ashley came through the gate, he didn't hold back his excitement and ran to her with open arms, embracing her as any child would embrace their mother after a long day's absence. Florence beamed, despite being well aware of the contemptuous eyes watching their exchange. She quickly ushered Ashley into the back seat of the Packard and circled to the driver's side. Before she could get in, a balled-up brown paper bag flew across her face.

"Don't think those Yankees on the Jew court are gonna tell us
where our children can go to school!"

Florence didn't try to find the voice's owner as she swiftly shut herself into the car and drove off, keeping her head down and eyes forward.

"Mama," Ashley said. He only called her that when his parents weren't around. "Don't worry. I will protect you."

"I'll be all right," she lied.

Florence was constantly impressed by his perceptiveness, and she believed he really would protect her if given the chance. Ashley, a delightful seven-year-old boy with sandy blonde hair, crystal-blue eyes, and an alabaster complexion, was blessed with his father's good looks and his mother's kind demeanor. But, unlike his parents, Ashley was full of questions with none of the airs his father wished he had. Unabashed and inquisitive, he'd ask the questions polite society was afraid to answer, and that would become an excuse for the Dunnings to have fewer visitors.

"Why can't Leelee and Leesa go to school with me?"

"Why does my white mama sleep all the time?"

"What is a nigger and why does my daddy hate them?"

Growing up with Florence's twins, Ashley felt a kinship that Evelyn didn't mind, but Jasper abhorred. He adored Leeland and Leesa, and they treated him like a little brother, to the point that Ashley saw himself as an "'honorary'" colored child and often expressed his wish that Florence was his only mother.

As Florence approached her own children's school, she noticed several children and a few of the parents standing out in front of the schoolhouse alongside the gravel road. The Frederick Douglass School for Colored

Children sat on less than an acre parcel and served as a throwback to the antebellum South. Several grades shared the same classroom, and the building was dilapidated and in need of serious repair, but the Negro families were grateful to have a place to educate their children. It was little more than a generation ago that colored families seeking to educate their children had to find transportation into Suffolk County or as far up as Newport News. If it wasn't for the modernization of the tobacco factory, current families would still be making the trip out of Lafayette County to educate their children.

A sheriff's squad car had pulled up to the front of the schoolhouse. Cleavon Jackson, a little boy drenched in tears, came out flanked by two deputies. One of the deputies put him in the back seat of the car, turned around, and gave a defiant look to the glaring eyes watching him. He hitched up his trousers, snorted, and spat on the ground in front of his feet. He then looked up towards the school's principal, Dr. Adele Drummond, tipped his hat, and patted his gun belt as he sauntered around to the driver's side, got in, and slowly pulled away.

As soon as he pulled onto the gravel road, Florence heard tearful mutterings. She made Ashley wait in the car as she looked for her twins. He was disappointed; Florence would usually allow him to run out and play with all of the children before they made their way home. Ashley enjoyed roughhousing with Leeland and Cleavon, and chasing Leesa and her friends to his heart's content. He wasn't allowed to get dirty at his school.

Florence pulled aside Abby, one of the other parents.

"Abby, what's happening?"

"Teachers aren't allowing them out until a parent shows up to collect them," Abby said. As she went on, Florence felt fear consume her as she peered past the classroom door, looking for the twins. The last word out of Abby's mouth was all she heard next. "Dead."

Florence went into a stupor. Abby saw her distress and grabbed Florence's shoulders to shake her out, nearly holding her up as Florence's knees began to buckle.

"Ms. Jenkins, did you hear me?" she asked. "Lincoln Jackson is dead. He was found hangin' from a plank right inside his shoe shop. Mr. Turner found him this mornin'." She rubbed Florence's shoulders. "You better go in there and get your twins., I'm sure they're scared to death."

Florence crept towards the dilapidated wooden schoolhouse door and steadied herself against the splintering frame. She peered through the shocked parents and bewildered children, and her eyes then blurred with tears. Whispered voices and collective sniffles only compounded upon her trepidation.

Leeland and Leesa huddled in the corner, the center of their crying friends. They were the calm in the eye of the storm, and the other kids seemed to have gravitated toward them. Florence suddenly felt a sense of admiration and pride, and they bolstered her strength. Leesa rushed into her mother's embrace, and Leeland hesitated for a moment, feigning control. He tried to gather up both his mother and sister, but soon realized his arms didn't fit the bill. Florence held them both.

Lincoln's son, Cleavon Jackson, and Leeland Jenkins were best friends – —the kind of best friends only nine-year-olds could be. They spent every moment they could together, having sleepovers at each other's homes and sharing each other's toys and wrestling each other to the ground. They both couldn't wait to be ten years old. Now, Leeland seemed helpless and confused, too young to know what to do next or what he was expected to do. He'd always thought of himself as the man of the family and the protector of his mother and sister. Now, he wished his father, whom he only knew through stories and life lessons from his mother, was here to help him now.

Ashley, in the Packard, had climbed into the front seat and pretended to drive the steering wheel, as if he was on a long-distance trek across Lafayette County. He was bursting with excitement to see the twins, but when he jumped out and ran closer, he could see Leesa crying and clinging to her mother. Before Florence answered what had happened, she rushed the kids into the car and they drove home in silence, save for the somber whimpers from Leesa. Leeland stared out the window in the back seat.

Ashley sat in the front, a spot he was unfamiliar and uncomfortable with. He wanted to be in the back with the twins. He looked up at Florence and saw tears slowly roll down her smooth skin like a droplets of rain. Ashley put his head down and folded his hands in his lap – —he'd taught himself to disappear.

***

In the center of Lafayette County sat the old plantation home of Montgomery Crawford, which held the Lafayette City Council Hall. Most of the Crawford parcel had been sold off and developed in the town's center, and the one-story, seven-bedroom home had been renovated under Courtland Parker's tenure, sparing only the dining room. Two bedrooms had been merged to form a boardroom, where the senior members of the Council now gathered. The cherry oak walls held paintings of the founders of the Lafayette chapter of the Ku Klux Klan—Crawford, Emerson Parker, and General Nathan Bedford Forrest—in full Confederate regalia.

As he sat on one of the two leather chairs before Courtland Parker's office desk, Jasper Dunning listened painstakingly as Parker plodded on and on about the "'good old days,'," something he'd heard only a few thousand times before. Jasper had been growing tired of playing Courtland's glorified secretary; he had plans for the future, but if he allowed himself to be stuck in this role, they might never get done. He would need to refill a few senior positions, to start, but this would require strategy.

Jasper shifted some papers on the corner of Courtland's desk in the pretense of straightening up, and when Courtland's gaze was away, Jasper slyly inserted a paper of his own. He lit a cigarette for Courtland when he finally returned to his desk from his pacing, and in the pause that was created, Jasper spoke.

"There is a rumor goin' around," he said. "And mind you, it's just a rumor. But I think it bears listenin' to." He waited for Courtland's attention before he continued. "There's a rumor that Sheriff Tisdale has become quite infatuated with a colored girl who lives in the Negro section of town. Now, I know, engagin' with a colored woman or two ain't anythin' to be alarmed about. Tisdale does have a propensity towards darker meat. But I hear tell, this one knows a reporter for that colored rag they call a newspaper in Roanoke."

Unmoved, Courtland took a thoughtful drag from his cigarette and squinted at Jasper through the plume of his own smoke. He said nothing, so Jasper continued, stronger.

"It has come to my understandin' that this reporter has ascertained some specific details about a collision that resulted in the deaths of two Negroes that were members of the NAACP some years ago. And those details have started to stir up some interest in the case."

This was a lie. But Jasper had full knowledge of Courtland's proclivities and knew bringing up slight inferences of past Council crimes would take residence in Courtland's ear until they festered.

"Now, I'm not sayin' this is true. After all, it is a rumor," Jasper went on. "But to my understandin', this reporter is known for breakin' big stories of what they call 'crimes of the Klan.'. Includin' some that has papers in Washington lookin' into stories of missin' Negro children." When Courtland stopped and stared, his attention seized, Jasper leaned closer with a whisper. "Tisdale is gettin' sloppy in his old age. And when you get sloppy, you get caught."

Behind his mahogany desk, Courtland considered the merits of Jasper's argument. He took a long drag of his cigarette and blew smoke into Jasper's face. Jasper merely leaned back and offered an ashtray to catch the growing stem of tobacco ash. Though Courtland's expression hardly wavered, he seemed pleased by Jasper's attempts to ingratiate himself.

Reveling in his kingship, he flicked his ashes into Jasper's palm. Jasper didn't miss a beat, wiping the ashes into the tray.

It was time. Jasper pulled his own paper from Courtland's stack and placed it in front of him on the desk. A typewritten order, waiting for his signature. An order that would put Jasper's plans into effect.

Courtland Parker understood the short-term gain of replacing the aging Tisdale, never considering the possibility of any long-term benefit for anyone other than himself. He expected perfect loyalty from the council members and regarded Jasper as nothing more than a flamboyant yes-man who was only in the club due to the Lord's good graces and Cartwright money. (The council members had taken to calling him "'Bumstead'" after the character in the comic strip *Blondie* – —a fitting name for someone benefiting from the hard work of others.) Jasper had no real power within the Council apart from carrying out Courtland's orders. Replacing the sheriff with an aggressive deputy would get Jasper's appointee to assume control of the sheriff's office, thus shifting the power balance of the City Council.

It was a combination of Jasper's wit and Courtland's overconfidence that led to the appointment of the new Sheriff Beauregard Clayton that same day. Jasper introduced the two of them as he hid his own delight. The plan was unfolding. Clayton appeared hesitant if only in front of Courtland; Jasper figured a nudge was in order.

"Sheriff. Guess I'd betta get used to that," Jasper said. "Sheriff, I hear that uppity Jackson nigger got his due. I understand you and him was childhood friends."

As if remembering something he had long forgotten, Clayton considered his words, giving Jasper Dunning a once-over. "Some folks get ahead of themselves," he said somberly, passing a look at Courtland Parker. "I suspect ... some more of our coloreds will be gettin' a bit ahead of themselves with this court rulin'."

In his usual subtle manner, Courtland installed his directive.

"Perhaps some boys will be out carryin' on to keep some peace," he said. "It would be just fine if you and some deputies could make sure they don't get into too much trouble, Sheriff." He then nodded in agreement with Jasper. "Yes, I do believe callin' you Sheriff will take some gettin' used to."

A fourth party remained in the office after having checked in on Courtland: Dr. Weldon Michaels, who remained only to pack up his bag while he pretended not to be listening in. He'd managed to slink around the office unnoticed all the while and had been able to collect some useful pieces of information. The *Brown v. Board* ruling seemed to be the opportunity the Council needed to agitate the white community enough to stir trouble. Tempers would flare, especially towards Negro troublemakers.

Lincoln Jackson – —whose entrepreneurial spirit and leadership in the colored community had not gone unnoticed – —had just died. His death was not a surprise to the Council, which could only mean one thing.

"Are you quite done, Doctor?"

Dr. Michaels shot up a glance at an irritated Courtland and collected himself. "Yes, sir."

Jasper, with a grimace, pulled Michaels aside. "Don't fuck this up, Wells," he hissed. They missed the curious look Courtland shot towards Clayton as Jasper then patted Dr. Michaels on the back and ushered him out of the room. When Jasper and Clayton lingered behind, Courtland kicked them out of his office, leaving them to scurry out after Dr. Michaels.

Weldon Michaels and Jasper Dunning shared a past both would prefer to keep secret. Michaels was the one who had christened Jasper with the Bumstead moniker while relating the story of how Jasper had won Evelyn's heart and her daddy's fortune to a few club members after too many drinks. Michaels harbored just enough resentment and envy towards Jasper to make him dangerous. If not for his good looks and homespun charm, Jasper would have remained the product of his sharecropper upbringing – —and because of that, Michaels considered Jasper his intellectual inferior.

The smell of tobacco and sweat followed them into the parlor as soft sunlight crept in through the upper windows, casting half-shadows across their faces. In private, Clayton now regarded Jasper with both appreciation and caution. Jasper had been the one to persistently bend Parker's ear with favorable words that ultimately convinced him to make the change in the sheriff's office. But Clayton knew now that he had entered a race with Jasper Dunning to take control of the Council. A once-trusted friend, Jasper had now assumed the role of the proverbial snake offering him the forbidden fruit, and Clayton would not allow the quiet battle between them to remain one-sided.

"It's too bad for you," Clayton said. "That colored maid's got herself a protector even *you* can't get around."

Jasper bristled, seething inside at the remark. He only offered a smile to disguise his emasculation at the implication of his household's inverted hierarchy. "We'll see," he said simply. "I think a major concern for your new position would be to regard Dr. Michaels and his propensity to let anything slip after he's had too much to drink. We both know he could say something untoward about the Council, or even the sheriff's office, that might end up in the ..." He paused and smiled. "Well, I just don't want to think where it would end up."

Jasper felt he had won this round, but as he departed, he couldn't let go of Sheriff Clayton's words. They stuck to him with particular annoyance, a sting of humiliation, a struggle for power in his own room, a persistent, aching thorn in his side.

A protector even you can't get around.

***

Still steaming, Jasper Dunning returned home in a foul mood, grumbling and cursing under his breath, only to see Florence standing by with his son Ashley. Ashley stared, unsure of how to approach him properly. Florence gave him a smile and a bit of judging.

"Go on, Ashley," she said softly. "You should always welcome your father home. He's had a long—"

"Don't you *evah*," Jasper growled, cutting her off with a finger thrust in her face as he approached her. "Don't you *evah* tell my son what to do in his home, you ..." As he noticed Evelyn at the top of the stairs looking out over the bannister, he held his tongue. He wouldn't engage her in her crusade to save the nigger woman and her pickaninnies, nor reignite the unfortunate encounter Clayton had sparked in Evelyn. He bristled and turned to his study, demanding his supper.

Not long after, once the children were seated at a small table in the corner of the kitchen, Florence took Jasper his dinner. She knocked and waited, heart pounding in her throat.

"Just bring it in and go!"

Florence scurried in to drop it off. The last thing she wanted was to do anything that would extend her stay in his presence. She hastily placed the tray on his desk, but just as swiftly as she turned to leave, Jasper deftly grabbed her by the wrist. He stared. She successfully managed to wrench her wrist free and leave Jasper's study without a word or a stray glance. Once outside, fear and dread enveloped her, and they never dissipated as she endured the rest of the evening, keeping her feelings at bay with busywork caring for the children.

Jasper drew comfort and courage from a quickly depleting bottle of Kentucky bourbon, not his first choice. Sheriff Clayton's words, Courtland Parker's toying with him, Dr. Michaels's smirking, and the abolishment of school segregation continued to replay in his mind over and over. They were the seeds that slowly fledged and blossomed into a rage. And he had simply backed down when he saw Evelyn at the top of the stairs – —her power over him was undeniable, and it made him seethe. Now, even his colored maid had refused and rejected him. He'd seen the look of relief on her face when they both noticed Evelyn.

Florence was not afraid of him, he realized. She lacked the proper respect of his position as the man of the house, the white man, and a member of the City Council. The fact that he was not in a position of envy, save the one afforded to him by marrying into the Cartwright fund, was beyond him. He could not carry on submitting himself to the facts that piled up around him.

Jasper gazed around at the dimly lit maple walls and suddenly discovered that this was the only room in his house that he felt truly safe – —but that this "'home'" of his, the estate, was clearly not his castle. He had been king once. *Before that darkie and her litter entered my home.* He stood and kicked over his leather chair, taking a deep swallow from his tumbler of bourbon. Rage consuming him, he threw the glass against the wall of his study, then swept the half-empty dishes from his desk, sending everything shattering and crashing to the hardwood floor.

When he flung open the solid oak door of his study, he happened to catch Florence just as she'd had her hand on the doorknob, likely coming in to check on the noise. The door slammed into her, and she fell to the floor of the hallway. All at once, it hit him – —*it was her.* Florence Jenkins was the source of every one of his problems. She was the reason he had lost his seat on the throne in his own castle. He deserved her respect, and she deserved to be put in her place.

Jasper went to grab her, but Florence was agile as she rolled away from the door, even as she swayed from the impact the door had on her head. Her nose bled. Her fear demanded that she run, but Jasper took a fistful of the back of her dress. "Not this time!" he snarled. The neckline rose up to her throat, choking her, and she tasted the blood from her nose as she attempted to breathe. Jasper dragged her into the dark, dreary study and tossed her around. Florence wondered if this was how a small child felt – —unable to control what happens to them. Florence's head crashed into the side of his fallen leather chair. Dizziness enveloped her completely now. When she went limp, Jasper restrained her arms and legs, and she lost track of time as it all seemed to happen in painfully slow motion.

She knew what was about to happen, but Jasper Dunning was stronger, angrier, and determined. A wild rage burned in his eyes.

Finally, here in his study, he marveled at the ease of which he was able to control her and exert his will. He quickly moved on top of her, and his superiority stiffened. He lifted her dress to stuff it in her mouth, stifling her screams as he ripped her underwear. He rushed to enter her with all the force he could muster.

Even in her dazed state, Florence could smell the mix of musk and alcohol. She kicked and screamed in vain. She wretched in agony. He forced himself inside her, and her entire body lurched, repulsed by his touch, his violence. Tears streamed down her face as she begged for Dillard, his face, her memories of him, his promise to return.

Mercifully for Florence, it ended quickly. Jasper lost steam and vigor after a few thrusts, but his violent anger raged on. It was then that she realized—he'd been unable to maintain an erection, and his dominance over her meant nothing. He rolled off of her, zipped up his pants, and grabbed her by the throat.

"There is plenty more where that came from," he growled. "If you even think of saying anything to Evelyn, or anyone, I will do the same to your little Leesa, and I'll kill you *and* your pickaninnies." Jasper tossed her head back against the chair, and Florence lay where she was in shock.

Both were oblivious to a pair of soft, blue eyes, wide with fear, that had watched the brutal attack in its entirety.

Chapter 7

Lafayette, Virginia

Friday, July 18, 1975
11.:39 a.m.

Dolores Peters, a registered nurse pushing her early thirties, had never had the best of luck in romantic relationships. She'd once had a torrid affair with a renegade doctor with inexplicable privileges at Lafayette General, where she got her first job fresh out of nursing school. The prolonged dalliance had forced her to compromise her ideals and dreams. After the relationship abruptly ended, Dolores shut herself off from her lifelong hopes of a storybook romance. That is, until she'd met Percy Hawkins.

Percy Hawkins was suave and generous. He made her feel again. It took a few months of dating for her to know that she could truly trust him, even though no one else seemed to. The trust they shared, she believed, meant something. And that meant if she really wanted the relationship she had with him to become something real, she knew she would have to lay down all of her past. She would make dinner, he would regale her with the news of the day, and little by little she would find a way to open up to him.

Percy ran late and missed their movie date, having had to stop by the crime scene in a second murder in Lafayette. "I've got some details that will blow you away," he said over the phone before he left his office. He'd received an anonymous tip and garnered information from some of the deputies at the scene. Over dinner, he spun a tale for his lady love.

"So I'm standing there with Sheriff Clayton, and I'm staring him down, telling him, 'You'd better not hold out on me or I won't be upfront with any information I get,'" Percy said. "You should have seen his face. He turned all beet- red and was like, 'Son, I won't hold out on you. You can trust ol' Bo Clayton.' And I said, 'Well, I sure hope so, Sheriff.' Then I walked out and went to file my story for tomorrow!"

Dolores nudged her chair closer to his until they were nearly touching now. "Percy, you are somethin' else," she said. "I can't imagine anyone talkin' to Sheriff Clayton like that. He's so big and mean-lookin'. I would be too afraid to talk to him, let alone challenge him." When she saw his off-smile, she realized he must have been irritated by her interruption. "You're my hero, Percy Hawkins," she added to soothe him. She refilled his glass of wine and urged him to continue.

"So these thugs," Percy went on. "Pierce and Stiles, they're pretty bad guys. They won't be missed. At least, not by anyone I know." He paused. "There was blood everywhere. Easy to see that some of the deputies were scared. I heard the new deputy, Grimes, threw up because he couldn't stomach it. I just laughed when I heard that. Can you imagine it?" He chuckled and returned to his meal, waiting for another exclamation of her admiration. When he didn't get it this time, he leaned close to give her a secret. "You know, people want to trust me and give me their side of the story. I have an honest face, and a particular way to make people want to tell me the truth. I guess I'm blessed like that."

Dolores sipped her wine and stared distantly, as if she wasere somewhere else, her food going largely untouched. Percy slurped up his spaghetti to make up for it. "That new deputy, Grimes. He seems to have Clayton's ear. But it doesn't appear to me that he knows what he's doing. I almost told the sheriff to let *me* take over the investigation!"

Dolores slowly stood from the table and walked out onto the terrace. Percy remained seated and waited silently, his story paused, rhythmically tapping his fingers as if to count the seconds till her inevitable and immediate return.

"Dolores!" he said finally, storming out onto the terrace behind her. "At the very least you could have asked to be excused. I was just getting to the good part, and now you've ruined it."

She turned to him with tears staining her face and a sheer terror shaking her body. It was a hot, humid night, yet she shivered with goose bumps. "I knew them," was all she could say, again and again.

"What do you mean, you knew them?"

"Gary Pierce and Don Stiles, right?"

"I said Pierce and Stiles," Percy said. "You know their first names. How?"

"They were ambulance drivers, weren't they?" Dolores asked.

"They used to be. I learned they were banned from driving after an accident transporting a young girl." Percy stumbled through his words in his attempt to recall. He was beginning to feel flummoxed, that he was losing control of the direction of both the evening and the conversation. He wanted to take back control, but his urge to show off his ability to grasp facts and force them into a story superseded any thorough follow- up with her.

"I think it was about three and a half years ago," Percy continued, "that the girl they were transferring died when the ambulance crashed. It was in the police report – —they were drunk and fighting as they were transporting her. The girl died in the accident, and these two were very lucky they didn't have to do time."

"What do you mean?" Dolores ventured. She pressed close to him, as if for comfort, but he only loosely held her.

"Well, let me see," Percy recalled. "From what I remember, the
deputy told me the boys could have been drinking, but ... No, they were hit by a drunk driver. Then, instead of trying to help the girl, they got out and started a fight with the other driver. That driver went to jail, but the judge didn't find enough evidence to send Pierce or Stiles to jail. They were fired. Been derelicts ever since."

"How old was the girl?"

"Just a teenager. Deputy Dawson told me her daddy swore he was gonna do something to them. He blamed them for her death," Percy said. "It didn't help when the story came out that her dress was torn when they got to her body after the accident. The father said she wasn't like that when they put her in the ambulance."

"What happened to the father? W, why didn't he ride with her?"

"Pierce and Stiles told him it was against company policy to let
him ride.," Percy shrugged. "But I just think they planned on violating that Negro girl from the moment they saw her."

"She was black?" Dolores tensed.

"Probably why the judge didn't feel the evidence was enough to put those boys away," Percy said. "The truth was, she had severe head trauma and might not've made it anyway." Percy gave her a smile. "That's a little tidbit I'll have for Sheriff Clayton in the morning. I bet he hadn't figured out anything on that angle."

"You mean that it's the father of the girl who kilt them?"

Percy preened. "I've practically solved this myself. Jefferson – —that was the father's name, Jeremiah Jefferson."

Dolores relaxed in his arms, appearing calmer than she'd been when she left for the terrace. She squeezed herself into his chest, and Percy finally reciprocated his own end of the embrace. "So you think this Jeremiah Jefferson did this to get back at them?"

"Sounds reasonable enough to me. Don't you think?"

"Guess so," she said.

But her heart couldn't calm down enough for her to take stock of her own words. She decided that tonight wasn't the best time to clear her past with him – —and furthermore, she was beginning to think there are some things in the past that should stay in the past.

"So, why were you so scared?" Percy asked her. "I mean, you ran right out in the middle of my story. And you were asking all these questions, like you knew what the answer might be."

Dolores stammered. "I'm sorry, honey, I was just ... scared. At the thought of all that blood. That kind of stuff doesn't happen in Lafayette." She let him hold her tighter. "And you just tell the story so well, I felt like I was there."

"Oh, that's all right." Percy led her off the terrace and into the living room. "There are some scary sides of life that you haven't seen. It can be traumatizing to hear in detail. Truth is, I'm a reporter, and I'm gonna make the big time. And if you're coming along with me, you'll have to get used to it."

Those words hung on her heart like a painting in the Louvre. *If I'm going to come with you*, she thought. That was more than what she could have hoped he would say.

"Of course I'll go along with you," Dolores sighed. "I will go as far as you need me."

***

The next morning, Dolores barely touched her coffee as she read the paper, knee-deep in the middle of Percy's article. When he walked in, she almost dropped her cup as it only just touched her lips.

"Ohn, you're reading my story!" he said, grabbing a pastry. "What do you think?"

Dolores forced a smile, trying to contain her fear as she wiped the coffee from the table. "Percy, last night you said you thought it was this black guy, Jefferson somethin', that was doing it."

"Jeremiah Jefferson, yeah," Percy said derisively. "So what?"

"Well, in your article, you say there is a note from the killer — —that he's going to kill two more people. If he only made threats to Gary and Don, why would he say he's going to kill two more?"

Percy offered the kind of laughter you reserve for a small child's irrelevant question. "He's trying to throw the sheriff off," he explained. "Probably thinks he's clever. Somethin' like, 'I'mma gonna fool them deputies into thinkin' it ain't me.'" He laughed again, but when he saw Dolores nearly in tears, not laughing with him, he gave her a look of bewilderment.

"How can you be so sure?" she asked him.

Frustrated now by being challenged and having his humor go unrequited, Percy responded tersely, "Because I know what I'm doing. I know human nature and I've been at this long enough."

He reassured her that once he went by the Jefferson place, he would wrap this up and meet the sheriff before noon. He boasted of the probability of an arrest as early as the afternoon. Though his irritation simmered, he kissed her forehead and headed out the front door.

Dolores grabbed her trim-line phone off of its stand, dragging the extended cord along with her as she paced her unit. She held the lever down to avoid the continuous buzzing of the vacant line tone as she collected her thoughts. She waited a full ten minutes, pacing back and forth, before she called Sheriff Clayton's office. She stared out of her terrace window before returning to the table to sit down at her table, repeating the fears that enveloped her thoughts out loud to an empty room.

"What kinda 'mergency do you have, miss?" Clare Miles retorted back at her over the phone.

"I'm not sure," Dolores said, "but I think ..."

"I'm sorry, ma'am, but you're gonna hafta speak up. It's very busy here, and the sheriff is in the middle of a murder investigation."

"I understand," she stammered. "My name is Dolores Peters, and I'm a nurse, and I may have worked with the two men who were murdered. They were ambulance drivers, and I know there was a note, and I think I know who might be doing this, and ..." She paused, realizing she was rambling and trembling, and could only hope she wasn't sounding hysterical. "I may know how the murders are connected and who's gonna be next. The note said four people, right?" Dread filled her suddenly. "My god, I hope I'm wrong, but I think ... God, please help me! I think I'm one of the four! I need to speak to Sheriff Clayton, now!"

"Okay, darlin', just hol' a second, I'll run an' get him."

Dolores heard a soft clack as the phone was set down on Clare's desk. She could hear something on the other end – —talking, yelling – —but no one was coming back to the phone. The rustling sound of the shower running in the bathroom reminded her that she should take one. *Did I turn the shower on today?* Her thoughts were a jumble, and her heart pounded wildly. She paced back and forth from the terrace to the living room wrenching the extension cord around the table and chairs, wishing now that she had gone with Percy to the sheriff's office herself.

Right now, she felt wholly alone. And then, suddenly, she didn't.

***

Percy's visit to the Jefferson home was fruitless. Jeremiah Jefferson had died in an automobile accident less than six months after his daughter's death – —despondent and drinking heavily, feeling responsible for the injuries she had suffered that resulted in the ambulance call.

"The judge shoulda put them boys in jail," Edda May Jefferson, Jeremiah's mother, told Percy. The grief was still heavy in her voice. "A colored man got no hope if the law can't help him."

She didn't wait for Percy's response. She slowly turned her aging body and closed the front door, leaving Percy on the porch to listen to the distant barking of dogs and the purr of a well-tuned engine revving next door. Feeling like he'd wasted his time, Percy left the Jefferson porch and headed back to his car.

"Why don't you let that old lady be?" a voice shouted out to him. "Her son's gone. What else you want?"

Percy located the voice by the purring engine. He changed direction, heading towards it and the mechanic standing there. "Good morning, sir," he offered. "Can I speak with you for a second? I'm with the *Lafayette Gazette*."

"Yeah, I knows you," the mechanic said. "I seen you on TV. I read your stories. I been sendin' you pictures and letters 'bout my little brother, who been missin' for almost twenty years now. But you never come down here askin' 'bout that. But I gave that new deputy a picture yesterday, when he come 'round askin' 'bout Miss Jefferson's boy. Says he's gonna look into it."

Percy bristled at the mention of the new deputy. It must've been Grimes.

"I doubt it," the mechanic continued bitterly. "You white folks only care 'bout other white folks. Don't come back 'round here till you ready to find out 'bout black folks."

He went back to adjusting the carburetor on his 1965 charcoal Electra 225 – —deuce and a quarter. Percy, standing there, went through his mind trying to place the letter and requests. Then it hit him.

"I do remember, sir," Percy said. "But there was never any mention of black kids missing in any of the papers. I'm sorry to say this, but if he was kidnapped, there's a statute of limitations on prosecuting anyone for that. You know, expired justice."

"Death ain't got no expiration date."

The mechanic stared at Percy, who quickly realized he wasn't going to get anything else out of him. He excused himself and returned to his car.

On the road, Percy sorted and compartmentalized what he knew. And he kept returning to the conversation he'd had with Dolores. Something was bugging him, and he couldn't put his finger on it. *Why did I let her get away without answering me?* he asked himself. *Does she know something? Is she hiding something?* Instead of heading to the sheriff's office, Percy detoured back to Dolores's apartment. With every red light he encountered, his patience grew thinner.

He pulled up to the curb and carelessly pushed open his car door, intending to make a quick dash across the street and up to her apartment. The sound of screeching wheels made him pause as a late-model crimson Camaro zipped past, barely missing his open door. He stumbled right into the path of a slow-moving pale yellow pickup truck and caught himself on the hood. Even as the universe seemed to want to stop him at every turn, Percy tossed a hand in the air at the driver and continued for the apartment.

She chose to keep secrets from me.

Galvanized, Percy rushed up the stairs to Dolores's apartment and banged his fist on the door. When there was no response, he used his key to get inside. Apprehension began to seize his chest. His notes heavy in his pocket, he suddenly thought of the killer's warning: '"*two to go.*".'

The sound of the shower running gave Percy a sense of relief.

Dolores was just fine. He'd let it go. He'd make them both some more coffee and after all this, after he got a chance to explain it all, after she got dressed and explained her side of things, they'd laugh about it. Clearly, he was missing a vital piece of information.

"Dolores! I'm home. How many sugars in your coffee?"

Only the echo of the shower answered him. It was all too easy for Percy to assume she hadn't heard him. Almost feeling amorous ——that maybe they could work this all out – —Percy left the coffee pot to approach Dolores's bathroom.

What he saw in the bedroom, however, stopped him dead in his tracks.

***

Clayton and Grimes stood while Percy sat on Dolores's living room sofa, in anguish, while forensics dealt with the bloody crime scene in the bedroom. Dolores's throat and an artery in her leg had both been slashed. The trim-line receiver telephone had been found by her body, the cord extended and twisted far from its cradle, silent. Because but the phone line had been cut.

"I knew something was wrong," Percy told them. "It was the way she looked at me when she read the paper this morning. Why didn't I just ask her? Why did I have my mind so made up?"

Percy reported the screeching car – —a crimson Camaro or a burnt-orange Firebird – leaving the scene in a hurry when he'd arrived. On file, a 1965 crimson Camaro was registered to Jeremiah Jefferson, but the lead seemed to end there.

"What I can't figure is why Dolores would have anything to do with Pierce and Stiles," Percy explained. "Gary and Don. She knew them." He hung his head forward, shaking it. "I should've talked to her instead of thinking I'd solved the crime myself."

"Sometimes we get our signals mixed and we cut off our ability to hear what other people are trying to say," Grimes said gently.

"What's that supposed to mean, Deputy?" Percy snapped. "I'm a reporter. I check the facts. I'm supposed to be able to look a person in the eye and know when they need to unburden themselves and tell me all about it. I understand what you're trying to do, but I'm no kid. I'm an adult that should've known better. Don't try to console me. You're doing a terrible job."

Sheriff Clayton gave Grimes a look, then took a seat in the chair across from Percy. He stared at Percy for a moment, as if thinking, until Percy lifted his eyes to meet Clayton's stare. It made him nervous, as though he was a student who'd just been called into the principal's office.

"Percy, you was at the Jefferson place when this happened?" Clayton asked. "What was it you was doin', an' why didn't you check with me before you high-tailed it over there?"

Percy assumed any sympathy he might have received from the sheriff had walked right out the door when he admitted to going behind Clayton's back. "I was following up on a lead, Sheriff."

"A lead or a guess, son?"

"More like reporter's intuition," Percy answered. "I remembered Jefferson made a threat towards Pierce and Stiles, and I wanted to follow it up. And I ..."

"Didn't think we already made that connection, huh?"

"Well, no, I was thinkin' I could—"

"Figure this out first an' make ol' Bo look like a fool?"

"No! No, that wasn't what I had in mind at all."

"Then why didn't you mention somethin' 'bout Jefferson last night?" Clayton implored. "I already sent deputies over to Jefferson's mama last night lookin' for him. He's dead. Hell, I was hopin' it was that crazy nigger, so's I could be done with it." He sat forward in his seat. "If you had tol' me what you was thinkin', I coulda tol' you my deputies were there already. You coulda been here with your lady friend an' she'd still be livin'. Did ya think about that?"

Percy didn't get much of a chance to reply, as a deputy interrupted the interview and handed the sheriff a note. Clayton shot him a terse look, then glanced at the note. "When'd you get this?"

"It came in after you left the station, Sheriff," the deputy said. "I was tol' to hand it to you directly."

Clayton folded the note and shoved it into his chest pocket. "Gotta go see the Council. I got no time for this shit."

"The Council?" Grimes asked in earnest. "Who's the Council?"
Percy looked between them. "It's a not-so-secretive group of Lafayette's rich and powerful who—"

"Ain't nothin' you need to worry about, Deputy," Clayton barked. "Percy, this time the note wasn't on the body. Where was it?"

"It was laid out on the bed next to her. The blood had started to soak the paper." Percy sighed. "You know, it really is different when the victim is someone close to you. I just wish ..." He trailed off into his own silent thoughts.

The coroner wheeled out the body – —a lifeless lump in a black body bag on a silver gurney that squeaked across the carpeted floor on its way out into the hot summer day. Percy watched it go by.

Deputy Grimes studied the killer's note, which had been bagged in clear plastic. "Sheriff," he said, "we've got to get the FBI involved. This is happening so fast and we've got no idea what's really going on. He's completing his countdown. Hell, he's got one left and he's mocking us!"

Clayton looked at Grimes as if he'd just received a cold slap to the face. "Abel, if you don't shut the fuck up 'bout the goddamn FBI ..."

"I already called the FBI!" Percy admitted defiantly. "I called them right after I called you, Sheriff. I saw that note and I know there is one more person he's after. I've got a friend at the FBI. Someone will get in touch with your office this afternoon. So whatever the Council has to say, you can tell them the federal government will be happy to help."

Clayton yanked Percy off the couch and pushed him up against the wall, balling his fists into Percy's shirt. The wall shook with the force of it. "Why, you little snot-nosed sumbitch! Just who you think you are to tell me how to run my investigation? I oughta arrest you for interferin'!"

Grimes was at the sheriff's back in an instant, pulling him off the reporter. The sheriff shrugged free and let Percy go. "Grimes. Outside. Pronto."

Once outside, the sheriff glared Abel in the eye, as if challenging him. "You speak with anyone in the FBI, Grimes?"

"No, Sheriff," Grimes said with a shake of his head. "You gave me strict instructions not to."

Turning away in disgust, Sheriff Clayton snatched the plastic bag out of Abel's hands and studied the note. He read it to himself and gave the deputy a look out of the corner of his eye. He appeared resigned, knowing that things were getting out of his control.

"What in the fuck am I gonna do?" he muttered. "I'm gonna get both the Council and the government breathin' down my neck."

"Sheriff?"

"Nothin'," he said. "Just thinkin' out loud." He handed the note back to Grimes. "You see there's one more word there, at the bottom?"

"Yeah, I saw it," Grimes replied. "He's adding a new word with each new note. But ... what's it leading to?"

1 down 32 go — Death makes life.

Chapter 8

Los Angeles, California

Monday, July 19, 2010
9.:11 a.m.

Houston's first day back at work came just a few days after the funeral. Though he was still in mourning, and further confused by his "'mother's'" deathbed confession, he felt that returning to a familiar routine would help him adjust. Still without a license, he took the bus to the office and joined the small crowd that had gathered around the communal coffee pot.

The smell of hazelnut cream filled the room, wafting up from the second pot of coffee that was always flavored because the first person to enter the office refused to make anything but the strongest coffee no one could stand. This was the work of Phil Cantoni. His name was most often cursed by employees who, anxious for morning brew, would dare to take a sip of Phil's concoction, only to rush to the sink to spit it out. No one ever watched him make it, but plenty would see him swill down at least two or three cups every morning.

The big wigs of the office usually wouldn't show up until almost noon, and most of the junior attorneys had their own single-cup machines; plus, the office manager, Elizabeth Taylor-Barrings, had a soft spot for Phil and allowed his quirks. No one quite understood why, and no one ever really challenged it, either. It was just one of those things that happened in the office, and all new employees had to learn to accept it eventually.

Houston greeted the anxious few—Scott, Michelle, and Renee—calling out to Michelle in particular. "Hey, Michelle, I ... uh," he started nervously. He wasn't used to having people do things for him without his having to ask. "I just want to say thank you, for helping me and Sabrina with the flowers. They were beautiful."

Michelle smiled genuinely. "You're welcome, Houston. It was a beautiful ceremony," she responded. "I'm actually surprised you're here today. I thought you'd take a few more days off."

Houston shook his head. "It's been a long two weeks, and I have a lot to catch up on. Phil and Oscar need me to finish."

Phil coughed his way into the room, as if announcing his presence. "Yeah, we're waiting on you. Your vacation's gone on long enough."

Oscar followed Phil in, patting him on the back. "I'm glad you're back, Houston. I was going crazy with no buffer between me and this old dude."

Houston rolled his eyes, but Renee got his attention. "I know you and I've butted heads a few times," she offered, "but I want you to know I helped Michelle with the arrangements and setting up the flowers at the church. I'm so sorry for your loss."

"Hey, Renee," Phil interjected,. "I know you Iowa girls have the hots for black men, but this one's taken."

Renee fumed and spun herself at Phil. She opened her mouth as a retort was loaded, cocked, and aimed, when suddenly Mrs. Taylor- Barrings entered the break room. Renee swallowed her retort, consuming the bile of her response. Phil, true to his nature, countered her dislodged anger with a smug smile.

"What's all this about?" Mrs. Taylor-Barrings inquired.

"Nothing much, Liz," Phil told her. "Renee here was just giving us her impression of a misanthrope."

Renee's anger fizzled quickly into embarrassment. Scott and

Michelle hastily left the break room while the others looked on. Elizabeth, confused but rather used to this, gave them a nod. "Ms. Peterson, when you have a moment, stop by my office." Code for *drop everything and see me.*

Not more than three minutes had passed when Renee gently announced her presence, tapping lightly on the doorframe, so as not to disturb Elizabeth's phone conversation. Finishing her call, Elizabeth gestured to Renee to take a seat. Renee did so, swallowing her nerves and putting on her best smile.

"So what's on the agenda today, Liz?" she blurted out. Once she realized the casual and unprofessional manner in which she'd addressed Mrs. Taylor-Barrings, she quickly apologized. She jumped to attention, as if she had spilled something hot in her lap, which nearly knocked over the cup of coffee she'd just placed on the ornate woven coaster on the edge of Elizabeth's huge mahogany desk.

Undisturbed by Renee's reaction, Elizabeth calmly punched her access codes into her laptop keyboard, then briefly paused, raising a manicured eyebrow just above the frame of her tortoiseshell-rimmed glasses. She pushed the sliding lenses back into their proper place on the bridge of her nose. She decided she wouldn't respond to Renee's gaff and went on with the day's activities. For Renee, Elizabeth coolly eased her anxieties as she slipped into her office manager role with aplomb. Her ability to simultaneously comfort and control was one of the many reasons Renee loved working under her, even if the thought of slipping up made her nervous. Nothing seemed to upset Elizabeth nor make her lose her temper.

After Elizabeth listed off the agenda, Renee gave a rundown of her accomplishments. She was quite proud of them, her confidence growing with each appointment and arrangement she'd scheduled. "I've emailed everyone this morning about today's meeting. I've also booked flights for Mr. Watson and Mr. Johnson for their meeting in the capital tomorrow morning. A car will pick them up from here at nine thirty. I've also arranged for a car to pick them up at their gate at Sacramento International. I've booked dinner reservations for them as well. And lastly, I ordered the ice cream cake for Phil's birthday party this afternoon."

"Taking initiative with confidence is what I've always admired about you, Renee," Elizabeth said with a smile. "I wish more of your coworkers were as assured and reliable as you are. I want you to know I apprecia—"

"Hey, Liz," Phil Cantoni interrupted, poking his head in. "I need to talk to you about this afternoon. I don't think I'm gonna be there. You know me, I don't like a fuss." He turned and started back down the hall.

"Just a minute, Mr. Cantoni,—" Elizabeth called. "Get back here!"

She hurriedly turned back to Renee. "Is that all? I'll see you around eleven forty-five before we get the meeting started." When she saw Phil had returned, slouching in the doorway, she nodded to him. "Mr. Cantoni, come in here and have a seat, please."

"Sure thing, boss lady," Phil responded, clearly inappropriate and unprofessional. He demonstratively sauntered past Renee to take the seat she'd left open. She looked to Elizabeth for any acknowledgement of his behavior, but she merely dismissed Renee.

To Renee, who had been abruptly cut short of her appraisement, this encounter struck her as odd. Elizabeth was almost placating Phil. Why was she being so nice to him? *He's such an asshole*. He'd made more than his fair share of belittling comments about her, from insults towards her home state of Iowa to off-color sexual remarks. Renee had often thought of making a formal complaint, but just as in the coffee situation, it would be more trouble than it was worth to complain about Phil's antics. Making a fuss about it would be in vain, so she could force herself to ignore it, but she couldn't understand why Elizabeth took it from him – —she didn't take shit from anyone, including any of the senior partners.

It was a mystery she was determined to solve.

***

Houston buzzed himself into the secure records room and made his way to his desk to get back on track. He had to complete the Cloud upload of the company's records and client files. Oscar sat at his own desk, alone, which made Houston pause.

"Where's Phil?"

Oscar simply shrugged. "Cranky old gringo went to have a piss for the fourth time this morning."

"Hey," Houston spoke up, "lay off the old man."

"Why are you always standing up for that guy?" Oscar said, defensive. "He's a weird, cranky dude and you know it. I really hope they renew your contract or make you permanent, because I know I won't be able to take working here alone with him. I mean, his conspiracy theory shit, hating everything and everyone, it takes a toll on you. You know?" He shook his head. "Fuck, I'm a likable guy and I don't have a problem with most people, but Phil ... he can be a hard pill to swallow."

Houston considered his words. "I guess I didn't realize I was always standing up for him," he said finally.

"Yeah, man. You do. Even more lately." Oscar eyed Houston. "I've been wanting to ask, what's up with you?"

Houston finally sat down at his desk. "I guess I was just thinking about my mom, and well ... I'm sure she could find something nice to say about Phil. So I guess it's my gift to her." Unable to give a more satisfactory explanation, he changed the subject. "Speaking of my contract, I should find out whether they're extending it or planning to hire me full-time by the end of next week. I could use a permanent gig, and I should be tryin' to get my ass back in school. Sabrina and I want to have kids someday, but first we need to buy a home and ..."

"Really? You want kids?" Phil Cantoni said, stepping in. His tone was oddly hopeful.

Oscar lifted his head from his desk in surprise. Houston, also caught off guard, chuckled.

"I want kids. Someday, I guess. I mean, it's a topic that's ..." He trailed off, almost waiting for an inevitable joke or jab from Phil, but it never came.

"Dude," Oscar said, "what do you care?"

"I don't."

Oscar rolled his eyes and shot Houston a grin. "Wow, dude. Dunno what you've got on him, Hou, but you're the only one he doesn't seem to completely dislike."

"There is nobody I like," Phil responded.

Houston and Oscar laughed to each other from across the room, which only confused Phil. Together, at least, they could tolerate him. Phil seemed to derive pleasure from pushing people into acting out of character, or into saying or doing something they would regret and apologize for later.

Dissatisfied that he didn't get a rise out of them, Phil waved them off and put his ear buds in to drown out their laughter.

***

It was not only Houston's morning coffee break but also his lunch break that had now been hijacked by Phil and Renee. He'd barely had a chance to eat when Phil roped him into an argument he didn't want to have, earning him an enemy in Renee. He started to wonder if Phil had set him up. In only a few minutes, the heated debate had escalated, and he could now feel the eyes of onlookers grabbing their lunches from the kitchen.

"Come on, Renee," Houston appealed. "Do we really have to do this now? I wasn't even talking to you. Phil's the one who started this;, why don't you yell at him?"

"Thomas Jefferson himself," Renee continued unabated, "said that slavery was corrosive to the slave and the owner."

"So you can quote Jefferson?" Houston responded, sighing. He was in it now. "Then you know full well that he was a rapist, too."

Renee dropped her jaw, incredulous. "Rapist? Who did he rape?"

"You know who Sally Hemings was, right? And who she was to him?"

Houston hoped to at least call her bluff and send her away with homework. He didn't need this right now. He couldn't appear disrespectful to the office that had graciously supported him over the last few weeks he'd dealt with his mother. He also knew the managing partner was deeply involved in the Monticello Authority, a Thomas Jefferson historical preservation group.

Renee, too, felt the attention of others, but she appeared to revel in it. This was an opportunity for her to show off the knowledge she had gained since learning of the Monticello Authority. She didn't look around, but she thought she spied Mr. Watson's secretary in her peripheral. She went on the defensive strike.

"I know exactly who Sally Hemings was," she retorted. "She was his mistress."

"Mistress?" Phil butted in mockingly. "Well, he owned her. So I guess that makes her a mistress."

Houston shot Phil a look and noticed his wicked smile. *Old bastard set me up.*

"Yes, he owned her," Renee said, ignoring Phil. "But he treated her with—"

Houston interrupted, "If you know they were slave and master, then you know she didn't consent! That's rape!" He shook his head. "Look, I don't think this is something we're going to agree on, so why don't we just agree to disagree?"

"But that's by today's standards," Phil added, pouring a bit more fuel onto the fire.

"Not only are you looking at it with today's standards," she said to Houston, "but you forget that she willingly returned to the US with him. He took her to France, and at the time she was considered free. She didn't have to come back with him, but she did." Renee declared it somewhat cheerfully, as if she'd won.

Houston only nodded. "Thank you for making my point for me.

Jefferson did take her to France and she was free. So free that she decided she wouldn't come back. Jefferson had to *beg* her with the promise to free their children if she did. *His* children!"

"But she went back with him."

"But he didn't free their kids, did he?"

"That doesn't make him a rapist," Renee argued. "That makes him a jerk."

"A jerk, yes. And a rapist. Because that means she was coerced and—"

"No, it doesn't."

"Looks like the big fella got you on that one," Phil remarked in his Southern drawl to a smattering of snickers in the kitchen.

Houston at least appreciated the backup. It almost made up for the fact that Phil had intentionally dragged him into the whole thing. Still, they had an audience that was eager to see the final result of the confrontation.

Silence suddenly fell over the kitchen as Elizabeth Taylor-Barrings and Neil Watson, the managing partner, stepped in to get coffee. Elizabeth paused in the doorway until employees laughed nervously, whispered to each other, and began to file out. Phil finally stood and slapped Houston on the back.

"Well, that's a buzzkill if I ever saw one," Phil mumbled. "I don't think you convinced her."

Elizabeth asked Neil into her office in an attempt to take back control of the room—which Neil could never do when Phil was in the room. He always avoided Cantoni unless Elizabeth was nearby, but in any case he still hoped Phil would leave him alone as he finally left the kitchen. However, Phil couldn't stop himself as Neil passed by.

"So Jefferson was a rapist," Phil said matter-of-factly. "Who'da thunk? Guess that puts a dent in your Monticello pride." He winked at Elizabeth and stepped out of the kitchen, leaving Neil to seethe over the argument he'd heard.

Chapter 9

Quantico, Virginia

Monday, July 19, 2010
12.:11 p.m.

A slew of blood evidence reports lay on the desk of FBI Assistant Director Abel Grimes. The report—known as the Combined DNA Index System, or CODIS for short—connects familial ties, through gathered blood and tissue evidence, with the FBI's DNA database of unsolved crimes. It was a mountain to go through, and Grimes spent a few minutes contemplating the time it would take to go through them all before his lunch appointment.

He leafed through one more pile when he noticed a yellow highlighted entry. He pulled out the sticky note that had been slapped on the front.

This is the big one! – A :)

Abel quizzically peered at the note, written by his capable assistant Audrey Cummings. As he read the highlighted text, it hit him. He grabbed a pen and notepad and started to scribble.

Beverly Hills, CA

African American male age 39 Y-chromosome match.

Grimes then didn't hesitate to buzz Audrey, who picked up the phone and answered, "Chief! You got my note? This is the one, isn't it?"

"It's not the biggest, but it's important to me on a personal level," Grimes said. "I didn't think this ID would ever appear. But since it has, I want all of our ducks in a row. I want to make sure the old evidence hasn't been tainted and the CODIS for this was obtained illegally. Get the Beverly Hills police chief on the line for me. And cancel my one o'clock."

"Already got a call to his office," Audrey replied. "A business meeting with city bigwigs that must be running long. But I'm expecting a return call as soon as he gets in."

"Great. If I'm not in my office, connect the chief to my cell."

As he hung up the phone, Grimes trailed off as another notation on the report caught his attention. The report stated the blood sample had been obtained from a DWI arrest, after a routine traffic stop had resulted in a refusal to comply with a sobriety test. With that, he thought, there was a slim chance the arrestee could still be in custody.

Grimes shut the door to his office before buzzing Audrey again.

"I know I'm gonna have to deal with that dick in the LA office. Is there any way I can get around procedure to get in and out of LA without him knowing I was there?"

"I doubt it."

"Yeah, I didn't think so, either. But I thought if there was a way to do this off the books, then maybe ..."

"Not if you want me to have anything to do with it," Audrey replied.

If anything, Audrey Cummings was by the book. It was the one time she didn't follow procedure that had placed her in a wheelchair, and she'd never forgotten it – —nor would she allow anyone else. To her, rules and procedures were an agent's best friend out in the field.

"Yeah, I figured," Grimes conceded. "I just don't like him, and he knows it. Besides, if he gets wind of what this means to me, he'll try to either grab the glory or fuck it up."

"Aren't you being a bit petulant, sir?" Audrey inquired. "You boys are never going to get over that, are you?"

She was met with a guilty silence. Ten years earlier, the two men had gotten into it and thus neglected to follow up on an anonymous tip that would have saved Audrey from a nearly fatal encounter with the Black Creek Killer. Rather than taking responsibility, the two men blamed each other for putting Audrey in a wheelchair, but Audrey still believed the tip wouldn't have changed anything.

"But ... as part of protocol," Audrey added, "I've called the LA field office and BHPD. Just so you know, the LA assistant director is currently in Washington, testifying before Congress."

Grimes smiled to himself. "He is, is he?"

Audrey confirmed his flight information and Grimes had less than two hours to make it. Because Grimes, too, would be testifying before Congress in a couple of days, he'd only be in Los Angeles for a two-day turnaround. But if he could get this case solved, it would be worth all the trouble. For the first time in over thirty years, Grimes allowed himself to dip back into the intense fear and adrenaline he'd experienced working in that small backwater town.

***

Rolling her wheelchair down the marbled floors of FBI Headquarters towards the elevator, Audrey Cummings noticed light emanating from the space under the door to Grimes's office. As she propped open the door and maneuvered herself in front of the federally issued desk, her cushioned wheels made minimal sound on the carpeted floor. Unaware of her presence, Abel continued to feverishly pound away at his laptop, stopping briefly to check his notes and pull pages from a ratty old evidence file he'd retrieved from the bottom of his locked file drawer.

"What are you doing here?" she asked. Grimes jumped, and she continued. "I booked you a three o'clock flight."

Quickly recovering his composure, Grimes kept his eyes on his work. "I forgot about an appointment I had on the Hill. I've been there a couple of hours, just got back a little while ago. I'm getting all my things together now." He saw her look of concern. "Don't worry. I switched to a five a.m. flight out of Dulles, and I should land at LAX by six. That'll give me enough time to get to the hotel and check into the Westwood office before I meet with…" He fumbled for a slip of paper where he'd written the name. "Captain Rhodes, Brian Rhodes. He faxed over the arrest report for Jenkins."

"I guess that's fine, then." Audrey could see the excitement in his eyes, and if she didn't know better she would guess he was on the verge of a giddy feeling he would never admit to.

"Besides," Grimes went on, still distracted, "I promised Darlene I'd take her to dinner at Ferragamo's since I missed our anniversary last month."

"Happy anniversary!" Audrey replied with genuine cheer. "How many years is this, fourteen?"

Grimes was clearly on a different train of thought. He took a moment to respond to her. "What? Oh, yeah, thank you. No, it's seventeen." He flipped through the file he had open on his desk. She could see that something was bothering him, and she stayed quiet to let him think it through. "They let him go. They didn't have enough to hold him, so, they let him go."

"Who?" Then Audrey caught on. "How?"

"Something about his father-in-law being a defense attorney and the Beverly Hills cops racially profiling him. Apparently, his father-in-law went in there and made such a stink the desk sergeant thought it best just to let him go." The disappointment held on to the last few words leaving his mouth.

"Wait a minute, they let him go? No charges were filed?" Audrey asked, flabbergasted. "If they didn''t file charges, then they shouldn't have kept the blood sample. Hell, they shouldn't have even taken blood! How are you going to explain that to a judge?"

"Hold on, Audrey. Let's not get ahead of ourselves. I just want to get out there and talk to this Jenkins character, see what connections I can make to Lafayette before we even think about taking anything to a judge." Grimes assembled the mess of files in front of him, now packing up. "I'm just paying a social visit. Not official agency business. Not yet."

Chapter 10

Los Angeles, California

Monday, July 19, 2010
1.:18 p.m.

Sabrina Jenkins sat nervously waiting in her obstetrician's office. A small pain just below her abdomen had grown from nagging to stabbing. Thoughts of miscarriage had clouded her mind with panic, forcing her to drive herself to the hospital. Sabrina was the kind of woman who was used to taking care of herself, and she was determined to be certain of what was happening to her body and her baby at every moment. In the exam room, while Dr. Wang performed tests, Sabrina checked her messages. One, from Head Attorney Will Shanks, wanted to know her progress on the pending lawsuit against the city; she had filed a few briefs and was awaiting a hearing, but the funeral had put things on hold.

Sabrina worked for Watson, Creed, Johnson & Cole: a small legal firm in Downtown Los Angeles with three attorneys, one paralegal, three secretaries, one file clerk, and a receptionist/mail clerk. The firm specialized in community-based *pro -bono* cases —Mr. Shanks was well known as a crusader for the underprivileged and the underrepresented— ultimately giving the place a familial environment. Shanks had been thrilled that an up-and-coming attorney, second in her class at Stanford, had decided to take a pay cut to work for his firm.

Sabrina was brilliant with mergers and acquisitions and corporate law, both national and international. She'd completed her jurist degree at twenty-four and passed the California bar two weeks before her next birthday. She refused several offers before moving to New York. After a few years, in the city that never sleeps, she was visited by a headhunter who convinced her to meet with WCJ&C, and he received a large commission when Sabrina signed a one-year contract with them. It didn't take her long to get noticed by a couple of the managing partners, Neil Watson and Oliver Cole. Elizabeth Taylor-Barrings also took an immediate liking to her, as well as the rest of the staff. She'd quickly become the office favorite, because of both her direct nature and her genuine ability to empathize, and her wicked sense of humor could make anyone feel at ease. Along the way, she'd made herself into a soft spot for even the unshakable Phil Cantoni, who once – —in his own sense of affection – —told her she could make a Klansman fall for her. The entire break room had broken out into laughter when they saw Phil's face turn red. When they were alone, his guard lowered, and he told her, "You remind me of someone once very dear to me." From then on, they considered each other friends.

"Sabrina?"

Dr. Emily Wang entered the room with Sabrina's chart in hand. She noted the anxiety in Sabrina's face while she massaged, maneuvered, and poked Sabrina's belly as if she were handling a plump melon.

"It's gas," she said, to Sabrina's relief. "Have you had any spicy foods recently?"

"A little last night, but I didn't think it would make me feel like this."

"You're completing your first trimester," Dr. Wang said.

"Sometimes a little spice is all it takes."

Sabrina sighed, feeling her anxiety dissipate from her body, even if she still felt the pain and discomfort. "Thank you."

"Have you told your husband yet?" Dr. Wang asked pleasantly.

"Tonight!" Sabrina responded with a smile. "I'm going to tell him tonight. I have it all planned. I'm going to make his favorite dinner, light some candles, and break the news while he eats dessert."

She didn't notice her smile had faded until Dr. Wang gave her a soft concerned look. "Well, don't get your hopes up too high for an overwhelming response," she said. "You've told me how Houston reacts seeing some men with their young children. Sometimes, men who are raised without a father can take the news in one of two ways: either they're ecstatic and overjoyed right away, or they're overwhelmed by the thought of not measuring up and will be somewhat reserved. It can be scary if it wasn't planned."

"We talked about moving into a home and starting a family," Sabrina said. "We were ready to plan and schedule it all out before we found out how sick his mother really was. She hid it for a long time." She sighed. "I think he feels guilty about it. So I wanted to tell him the moment I found out I was pregnant, but I didn't think him learning his mother was dying would give him room to celebrate a new baby. Bad timing, you know?"

Dr. Wang nodded. "Birth is the celebration of the beginning of new life. When our first child was born, my husband said that he was now responsible for someone else dying."

Sabrina gave her an incredulous look. "What?"

"I thought it was the silliest thing," Dr. Wang said. "He said that because he created a life, that one day that life would end."

"And what did you say to that?"

"I just about smacked him on the back of his head to knock some sense into him," she laughed, making a swinging gesture. "He snapped out of it and just cried because he was so happy. I'll never understand why men think the responsibility of the world has to fall on their shoulders." She gave Sabrina a reassuring smile. "I'm sure Houston will be as happy as you expect him to be."

Sabrina went home feeling better than she had for the last few days. Houston's immediate response to the news would be happiness —— she knew it.

She caught the answering machine picking up a call just as she entered the front door, hearing Houston's voice recite a voicemail recording that she'd always thought sounded more professional than homey. She hesitated, waiting to see who the caller was and whether they'd leave a message. As soon as she recognized the voice of Houston's Aunt Ethel, she swiped the phone from the receiver.

***

"Dude, I cannot believe you said that shit in front of Watson!" Oscar leaned forward in his chair, glaring at Houston. "You know he did his undergrad and law school at Virginia. He's even proud of coming from the same state as Jefferson."

Houston cut Oscar off as he turned the spotlight to Phil. "Phil, you set me up, didn't you? Why?"

Phil only chuckled. "You probably won't believe this, but it wasn't a setup. I was actually enjoying our conversation. I didn't ask her or encourage her to join in. She took it upon herself to do that."

"Yeah, but once she joined in, you just fanned the flames, right?"

Phil coughed through his words. "No, not really. You know, Renee can be a pill sometimes. Sabrina used to do such a good job of keeping her in check. I thought you'd be good at it, too. You know. Keep it in the family, that sort of thing."

"You're a twisted old dude," Oscar interjected. "Now Houston's going to get fired because of you."

"He ain't gonna fire me!" Houston jumped in. "I'm a contract worker, remember? And the contract work hasn't been completed yet."

"Yeah, bro, but what if Watson won'ʼt let 'em renew your contract?

I'll be stuck with this ol' gringo here by myself. Damn, Phil! I thought you liked Houston!" hHe said quickly to Phil, before returning to Houston. "Why'd you have to say that shit in front of him, of all people?"

Houston dropped his head into his hands. "I didn''t know he was there! Fuck! I thought it was just a couple of people getting their lunch. I tried to back out of it, but you know Renee, she likes to push."

"*Hombre negro*, you know she's a brown-noser. She probably knew he was coming and wanted to strike up a conversation with him about it. But you—"

"Honestly, I think you got the best of her," Phil chimed in.

Houston was prepared to respond to Phil, but a notification from the receptionist told him he had a call waiting. "Fuck me," he whispered, glancing at Phil. Houston began to feel the dread of the position he might have found himself in.

"Honey, it's me." Sabrina's words landed in his ear like a butterfly on a rose petal. Relief washed over him.

"Baby, I'm glad it's you. You seem to know exactly when I need to hear your voice the most."

"Why? What's wrong?"

Houston told her all about his encounter with Renee. It sounded silly when he recounted it, but worry still ate at him. He awaited her response, anxiety eating at him.

"Well, yeah, Jefferson was a rapist," Sabrina said finally. "Who doesn't know that?"

"This is why I love you," Houston said, his heart melting. "You've got my back and you're not even here."

He swore he could almost hear her smile. "So anyway, I've got a message for you from Aunt Ethel."

"Does she want her car back?" he asked. "You didn't tell her it got impounded, did you?"

"Of course not. She's left a few messages on the machine."

"I was a bit embarrassed to talk to her after ... you know," he said. "I figured I'd take the car over to her after I get it detailed."

"She says she's not worried about the car," Sabrina replied. "But she did say she has something for you. From your mom. Something she wanted you to have after she was gone."

Houston hadn't thought about his mother or her last words all day. The rush of anxiety required caution as he attempted to hold his emotions in check. Sabrina had delivered the news with careful gravity, but it still hit Houston hard. His silence must have worried her, because she spoke up again to ask if he was okay.

"Did she tell you what it is?"

"No," Sabrina offered. "It's something your mom wanted you to have, so I'm guessing it's pretty important. Ethel wants to give it to you personally."

"Oh." Houston still didn't want to think about what his mother had confessed to him on her deathbed. He'd been starting to wish she had never told him in the first place. He didn't want to let his emotions get the better of him while at work, and he didn't want to say anything in front of Oscar, so he changed the subject. "Hey, look, I'm up for contract renewal next week. I'm supposed to meet Elizabeth tomorrow to talk about an extension."

"Please tell her I said hello," Sabrina said, going along with the change of direction. "I'm sure they'll keep you. Just make sure to up the fees this time. We'll never get a house on your current salary."

Her attempt at humor got an obligatory chuckle out of him. He changed the subject once more, looking forward to dinner and a beer when he got home. He expressed he didn't want to drink alone, which made Sabrina hesitate, but she left it there. "See you then, *mi amore*."

When Houston hung up the phone, he noticed Phil watching him. He wasn't sure of the feeling this gave him.

"What?" Houston asked finally.

Phil waved him off. "Nothing."

The gesture got under Houston's skin. He stared until Phil noticed him again. Phil turned his head and smiled in a way that seemed to convey both sadness and glee. "You sound like you've got quite a woman with her. You're a lucky man, Jenkins. Don't fuck it up."

"Thanks," Houston said, hesitant. "So why did you set me up?"

In typical Phil fashion, he responded with a convoluted answer. "She just butted in. I figured you could handle her. If not, then you needed help. And I helped."

"So you're admitting it and denying it at the same time."

"I did, didn't I?" Phil smirked. "Oh well, what are you gonna do? As ol' blue eyes says, that's life."

"What in the hell are you ..." Houston shook his head. "Never mind. Sometimes talkin' to you feels like a waste of time. But I know you like Sabrina, and she likes you. So I know you're not the piece of crap you pretend to be."

Phil shrugged. "I don't pretend to be anything. I just am what I am. Maybe that's not good enough for you."

"Whoa, whoa, whoa, hold up," Houston interrupted. "You ain't gotta be good enough for me. Just don't be such a Cantoni all the fuckin' time, all right?"

Phil's hesitant chuckles were sprinkled with coughs, revealing more than just congestion. "Careful, Jenkins. For a moment, you made it sound as if you like me. What would Oscar say about that?"

"I don't give a fuck what anyone says." Houston could feel his anger rising and his frustration with a conversation that really wasn't going anywhere. "Look, man, I just thought it was kinda messed up, you ..." He softened his tone as he witnessed the pallor in Phil's face change to gray. "Hey, man, are you okay?"

"Yeah, I'm peachy," Phil responded, trying to get up. "You're a good man and I know you''ve stood up for me with Oscar and some of the other people in the office. I just wanted you to know I appreciate that. I know I'm not an easy man to get along with."

Houston was starting to feel a little uncomfortable with Phil's confession. He was somewhat embarrassed and tried to deny that he'd ever defended Phil. But Phil offered that he'd heard it from Elizabeth, which meant it was true, and Houston knew it.

"You're a good guy, and I only give you a hard time ..." Phil hesitated, and Houston thought Phil's eyes shone. "You remind me of someone, my ... my brother."

Houston started to feel a bit uneasy, hoping that Oscar either wasn't in the room or wasn't listening. Houston wasn't quite sure how to accept Phil's expression of sentiment. He tried to make a joke about it at first, but soon he realized that Phil was serious. Houston attempted to cover up his own awkwardness with an inquiry.

"I didn''t know you had a brother. I guess I never thought of you having a family. Do you get to see your brother much? Is he still alive?"

Phil shook his head and waved his hand, as if brushing off the questions. "You're a lucky man. You won the heart of an amazing woman. Not many of them around anymore. So, you had better not fuck it up—or I'll cut your nuts off."

And with that, whatever brief moment of reflection Phil Cantoni had been seduced by was gone. But Houston could see the change in Phil's demeanor, and he sought to get back to the more genteel Phil he'd never seen.

"Why do you admire Sabrina so much?"

"She also reminds me of someone. A love from long ago. And I trust her judgment." Phil tried to shrug through it. "For some reason she chose you, and that must mean you're worthy of something."

Phil returned his gaze to his desktop computer, which had been showing a blue screen for the past several minutes. He seemed to be signaling that the conversation was over. Taking the hint, Houston offered, "Your computer needs to be rebooted."

Phil threw up his hands. "Duh!"

Chapter 11

Los Angeles, California

Monday, July 19, 2010
3.:45 p.m.

As Houston set up the nightly backup of the computer system, he noticed that Oscar had snuck out a bit early and Phil was uncharacteristically still at his desk far past the usual quitting time of three thirty3:30 p.m. Houston glanced at his wristwatch, then at the time stamp on his desktop, to make certain he wasn't missing anything. He looked up to see something he recalled seeing before: Phil Cantoni wincing in pain and sitting at his desk merely looking drawn and quartered. It dawned on him how frail Phil had become over the last few weeks. He'd wanted to say something when he first noticed, but dealing with the long-term illness of his mother kept him from showing Phil any genuine concern.

He knew Phil was very private and very defensive when inquiries were made about his life. They had worked together for almost two years, and Houston realized he barely knew anything about him, other than the few times the subject of sports came up. He never knew Phil had any family until he'd admitted it before. Phil was fairly tight-lipped about the rest of his life.

Houston felt an sudden surge of regret, compelling him to reach out. He wasn't sure what to say. As he approached, he could see Phil wince once again and he became concerned. "Are you all right?" he asked. "You look like you're in a lot of pain. Can I get you something?"

Phil held a dark blue handkerchief to his mouth and peered up through glassy blue eyes at Houston, who now stood in the opening of Phil's cubicle. It was a moment, a pensive moment, that Houston would later realize made Phil so very difficult at times. Phil stared at Houston, then muttered, "Yeah, I need you to leave me alone and to mind your own business." He turned and coughed heavily into the handkerchief.

Houston turned to walk away, rejected, then suddenly turned back towards Phil. He didn't want to let this opportunity pass. "Hey, man, I just wanted to—"

Phil raised his hand to cut Houston off and took in a shallow breath. He cleared his throat and sputtered through gasps for air, "I'm okay." Then he shooed Houston away with a wave of his free hand as if he was irritated with Houston's presence.

Houston refused to let Phil off that easily. "Dude, I'm trying to help," he said, defensive.

Phil relented in a manner that appeared appreciative and confused. "Thanks, Houston," he said, struggling with his breath and his words. "I know you're ... you're ... just ... trying to be a friend. Like you always have." Phil stood and slowly maneuvered himself between Houston and the open pathway from his cubicle. "I'll be all right. I've just got to get home." And with that, he grabbed his keys and empty coffee mug and made his way towards the door.

Houston tried again, but was once again rejected with a wave of Phil's hand and the closing of the computer room anterior door. His first thought was to go after him, but as the door closed, he thought better of it and decided to let it go. Houston went back to his desk with Phil's comment stuck in his head. *Like you always have.* In a way, it made Houston feel good, to think that of all people Phil would think of him as a good guy. He didn't know why, but it made him feel a little better. On that note, he decided it was beyond time to go home.

As he exited the elevator to the main lobby of the building, he was surprised to see Phil talking to one of the partners of the law firm, Oliver Cole, the one attorney Phil seemed to treat with deference and respect. Phil appeared to be okay, standing straight, talking and laughing, no longer coughing. Even the color had returned to his cheeks. Not wanting to interrupt what appeared to be an intimate moment between genuine friends, Houston retreated into the elevator and went through the parking garage drive out to the street instead.

***

Houston was not used to taking public transportation, completely unaware of the hassle of riding a bus on Wilshire Boulevard during rush hour. His first mistake was not paying attention to where he was going and catching the wrong bus. Houston took a seat near the rear exit, welcoming the chance to sit and clear his head. Thoughts of Phil, and fear that his conversation with Renee could affect his employment, distracted him. He immediately regretted taking a stand just to shut her up. *Some people just have to have the last word*, he thought. *I should've just shut up and let her have it. But damn, is she irritating. She just has to have something to say even if no one's talking to her.*

Houston noticed a gamely elderly woman, carrying more grocery bags than she should handle, wiggle herself toward the rear of the bus. Houston gladly cleared a route for her and offered his open seat.

The elderly woman thanked him profusely, appreciative of his manners., "Thank you so much, young man. Your mother did a great job with you," she said.

Houston gave her a gracious smile, though a part of him wondered why she would assume it had been his mother and not his father. Did she know? After all these years, he'd grown paranoid that people could tell, just by looking at him, that he'd been raised without a father.

"You know, I don't usually ride the bus at this time," the woman told him, as if she already knew him. "I had a doctor's visit and needed to pick up some extra groceries. I spent more than I intended at the market, so I didn't have enough for the cab fare."

Houston nodded. "Me neither. I'm just getting off work. I usually drive, but I thought riding the bus would give me time to think." Part of him regretted responding. He didn't really want to have a conversation with a stranger on the bus. But then a seat opened up next to her, and he found himself seeking out conversation. She was pleasant.

"Houston Jenkins," he offered.

"Katherine Kobashigawa. Just call me Kate;, you'll never remember my last name." She grinned. "Besides, Kate sounds like a young lady's name."

Kate didn't live too far from him, so Houston offered to assist her with her bags. They slowly walked towards the end of a long cul-de-sac. Neighbors waved and greeted Kate; a young couple apologized for being late on their rent, and the woman kissed Kate on the cheek, thanking her for her patience. Once they made it to Kate's small apartment, she offered Houston a dollar and he refused.

"I'm happy to stop by and see you every once in a while," Houston said. "Help you if you need it."

"That's all right," she said. "I've gotten along fine all these years by myself."

"It's really no problem."

"Thank you," she said, appreciative. "I may need help this weekend with something ..."

Houston smiled. "I'll come by and bring my wife. I think you two would just love each other."

Kate reminded Houston of his mother in her waning years, and it left him with a soft spot in his heart for elderly, independent women. It made him remember how much he missed her, but fondly. The wounds of her passing remained fresh; so much had gone on in the past couple of days –

—returning to work, arguing with Renee, trying to plan out his future with Sabrina, starting a house and a family – —that he felt he'd hardly given himself time to truly mourn, let alone inquire about Florence's last words. He almost wondered if it didn't matter; he'd never had a father, but even if Florence had been his grandmother, she'd still raised him as a mother would. That was enough.

***

Houston made the six-block walk to his apartment still stuck in his own head. Without realizing it, he'd made his way up the stairs and into his apartment, when the smell of Spanish rice, beans, enchiladas, and corn greeted him. The aroma was so strong, and he floated on the fumes, stomach growling.

"Houston?" Sabrina called from the kitchen. "Are you home?"

Houston gratefully made it to the kitchen table and joined her for dinner. He kissed her, she kissed him, and she left him wanting more as he opened his eyes to see her smiling at him with a loving gaze. She didn't say another word; neither of them needed to.

They ate in silence for the next few moments, until Houston went to get another beer. He opened one for him and then reached back into the refrigerator to get one for Sabrina. She turned back to him.

"That's not for me, is it?" she said, just as the second bottle cap cracked. "Honey, I ... No thanks," Sabrina said. "I don't feel like a beer tonight, actually. Sorry."

Houston frowned, irritated. "I told you I didn't want to drink alone. I just opened it."

"I tried to stop you, come on."

Houston poured the second beer into the kitchen sink before she could say anything more and returned to his seat at the table. Sabrina attempted to diffuse any rising tension, but once he ate, he sighed. "I'm sorry. I shouldn't have reacted that way. And I know what you're gonna say, that it's okay, but it's not."

Sabrina felt a "'but'" coming on. "But ... ?"

"Well ... sometimes I feel like I'm being babied," he said. "Because of my mom dying."

"Oh, honey," Sabrina sighed. "I'm sorry if you think I've been babying you. I would never. I may want to protect you, but ... Can't you see?"

"My mother used to do that to me," Houston went on, laughing a little. "You know, we haven't had a chance to talk over dinner in a while."

Sabrina relaxed. "Of course. Let's get our dinner rap on. You first."

Amidst the rest of the day's confusion, Houston struggled to think of something to talk about. Then, after a moment of silence, it came to him. "I met this cool little old Japanese lady on the bus," he said. "She's probably super- rich. But she was riding the bus carrying all these groceries. I helped her and walked her home. Everybody on the block was greeting her. The way the people talked to her reminded me of my mom. I told her I'd bring you by to meet her ... Can't remember how to pronounce her name. Told me to call her Kate, or Mrs. K. She lives over there off Bronson."

"Katherine Kobashigawa?" Sabrina asked.

"Yeah. How do you know her?"

"She's a client of Will Shanks," she responded. "She actually helps fund some of the *pro bono* work he does. And she *is* really rich. I think she owns that entire block."

"Damn, I knew something was up," Houston said. "She walked down that block like the Empress of Japan. Everybody running up to her. I'm surprised someone didn't call the police, thinkin' I was tryin' to rob her or something."

"Don't be silly. You don't have the face of a criminal," Sabrina said. "But yes, I'd love to meet her. I've only seen her once in the office. Mr. Shanks usually goes to her place to talk."

Houston nodded. Then he finally admitted something that was eating away at him. "I think Phil Cantoni is really sick."

Sabrina frowned with genuine concern. "Really? Why do you say that?"

"I'm not sure. It's just a feeling I get when I look at him. I couldn't remember ever seeing him so frail." Houston could see the look of concern cover his wife's face. "Not to gross you out, but he was coughing up a lot. I'm not exactly sure, because he's got dark handkerchiefs. I think it's so no one will notice the color.... I tried to ask him about it, but he gave me his typical pain-in-the-ass response. But then, he actually had a moment of humanity, and said that he knew that I had always tried to be a friend to him. I couldn't believe it. Now, I'm thinking ... maybe he just said that to stop me from asking about his health. Because he turned right back into a sourpuss the moment he knew what he said caught me off -guard."

"Perhaps, he was being genuine and wanted you to know that even though he can be a jerk sometimes, he did realize that you actually tried to be nice to him in spite of his efforts to deter you," Sabrina said, letting her idea sink in with him. "And even though he's never said anything before, he wanted to say so now, because he might not get a chance later."

The end of her last statement hung in the air as if it wasere being considered by a jury. Houston shook his head, letting the words work their way down, and he begrudgingly agreed. "He did seem sincere before he ..."

He drifted off, picturing the frail man in his head. When Sabrina caught his attention, he returned her look with a shrug.

"So, you really think he's that ill?" she asked. "I'm not sure, but I think he's close to seventy."

"Seventy what? Years old?" Houston said, incredulous. "You've got to be kidding;, he looks nowhere near that old. Though if you saw him today you could see it."

"He really looked that bad, huh?"

"Yeah. And then I saw him and Mr. Cole hugging in the lobby."

"Oliver Cole?" Sabrina asked. "They've been friends for a long time. Oliver knows all of the secrets of the firm and he's supposed to have some juicy ones on Phil, Elizabeth, and Neil. Along with some of the other partners. But they keep it on the down low on account of Oliver arranging some deal with Phil and Neil."

"Are you sure it's not Phil who has the dirt on Neial and Elizabeth?" Houston ventured. "Because Cantoni walks around there like he owns the place sometimes. I'll bet Phil's got evidence that they were having an affair. And Mr. Cole wrote up papers so that Phil could never be fired in exchange for him ... What do they call it when you can't say anything about ... ?"

"A gag order," Sabrina chimed in. She could see he was in full-blown conspiracy theory mode, and Sabrina just loved the way his face would light up when he concocted his far-flung ideas. She was happy to see him thinking and reacting to things other than what he'd been dealing with. Maybe he was ready to move on.

Houston continued on about how most people in the office shared his perspective. Sabrina smiled and reached for his hand, stroked and kissed it. Houston gave her an awkward smile, unsure of the unwarranted affection. He started to feel like she just wanted him to stop talking, as the feelings of being babied started to creep back into his mind. He took somewhat of an offense to her gestures, pulling his hand away while trying to finish his revelations. Sabrina, too, was getting slightly irritated because the evening was not following her game plan. She pulled herself closer to him to nibble at his ear.

Houston pulled away, irritated but smiling. "You know, if you're not interested in what I have to say, you can just tell me to shut up."

Unsure where the hostility had come from, Sabrina tried to assuage his feelings. "*Mi amore*, I am always interested in what you have to say. I just wanted to snuggle up next to you. What's wrong, my love? Are you still bothered about what happened with Renee? Should I go over there and put her in check?" she said, loving and a bitg silly.

But Houston took it differently, laughing through his growing irritation. "That's the same shit Phil said. That he thought I couldn't put

Renee in check like you could," he said. "I don't need you to protect me. I know you think you're right all the time, but sometimes you're not. I'm a grown-ass man and I can take care of myself. I know everyone thinks you're the best thing that's happened to me, but I'm good on my own, you know!"

It came out more adamantly than he'd wanted. Constant reminders of not growing up with a father figure around had been driving at his core since his mother became ill. Houston had challenged himself to handle it like a man, but he was losing himself in self-pity and paranoia. His wife seemed to be his savior more times than he admitted, or wanted. Affronted and emasculated, he overreacted to the comments tossed at him earlier, caught in what he couldn't control nor explain, becoming unglued. Was it her fault? Was it his? *You've fucked your life over – —now you're gonna fuck over hers.*

Sabrina's first reaction was to reach out to calm him, but she, too, was dealing with emotions emphasized by the hormonal changes her body was conjuring as she now lived, breathed, and ate for two. The confluence of emotion and hormones pushed her into a defensive direction. Her response was not unkind, but more to the point.

"You're a grown man. I get it. I always have, and you don't need my help with anything," she said. "But if you were paying attention to more than what I was saying but how I was saying it, you wouldn't need my help understanding that my comments weren't meant to belittle you. But to support you. You know, I'm your wife, that's just what I do. I'm sorry you're going through a tough time with the loss of your mother. And maybe seeing Phil as the old decrepit man he is makes you feel strange and emotional, too. I'm sorry, but newsflash: death happens. But so does life!" Her own words began to undo her, and she stared at him and smiled through the tears welling up in her eyes. "This isn't how I wanted our evening to turn out. When you're ready to treat me with the love and respect I defer to you, then come to our bedroom and we can talk. If not, I'm sure the couch will not complain so much about your company tonight."

As the bedroom door closed behind her, Houston reflected. He would always give Sabrina credit for her insight and instincts; it was one of her qualities he envied and admired. But this time she was completely off base. *I don't give a rat's ass about Cantoni.* But he did. They both knew that Houston cared more for the onerous old white man than he would dare admit. He didn't touch the notion of his grieving, because there was too much eating him inside to put a finger on exactly what she meant. He replayed the evening in his head, moving over to the couch and feigning comfort as he searched the cable channels for a distraction.

Every image of a woman smiling on the television made him think of Sabrina's eyes swelling up with tears. He was responsible for that. And with that realization, he knew he must do something about it. He turned off the television and softly knocked on the bedroom door. He entered cautiously, trying to navigate his way into the dimly lit room. Sabrina had lit a candle in the corner of the room and was meditating in the lotus position on her side of the bed with one of her ear buds securely in her ear and the other tucked under her pajama top. The flickering light danced around her face, shadowing her expression, so Houston wasn't exactly sure how to read her.

Houston offered, with a scant amount of uncertainty and in a soft tone, "Hey, baby ..." He waited for a response. When she didn't respond, unease crept into his mind. He called to her again, and still no response. He fought back the circling butterflies. Houston was not a confrontational soul. He was a peacemaker – —or, at least, he wanted to be.

He preferred to calmly resolve any conflict and saved his anger for situations that he could control.

As he got closer to her, he could faintly hear the sounds of violin strings and piano keys emanating from her ear buds. She couldn't hear him. The knot in his stomach subsided. He wasn't sure what exactly had made her cry, but his wife wasn't one for crocodile tears. Something was obviously troubling her, and he hadn't picked up on it. Then it dawned on him: she had been sleeping more and gaining some weight. Perhaps she was irritated at her weight gain.

He sat next to her and picked up one of her hands. She opened her eyes and offered a soft smile. Whatever had been bothering her no longer appeared to be an issue. He felt a brief reprieve of guilt, and he kissed her on the forehead, gentle and with all the love in the world.

Sabrina cupped his face in both of her hands and whispered lovingly, "I know you're going through a lot, sweetheart. I'm sorry. But I didn't deserve you snapping at me like that. I would never do that to you."

Houston tried to take control of his face, but she held firm. He knew he'd screwed up and needed to apologize, now. She was not going to wait.

"I'm sorry, honey," he said. "I really am. I never ever wanted to react to you that way. You are my everything, and you deserve the best from me. I know I haven't been—"

Sabrina directed his mouth to hers, kissing him passionately. Once again, she proved her way of ending a conversation was better than his. When he felt her stop, Houston opened his eyes to see her smiling at him. He started to speak and she raised her forefinger to his lips. She took his hand and placed it gently onto her belly where she was beginning to show. Houston eyed her quizzically. Sabrina beamed, without a word, her eyes swelling with excitement and more tears.

It was then that it all dawned on him: his beautiful and loving wife was pregnant. The world stood still, and he took a deep breath as the realization saunk in. He held her close as he lovingly kissed the tears from her eyes. He started to speak and she quieted him, wanting to enjoy the moment. Words at this time would be pointless. He held his wife close to him and slowly rocked her back and forth. Sabrina nuzzled her head under his chin as they went from sitting on the edge of the bed to lying in each other's arms on top of the goose-down quilt. Sabrina released a deep visceral sigh of satisfaction as Houston brushed away her bangs to kiss her forehead. They continued to hold each other in silence as the candle flickered its final light and the faint sound of Gustav Mahler's Symphony No. 8 played to its conclusion. Houston and Sabrina fell asleep in their tangled embrace.

***

Neil Watson called Elizabeth Taylor-Barrings into his office and asked her to have a seat. He didn't appear upset, but his stern tone and gaze told her that something was bothering him. When she sat, he handed a file over to her.

"I want to have a word with you about Houston Jenkins and his employment contract renewal," he announced with full authority.

Dumbfounded, Elizabeth only said, "Sure, okay." It was rare to catch her off guard. It was even rarer for Neil Watson, the senior managing partner at Watson, Creed, Johnson & Cole, to take an interest in any temporary staff's employment contract. "What about him?"

"Have we had any complaints about him?" Neil spoke in a suggestive tone. It wasn't exactly a question.

"None that have crossed my desk," Elizabeth answered, though she expected she knew where the conversation was headed. "The staff here seem to like him. He's a bit forthcoming, but not obtrusive. One of the paralegals has a crush on him, even. Why do you ask?"

"Do you know if anything untoward has occurred between him and the paralegal?" Neil asked. "I mean, we can't have any philandering going on here." He flashed the interrogation style he often used to direct a witness's testimony towards the answer he wanted: ask a question, then cajole the answer that best suited the line of questioning.

"No, it's quite innocent," Elizabeth responded, trying to avoid losing her place in the conversation's direction. "Houston is married. And as far as I can tell, very dedicated to his wife. Who used to work here, if you recall."

"Has anything come up missing in the record's rooms? Are there any old case files that have been recently disturbed?"

Elizabeth frowned. Neil was grasping at straws. She knew the real problem Neil had with Houston Jenkins; she just wanted him to admit it and stop playing lawyer with her. "Neil, I can't think of a single solitary thing about Houston Jenkins that deserves this line of questioning. What's your concern about him?"

"Jefferson!" Neil Watson finally spait out. "Thomas Jefferson! A rapist!" His anger now simmered to a boil. "Thomas Jefferson, a father of our country, to be spoken about in such inglorious terms! I've heard some of the comments he's made about supremacy, too."

Elizabeth sat back, letting him get it all out. She was only surprised that it had not taken much to coax it out of him. She was so used to the lawyerly response – —stating a topic without addressing it.

"We have more than a client or two with Monticello connections,"" Neil added. "Do you really think they would want us to have employees with his attitude working here on their cases? Do you? And how do we know he hasn't copied something out of one of those files he's transcribing for us?"

Elizabeth picked up on his inference and tried to assuage his fears.

"He's not ... Neil. That's not his job. But he is an independent contractor and his contract is up for renewal in a week or two. Perhaps, we can——"

"It renews after the end of next week, according to that file." Neil pointed at it as if it were alive. "I don't really see the need to renew it. Do you?"

"He hasn't finished his work," Elizabeth started.

"Good! Then we have a reason not to renew. He didn't complete the job he was contracted to do."

"That's not what I mean," Elizabeth responded. "He completed the first wave and is currently working on the second wave. He's transferring our antiquated system out of the dark age and into the modern age. He set up image machines and oversaw the purchase of those new laptops and tablets everyone is so thrilled about. The paralegals have faster access to legal precedents and can track case filings much better than they could before, thanks to what he's done. And so far he's kept us on budget."

"I think my wife's cousin's son does the same thing. Why don't we just hire him on a permanent basis and tell Mr. Jenkins that we're moving the responsibility in- house and his services are no longer needed?"

"It's her nephew, and you didn't like the way he wore his hair," Elizabeth said. "Besides, there was something about nepotism that you mentioned as a reason *not* to hire him in the first place."

""Well, we made the AA hire, so now we can hire my nephew," Neil said. "There isn't any concern about nepotism, because Jenkins won't come on full- time. Isn't that right? And we need a full-time employee to finish the job."

"We were supposed to address the full-time status at the renewal of his contract."

"I don't think that's necessary. Do you?" Neil Watson stared at Elizabeth, exerting his full power as managing partner. "It's settled, then." Elizabeth took a moment before responding, accepting the inevitable. "It's late and I'm not certain he's still here. I'll have accounting make a check equal to what would be the end of his contract next week as severance and I will give it to him in the morning." The part about the check was an afterthought. She said this while looking directly into Neil Watson's eyes, so that he understood she would not budge on this.

Neil Watson winced at the thought of paying someone for not working, but accepted the inevitable and decided it best to settle there than litigate further. After a moment of reflection, he concluded, "So, then it's done. He'll be out before I leave for Sacramento in the morning." As if he had to have the very last word on the subject. Then, as if their discussion had been about the weather, Neil changed the subject.

Elizabeth Taylor-Barrings opened and stared into the employment file of Houston Jenkins and immediately thought of his wife, Sabrina.

Elizabeth had always been fond of her and knew what a capable and formidable trial lawyer she was going to be. Elizabeth closed the file, stood up, and walked out of Neil's spacious corner office. Neil watched her leave with a look of satisfaction.

Chapter 12

Lafayette, Virginia

Saturday, August 15, 1959
2.:39 p.m.

For the fifth time, Jasper yelled at his son Ashley from the other side of the sitting room window. Evelyn, who couldn't stand her recalcitrant husband's outbursts any longer, turned on him.

"Leave him be, Jasper!" she snapped. All she wanted was a peaceful afternoon. "He's just having fun with the children. They're like family to him."

"Those children? Like family?" Jasper spewed with venom and disgust. "How can you let them continue to stay here? Those pickaninnies are losing respect for their place here. They think they can run around like they own the place! And that woman ..."

"You leave that woman and her children alone, ya hear!" Evelyn hurled at him like a fastball delivered to force the batter to back off home plate. She didn't have to say anything further – —Jasper knew enough not to question or challenge his wife. He could feel the heat of her intense protection over the entire Jenkins family. Her acrimony towards his words confirmed that he would be fighting a losing battle.

Jasper felt he desperately needed to regain his wife's trust and thought of no better way than to acquiesce to her way of thinking. "You are right, my dear. Perhaps I am being a bit hard on them. I appreciate you forcing me to recognize my ill will. This lady and her ... her *children* require a gentler hand than what I've previously offered." He slithered out with the sting of venomous honey as he moved towards the bar and offered to refresh her drink. He knew he needed to submit to her to regain her trust, and he smiled, knowing she wasn't prepared for his response as she started to speak over him before what he said actually sunk in.

"Jasper, it's just that you've been ... you've been ..."

He watched the inner workings of her mind turn as she battled with his previous behavior and his admission offering amends. She paused, not certain what else to say as he moved across the floor, stirring the mix of bourbon and ice. Evelyn gave him a peculiar look as she watched him glide across the room, as if she were watching the man she had fallen in love with, reborn. He hesitated for a moment, wondering if her expression was due to her catching a glimpse of him or just seeing him as he wanted her to see him. He reminded himself that the Lord was on his side, and he knew what she saw was not what he did, but what he had become. He placed a small kiss on her forehead, put the drink in her hand, and whispered, "My dear, I know I allowed my envy to cloud my judgment. I thought I was losing my family."

"But you were so cruel to Florence and the children."

"I can only apologize to you, my dear, for my actions. And admit that I have allowed my duties at City Council to distract me from what is needed from me here at home. I thought I was being replaced. I can see now, you must think I've abandoned you and our son."

"Well ... I ...," Evelyn stammered, caught completely off guard. He was giving her the direct attention and affection she thought she'd lost from him. Since the Jenkins family had moved into their home, the distance between them had seemed to grow wider and faster than before. Evelyn told herself it was because she had forced him into having a child when he wasn't ready. But now, she felt she was going to have to rethink that.

"It's just that I know deep down what kind of man you are.... I mean, what kind of man I married. And I just never thought that I would see that man again. It would mean so much to me to have that man back. To have you back, Jasper."

He placed a soft kiss on her lips. "I know, my dear, and I apologize once again. I've seen where I allowed jealousy to take control of my heart. You were only in need of assistance with a newborn child. And you opened up your kind heart to save a woman who reminded you of your youth. I should have understood that. Will you forgive me?"

Evelyn's mind was working overtime as she reconciled who Jasper had become and what she thought he was. Perhaps, she believed, the good Lord had answered her prayers and patience. She offered a heartfelt smile. "Oh, Jasper, I have prayed that the good Lord would show you the error of your ways. That He would see fit to open up the kindness you've shown me before. That He would rekindle that ... somehow."

She held her drink at bay, until Jasper touched her hand to remind her, and suggested, "Let's offer each other a small toast of remembrance for our past and towards our future, my dear. The Lord has been good to us."

He smiled as she took a reluctant sip of her drink.

***

Even though the decision of *Brown v. Board of Education* had passed over five years ago, with the Supreme Court's recommendation for swift and immediate implementation, true and actual implementation in the South was deliberately slow. And in the county of Lafayette, Virginia, it was practically nonexistent. Florence wanted her children to get an education not afforded to the colored children of Lafayette County. So she would take the twins and Ashley on long drives into the nation's capital, where she would feel less wary that someone would harass her or the children. The Smithsonian Museum and the Lincoln Memorial soon became their favorite places to visit. They would spend all day in the museums and get lost in the history of the nation. Florence would find ways to incorporate her own history into their visits. She told them what life was like for her as a child, before her parents died; about what it was like growing up with the Jenkins family; how she and their father realized they were meant to be. She'd talk lovingly about how dedicated Dillard was to his education and to being a soldier. She'd talk in measured tones about how slowly it took for things to change as she grew, and contrasted it with what had occurred in recent years. The world was changing faster around them now; the boycotts and the marches were making headlines in papers all across the nation.

Reverend Dr. Martin Luther King, Jr,. had become the bane of the existence of many Southern whites as the news of busloads of northerners, both black and white, created a buzz every time they passed through any part of Virginia on their way to the Deep South. People concerned with the very Deep South took for granted that changes were happening elsewhere – —they weren't. Virginia's refusal to go along with the call for civil rights was more clandestine than her Southern cousins, even though their methods were just as frightening. g. In a few weeks, A few years earlier, the death of Emmett Till in Mississippi would grab the national headlines and become a focus of racial injustice, as an anomaly only occurring in the Deep South, when in actuality it occurred as far north as Massachusetts and as often as the change in seasons.

Leesa and Leeland were into their teenage years and enjoyed these outings to the capital. They had many questions about their heritage that their school lessons didn't cover. Florence hoped these trips would inspire them to respect themselves and see their father's life and legacy through her eyes. She strove to embed them with dignity, integrity, and love for themselves. It never occurred to her to adjust her lessons to fit the understanding of Ashley Cartwright, a child of privilege and a descendant of slave-owners.

Ashley enjoyed and learned from the museum trips as much if not more than Leeland and Leesa. He showed extraordinary maturity and acceptance of the way the world worked. He was not ashamed of his family's history, nor was he proud of it. He accepted it for what it was, admonishing himself to do better. He knew he couldn't change the past, but was quick to realize his actions on a daily basis would shape his future. He enjoyed hearing fond memories from Florence, who in many ways he wished wasere his real mother. He received the love from her that was absent from his parents. His mother was distant and cold, while his father cared more about the City Council than his own family. Ashley knew his deep association with the Jenkins family would be a point of contention in Lafayette. He also understood that the wealth of his own family allowed him to explore the limits of their relationship. Ashley could feel the pain in Florence's words when she spoke about her husband and father of her children. He believed the one person Florence needed more than anyone was her husband, Dillard.

As the kids engaged each other on the road, Ashley then and there decided he would live in the way he thought would fulfill the promise of Dillard Houston Jenkins. He decided to be part of the solution, not like many of the whites in Lafayette he saw as the problem, especially his father. He felt a visceral reaction whenever he was in Jasper's presence. Ashley was wreathed in silence, untying the knots that gathered in his stomach whenever he recalled his father's rape of Florence. He had been horrified. He felt small and helpless. He was familiar with the sting of his father's backhand and had witnessed the pain Florence experienced. He was frozen in fear and horror as his tears streamed down his cheeks in silence. When reflecting upon that moment in his adult life, he would come to realize that he had been in shock. Ashley would also come to realize that the hate he harbored for his father was really in part towards his mother, Evelyn. He hated that she had married such a man, and even more so that she did nothing to stop him. Ashley knew that Dillard Jenkins would protect his wife and family. And so would he. He closed his eyes and made his own promise.

Today was one of the most special trips to the museums of the capital simply because of the presence of Andrew Walker, an unrecognized war hero and fellow soldier of Florence's late husband. It was Andrew Walker who explained to Florence the circumstances and conditions the soldiers faced when her husband was killed in action. Andrew was one of the soldiers who constantly wrote letters to the Veterans Administration and the Secretary of Defense, trying to force recognition of his Brothers- in- Arms and the exploits of the 761st and 769th infantry and tank divisions – —but to no avail. Andrew Walker would remain vigilant and continue to express his feelings about the treatment of the colored soldier. He would regale the children with stories of the amazing camaraderie shared amongst the Black Panthers and their struggle for acceptance in the white man's army.

Andrew had taken his story to the press and straight to Washington, DC, to address the committee on foreign wars. He even sought the assistance of the Virginia chapter of the Veterans of Foreign Wars;, but, other than a few press clippings, recognition was never realized. He had become little known in the broader community, but he was well known by the black soldiers who appreciated his voice. His voice was also heard by the Lafayette City Council and the Klu Klux Klan, who believed that niggers didn't deserve to wear the colors of the US Army – —let alone be recognized for dying in service for America: a country that wouldn't accept them and didn't want them to "get too big for the britches,", as the Klan would explain it.

Under the shade of a large ficus tree in the Smithsonian courtyard, Florence set up a picnic for the children to eat their lunch, while Andrew treated them to detailed stories about traveling by tank into the French and Italian countrysides and finally into Germany, where Negro soldiers met Europeans. "The civilians in France and Italy would come up to us and hug and kiss us. They treated us like heroes! They weren't scared of us!" he exclaimed in a bemused tone. "Them American white boys didn't like it one bit," he continued. "They tried to get us in trouble just because they was jealous of how we was liked.

"Man, let me tell you, it was like nothin' we experienced here. That's a fact sho. Sometimes, them French and I--talian girls, pronouncing the capital "I" sound, would walk right up to you and touch you and bring you food. I'll tell you, you should have seen the look on them white boys' faces because they couldn't do anything to stop 'em. No matter what they tried to do."

Andrew let the memory glide over him, and it would bring a smile to his face. He'd often speak about the true patriotism of his fellow colored soldiers and what they endured both Stateside and in the battles of Europe at the hands of the American military system. He told the children the reason it took so long for the Negro soldiers to face the enemy was because the military leadership and the national press didn't want to send pictures home of coloreds shooting whites. "They really didn't want our help until they realized they needed it. General Patton believed in us and gave us a chance to prove ourselves. Them Tuskegee boys shot down them Germans planes and those white boys dropping the bombs wouldn't fly without 'em. But they never let them fight those Krauts on their own. I think the war would have ended sooner if they'd'a let us join the fight sooner."

A timid voice asked a question Andrew had to contemplate before he could answer. "Mr. Walker, why did Negro soldiers fight so hard for America?" Ashley inquired. Andrew was so lost in his thoughts, he almost forgot it was a little white boy asking. Usually, Andrew held himself in a certain reserve around whites; men, women, or children. Too many times he'd witnessed harm come to people that looked like him because of the whim of any white person willing to point a finger. But with Ashley, he felt that the boy's love for the Jenkins family,. and his respect for Andrew, was genuine. Unwittingly, he felt comfortable around a white person for the first time in his life.

"Well, since the end of slavery, we believed that once America saw all we wanted was to prove we could love this country, too, white folks would understand and treat us like they treated themselves. But I reckon it don't matter what we colored folks do. White folks never want us to get the same things they git. Never." More dejection than spite. An accepted reality.

Florence picked up on the shift in Andrew's mood and directed the children's attention to hope for the future and what they could do themselves to evoke change. She knew that Andrew's stories of their father were the kids' favorites. But she also knew that his intermittent visits would bring additional scrutiny. During his visits, she wanted her kids as far away as possible from the likelihood of trouble. She didn't want to tell Andrew of the danger his presence would bring. So she planned special trips when Andrew would ask to visit. Her idea was to expose her children to places outside of Lafayette in the hopes that her children would one day want to do the same: get out of Lafayette County, move to any one of the bigger cities in the northeast or to the West Coast, where better opportunities were available to them.

She knew that Andrew's visits were a part of his commitment to her husband to look in on his family. She couldn't help but feel that some of Mr. Walker's concern for her well- being had grown into affection. These were the times she missed Dillard the most, and she knew the children and their lives would have been different had he survived the war.

Florence would sometimes hold her breath watching the children listen to Andrew and imagine Dillard holding them and laughing with them. Andrew was nice to her children, but he wasn't her husband, and he wasn't their father.

***

In front of the modest home of the family of the deceased Lincoln Jackson, a squad car sat in an unusually cool summer afternoon while its occupant debated whether to make the trek up the unpaved dirt road to the front door. It had been a long time since his last visit, and he was unsure how he'd be received. Bo Clayton was not afraid of anything, least of all the anger of a Negro widow of a one-time friend. He knew in his heart this visit should have occurred years ago. Since the circumstances surrounding the death of

Lincoln Jackson had yet to lead to a conviction or even an arrest, he knew he had to make a personal appearance. This was one case he wouldn't handle by the Book of Clayton – —but rather by the Book of Lafayette City Council.

Bo and Lincoln had shared a childhood friendship that had survived the ranting and raving of Clayton's overtly racist mother, but couldn't survive the overt subjugation of the Lafayette City Council. Bo knew, in his heart, his father would be disappointed in him – —just as disappointed as Bo was with his father for running away with his Negro muse and leaving him behind, alone with an overbearing and hateful mother. Bo, having hoped to become a man worthy of respect, had become a product of his upbringing and socialization. After Bo's father left, he separated himself from Lincoln, even though his friend would continue to speak fondly and respectfully of him. Lincoln's brutal murder had taken a toll on the Jackson family and especially on his son Cleavon – —so much so that it got the attention of the City Council, which meant, more and more, Jasper Dunning. Jasper convinced the Council to use this grief to their advantage: by using the man Cleavon's father respected to engender that end.

While he continued to sit in the car, gripping the steering wheel, Bo was rudely shaken by a loud crash and a barrage of foul language. He quickly regained his sense of awareness and immediately turned his attention to the image in his sideview mirror. A shabbily dressed, elderly black man kicked the remains of a broken liquor bottle that had slipped from his feeble hand onto a large rock on the dirt road. Bo recognized the man as someone who, on more than one occasion, had endured the hospitality of the Lafayette County Jail for drunken and disorderly conduct. His immediate reaction was to take this assault on his memories as an offense he would have to rectify. But for some reason, a reason he himself could not rightly understand, Beauregard Clayton lifted his large frame out of the car and gingerly approached the pitiful drunk. The inebriated man immediately recognized the sheriff and started to physically shake with fear as he approached. Too many times he'd been on the receiving end of the sheriff's intolerance for anyone so drunk they'd stumble into a squad car while he was in it.

It's too early for this shit, Bohe thought. HeBo snatched the man's bony arm and lifted his entire frame up off the ground, then let him go with a gentle touch unrecognized by anyone on the wrong side of Sheriff Clayton. Bo stood him upright, straightened out his shirt, and leaned in close.

"Alouysius, you know I don't have to see you like this," he whispered, then reached into his own pocket and seized the man's hand, placing two dollar bills squarely in his palm and closing his fingers around them. He forcefully turned the inebriated man around, pointing him in the direction of the local Negro diner. "Now git to Josephine's, git somethin' to eat an' sum coffee before you git home to May. Now scoot!"

Unbeknownst to the sheriff, a small group who had heard the crashing glass came out of the Jackson home onto the porch in time to witness the sheriff's charity. There was a collective sigh as Al stumbled away. He appeared to walk with urgency and purpose after having just escaped what could have been a harsher fate. Neither the sheriff nor the onlookers could tell if he were sober enough to understand what had just occurred. Al simply waved his hand as he stared at the bills in disbelief, before he stuffed them into his pocket.

Turning away from his charitable recipient, Bo hesitated just a moment, collecting his thoughts as he raised his head towards the Lincoln residence, seeing the looks of relief on their faces. Bo scanned the onlookers as he picked out Mrs. Jackson, who had placed her palms together pressing against her mouth, as if thanking the good Lord the sheriff had shown mercy. More of the Jackson men from inside the house came out as a result of the whispers. He tipped his hat to Mrs. Jackson, giving everyone else a defiant stare as he slid back in his squad car and drove away. Mrs. Jackson took the sheriff's unnatural kindness as confirmation of her husband's past acknowledgement of their friendship. She prayed that justice would finally come her way. Her prayers would not be answered.

Realizing that more than a few eyes had witnessed his kindness, the sheriff decided he would pursue a meeting with Lincoln's family at another time. He slowly pulled away in the squad car, peering at Mrs. Lincoln in his rearview mirror. He tried to replay the moment, and he couldn't quite grasp the meaning of it all or how it had come about. He chalked it up to his penance for abandoning Lincoln and never gave it another thought. He would have to find an excuse to commandeer Cleavon when school started back up in the fall – —to recruit him for the Council's purposes.

***

Urging the children to get to bed after such an eventful day had been an arduous task. But the three of them had finally fallen asleep and Florence steered her exhausted frame nervously to the foyer, where Andrew Walker had been waiting patiently. The drive back from DC had been a long one: one that consisted of a traffic stop just outside of Bethesda, Maryland. The officer claimed Florence was driving over the speed limit; however, when the white policeman, an ex-infantryman, recognized her passenger, Andrew Walker, he relented and issued Florence a warning as he spoke with great deference to his brother-in-arms and his dedication to his fallen comrades. The encounter made Andrew and his war stories loom large in the children's eyes, especially those of Leeland. The genuine respect from a white police officer towards a Negro veteran left an indelible mark that drove Leeland to find that same respect – —the respect he believed was owed to his father.

Florence stepped into the foyer, not certain if Mr. Dunning was home or if Mrs. Dunning was still awake. When Andrew's gaze fell upon her, she could see his eyes brighten and his smile grow warm as he took her in. She placed her index finger to her full lips, begging quiet. She led him to the kitchen and offered him a cool glass of sweet tea. He accepted graciously and waited for her to sit across from him at the small service table in the corner.

Andrew could sense that she knew of his intentions; he also sensed that her relationship with Dillard wasn't over for her. Andrew reached across the linoleum tabletop for her hand. Florence initially pulled back, then relented. She didn't want to feel uncomfortable with him, and if he made any advances towards her, her heart would make her feel that way. Andrew started to speak as he rubbed the back of her hand, but Florence stopped him abruptly, almost in tears.

"Andrew, you know I'm fond of you.... I just need a little ... more time to get my heart and head in the same direction," she confessed.

Andrew offered a soft smile, respecting her feelings. "Florence, now you know I would never rush you into anything you ain't ready for. Dillard and me were like brothers from way back. And I know he'd want me to look out for you and the children. I'm not tryin' to say that it's just because of Dillard that I, uh ... but it's because I want to."

"Andy," she said, only ever calling him that when they were alone. She understood the intimacy of the relationship they all shared and his reverence for her husband.

"Florence, I owe my life to Dillard. And therefore I owe my life to you. I worry about you and the children here in this house. Here in the South. The way things are here for Negroes hasn't changed. And both Leesa and Leeland are growing fast. They need a man around. Especially, Leeland."

Overcome by the awkwardness of the moment, Andrew got down on one knee. He wasn't exactly sure how this had happened, but all of a sudden it felt right to him. He looked into her eyes and recognized the unease behind her cautious smile as she wiped away a tear. He noticed the subtle shake of her head. Andrew rubbed her hands, stood up, and gently kissed her on the mouth, wiping away her tears. He understood.

"This will probably be one of the last times I get to see you," he said softly. "I'm heading out west. I know of some colored folks who were able to purchase some homes and land. Some near where Ethel is. I've already spied a place big enough for me, and you and the children, should you ever decide to come out. I will always be here for you and Dillard. I promise."

Florence tried to explain, but couldn't find the words to say what she knew the both of them were thinking. *It's not the right time.*

Andrew let himself out through the service room back door. Deep down, he knew it would never be. Florence Jenkins was a woman dedicated to love and family. She believed allowing another man to enter the lives of her children would lessen the memory of their father. Andrew finally understood that, and he smiled and said a brief prayer, admitting to Dillard what a lucky man he was. As he turned to leave, he saw the lights switch on inside, as the door closed behind him.

"Florence?" Evelyn called out in a hoarse and exhausted voice from the balcony upstairs. "Is that you, dear? Florence!"

Florence hurried to the distressed call. Reaching the top of the stairs, she found Evelyn out of her wheelchair, lying prone on the ground with her boney fingers clutching the railing of the bannister. Florence rushed to her side, sitting next to her at the edge of the staircase. She gingerly repositioned Evelyn, placing her head to rest on her lap as Florence had now positioned her own back against the bannister's railings. Florence stroked her forehead and sweetly asked how she had made it out this far without her chair. She raised the frail woman to her feet, and they slowly walked towards the master bedroom down the hallway. All of the bedroom doors on the floor were closed except for Evelyn's ――although Evelyn and Jasper remained married, they lived in separate bedrooms.

Candles provided flickering shadows as they moved across the landing. Her wheelchair was just outside her bedroom door, braced against the bannister, wheels turned inward. Evelyn had been secretly trying to regain her strength. When she found herself alone, she would use the bannister to stand and take a few steps each day. She usually made it back to the chair before anyone would noticed. Florence had witnessed her efforts before, knowing this was something she needed to accomplish on her own. She tried to deflect the consequences of her efforts, and in a jovial manner she said, "So this is where all the trouble began."

Evelyn clutched Florence's arm as tightly as her frail hands could. Florence started to speak, when Evelyn interrupted her.

"Florence, I want to thank you for everything you do for this family. For the way you are to Ashley and me. You take care of him like he was one of your own. I know that sometimes, he wishes he was.... I don't know how the two of us would get along if you weren't here, sweetie;, I just don't know."

Florence placed Evelyn into her wheelchair and rolled her to the side of the canopy bed while she pulled back the comforter and silk sheets. She slowly lifted the frail woman into bed and adjusted the pillows around her.

She sensed Evelyn had been listening in on her conversation with Andrew. She smiled and again gently stroked Evelyn's head.

"Now, Ms. Evelyn, you know that you have always been there for me when I didn't even know I needed you. I'm not planning on going anywhere. My children love you and Ashley. I couldn't think of taking them away from here."

Reassured, Evelyn reached out to Florence and squeezed her forearm once again. "I will take care of you and your children. I know that Jasper can let the evil in his heart get the best of him, but I will protect you from him, too."

The specter of Jasper's crime against Florence tried to push itself into Evelyn's mind, but she fought it off, thinking of the conversation she and Jasper had had earlier. She wanted to trust him, and in order to do this she needed to convince herself she hadn't seen it at all. Her heart wanted to believe the good Lord was answering her prayers, but her head was telling her not to listen to her heart. It kept telling her the prayers the good Lord was answering were for the care and nurturing of her son. The prayers for her son won out, as she blocked any thought of Jasper from her mind and she pushed forward, allowing her genuine concern and bridled guilt to direct her thoughts.

"I will take care of the children," she said again.

She pledged all the protection and comfort her name could afford. She promised when the children were of age, she would make sure they would benefited from the Cartwright trust.

Florence didn't respond. She only smiled, rubbing warmth into Evelyn's cold hands. She sat quietly as Evelyn quickly fell asleep. A tear rolled down her cheek as she gently kissed her on the forehead and raised the bedsheets and comforter to cover her. She wiped away the tear, convinced that in their own way, both Andrew and Evelyn made offers of love and security. Florence knew all too well of the real dangers that could befall her children. She remained in constant battle between her fears and aspirations for the twins. She drew strength from the love she shared with Dillard to face the uncertain future for Leesa and Leeland.

***

Earlier that day, after sending the sheriff on his errand to gather the Jackson boy, Jasper Dunning connived in the corner of the Lafayette City Council's anteroom with Dr. Michaels. He urged Michaels to spare him more of the Wu Mei, having given his wife the last drop in her bourbon.

Jasper spoke with newfound enthusiasm. "It occurred to me that my journey was never in my own hands, but in the hands of the good Lord himself. I believe He placed me in the unenviable position to test my resolve. It is obvious: the Almighty has ulterior plans for me and my unique abilities. Looking back over my life, I can clearly see how the hand of God has influenced me." For added emphasis, he pointed out where it all started: "I see now that it was indeed the good Lord's hand that prompted me to take an interest in Evelyn, to add calm and control over her indecisive shyness. And it's become clear that the good Lord wants me to take the helm of the City Council. Why else would He place me as Courtland's right hand?" he asked Michaels, sensing there would be no dispute in his proclamation.

Weldon Michaels merely stared at his friend, seemingly unfazed by the direction of the conversation, but more in fear of incurring Jasper's wrath. Dr. Michaels had witnessed Jasper when he was interrupted during moments when his certainty was to remain unchallenged.

Jasper continued, "The utter ridicule I've endured—no, *suffered*—at the hand of the Lafayette *ill-ete* for not being one of them. This is indeed the Lord's will. And to think I almost succumbed to the evil machinations of that venomous colored woman and her vile children. Just to know that the good Lord has placed my salvation within my grasp gives me newfound patience. Surely I have survived my ceremonial forty days and proven myself worthy?."

When Dr. Michaels remained silent, Jasper hesitated, gathering his summation to drive his point home.

"You see, Weldon, it was the sin of pride that made me think I could deal with it all at once. Unlike Adam and Eve, the snake I need to deal with has two heads. I need to grasp control of one head before I can destroy the other."

He would bide his time with Evelyn, playing the doting husband, as he would move with explicit authority to redirect the family fortune to singular holdings that bore only his name. Providence and God's will would show him the way to ridding his home of the Jenkins for good. He chose to concentrate on grasping control of the City Council.

"The Wu Mei has had sketchy results so far," Jasper told Michaels. "So I've reconsidered how I want to handle Evelyn. Of most important concern to me is Courtland."

Michaels lowered his voice. "I've told you, you must be consistent with the dosage and timing," he whispered. "Wu Mei, *when handled properly*, will cause a *slow* descent into hysteria, and finally death. You *must* use it on a daily basis and no more than one drop at a time for the benefits to show *consistent* results."

The solid oak door opened to Courtland Parker's office. Jasper had been inside enough times to no longer be inspired by the ornate refinements and detail put into the construction of the room. No longer did the portraits of the Confederate generals, positioned to draw the attention of anyone entering the room to the majestic built-in maple desk with matching throne chair, hold any sway with him. He did, however, retain his appreciation for the large painting directly behind the desk depicting the victory at Fort Sumter. Jasper often daydreamed that this would be his office and his rear sitting in the soft leather chair as he discussed City Council business. He now believed his time would come sooner than later.

But first, he needed to close any lingering doubts Courtland may have held towards him. He entered the room apprehensively, uncertain of why he had been summoned. As the door closed behind him, he could see that one of the two elegant chairs in front of the desk was occupied. He didn't recognize the occupant until he stood at the back of the chair right next to him. Former Sheriff John Tisdale sneered at him with a halfhearted welcome.

"Jasper," Courtland offered. "Have a seat."

John Tisdale gave an agreeable grunt and snidely mumbled, "Bumstead," for his excuse of a greeting as he shifted his position, scooting his chair away from the one offered to Jasper.

"Gentlemen, we are about to embark on a mission that will change the direction of our fair city. We are going to open up our city to people who have been looking to change the colored section of town. These people believe they can make better use of the land currently occupied by them."

Courtland's secretary suddenly cracked the door open with news of the new sheriff's return from his errand. Courtland dismissed her.

"Jasper, you are not yet privy to all the goings on here," Courtland said, gesturing for him to stand. "Wait outside. John and I need to discuss a few things with Sheriff Clayton."

Jasper despised those who wielded power over him. It ate at his very soul. He was adept enough in the politics of power to understand it wouldn't be gained by submission, but it could be, by theft. So he followed orders, secure with the knowledge that it was he who engineered the secret discussion they were now having. Only time and God's will would tell him just how far he would have to go before the mantle of leadership was his. His newfound patience, he believed, was his best virtue.

Minutes later, Courtland Parker, John Tisdale, and Beauregard Clayton emerged from their meeting with a unified look of satisfaction. Courtland and John huddled together, mumbling a few words into each other's ears while casting glances at Jasper, while Bo made a quick exit. Courtland excitedly called the sheriff back before he exited from view and whispered in his ear about his search for the Lincoln boy. Although the sheriff's response was inaudible, Jasper could clearly hear Courtland's disappointment when he stated in a derisive manner, "Never mind, maybe I'll give that project to Dunning to settle for me." John Tisdale made his exit as Courtland motioned for Jasper to reenter his office and have a seat.

Jasper entered the room with increased curiosity, now aware his instincts weren't always on point. Thoughts scrambled in his head as he tried to search for a verbal clue that would reveal the office's previous conversation.

"I take it Tisdale had some final words of wisdom to share with his protégé," he said.

Courtland poured two drinks from the built-in wet bar and handed one to Jasper, softly patting him on the shoulder as if admiring a painting Jasper just created.

"Jasper," Courtland said,. "iIt has come to my attention that a Negro soldier was seen leaving your home rather late last night. And that he has been stirring up trouble trying to take recognition away from our boys, the real heroes, to get medals for some Negroes who never should have been allowed in the Army in the first place." He allowed the words to hang in the air for a moment, searching Jasper's face for any recognition, then continued. "Jasper, the kind of trouble this Negro can stir up will only create unrest with our coloreds. Besides, he has a tendency to involve the press to further his agenda. We know he fancies that Negro maid of yours and we are of the opinion that he might be trying to make his home here."

Jasper was completely unaware that his residence had been under surveillance. He knew the Council kept tabs on any colored of any

importance that came into town, but it never occurred to him that his home life would have become the object of attention. Jasper didn't know how to respond, so he listened as Courtland dictated how the Council would handle the possibility if the Negro soldier did indeed take up residence in Lafayette County. Jasper tried to offer his assistance, but Courtland deferred.

"I have something else of a personal importance to me for you to handle."

Chapter 13

Lafayette, Virginia

Sunday, July 20, 1975
10.:36 a.m.

Wearing just his pajamas pants and a plaid bathrobe, Weldon Michaels took his time cooking a slab of bologna and frying a pair of eggs in his small kitchen. As he poured boiling water from an old saucepan into a cup of instant coffee, he heard his paramour in the bathroom yell out, "I'll be out in a sec, hon!" His patience was reaching its limit as he tossed the plate of food and cup of coffee onto the table. Just as he'd set his place, she entered the kitchen with a face fully made up and a smile as bright as the sun. "Ta-da!" she exclaimed. "Sorry, sugar, I don't have time for breakfast."

Weldon pointed to the bills on the table. "Didn't make you any. I want to eat in peace. Here's your money. You can go."

The young lady picked up the cash and started combing through the wad of singles with a frown. "A gentleman would have added enough for a cab fare."

"A gentleman wouldn't be paying a whore," Michaels responded.

He rounded the table and guided her to the door.

She went, attempting to reclaim her pride along the way. "Don't ever call me again!" She paused at the open threshold, thinking her statement could cause him to rescind his bad behavior. Instead, he placed a hand on her shoulder and pushed her out.

"You can count on it," Michaels said.

He shut the door before she could respond, and sat down to enjoy his meal, muttering about the size of her bottom and the smell of her cheap perfume. He could hear her yell about the diminutive size of his penis as she called him a dictionary of names. He laughed through her final words. There was a time he could have drugged her and saved himself twenty dollars.

Michaels was just starting his overcooked breakfast when the telephone rang. Of all times. He picked up the receiver, but before he got a chance to chastise the caller's timing, he was met with a disdainful greeting. "Wake up, Michaels. This is J. Dunning." The words slid into his ear as if spoken by the serpent with the proverbial apple. "I'm callin' to tell you, from the looks of it, someone's comin' to kill you."

The thought immediately turned Weldon's stomach, but he recoiled at the idea he would believe anything Jasper Dunning had to say.

"I know a sergeant over in the second precinct there who owes me a favor," Jasper continued. "If you stay put, I'll see if he can spare a deputy to come sit with you until we can end this."

Weldon remained silent, as if waiting for Jasper to shed his skin of calm authority. Jasper went on with the diction of someone who safeguards the key to everyone's secrets.

"Some of your friends already got themselves murdered ..."

Jasper paused, allowing time for his words to sink in.

It took Weldon several seconds to catch up to what Dunning was saying. In the back of his mind, Weldon always knew this day would come, and he knew Jasper was relishing in the moment, pretending to be his savior. He wouldn't let him have the satisfaction.

"Some of my friends, Bumstead?" Michaels asked. "You know I don't have any friends."

"I don''t have time for this, Weldon. Those ambulance boys of yours were murdered and you had better take heed to my words."

"Well, I appreciate your concern, Bumstead," Michaels cut in. "But I''m sure I can take care of myself."

Weldon wasn't in any danger. There weren't but a few people who knew where to find him; even less who would be interested in finding him. When his medical license had been stripped from him, nearly everyone he knew had disowned him. He'd only retained contact with Jasper Dunning and a reluctant Dolores Peters. And even Dolores had forgotten about him now.

Jasper's tone of voice completely changed, turning into something that sounded like genuine regret. "Weldon," he said, "Dolores was murdered yesterday morning. I tried to reach you, but you must've been out all day."

Weldon gasped and nearly shuddered. A situation he had thought only a ridiculous notion now seemed highly possible, if not certain.

"If Dolores is really gone, then the only one left who knows how to find me is you," Michaels said. He paused, then laughed. "If your malignant courtesy call is true to your nature, Bumstead, then you had better take heed of your own words. 'Cause after me, you'll be next. And I'll wait for you at the devil's doorstep. You bastard!" He slammed down the receiver.

Weldon, took a moment to gather his thoughts. He could see Dolores's smile as his thoughts ran by. He immediately halted any remnants of regret and rushed to the bedroom. He opened his closet and pulled out his .22

revolver, an old scalpel, a ballpoint pen, and a legal pad. Before leaving the bedroom, he meticulously opened the box of ammunition he kept with his gun and loaded the bullets, kissing each one of them before he placed them in the chamber. He attempted to return to his coffee and breakfast, but his desire to eat had ended with the sound of Jasper's voice. He scraped the cold food into the trash can, sat down at his grimy kitchen table, and wrote across the top of the legal pad:

'The Real Crimes of Weldon Michaels and Jasper Dunning.'

Weldon Michaels cut his own reality on both edges of the sword of misfortune. Since the Virginia State Medical Board had stripped him of his license to practice medicine some years ago, Michaels was forced to drop the '"Dr'." from his name. Rumors of his addiction to drugs and alcohol, presented with false evidence that he had participated in medical procedures while under the influence, had led to his downfall. Weldon always thought his losst of favor with the Lafayette City Council had begun with his disagreements with Jasper Dunning. He could almost

see Jasper's conniving hands directing the inquiry. And yet it was his relationship with Jasper that saved him from doing any time in jail – —he just couldn't prove it without further implicating himself. So he took Dunning's advice to accept the monthly stipend and retire in another locale not too close and not too far away from Lafayette County. The City Council wanted to keep tabs on the good doctor. After all, he knew just enough to be dangerous. Underneath the armor of false bravado, Weldon's cowardice was his Achille's heel. And a coward with dangerous information was a coward worth watching.

So, a coward, Weldon Michaels wrote.

'...The proclivities of Courtland Parker didn't stop with the nubile Negro girls he ravaged. His subtler tastes were for the prepubescent black boys and their budding adolescence that drove his desire. Courtland's preference for the feistier Negro often left him scarred. That's where I came in with the proper sedation to alleviate just enough of the fight in them to give Courtland the challenge he desired. If Courtland was in a generous mood, he'd share his offerings with certain members of the Council. And on certain occasions I myself would partake in the sweet blackness of youth. I believe this might have led to my ostracism. It wasn't enough that I performed the termination of pregnancies for the myriad young white mistresses of the Council members. It was my desire to satiate my own taste that violated an unwritten law of Council privilege ...'

After more than three hours, his writing hand was getting stiff. Weldon had written several pages of the medical procedures he'd performed, contributing to the illicit crimes committed by the members of the Lafayette City Council. Afternoon had come, and with it a rise in the temperature of his stuffy, stale apartment. He swallowed some aspirin and felt it was a good time to end his ramblings in a coherent fashion, skipping several paragraphs of further explicit detail to reach his ending, and read his work aloud to himself.

"It was Jasper Dunning," he said to his apartment, "who enviously eyed the Council leadership and who initiated the plan to wrest the mantlel from Courtland Parker. In doing so, Jasper abandoned the methodic destabilization of his beloved Evelyn to suit his desire for a broader path of power and control. Never one to partake, Jasper Dunning became the ever-present eyewitness to the pleasures he dutifully detailed for his more nefarious ambitions. And it wasn't until my unheralded departure did I unveil hidden facts with certainty of the implicit support and protection engaged by Sheriff Beauregard Clayton. His beholding to Jasper was his undoing, as was mine."

Michaels read it with a Shakespearean performance. He wanted it to generate a full picture of the distaste he harbored toward his one-time facilitator. Now uncertain that the ending had the proper accord, he stepped away from the kitchen table to take a mental break.

As he slowly approached the terrace window, Michaels regarded the clear skies and the afternoon breeze that sailed through the trees, a warm, gentle summer wind that begged to enter. He obliged. It raced into the second-floor unit and permeated the small living room as it crept its way down the narrow hallway, chastising the stale stench of tobacco, alcohol, and cheap perfume that always lingered. Michaels thought for a moment to open the large windows in his bedroom, when he was struck by an idea: one that might help him live through the night.

After hours of cathartically putting pen to paper, with the assistance of a few additional swigs straight from a bottle of Kentucky bourbon, the loss of Dolores Peters seemed to abate his melancholy attitude, and anger began to set in. Drunkenly, Michaels reclaimed his bravado. He would turn the tables on his assailant and leave Bumstead Dunning holding the bag.

Still in his bathrobe, pajama pants, and bedroom slippers, Weldon Michaels sauntered down his tree-lined street, soaking up the sun and the warm breeze. He had a distinct lilt in his gait as he hummed a Mozart tune stuck in his head. He'd buy a few essentials – something to eat, for certain, after his ruined breakfast – and some candles or incense. He'd draw the shades and close all the windows and curtains, making his bedroom dark and stuffy, and fill it with a smoky haze to disorient any unwelcome visitors in the night. Convinced of his own brilliance, Michaels further believed that once the body of the perpetrator was discovered, along with the detailed crimes he'd just penned, he would finally have his revenge on Jasper Dunning and the Lafayette City Council. What a scandal they'd have to chase – —what delicious revenge he would have.

In his peripheral, a pale yellow pickup truck lingered at his corner. When he swiveled to take a look, the driver turned the corner and picked up speed as it pulled away. A lost tourist, perhaps, visiting the confines of Virginia Beach. He considered that he was being watched when he heard someone in another vehicle yell something about his clothes, calling him a hobo, and after the distraction, he had lost sight of both cars as they drove off.

Weldon combatted his tinge of embarrassment by opening his robe to reveal his sunken chest and pot belly, which extended beyond the waistband of his pajamas. He finally entered the store and dared anyone to make an untimely comment about his wardrobe.

As he returned home, Weldon thought he spied the pickup truck again, casually perusing his street. Thinking he would get a better view from his balcony, he rushed into his apartment, set down his groceries, and pulled the .22 out of his robe pocket. He slid himself next to the wall, slowly behind the curtains, and pulled open the sliding glass door so he could ease himself out onto the balcony. From his vantage point, he could clearly see the road, save for some of the vehicles parked along the curb. He leaned over the edge, and if he stretched, he could see just beyond the tree branches that obstructed his view. He gave the street a once-over.

He was being paranoid. He just didn't know anything about any of his neighbors' comings and goings or what cars they drove. The truck had nothing to do with him – it was all Bumstead in his head. He refused to let Jasper get to him. Several hours passed as the afternoon turned into evening and Michaels prepared his bedroom. He felt secure and certain that when and if any attempt on his life would occur, he would be the one controlling the outcome.

A thump against the balcony startled him. He turned off the lights and made a quick dash back into the bedroom. He stopped for a moment to listen to the night. Not hearing any additional sounds, he took several deep breaths to calm his hammering heart. Taking note of the hot summer night, he thought it was unusually quiet for a Sunday evening, no chirping birds or automobile traffic to speak of. He turned the lights back on, then saw a shadow on the dimly lit balcony. The door was wide open. He reached for the revolver he'd placed at the edge of the table and slid the door shut. The shadow disappeared, merely caused by a mirage of reflected light. Relieved but still nervous, he closed the drapes tight.

Settling down to eat a hot sandwich of tuna, cheese, and a fried egg, with a can of beer and a bag of chips, Weldon sat in front of the television and placed the revolver on the arm of his recliner. He took three large bites of his sandwich, barely breathing between bites, and washed it down with beer. For the first time all day, he felt relaxed enough to fully exhale and lie back in his chair. Letting himself relax, he propped up the footrest and shut his eyes. The beer can made a soft tinny thud as it hit the carpeted floor and lay there, draining itself.

An incessant banging on the front door ruptured the peaceful sleep Weldon had slipped into. Disoriented, with a throbbing headache, Weldon wrestled himself away from the blaring television set and wiped breadcrumbs and tuna from his mouth and chest. The banging on his door continued.

"I'm coming, I'm coming! Stop your goddamn pounding." He paused before he reached for the doorknob, glancing at the clock to catch up on the time he'd lost: two hours. "Who is it?" he called through the door. "What do you want?"

"Dr. Michaels, my name is Officer Tanin. I'm here to give you a look to see if you're doing fine. May I come in?" the voice asked with all the accoutrements his Southern charm could muster. Then he added, "I'm from the second precinct and a Mr. Jay Dunning requested a visit."

Weldon slowly opened the door and leaned his head out. "Show me your badge," he demanded, addressing the officer in full duty uniform. Officer Tanin just pointed to his chest and briefly covered his nose against the stench emanating from inside the squalid unit. He stepped in and around Weldon Michaels, sizing him up, with full benefit of the doubt that he was ever a medical professional. "Are you all right,

Dr. Michaels? Have you been drinking?"

"Yes, I have been drinking!" Weldon responded emphatically. "And I plan to do some more! Are you here to arrest me or look in on me? You and Jay Dunning can both go screw yourselves. I have everything under control here." Realizing that he was speaking to an officer of the law, and that he'd left his revolver on the arm of his recliner, he changed his tune. "Please excuse me. I've been under some undue pressures and I apologize for taking it out on you. Have a look around to your satisfaction."

Officer Tanin stepped inside and glanced around, while Michaels crept to the recliner to feel for the gun. It wasn't there.

He looked to the carpet, hoping it had fallen, and did his best to casually look on the floor, the cushions, the carpeting under the chair. He found it on his dinner tray – —didn't recall placing it there, but who knew what he'd done before he'd fallen asleep?

Tanin barely made it through the living room when Weldon steeled up. "Okay, you've seen enough." He opened the front door and gestured for the officer to leave.

"If everything is fine, then I'll be going," Tanin said, seeming all too happy to comply. He'd held his breath for as long as he could – —the various scents of Weldon's apartment had assaulted his senses. Turning to the door for a quick exit, he reassured the doctor he would give the building a once-over before leaving, and other officers would be close by but wouldn't disturb.

A neighbor's door creaked open. "Is he finally being arrested?" she asked.

Officer Tanin laughed it off. "Not yet. Good night, ma'am."

When the officer was gone, Michaels waved. His neighbor went on to tell him he was trash and shouldn't be allowed in the building. He flashed his revolver at her, relishing in the priceless picture of her shocked expression. He slammed his door shut and returned to his recliner.

A soft, warm breeze eventually pushed through the drapes of his open balcony door. He jumped out of his seat, spinning his head around the room, securing the revolver in his hand. The sliding door was just barely ajar. He shut and locked it and kept the drapes closed.

An eerie feeling began to take hold of him as he felt the hairs on his neck stand up. After thinking, he was certain that he had closed the door. And his bedroom door, too, come to think of it – —which was now also ajar. He cocked his revolver and crept down the narrow hallway, sliding his back along the wall. Michaels threw open the door and flicked on the light to startle whoever was in there.

No one.

Maybe no one was coming. Maybe Jasper Dunning had simply sought to drive him crazy.

The weight of the day hit him. As Michaels dropped two tablespoons of instant coffee into his mug, the television abruptly switched on, blaring his favorite mystery program on CBS. Weldon whipped out his revolver and pointed it straight at the figure who now stared at him from the darkness.

He pulled the trigger to the click of an empty chamber.

***

6.:23 p.m.

Deputy Abel Grimes finally requested off-the-books assistance from the FBI – —in particular, a former college classmate and friendly rival who had competed with him since the day they first met in their criminal law class. Both Grimes and Pullman were recruited by the FBI, but where Pullman saw the FBI as a place to land and develop a career, Grimes only saw being an FBI agent as a hindrance to his aspiring political career governing in the South. Abel hesitated, but ultimately made the call, knowing the acerbic relationship he had with Agent Pullman would aggravate him as much as this case had.

"Look, Pullman," he said, "I really do appreciate your assistance, but—"

"*Guidance*, Grimes. Let's get it straight," Pullman said. "You're asking for guidance on a case that really should be handled by the agency. Shoulda called it in from the start. That's not a good way to start a law enforcement career, if you ask me."

"You don't know how things work in these backwater towns, Pully," Abel said. For years he'd known disrespectful nicknames would have Pullman seething in bridled anger. "Hell, I'm still trying to find out if this city is incorporated. They keep things very close to the vest here. Not very welcoming to outsiders. And definitely not fans of the Feds. So yes, protocol is not something that happens here. You can step off your high horse any time now, Pulls."

Agent Pullman took a heated pause before he continued. "I'll ignore that remark, Grimes, because I know you need my help. Now, let's go over this again, and I suggest this time you write it down, because I won't be repeating myself. The connection is obvious. Why you didn't figure it out just reaffirms why you finished behind me."

Now, hours later, Pullman's words still bounced around in Grimes's mind as he tried to connect the victims to the facts. Abel had been concentrating on developing a profile – —not a connection between the victims. Agent Pullman had pointed out the possibility of a larger connection and the likelihood that the victims hadn't been chosen at random. Abel reexamined his notes.

Dolores Peters, from everything he'd seen, was a good nurse with good standing. Why or how she would have a connection with those petty thieves ... There was something no one was telling him. Why was the City Council involved? If they knew about the next victim, why weren't they doing more to help him?

Sheriff Clayton was not as forthcoming as he pretended to be. He had a sketchy connection to the council, but Grimes hadn't yet pinned down what power they had over him. Grimes, an outsider of Lafayette County, knew little of the town's history as well as the Council's inner workings. Unofficial procedures; unorthodox policing techniques just shy of criminal; things he ignored and chalked up to life in the South. He'd convinced himself that they were all things he'd have to accept if he hoped to be a successful politician. As unfortunate as it was, he couldn't fix it – —not yet.

Grimes had gathered enough information about a certain Dr. Weldon Michaels and his checkered past, but his connection to the

Lafayette City Council was still unclear. But somehow, in all of this, Michaels was the key to the city. If Grimes could turn him, he'd unlock the secrets behind the Council and its hold over the sheriff and the city.

Pullman was right, and he had to get to Weldon Michaels – fast. He was scheduled to accompany Sheriff Clayton and the City Council head, Jasper Dunning, in the morning to see Michaels, but Grimes knew that if he waited for them, Michaels would be dead by morning.

Grimes arrived at the Virginia Beach police station second precinct just after eleven in the evening; his adherence to proper protocol prevented him from knocking on Michaels's door without formal assistance.

Over two hours later, homicide detective Barry Baker and another

officer got the okay to bring Deputy Grimes to Weldon Michaels. Grimes didn't ask any questions – just grabbed his effects and followed them out of the precinct. In the back seat of the patrol car, Grimes felt as though he was in another era. He could smell the difference between Lafayette and Virginia Beach in the air. He hadn't realized how stagnant the town stayed until he sat back, listening to the officers talk to each other.

At Weldon Michaels's apartment, Deputy Grimes got a chance to witness a professional police investigation unit address a crime scene. He was handed a pair of gloves while Detective Baker, referred to as "'BB'" in the station, escorted him. BB had undergone crime scene forensics training with the FBI and was the Virginia Beach Police Department's lead detective.

Grimes felt as though he'd stepped onto a movie set. The officers had cordoned off the apartment, and one was taking notes from a neighbor just beyond the apartment door. All the lights had been turned on in the unit. Grimes watched as the blood-soaked sheet was removed from Weldon Michaels's slumped body in the recliner.

"Do you recognize him?" Detective BB asked in a matter-of-fact way.

After staring at the bloated face now losing its pallor, Grimes said no – he'd never met Michaels nor seen him before. The detective nodded and left the body uncovered.

A note, already in a plastic evidence bag, sat on the kitchen table. Grimes approached to get a closer look, but another officer took it away. By the minute, Grimes was feeling less like a deputy and participant in the case and more like a limited observer.

Several officers were talking outside when one of them called BB outside to speak with the neighbor who reported the murder. Grimes walked to the door to see if he could glean anything out of the conversation. He learned another officer had visited Michaels earlier and was being called back to the scene.

The policeman who had driven him and BB to the apartment stood in the doorway looking at Grimes in a suspicious manner. Grimes took the hint and eased back into the room. He tried to engage the officer, but received little response.

Grimes asked if he could check the rest of the apartment. The officer looked to BB for permission. BB gave Grimes a once-over, then waved his approval.

With the officer at his heels, Grimes ventured into the bedroom, looking for a point of entry and any signs of a scuffle. He returned to the living room and studied the blood splatter on both sides of the dinner tray, that had apparently been knocked over, and the smeared blood on the television dials. The blood had formed a moat around the recliner as the doctor had bled out.

The coroner arrived wheeling in a gurney to carry out the body. As the body was lifted, Grimes could see that rigor mortis had already set in. He estimated Dr. Michaels had been dead for just a few hours. He thought about the two hours he'd sat in an interrogation room waiting for clearance from Lafayette. He knew he would hear about it from Clayton, but he couldn't help but think of those two hours as time for the murder to occur more than they were for his verification. Their professionalism seemed to be more of a show for him than real concern for a victim.

A small knife-like object fell into the recliner's cushion from underneath the body. Grimes took a closer look and noticed a small glob of skin and muscle covering the underside of the blade. He grabbed an evidence bag and tweezers from the coroner's tray and picked up what he recognized as a scalpel.

"What's that you got there?" an officer asked loud enough to get the detective's attention.

Grimes remained professional and responded, "This scalpel fell from the body and I was just bagging it for evidence. I think it was stuck under the leg. It scraped off when they moved the body."

As the officer approached, Grimes nicked off the slab of skin and tissue and quickly palmed it into one of the small bags in his pocket.

When the body of Weldon Michaels was discovered, Deputy Grimes knew it would make national news. He wanted his name to be among those that would become synonymous with the solve – —he had a career-making case right in front of him and the last thing he wanted was to let it slip out from under him.

It was tragic yet fateful that one of the victims had been dating a reporter for the local news station; the only television station in Lafayette;

a station that would follow the investigation and the officers, bringing attention to the personalities involved; a station, Grimes would later find out, that was owned by a member of the Lafayette City Council.

The policy of the FBI was not to get involved in local affairs unless requested by the local law enforcement or a politician. Then again, if a case made national attention, the Federal Bureau of Investigation was always there to lend a hand. The FBI had profiling experts and even offered to teach local law enforcement the proper techniques in high-profile cases. A serial killer in a small town in Virginia was such a case. This one, however, would not receive the attention it needed simply because of the involvement of the Lafayette City Council.

When Sheriff Clayton caught wind of Grimes's communication with the FBI, he was ready to have him hogtied. Instead, he relegated Grimes to filing duty at a small wooden desk in the back of the station as he immediately put a stop to what was turning into an in-depth and rigorous investigation. Sheriff Clayton made it clear, in no uncertain terms, where Deputy Abel Grimes's career and future were headed if he ever took such initiative again.

"We haven't even gotten a chance to review the evidence from Virginia Beach," Grimes insisted. It was all he was able to get out before two fellow deputies restrained him. Bo Clayton closed the distance between them with amazing speed for a man his size. His face went red with rage and the veins in his temples protruded. "Bo, please!"

"It's Sheriff Clayton to you, son!" Clayton snarled. "And ya don't tell me how to run an investigation. If I say the matta is closed, then daggummit, it's closed! Your job is to do like I tell ya, when I tell ya, an' nothin' else. I'm the law in this here county, not the goddamn FBI. You understan' that, boy? Am I makin' muhself clear?"

"I know I overstepped, Sheriff, and I should've at least let you know," Grimes said. "I mean, I should've got your permission to go to Virginia Beach early. But I just had a hunch that the morning would be too late!"

"What you did was get yourself smack on the wrong side of the Council and out of a job, son!" Clayton snapped. "Things work different here. Or don't you know that yet?"

Abel was dumbfounded. Up to this point, he'd managed to remain on Sheriff Clayton's good side, relatively speaking. He'd believed that even though he'd been a deputy for a short time, he'd gotten to know how to read the sheriff. What he discovered, however, was that Bo, as well as the South, didn't always comport with the scenario he'd developed in his personal profiles.

Abel didn't answer Clayton's question – —there was no need to. He lowered his head to avoid Clayton's glare. The sheriff hastily turned around, making certain that anyone within earshot also received his harsh, red-faced message.

"I'm the law, and what I says goes! Anybody here don't like that, you come see me!"

Clayton stormed into his office and slammed the door. The entire precinct then heard what sounded like a coffee mug crashing against the concrete wall.

***

11.:43 p.m.

In a dimly lit and sparsely furnished apartment, the glare from a thirteen-inch television screen cast flickering shadows. A light from an opened refrigerator door swallowed the shadows as they reached the kitchen table. The only other light, emanating from the glow of a full moon, crept eerily through the balcony window. A gloved hand increased the volume on the television, before securing a small note onto the open refrigerator door, leaving a splotch of blood thick enough to drip a trail down the front panel. The red line of blood turned black as it slid down the page and onto the avocado-colored appliance, leaving a small splatter on the greasy floor.

The last note contained a zero with a line through it, the same ancient hieroglyphs, and a final message:

Death makes life precious.

Chapter 14

Los Angeles, California

Tuesday, July 20, 2010
7.:17 a.m.

Houston took his time getting out of bed as he lay there recalling his dream. It wasn't unlike a recurring dream he'd had as an adolescent: one of his father. Houston could only remember bits and pieces of the dream as it quickly dissipated from his memory, leaving only the most visceral parts playing in his head. He could see the faceless man hovering over him as a little boy, playing in the sand at the beach, reaching up to pull on the man's gray trunks. *"Daddy! Daddy!"* he'd call. *"Come on, take me to the water, Daddy ..."* He looked up, seeing the broad shoulders of a dark-skinned man and the outline of a rugged face with piercing eyes, silhouetted by a shadow cast by the sun. As he put his hand up to shade his face from the glare, he felt the imbalance of a weight shifting and slipping out of his other arm. He tried instinctively to adjust the balance. He looked down just in time to see a small child slipping out of his grasp and into the surging waves, disappearing into the sea foam. The splash of the water would hit his face and wake him from his dream.

Houston struggled to contemplate the meaning. A tear squeezed its way out of one of his eyes, as he blinked to stem the emotion. It quietly rolled down the side of his temple to nestle securely into his ear. Unaware he was being watched, he continued to stare blankly at the ceiling until a soft, warm hand wiped away the remnant of the tear line from the side of his face. Startled, he jumped up. "Holy shit, I'm gonna be late," he stammered, coughing as he hurried out of the bedroom and into the bathroom without looking back.

He quickly turned on the shower as a distraction from the inevitable question he knew was coming from his wife. He wanted an excuse for not hearing her when she knocked on the door asking to join him. He moved to the sink and splashed cold water onto his face to explain away the redness of his eyes. He stared at his reflection for several minutes before it dawned on him: she wasn't asking to join him. He hovered over the sink, staring at his reflection, paying little attention to the whiskers begging to be removed. Houston picked apart his face little by little, trying to discern any resemblance to the shaded face of the man in his dreams. He stared at the curve of his forehead before he picked apart the prominence of the high cheekbones providing cover for faint dimples that accented the wisp of gray stubble on his slim cheeks. He placed a palm on his cheek and followed the stubble down and around a firm jawline. He tried to picture the mouth and nose as he could feel the strength of the piercing light brown eyes he dreamt staring back at him. The steam from the shower started to fog the mirror before he gave full thought to what he was feeling.

Underneath it all, he felt it was his fault he didn't have a father. Psychologically, he could reason his doubts and fears away, but emotionally, he hadn't allowed himself to fully accept that he was without blame. He stood under the shower and silently cried, allowing the torrents of water to compete with tears as they streamed down his face. Oddly, he felt safe allowing himself this moment. He ended the shower deciding he would think of it no more. He would dedicate himself to being a great father and conquer his fear of feeling unworthy of fatherhood. He quickly dried himself and addressed his taunting whiskers. Wrapping himself in his towel, he tried to sneak back into the bedroom to get dressed, assuming Sabrina had gone back to sleep.

"Are you all right, sweetheart?" Sabrina asked from the hallway behind him as he opened the bedroom door. "I made you something to eat." She offered him an egg sandwich.

"Yeah, baby ... I'm all right," Houston responded awkwardly. His wife knew him better than anyone, and he knew that no matter how much water he splashed onto his face, she would still know he had been crying. He tried to keep his face turned as he slid his pants up and sat on the bed to pull up his socks.

She placed the small plate on the bed and handed him a short-sleeve shirt from the closet. She held it up to him. "I like this color on you," she said. "It highlights your eyes."

That was when he knew that she knew. Houston stumbled for words, and Sabrina just kissed him on his lips. Houston leaned his head into hers. He felt a tear land solidly on his slacks. He looked up to see her smiling as she wiped away her own tears.

"I know you're going to be the best father our boy could ever have," she said confidently.

Houston smiled at her, not knowing exactly what to say, as he held back his own tears and forced himself to laugh. "Oh, so you know we're gonna have a boy?" he challenged.

"Honey," she offered, strengthening her resolve, "now you know I may not always be right, but I'm never wrong."

They both started to laugh, easing their intimate sensitivity into normalcy. Hugging each other, Houston snuck a quick look at his watch. Feeling him turn over his wrist, Sabrina quipped, "You're going to be so late. You're taking Aunt Ethel's car, right?"

"Yeah, I guess I better," he admitted. "Oh, shit!. It's really late.

Gotta run, baby." He gave her a quick peck on the mouth and rushed down the back stairs, only coming back to grab the egg sandwich she'd made for him.

On his way to the office, Houston convinced himself he was only just now noticing a bigger police presence on his route. He didn't recall noticing any patrol cars yesterday. He entertained the notion of being followed and chalked it up to having some lingering paranoia from his encounter with the Beverly Hills police. He shook off the thought and made it to the office unscathed. He made it to the office just a few steps behind Oscar as he buzzed himself in and entered the oversized cherrywood doors into the lobby.

Houston made his way to the computer room, but decided not to enter. He knew Phil would be in there, and he was hesitant to encounter him. He wasn't exactly sure how to approach him or what to say, whether he should show any considerable concern or none at all. He took a full swallow of his coffee and plunged forward, deciding he needed to find out why he was so concerned with a man who skirted the edges of compassion with enmity. Phil clearly wanted to be disliked, but Houston wanted to know why. Phil had the capacity to be genuine and thoughtful, but he contained it.

"Yo, bro! Hold the door for me, my hands are full!" Oscar called from down the hall. He carried a plateful of tiny blueberry and chocolate chip muffins in one hand and a mug of coffee in the other.

"What's that?" Houston pushed the door open with his back, balancing his own purchased muffin on top of his coffee cup.

"Somebody brought in sweets. So I made sure we were covered back here. Come on, dude, this shit is starting to get heavy."

Houston gave a solid push to the heavy door with his back to let Oscar in. "You're so anxious to get to work, you're drinking the shit that Phil makes?"

Oscar shook his head in response. "Naw, homes;, the old gringo's coffee was gone by the time I got there. I guess they only allowed him one pot this morning. My bet is whoever got the muffins probably ditched his shit and made regular coffee for everybody else."

Houston placed his cup and the last bite of muffin on his desk. He leaned slightly over his cubicle to see if he could catch a glimpse at Phil. "He must not be here," Oscar chimed in.

"Why do you say that?" Houston asked with more concern than he intended.

Oscar responded with a chuckle. "Just think about it. Something must've happened to Phil, right? He always makes two pots of coffee. As if he's daring anyone to disturb it. And no one does. Not even Elizabeth goes in there for coffee, right?" Oscar let that sink in as Houston tried to feign indifference, then he continued. "I heard Phil got fired last night. He and old man Watson got into it about the Jefferson shit you started."

"Are you serious?" Houston dropped all pretense of his lack of concern. He dropped his chin into his palm, debating whether he should let Oscar know what he'd witnessed in Phil the day before.

"Yeah, bro. What do you think?"

The thought of Phil coughing up a storm flooded Houston's thoughts as a look of panic came over him. He wondered what he should share with Oscar. Oscar seemed to be doing his best to hold back his laughter.

Houston finally sighed. "Hey, man, I think Phil's really sick. I mean, like ..." He stood up to fully engage his friend, when he saw the impish grin exploding from Oscar's face. Houston quickly turned around and saw Phil staring at him with a blank look on his face.

"Slow your roll, black man. I'm fit as a fiddle," Phil announced with a wink at Oscar.

"What the fuck? You old bastard! You were listening all along?"

Houston's remarks were drowned out by Oscar's roar of laughter. Phil walked past Houston as nonchalantly as usual. Houston became defensive. He felt kind of sucker-punched – —he'd felt genuine concern for the old geezer. *I don't need it. I've got too much other shit to deal with,.* Houston groused, and returned to his desk. "Ha-fucking-ha! Laugh it up!"

Just like that, Phil returned to his cubicle. Oscar continued to chastise Houston, and Phil wanted no more of it. He inserted his ear buds and tuned them out.

"Dude, I think your black magic is wearing off on the old white man," Oscar chuckled. "He's never played a joke on you before. And definitely not with me. What's up, you two get into a fight or something?"

"Naw, man. It's nothing. Just leave him alone. Apparently, he's got things to do, since he's tuning us out."

The morning passed with little interaction among the coworkers as the lunch hour approached. Oscar grew stir-crazy and lobbied Houston to join him for lunch outside of the building. Houston appeared more concerned with Phil than anything Oscar had to say, until Oscar brought his concerns to the forefront.

"Dude, why don't you just go ask him what you want to ask? You keep looking over there like a puppy dog."

"Huh?" Feeling slightly embarrassed, Houston looked for an excuse to share his concerns. "No, no, I'm just ... Hey, does Phil look all right to you?"

"He looks the same as always."

"You don't think he looks skinnier and paler?"

"He was a skinny old white man when I met him. And he's a skinny old white man still. He hasn't changed one bit. And his attitude still stinks as much as it did the first time I laid eyes on him."

Houston didn't have a response, but was saved from answering when a call came over the intercom from the receptionist: "Hey, guys, is Phil in there? If he is, tell him to take his phone off 'Ddo not disturb'."

Houston jumped up to see what Phil was doing and could see him leafing through some old black-and-white photos and faded Polaroids. To Houston, it appeared Phil was arranging memories he had gathered throughout the years. Houston tried to sneak a telling look over Phil's shoulder, but was only able to get a glance, as Phil felt his presence and quickly shuffled the contents into his drawer and locked it. He pulled his ear buds out and revealed he was blasting "'Heart of Gold'." Phil looked almost embarrassed, like a caught child.

Phil rested his forehead in his palm, using the base of his thumb and forefinger to rub his eyes, before sliding the rest of his hand down his face as he verbally let go of and acknowledged his exasperation with a groan. A second call came in from the front desk.

"Phil? Elizabeth is asking to see you."

"Okay, I'm coming,." Phil responded, knowing the receptionist couldn't hear his reply. "Can't keep the boss lady waiting."

As he stood for the door, he paused as if he had lost control of his balance and steadied himself, grasping Houston's arm. Realizing he needed help, Houston tried to prop Phil up, but Cantoni pushed himself clear, then returned a look of thanks and assured Houston he was okay.

"I just got up too soon, is all. I'll be okay. Thanks."

Once Phil was gone, Oscar gave Houston a look. "I think you're right, dude. I think something is wrong with him. I ain't never seen that old dude look so old before. You know, I think I saw him cough up something the other day. Like blood."

"Seriously?" Houston asked, chiding Oscar. "Why didn't you say anything?"

"What am I supposed to say? And to who?" he responded defensively. "You think Phil wants anyone to know what's going on with him? You think he wants anyone to care? Shit, if I said something, you know he'd be pissed off."

Houston shook his head, acknowledging Oscar's sentiment. "I know, but fuck, it seems like somebody should do something to help him."

"Somebody? Who?" Oscar retorted. "That old dude don't want no one to even like him. How's he gonna accept anyone helping him? You got it wrong, homes. Phil's the only man on earth who wants to die alone."

Oscar's words hung in the air, kept afloat by silence.

"Fuck it!" he continued. "Why waste your time tryin' to help him out? Just what you need after burying your mom. I don't think you need the frustration or aggravation, bro. Let him be. That's what he wants."

Houston fell silent in false agreement. Avoiding further discussion, he simply nodded and finally said, "I guess you're right." But he just couldn't let the dread he felt go. The brittle bones he'd felt underneath Phil's thick flannel shirt gave him pause. He could've broken Phil's arm. Perhaps that was the reason he wore flannel in the summer heat – —to hide. And against Oscar's warning, Houston only became more concerned.

***

Phil stood in the immaculate office of Elizabeth Taylor-Barrings, consoling her while she sobbed uncontrollably. For the past while, he'd been reminding her of her position with the law firm and the example she needed to set for the staff. He'd engineered Elizabeth's imposing frame over the chaise lounge in the corner of her office and then poured her a sip of Jamaican rum she'd had stashed in her cabinet.

"Liz, against all odds, you and I are friends. Actually, I feel fortunate to call you and Oliver friends," Phil offered. "At least I know I'll have two people mourning me. But it's my time. I want things to end this way."

In the last few weeks, Phil had become complacent with the disease that had taken over his body. At first, the plan had been to fight the cancer, to cut a section of his colon. The oncologists actually thought they had the right plan to fight it, but recent testing revealed it had spread and completely consumed his pancreas. It was a very aggressive strain in an advanced stage. His doctor prepared him for the news, and he fully accepted it was a fight he couldn't win.

Oliver Cole gingerly opened the door, late for their meeting. He stuck his head in, saw that Elizabeth was recovering from tears, and sighed. "Cantoni, do I have to do to you what you did to Creed for making Elizabeth cry?"

They both gave him stunted smiles. Phil held up the bottle of rum and gestured to the three tumblers sitting on the coffee table between them.

"Get over here, Jew boy. I'm going to meet my savior, the one good Jew, and I've got lots to tell him about you."

Oliver wouldn't acknowledge the tears that filled his eyes, so he took the rum from Phil and poured himself a drink. "Well, it's not that I don't trust you, Cantoni," he said. "But let's face it, I don't. You might slip something into my drink and ..."

The shroud they'd placed over the gravity of the situation began to fall. Oliver gulped down his liquor and gave Phil what was meant to be a bear hug, without squeezing too hard, but close enough that the emotion of the moment wasn't neglected. They sat together in silence and drained a good amount of rum. Elizabeth composed herself.

"Well, it's been charming, but I've got to go," Phil said finally, breaking the quiet in his usual manner. He held back a cough. "Remember what you promised. Don't visit me. The last thing I need is some Athena and her handmaiden embarrassing me in front of the lovely ladies washing down my Herculean body as they prepare me for the gods."

They all shared a laugh, and Elizabeth shared the sentiments of the partners not present. "Both Neil and Charles are in Sacramento and would want me to express their appreciation for your service here," she told him. All three knew it wasn't the truth – —it was just one of those polite things people say in times like this to make themselves or others feel better.

"Now, if that ain't a hunk of bullshit, I don't know what is," Phil laughed. "Liz, you didn't need to say that. I know those crackers probably wish I was already dead."

***

At the front desk, a tall, salt-and-pepper-haired man was waiting patiently when Beverly, the receptionist, returned. Apologetic, she ran up to address him. "I'm sorry. I didn't hear the doorbell chime," she said;. tThen frowned a little. "How exactly did you get in here?"

The gentleman, realizing he must have violated protocol, shrank back. "I was just about to ring the bell when a group of young ladies came out," he admitted. "I inquired if this is where Houston Jenkins works. They said it is, and told me to come to your desk and ask for him. I apologize if I startled you. May I see him?"

Beverly quickly understood the confusion and decided the man in front of her wasn't at fault – —but when those girls return from lunch, she was going to let them have it. "You missed him by about five minutes. He's gone for lunch."

"Do you know what time he'll return?"

Beverly Brazille believed she could read people, but what she was reading from this man was a mystery. He'd never given his name or his relationship to Houston, and he wasn't carrying anything, so she didn't think he was a process server. She gave him a quick once-over, noticing the frayed collar of his worn jacket, but otherwise he was clean and well groomed. She decided it would be best to be minimal if anything with information.

"No, I can't say that I do," she said. "I'm usually gone to lunch when he returns, or he might be using his time to run some company errands. But if you'd like to give me your name and number, I can have him call you as soon as he returns." She gave him a forced smile and a stilted lilt in her voice.

The gentleman nodded. "I noticed there's a cafeteria in the building. Do you know if he's eating there?"

"Houston doesn't like the food there, so he's gone out of the building," she dissembled. "Like I said, you're free to wait, or come back if you like."

The gravelly-voiced gentleman realized she was being obstinate and tried a sympathetic approach. He cleared his throat as if it would clear the crushed rock sound, then spoke softly. "I'm a friend of the family. I didn't get the right opportunity to speak with him at his grandmother's funeral," he told her. "And I just wanted to check in on him. Yes, I'd like to leave my name and number."

Beverly handed him an embroidered company notepad and a pen.

After quickly scripting his information, he tore the slip of paper free, folded it, and handed it to her.

"Would you please have him call me when he has the time?" he asked. "I really would like to see him. Please let him know that I apologize for the abrupt end of our last conversation, and for showing up here without calling ahead. I appreciate your time. Have a great afternoon." The man dipped his head slightly as he turned and left the suite. He didn't wait for her response, but took a casual look back, watching her unfold the paper and read its contents.

Beverly glanced over the torn slip, turning it over in her hands. The number was not from any recognizable local area codes. She placed the folded slip on her desk beneath her mouse pad.

Chapter 15

Westwood, California

Tuesday, July 20, 2010
7.:23 a.m.

At the Westwood offices of the Federal Bureau of Investigation, Abel Grimes muttered to himself as he downed his third cup of coffee. A knock on the prefabricated wooden door stirred him out of his reverie. "Come in," he called.

Federal agent Amir Nooryani poked his head into the small but efficient office. He introduced himself as the Los Angeles division liaison during Grimes's two-day visit, and then immediately apologized for the small accommodations.

Raising his hand to stop him, Assistant Director Grimes halted the agent mid-sentence with a direct question, while looking him up and down. "How long have you been with the Bureau, No-rani?" he said distractedly.

"I must admit, I am relatively new to the Bureau in years, sir," Nooryani answered. "But I graduated top of my class at Cornell in criminal justice, I have a law degree from Stanford, and I was in the top three graduates at the FBI Academy. I've been here in the Los Angeles division for three years now."

"That's great, No-rani," Grimes responded. "I, uh ..." He was still reviewing his notes. "I wasn't asking for a résumé, no matter how impressive. I just wanted to know if your boss stuck me with a newbie who can't tell the difference between shit and apple butter." He looked up from his notes to focus in on the diminutive agent standing in front of him.

Agent Amir Nooryani was known around the Los Angeles branch of the FBI as a competent and efficient agent, with tenacity beyond his five-foot-seven, one-hundred-fifty-pound frame. He spoke six languages fluently: Farsi, Arabic, English, French, Italian, and Spanish. Although he had a reputation as a by-the-book clinician, he was not afraid to think outside the box. His straightforward determination belied his impish humor. He smiled, enduring the remarks and the mispronunciation of his name.

Director Grimes stopped what he was doing and stared aton the agent, noticing an expression of bemusement with subtle irritation. Abel took the opportunity to chastise the agent further. "You see, Agent, my specialty is profiling. And I can tell when I've gotten under the skin   of—"

Nooryani cut the director off. "I graduated third in my class at the Aacademy;, I know when my chain is being pulled. Sir."

Grimes laughed appreciatively. "Now listen here, No-rani, I know all about you and your accreditations. How you were born in Tehran and came to this country as a three-year-old. You're a naturalized citizen and have excelled in your job. What I want to know is if you're number three in your class, why wasn't I given the number one in your class to assist me?" He pointed to three classified personnel folders on his desk as he stood up to look out of the twenty-first-floor window overlooking Wilshire Boulevard.

"You're toying with me, sir," Amir confirmed, sensing the levity in Grimes's line of questioning. "I know you would have easily accessed my files for this information. Knowing of your relationship with my boss – — it is well documented – —you would look over the possibilities of what agents would be assigned to you. Well, sir, I volunteered for the assignment. The way Assistant Director Pullman described you, not too many agents wanted the job. So I stepped up to get a chance to work with the leader whose team captured the Black Creek Killer."

Grimes turned away from the window and returned to the desk. "How do you explain that Assistant Director Pullman was able to get two of the top three agents from your class assigned to him?" he asked, diverting the subject.

"I don't know," Amir admitted. "It didn't occur to me."

"I believe there has been some serious politicking going on, No-rani."

"It's 'Nooryani,', sir," Amir said finally.

"And so it is, Agent Amir Nooryani," Grimes confessed, reaching out towards Amir for a handshake. Amir took his hand and the assistant director looked into his eyes and apologized for the mispronunciation. Agent Nooryani humbly and gratefully accepted his apology.

"Why the hesitation, Amir?" Grimes asked in earnest.

"Well, sir, it's not often an agent, uh, *director* of your status will admit an error and apologize for it. Certainly, not Director Pullman."

"Well, you'll find there are quite a few differences between me and Pully, Amir. Do, you mind, if I call you Amir? I usually like to work on a first-name basis, especially when doing fieldwork. That way, the locals don't exactly know who is in charge."

Amir posed a quizzical smile. "Not at all, sir."

"Not used to being addressed informally by a superior?"

"Well, I was just thinking, if we're out in the field together, they'll need only to look at us to see which one is in charge, sir."

"Not if you stop calling me 'sir'."

"Then may I presume to call you—"

"No, you will call me Director Grimes," Abel interjected. "I haven't spent all these years hunting down criminals and enduring politicians to be called Abel by some newbie." He gave Amir a sly smile and a wink, breaking any remaining tension with a chuckle. He made a show of purveying the room as if anyone may be listening, and then whispered, "Call me, Abel. Let's not stand on formalities."

Amir smiled and simply responded, "Shit stinks, sir."

"What?"

"The difference between shit and apple butter," Amir confirmed. Grimes let out a belly laugh and directed Amir to sit down.

Amir elaborated on the nuances of doing business with law enforcement in Los Angeles County and the cities encompassed within. "Beverly Hills, Hollywood, Culver City, Santa Monica, West LA,

Sherman Oaks, and the other valley cities," he explained. "All of them are controlled like fiefdoms. And like dukes and duchesses, you have to pay homage to get what you want out of them. Once the cities know they hold a piece of information or a suspect wanted by the Bureau, they'll barter to get some credit or to be seen on stage. For them, it's the prestige – of the appearance of conducting a joint investigation with the FBI – that gets officials reelected." Then he added, "And as bad as they all are, none are as bad as the sheriff's department. You are so lucky this case didn't fall into the hands of the LASD!"

Abel agreed, having run into similar obstacles before. His first thought was to assume Director Pullman had a hand in the disagreeable attitude of law enforcement in the area, not to mention big-city politics and media environments. The bigger the media draw, the bigger the obstruction from local officials. He often bemoaned the trouble he had with Congress and their control of the federal government. "So what are you telling me, Amir?" Abel asked him.

"Captain Rhodes changed his plans to meet you for breakfast and wanted you to come into his precinct to meet in his office after morning announcements. That way, he'd have full show of force from the rank and file and he could make a big production about how police efficacy can lead to apprehending suspects not even on their radar," Amir said. "I emphasized that you, and my own AD, would appreciate any and all courtesies he could extend. I also alluded that there could be a spot next to the podium once a news conference is convened. He said he would have a couple of units keep an eye on our suspect and would be ready to pick him up and bring him in for us. After speaking with Agent Cummings, I personally picked up a copy of the police report and matched it to a copy of the CODIS, which you have here in the file. I told Captain Rhodes that you would be in touch should we need anything. And thanked him in advance for his cooperation."

Grimes admitted, "I thought I was impressed by you on paper."

Amir smiled, accepting the inferred praise with aplomb. "So, how would you like to proceed, sir?"

"I have some details I need to attend to and some phone calls I need to make," Grimes said. "Making a mad rush to get here probably wasn't the best idea I've had lately. Having gotten here so fast, I didn't give myself time to think about what's going on here and what I'd like to ... *need* to accomplish. I'm waiting to hear back from a police captain in Virginia Beach, since Lafayette no longer exists."

Amir gave him a puzzled look. Abel decided to shift focus to the case itself as he editorialized it for his eager audience.

"In the summer of '75 in Lafayette County, Virginia, I was a rookie working for a well-known county sheriff, Beauregard Clayton. A big burly heap of a man who controlled the room just by being in it. He could exact fear and pain by the intonation of his voice. He was law and order for the South then, not always nice, but as fair as a redneck could be. As far as I could tell, he never let his prejudice show, if he had any. But that's besides the point. Bo was good at his job and kept Lafayette County in order. I mean, he knew about everything and everyone, with the exception of some dealings with the City Council. Which is one of the reasons, perhaps the main reason, I left the force and gave up any hope of being a politician and entered the Academy at Langley.

"I originally saw myself as Governor of Virginia. I had high hopes and political aspirations as a young man ..." He trailed off, then restarted. "But I digress. There were four brutal murders: two volunteer ambulance drivers, a nurse, and a doctor. The murders of the first three actually took place in Lafayette County, and the death of the fourth, a medical doctor, occurred in Virginia Beach. These murders were conducted with such precision, a single swipe with a large serrated steel blade across the femoral artery – —it was almost impersonal. But, of course, the closeness of the attacks shows it was very personal. Especially in the doctor's case: his murder was brutal.

"At each crime scene there was a note counting down from four, and a message that eventually spelled out 'Death makes life precious'.' Whoever the perp was, he was taunting the sheriff——hell, the entire county – —like it was a game." Grimes scribbled on a piece of paper to illustrate the notes, numbers, and symbols for Amir. "And then there was a symbol at the end of each note, something like this. We figured part of it was the Sumerian symbol for God, Dingir, but it was inside what looks like two arms going upwards, like this. I know my rendering is kind of crude, but I was never able to find out what that last symbol meant, if anything.

"After a deserter of the Vietnam War, who happened to be the son of one of the City Council members, was found burned alive in his car, the investigation was stopped and almost all of the evidence was destroyed —
—with the exception of what I was able to make away with when I learned what was happening. Then I quit and entered the Academy. Fortunately, I made some friends in forensics and they went and labeled some of the blood evidence for me and logged it into CODIS for future reference. I never thought anything would ever come out of it and had practically given up hope. Until Agent Cummings saw the connection and brought it to my attention."

Amir studied Grimes's crude rendering of the last symbol as he spoke. His brow furrowed in concentration, and he almost didn't appear to be listening.

"Ka," he said finally.

"What?"

"Ka," Amir explained. "It's an Egyptian symbol that means '
assisting in death'."

"Are you certain?"

"Almost positive."

Grimes took the page back and thought out loud. "You know, there was the consideration of a black ... uh, African American suspect," he said, correcting himself, "whose daughter was raped by one or both of the ambulance drivers. They were never charged." He frowned to himself. "Looking back, I guess Bo Clayton was a son of a bitch after all."

Chapter 16

Los Angeles, California

Tuesday, July 20, 2010
1.:25 p.m.

Having returned from lunch, Houston and Oscar took their time getting back to their offices. Houston had tried to avoid any interaction with Cantoni, and Oscar claimed after enjoying a beef dip sandwich that the only thing to do was take a nap. "Man, I'm gonna need some coffee if I'm gonna do any work now," he groaned. "Fuck, that sandwich was good. Right?"

"Yeah, but I still don't know how you can put away two of them," Houston teased. "You keep grubbin' up like that and you're gonna end up fat. Like you're ..."

"Don't even say it," Oscar chuckled. "You know I don't eat like that all the time. And I know I'm not gonna eat dinner. So fuck you, homes. I ain't gonna get fat. Walk with me to the kitchen to get some coffee and burn some calories with me. In case people are still in there eating and I have to fart, I can blame it on you."

Houston laughed and followed Oscar to the kitchen. Waiting in the doorway, Houston used the opportunity to think about the work he had for the rest of the day. He was snapped out of his thoughts when Beverly, exiting the kitchen, bumped into him. "Sorry, Houston," she offered. "Hey, do you have a minute?"

"What's up?"

"Well, I'd rather not say anything out here in the open," Beverly said. "Just walk back with me. I've got something for you. Unless you're busy."

"I was just waiting for Oscar," he said, loud enough to draw his coworker's attention, a little uncertain of Beverly's cryptic messaging.

"He's lying, Bev! He's not waiting for me," Oscar chuckled.

Houston laughed it off and followed Beverly per her request. She realized he might be feeling awkward about it and assured him, "Don't worry, it's not what you think."

Houston noticed her bouncing as if she had a secret she could no longer contain. When they arrived at her station, she gave him a wry look, then sat in her seat and spun around. "You had a visitor today," she announced, as if the game was over. "A tall, ruggedly handsome older black man. Carried himself like he was in the military. My dad was in the Vietnam War, you know, so I know how military men act with civilians." She then pulled out what appeared to be a small folded paper from underneath the mouse pad on her desk and held it to him. "Here."

"What is it?" Houston responded, hesitant. "It's a note, silly. What does it look like?"

Houston unfolded it carefully with a frown on his face. "What's going on, Beverly? Why are you acting weird?"

"Am I acting weird? I don't mean to. I guess ... I just felt like I might have met your father?"

"My what?!" Houston exclaimed. His mind had been racing ever since she'd mentioned wanting to discuss something with him, but this was the furthest thing from it. "Who told you—? —You met my father?" he demanded, voice rising as he tensed up.

"I'm sorry, Houston. I don't mean to upset you," she said. "But this very nice man came looking for you. He said you two spoke at your grandmother's funeral. I thought it was your mother, but I figured ... maybe he knows something. So ..." She drifted off, apologetic. "I apologize."

Houston started to calm himself, recalling his very brief encounter with the man she described – the mysterious man at the funeral? Admittedly, with all else that had been going on, he hadn't thought about the man since the night he was arrested. "No, no, that's okay, Bev. I understand. I probably would have made the same conclusion. Did he say he was my dad, or ... ?"

"No, not exactly," she said, hesitant, thinking of what to say to reiterate her explanation. "It was just the way he carried himself. Kinda reminded me of you. Just a little bit, maybe.?"

"I really didn't get a chance to talk to him at the funeral," Houston explained. "He came up on me all of a sudden. Said he knew my mom and my grandmother, then he rushed out. Like he'd seen a ghost or something. I didn't really catch his name."

"Well, now you have it. So are you going to call him?" she asked.

"It's not a local number. I think it's from the East Coast or around there. I took a little peek at what he wrote. I wanted to make sure he wasn't threatening you."

"I don't know. I'm not calling anyone now," Houston responded, ignoring her remark about possible threats. What for? "I wonder how he knew where I work. Hell, I wonder how he knew about my mom's funeral in the first place."

Beverly nodded, sympathizing with his confusion. "If you need to talk, I'm here for you."

"Yeah, I know. Thanks, Bev. I appreciate your concern," Houston said. "Sorry I went off on you."

Back in his cubicle, Houston debated on what to do about the note.

He didn't want to rush into making a decision without careful thought. If this person was indeed his father or someone who knew his father, Houston had myriad feelings to unpack and arrange before any viable contact could be made.

He put a hand on the phone to call Sabrina, hoping she could offer some advice. He glanced about the room to make sure he had ample privacy, when he noticed all of Phil's belongings had disappeared from his desk. He'd cleaned house. What the hell was going on?

Just as he'd been about to pick up the phone, it rang. He answered, now on edge. "Hello?"

"Hello, my love! How are you doing?"

Does she have a sixth sense? "Hey, sweetheart. Damn, I was just gonna call you."

"I just wanted to check up on you, since you obviously didn't want to talk this morning."

"So you noticed that?"

"We don't have to talk about it now, honey. I'm just letting you know I'm here when you're ready," Sabrina said. "How's Phil doing?"

"I don't know," he responded honestly. "He seemed okay this morning. Almost like the usual Phil." With his free hand, he held the piece of paper between his fingers. He wanted to bring it up with her. But with everything else – —his mother's death, Phil, his job – —he knew calling this gentleman could lead to a host of things he wasn't prepared to talk about yet, especially while he was still at work.

"That's good, isn't it?"

"I guess so. But I think he's been gone since lunch. He hasn't come back to his desk yet. And it looks like he's cleaned everything out ..." Looking at his desk again, Houston noticed some pictures sticking out of the cryptic drawer. It was peculiar that Phil would leave anything behind, especially related to the crypt.

After a long pause, Sabrina asked, "Hello?" Did I lose you?"

"Sorry, I just noticed some old pictures sticking out of his drawer. Looks like some black-and-white photos."

"You're not looking at them, are you?" she scolded. "Honey, that's his privacy you're violating."

"I'm not looking. I was just stuffing them down in the drawer."

"Houston,. I know what you sound like when you're lying."

She was correct – —Houston had stretched the phone cord over to Phil's desk as he took a look at the photos. "Just a quick peek," he responded. "Pictures of Phil and ... some black kids he must've grown up with. Didn't know Phil had black friends."

"Don't be silly,"" Sabrina said with a chuckle. "Now put them back. Oh, and, *mi amor*, your aunt came by this weekend."

"Shit, I was hoping to keep the car for a few more days," Houston responded. "It's getting detailed in the garage and I need to fill it up, too."

"Well, she wasn't here to pick up the car. She had a box of things your mom wanted you to have. I put it in the bedroom;, it's a shoebox, and you can take a look at it later. Oh, and she said we can keep the car for as long as we need it."

"I could need it forever!"

"Houston!"

"I'm just kidding. I better get goin'."

Sabrina thought it curious that he ignored the box, but wouldn't press him on it. "Hey, don't forget to remind Israel about dinner tonight, okay?"

"Remind him? Are you kidding? He's been reminding me about it every chance he gets."

Houston hung up the receiver and started to mill around the office. Before he realized what he was doing, he found himself rummaging around Phil's desk again, looking for a clue. But it's hard to find something when you don't even know what you're looking for. In a moment of clarity, he realized what he was doing and stopped himself. "I must be losing my fuckin' mind."

He returned to his desk and started working with renewed concentration on the job at hand. A few minutes later, Oscar raised his head and asked, "What'd you find, homes?"

"Nothing. I don't even know what I was looking for." Feeling guilty, he added, "Phil left some pictures out and I was just stuffing them back in his drawer." He immediately realized when he said it that it didn't make sense. He waited for Oscar to chastise him and was relieved when his coworker just smiled, shrugged, and let the inquiry end as he refocused on his work.

When the evening approached, Houston closed down his desk for the day. He collected the backup disks and brought them to the safe. He looked over at Phil's desk, then checked with Oscar and received confirmation that neither of them had seen Phil since that morning. Houston was just deciding to see if he could catch any of his coworkers to ask about him, when he came upon a small gathering of people at the door of Renee Peterson's office. The mood was somber, and Renee was saying a few words as Houston joined the crowd.

He could hear the conversation was about Phil and his illness. They were taking turns commenting about how little they'd noticed his physical changes in the last few months. No one really paid much attention to their crusty coworker, when in reality none of them actually cared for him and his cantankerous personality. It was almost as though they felt a comfortable camaraderie as they derided their fellow coworker.

"I don't think he ever had anything really nice to say to anybody."

"I really think he went out of his way to be nasty. Especially, in the last few months."

"Do you think he knew he was dying?"

Renee saw Houston standing in the back taking it all in, and decided to rein in the conversation. "Well, I think he most likely knew and didn't want anyone to miss him. We all know how he was and that he was antisocial," she declared to a nodding of heads. This acceptance of her opinion gave her impetus to speak brazenly. "But what I don't understand is the hold he had over the senior partners, especially Elizabeth. I mean, it was like he had a file on them or something. You know, he probably ..."

Her statement went unfinished as she recognized one of the subjects of her intrigue standing right behind Houston, frowning. Renee felt her face redden as she acknowledged Mrs. Taylor-Barrings's presence to the maddening crowd.

A deafening hush took over the group as Elizabeth, even with her demanding presence, showed vulnerability. She smiled warmly with a trace of water in her eyes, then blinked it away as she turned her focus to Houston. Standing nearly eye to eye with the six-foot-two man, she gingerly placed her arm on his shoulder and displayed a softness not many in the office were used to. "Houston, would you mind coming into my office?" she asked with patience.

Houston just nodded and followed her as she turned down the hallway. The group at Renee's door tried desperately to slip away quietly and hopefully unnoticed. Elizabeth wasn't a demonstrative person and rarely showed much emotion. The sight of water in her eyes, and the possibility of her hearing not just the tone but the crux of the conversation regarding someone she obviously held dear, made an impression on everyone that watched as she and Houston departed their company.

"Have a seat, Houston," Elizabeth suggested with a gesture, as she had not yet fully collected herself. She picked up a file that lay on the corner of her desk as they both sat, and she met Houston's gaze with a hesitant smile.

Houston could see she was a little uncomfortable and figured she had news about Phil to share, and perhaps about him taking on more responsibility. He thought he would broeach the subject first. His own unease made him speak a little faster and with a cracked voice.

"What, um ...? What happened with Phil?" he asked. "I don't think he came back after lunch."

Elizabeth stopped to consider her response. She let out a heavy sigh and fought back the tears welling in her eyes, then grabbed a tissue and slowly removed her eyeglasses. She gave Houston a deep and sincere look. She forced herself to remain professional, even though her heart was breaking. Then, with heartfelt hesitation, she uttered, "That's right. Neither you nor Oscar were present when Oliver and I called a quick meeting right after lunch. Well, I'm sure you've been aware of the weight loss and coughing Phil has endured over the last few months." She looked to him for his agreement, and Houston nodded his head on cue. "Well," she continued, "Phil is a very sick man. Phil was diagnosed with colon cancer a few months ago, and we thought that he had beat it after having a portion of his colon removed. Unfortunately, he was recently diagnosed with advanced pancreatic cancer."

Houston remained silent, consuming her words respectfully.

"Phil wasn't one to ..." She corrected herself. "Phil isn't one to make a big deal of anything when it comes to himself. So we accommodated his wishes and kept it quiet until he left for hospice. He doesn't have any family that I know of or that he will admit to. And he didn't want to wait out his time at his home with just his cats."

Houston blurted, "He has cats?"

Elizabeth paused, showing no irritation at the interruption. "Yes, he has two, I believe. He was ... He's very fond of them."

"I'm sorry, I just didn't think of Phil as a pet lover."

"There is quite a bit about Phil that you and apparently the rest of the staff don't know," she said defensively, as she pushed the conversation back on track. "So he wanted to be ... No, let me rephrase." Houston noticed the confidence return to her voice and thought this conversation must be cathartic for her. He assumed he was helping her by listening, and he started to feel better that he was the one who had broached the subject. "Phil chose to be here, and as far as I know he chose the people he regarded as his friends carefully. And he wanted to be around them. As you may know, Oliver Cole is his attorney and friend. Both Oliver and I have known Phil for as long as he's been here. That's over twenty-five years. He was very fond of Sabrina. But then we all are," she said out of the blue, "and he was fond of you and Oscar."

"Me and Oscar?"

"Yes. He said that Sabrina reminded him of someone from his past and, actually, that he got a kick out of chastising you and Mr. Mendoza. He spoke as if the two of you were in on the joke."

Houston let out an honest but nervous chuckle. He wanted to step lightly, knowing her reverence for Phil. "Really – —so he got a kick outta that? I can't begin to understand how."

He thought he noticed a hint of irritation starting to show on her face. Then she confirmed his suspicion.

"You're an intelligent man, Mr. Jenkins. I'm sure you were able to see past Phil's façade of the grumpy old man. Sabrina did. Deep down, he was a damaged soul, who had compassion and bravery. If there was anyone who proved to be a walking enigma, it was Phil Cantoni."

"Yeah, I know," Houston said. "But I just can't understand why someone would work so hard to not be liked when being liked was what he really wanted."

"I don't think he wanted to be liked, necessarily. I believe Phil put a premium on intimate relationships. And really didn't care to foster any of the ancillary relationships that most people tolerate just to be polite."

Houston remained silent, averting his gaze while nodding his head in agreement. He turned to see a look of frustration mounting in her expression. He realized she probably didn't want to talk about Phil. It was already past official works hours, and Houston assumed she wanted to discuss his future employment. While his eyes were turned away from hers, he spotted his personnel file on her desk and sought to segue into the discussion about his future with the company.

I guess with Phil gone, they're really gonna need me to be

permanent. Not to be a dick and take advantage, but this might be a good time to ask for a raise.

"Does that mean you're going to want me to come on permanently?"

Elizabeth reached for the personnel folder lying at the corner of her desk and let out a huge sigh as she fingered through the papers and pulled out Houston's employment contract. She laid it on her desk and placed her manicured hands on top of it, lightly tapping her fingers. Houston could sense she was searching for the right words, witnessing she was somewhat emotional about this as well. She paused, then stated with determined yet noticeable regret, "Houston, you've done a remarkable job getting all of our systems up to code. Frankly, I would have preferred to be in the position to offer you an extension or even a permanent position. But, unfortunately, we've decided to go in another direction for our IT needs."

The words hit Houston like a punch in the gut. He heard her annunciate clearly that they were not renewing his contract, yet for obvious reasons he couldn't understand it.

"You're firing me?" he asked incredulously. "But with Phil gone, that means you're leaving Oscar to handle everything by himself. And I've got at least another week or two on my contract. Don't you want to think about it?"

"I'm sorry, Houston, but this decision was taken out of my hands. Management has simply decided to go in another direction."

As she spoke, it felt as though time were slowing down. Houston collected his thoughts and measured his reaction. The last thing he wanted was to get emotional in a law office. He could hear her speaking, but none of it was coming through. What could have been the impetus behind the sudden action?

It was about that Jefferson shit you said in front of Watson. He could hear Oscar's words in his head now.

Houston looked her in the eye and asked directly, "Is this about the Jefferson remark I made to Renee? I thought the office was happy with my work. I've never been fired before." Before he realized it, he had asked two different questions, leaving her the option to decide which one to answer.

"Believe me, Houston, I am sorry for the abruptness of all this, and with everything that's happening. I know this doesn't make any sense, but all I am able to say is that the office ..." Then it appeared she tried to offer some comfort to allay his distress, as she looked him in the eyes with sincerity. "Yes, we were very happy with the progress you made. But, unfortunately, bringing you on in a permanent capacity would expand our budget further than what we can offer. We didn't feel it would be fair to you to ask you to stay and reduce your compensation."

Houston heard what she said, but his feelings told him otherwise. *If I had just kept my mouth shut about Jefferson, I bet she would be offering me the permanent position.*

Elizabeth continued, "Houston, you know I am fond of you and have always mentioned how appreciative I was of you accepting the contract. If I could, I would do things differently, but ..." She stopped herself mid-sentence, wiping the corner of her eye. "I know it's not much, but I've taken the liberty to pay you for the last two weeks of work on your contract. And I have a letter of recommendation for you as well. Normally, it is our procedure to have security follow you to your desk and then escort you out, but since it is after hours and security is at minimal response now, I would consider it a huge favor if you would come in and clean out your belongings in the morning."

Seeing her ride an emotional rollercoaster made Houston consider what she was going through. He understood that this was not what she wanted, nor was it easy for her to do this and balance her feelings about Phil. He decided to acquiesce to the inevitable and move on. He couldn't be upset at her for a decision that was taken out of her hands. He knew what it felt like knowing someone close to you was on the brink of death, and he felt for her.

He agreed he would return in the morning for the items he felt were important. He knew he could have demanded she allow him to take it all now, but doing so would make him look like a retaliatory jerk —— and he honestly liked her. He didn't want to put what relationship they had through that.

Houston could tell from her nonverbal response that she appreciated his understanding. He stood to leave, but then she did something he wasn't ready for. She moved around her desk and gave him a hug.

"I'm sorry. I know this has been a really tough time for you and Sabrina," she offered, gentle. "Please don't think this has anything to do with how you took the time to take care of your mother in her finals days. You are a good man and a resilient one, and I know you will not let this minor issue hold you back."

Chapter 17

Los Angeles, California

Tuesday, July 20, 2010
5.:45 p.m.

Houston sat in his aunt's Lexus, not having remembered how he got there.

Fired. *Fired*. He said it to himself as if saying it made him register the reality of it.

He'd never been fired before. What was he supposed to do now? Why had he agreed to bring himself back tomorrow?

As he pulled up to his home, he recognized Izzy's car, but didn't see his friend as he pulled up along the side of it. He parked and made his way to his apartment. As he got closer to the door, he could hear the TV, but he couldn't tell exactly where it was coming from until he opened his front door to a very comfortable Israel Tate lounging on the sofa, flipping channels. This immediately irritated him, but he didn't know why. This was not an uncommon sight.

"Hey, man," Izzy offered.

"Where's Sabrina?" he asked, stepping into the kitchen.

Israel could sense his best friend's heightened irritation and chose to ignore it rather than address it. Israel kept flipping channels until he found a program he liked, while Houston paced the apartment like a lion marking its territory.

Izzy called attention to the program he was watching. "Damn, man. Eddie is so fuckin' believable as Sherman. He reminds me so much of Marty, I almost wanna cry."

Taken aback by the new subject tossed into his lion's den, Houston responded venomously, "He doesn't look anything like Marty! You must be out of your fuckin' mind! Marty wasn't that fat or that insecure. What in the fuck are you talkin' about?"

"I didn't say that he was an exact replica. I said that he reminds me of Marty. You know as well as I do that Marty hid a lot of pain."

"Oh, so now you're fucking Dr. Phil? How the fuck do you know what pain Marty was going through?"

By this time, Izzy had paused the TV as if waiting for his cue to play a specific scene to prove his point. "Just take a look at this scene, Ferrigno, and tell me if he doesn't remind you of Marty." Houston still chuckled at the Ferrigno dig, but watched the scene in vexed silence.

"See, right there, Lou. If that doesn't remind you of Marty, then whatever's crawled up your ass has now made it to your brain."

As if transfixed by the scene and his friend's comments, Houston stared at Izzy and said, "I got fired."

"No shit?"

"No, asshole, I'm joking. What the fuck?" Houston sighed loudly.

"Yeah, I got let go. Not only did they decide to cancel my contract early and not offer me the permanent position they promised me, but now I have to go back in the morning to collect my shit and my check to take the loser's stroll outta there. Probably escorted by security."

"That's fucked!"

"Thank you, genius!"

"Hey, Hou, let's dial back that rage a little bit. You have the right to be pissed, but don't take it out on me. Especially when I'm here to do you and your wife a favor by meeting some spinster who can't get a date."

"Damn, everything ain't about you. Also, Sabrina's pregnant."

"Oh, shit! You're fucked!"

"Thanks, Einstein. Tell me something I don't know."

"Hold up, you're having a baby, dude. You should be happy! Not only that, you're having a baby with Sabrina!" Izzy gave him a big grin. "So kiss my ass if I'm not feeling sorry for you. You didn't want to stay at that job anyway. Now you can get your ass back in school and get the degree you were so fuckin' close to gettin' before you dropped out." Silence fell over the room as the television program kept playing.

Izzy went to the kitchen and grabbed two cold beers from the fridge, one for Houston. "You could use a drink."

"That's not all," Houston went on, taking it. "You remember that old man with the gravelly voice at the funeral? Apparently, he showed up at my job today. The receptionist said he looked like he could be my father."

"Are you serious? What did he say?"

"I don't know."

"Well, where'd she get the idea he's your father?"

"She said he kind of looked like me."

"Is she white?"

"Yeah. Why?"

"Because all black people start to look alike to white folks. I remember him. I didn't think he looked like you ... Well, maybe, a little bit around the ears. Both of y'alls ears stick out."

"Really?" Houston felt his ears. "Fuck you. My ears don't stick out."

Israel laughed and clanked his bottle of beer with Houston's as if toasting their friendship.

"Thanks," was all Houston would say, before Izzy took control of the direction of the conversation.

"Look, man, all I know is that this Patricia better be good looking or I will kick your ass like I was about to in high school."

"I don't know shit about her. Never met her before. But if Sabrina, says she's cute, she's probably too cute for you. And for the record, you ain't kickin' nobody's ass." They both laughed, and then Houston finally asked what he'd been wanting to for a while. "By the way, how in the fuck did you get into my apartment?"

***

Sabrina appeared harried when she arrived home, but she was a sight for Houston's welcoming eyes. She glowed like a rose in blossom, and when Houston immediately thought of the glow of pregnancy, he became a believer. He embraced her as if he hadn't seen her in a week.

"It's bad enough you two are procreating. No one asked you to show us how's it's done," Izzy said from the couch. "Now come on in and let's get the introductions started."

Sabrina had made it her mission to set up Izzy with her friend Patricia – a five-foot-seven, brown-skinned beauty with ringlets of natural cinnamon brown hair bouncing off her shoulders. Izzy took her in with complete silence and didn't notice, with his staring, that he'd become the center of attention.

"You're pregnant?" Patricia exclaimed. "Girl, you didn't tell me you were expecting! Congratulations! You're going to make an amazing mother!" She gave Sabrina a celebratory hug.

Overwhelmed by the sudden attention and unexpected revelation, Sabrina accepted the hug with an emotional burst of joy. "I'm so excited!" she said, though she turned to Houston. "A word, baby?"

When she pulled him into the next room, alone, she frowned. "I should've known you'd tell Israel."

"I didn't think it was supposed to be a secret," Houston said apologetically.

"But that's just it. You didn't think about it," Sabrina answered. "I wanted us to tell everyone together, to make an announcement. This is our first baby and I wanted it to be special."

Realizing he didn't diffuse as much of the bomb as he had hoped,

Houston rubbed both of her shoulders and arms, as if he were fighting off rising goose bumps, and gingerly kissed her on the forehead. "Sweetheart, it can still be special. I just told Iz because ... Well, actually, it kind of just slipped out. I'm excited to be a dad and I just wanted to tell somebody." Then he added, "How was I to know that loudmouth was going to blurt it out to you and your friend as soon as he saw you? You know he's like a brother to me and I don't have anyone else to talk to."

"Israel? Really? Come on, Houston, you know he can't keep a secret." *Uh oh. Full first name, still kind of pissed. Admit your mistake now and cut your losses.*

"Yes, you're right. I should've known. He really can't keep secrets," Houston agreed.

"We can talk about this later. We've got guests." Then Sabrina added, "Well, at least he doesn't know about the announcement party my parents want to give."

"You're parents knew before me?"

"Oops."

"Oops, my ass. You're giving me a hard time about telling someone who amounts to my brother and all the while you told your parents already? And just how long have they known?" Houston demanded, starting to show a bit of irritation himself.

Being on the other end, Sabrina brilliantly assuaged his feelings while ignoring his questions. "They were happy for us, sweetheart. My mom and dad are excited and proud to become *abuelos*."

Houston immediately picked up on how the tables had turned. He kissed her and gave up the fight. "It's a good thing you're so sexy," he said, "or I'd be pissed."

"No, you wouldn't." She smiled coyly as she left to rejoin their guests.

Houston left to pick up dinner from Hunan Bistro. He found himself staring at the bill he'd just paid while he sat in the restaurant parking lot. *Fuck, did she have to order the whole kitchen?* Now that he was without employment, he was severely contemplating the cost of living. They'd both gotten started late saving their nest egg for a home and eventual retirement. With this setback, things wouldn't be easy for the foreseeable future – especially with a child on the way. Houston's stomach curled up in knots. *What the fuck am I going to do with a baby? I can't be anybody's father. Fuck, I don't even know the first thing about being a father.* Sabrina had never had to worry – she'd grown up with two loving parents.

Houston entered the apartment to a hungry crowd. "It's about fucking time! I'm starving!" Izzy called. Much to the chagrin of his best friend, Houston waved him off. Izzy took the hint. Houston attempted to lighten the mood with jokes that didn't land; he tried to fix it by kissing

Sabrina on the cheek and holding her chair out for her. Never one to embarrass her husband, Sabrina took the peck in her stride and thanked him for his chivalry.

Most of the dinner went by without incident. Houston tried to put his irritation behind him, and when he realized he didn't have anything positive to add, he kept his mouth busy drinking. Sabrina could sense something wholly different was eating at Houston, and she felt for him. Patricia, as it turned out, was a lone conservative at a liberal table. Politics became an unavoidable topic of conversation and, eventually, argument. Tensions rose, and when Houston's drinking got the better of him and caused him to lash out, Sabrina stood from the table.

"Houston, a word, please!"

The conversation had taken such a turn that she felt this was the only way to end it. He followed her into the bedroom so they could have a moment alone and undisturbed, leaving their guests to get to know each other. She sat on the bed.

Houston fidgeted. "What's up?"

She took a deep breath and exhaled, then patted the spot next to her. "Come here. Let's talk," she said in a slightly pained voice, masking her frustration and impatience.

Houston knew exactly what was eating her and refused. "Nah, I'll stand."

"Well, would you at least come in and close the door?" she implored, as an irritated teacher would to a small child. And like a small child, Houston responded in kind, refusing to do it. So she stood and pressed her back against it, shutting the door and blocking his exit.

"Okay, so the door's closed," he said. "Now what?"

Sabrina softened her approach. "Honey, what's wrong?"

"What do you mean, what's wrong?"

"Come on, sweetheart. You've been bothered by something all night. I've never seen you drink like this, and the way you picked on Patricia – that wasn't like you."

"Hey, I didn't bring up politics, she did."

"I'm not talking about that. I'm talking about *you*, and what's eating you."

Houston felt cornered, and with a ready response, he deflected. "Can you believe her with that tired smaller government BS?" he retorted more than asked. "She didn't like it when I pointed out there's no such thing as smaller government. Because giant corporate government will take over and the voter won't have a voice."

"Yes, baby, you did make a valid point," Sabrina calmly reassured him. "But I'm not talking about that now. I'm talking about you. I feel like you're avoiding what's really bothering you. You know you don't have to hold anything back with me."

Houston, conflicted, could feel the façade crumbling. Reluctantly, he realized he had a choice: either to open himself up and allow his wife access to his fears, or to reinforce the battlements. He chose the latter.

"You're just upset because I told Izzy about your pregnancy," he stated defiantly.

"Sweetheart, I'm not upset," Sabrina insisted. "I know that you and Israel have a history. I'm not trying to interrupt that. I'm just concerned because you aren't being the Houston I know. Please tell me what's bothering you. Is it your job? Is it me or the baby? I'm just asking you to talk to me, *mi amor*. Don't you know I'm here for you?"

How can I tell her I got fired? She'll give me that look. I can't take that right now.

"Nothing's wrong with me!" He pushed his way past her, out of the room, walking out to the muffled words of Patricia and the blatant stare of Israel. Not certain if they were privy to the confrontation between hime and his wife, he just offered, "Fuck it!" and walked out the front door, down the stairs, and into the street.

More embarrassed than hurt, Sabrina joined Patricia and Israel with traces of tears in her eyes. "I'm sorry tonight got out of hand. This is not what I had planned," she offered with a forced smile. Both Patricia and Izzy went to her side to comfort her. Sabrina buried her head in Israel's chest and let the tears flow.

"Izzy, what's wrong with him? What's bothering him? He's hiding something bad and I know it. But he just won't let me inside to help him." She begged Israel, clutching at him, "Do you know what it is?"

Put on the spot, Izzy responded unwittingly, "He got canned. Other than that, I don't know. If you like, I'll go talk with him."

Patricia nodded. "I've got Sabrina."

Israel joined Houston outside, where he stood in the middle of the empty street, pacing. Izzy stormed up to him.

"What in the fuck is wrong with you?" he demanded. "You've got your pregnant wife upstairs, *crying*. Do I need to put my foot up your ass? Tighten up your cha-cha, nigga!"

Houston met him with a blank stare ———a look that admitted he deeply regretted the way he'd handled things. He had nothing to say for himself, so Israel went on.

"I'm takin' Patricia home, so you can get your ass back on the floor. I'll check with you tomorrow."

With that, they shook hands and embraced chest to chest. Israel had given him a much-needed verbal beatdown, a slap in the face that made him buck up, swallow his pride, and find the determination to fix things. Israel shooed Houston up the stairs, and as Houston stepped back in, Izzy beckoned Patricia to get her purse and come with him. They heard him boast to her about a late-night establishment he knew of where they could continue their evening in peace.

Sabrina glanced blankly at Houston as she strolled to the bedroom. Houston made sure the door was locked and called to his wife, who didn't acknowledge his attempt and closed the bathroom door. He realized he had an uphill battle ahead of him.

He cleaned up the dining table, then the kitchen. He put away the dishes and contained the leftover food. It gave him time to reflect and gather his thoughts before he could finally could bare his soul to his wife. He knew she would be expecting him to come running into the bedroom, begging for her forgiveness, but he wasn't ready yet. He was caught completely off guard when he heard her say, "Good night, Houston. I'm going to bed," without passion or concern.

Houston immediately stopped what he was doing and rushed to the bedroom. Sabrina sat in the dimly lit bedroom, sitting up on his side of the bed with headphones on her belly, playing classical music for the baby growing inside of her. She gently rubbed her stomach in circular motions. Even so, tears streamed down her face. Houston, overwhelmed by this sight, felt the full weight of just how much he had hurt her. He approached her with the realization that he didn't need to hide anything from her. And if he had been completely open and honest with her in the first place, all of this could have been avoided.

Houston wiped away her tears, which made her flinch, as she'd been almost unaware of his presence. He took her face in his hands and kissed her softly on the mouth. She welcomed it through tears and started to speak. He didn't let her finish.

"You were right. I shouldn't try to keep my feelings from you. I was an unbelievable asshole tonight. Can you possibly forgive me? Again?" he entreated.

"You can't speak to me the way you did," Sabrina responded. She softened. "But of course I'm going to forgive you. You're not getting rid of me that easily." She took his hand and placed it on her belly. "I think he knows something was wrong tonight. I started to feel a little queasy."

"It's probably because you didn't eat enough and ... and I upset you. I did. I'm sorry."

His admission hung in the air as they stared at each other, their eyes bouncing back and forth at the other, taking in all of one another.

"I lost my job today," he admitted with a sigh. Sabrina remained silent and gently stroked his brow. "I ain't never been in a position where I didn't of Ashley's bravery, too, in the face of his father's rage. *It's not always about those that share your blood*, he knew, *but those who will shed their blood for you.*

The twins were budding high school graduates and would be off to college the following autumn, yet they all huddled as small children together on the kitchen floor with Ashley in their midst. Florence could feel the anger elevating in her son. She knew her history with Mr. Dunning would hurt them and was afraid of what Leeland would do if he knew the truth. Her son had grown into a strapping young man, the spitting image of his father. Florence said a quick prayer to her husband, asking for his strength to help her guide their son.

Florence spoke up softly. "It was my fault. I was careless with the money Ms. Evelyn leaves for the groceries and little things we need. I went into next week's budget, and Mr. Dunning thought I was takin' the money for myself. He started yellin' about me stealin' money." She knew the explanation was uncharacteristic of her, but kept on. "I tried to tell him it wasn't for me. And I must've yelled back at him, because I was tired and I didn't want Ms. Evelyn or Mr. Dunning to think I would ever steal from them."

Leeland took in a deep breath, looking to his mother and then to Ashley, deducing her story didn't comport with what he could see. He knew she wanted to keep the peace and would live at the mercy of the Dunnings until he could take the mantle of provider.

He questioned Ashley with a discerning eye for detail. "Mama,

Ms. Evelyn knows you wouldn't steal from her. Ash, what happened? What did your dad do to my mama?"

Never before had he made such a distinction – –*his* mama. He usually included Ashley in everything they did as a member of the Jenkins family. Ashley harbored ill feelings for his own father, that much was obvious. He hoped that, now, he could force Ashley to make a choice: defend his mother by telling the truth, or protect his father by adding to the lie. Leeland drew a line in the sand and challenged the boy who called his mother "'mama'" to cross it.

"Ashley was just tryin' to stop Mr. Dunning from getting angry," Florence tried to continue. "He rushed over to try to calm us both down and knocked his father down by accident. Then Mr. Dunning must've thought he did it on purpose, because he got up and slapped him across the face. Then Mr. Dunning called him names;, that was when Ashley grabbed the knife."

Ashley sat patiently listening to Florence distort the facts, going over the scene cemented in his head.

I was sitting at the small kitchen table when Jasper came in, unaware of my presence. He snuck up behind Mama and pressed himself against her while she was doing the dishes. Then he reached his hand around, touching her, and said, "'I know you're tryin' to turn Evelyn against me. I believe you need another lesson on who really runs things here.'" Ashley gingerly rubbed the bridge of his nose as he focused on his anger. Yeah, you made my nose bleed, but only after sucker punching me when Mama pulled me off of you. You son of a bitch. If you ever try to do anything like that to her again, I will cut your dick off while you sleep.

He knew full well why she was hiding it. He knew Leeland was raring to go. He put himself in Leeland's place, knowing the rage building inside him. He knew what Leeland would do if he knew the truth. Ashley looked him in the eyes and said, "Lee, you know I wouldn't ever let anyone hurt Mama. Anyone."

Neither Leeland nor Leesa questioned the validity of the story, even though they knew vital details where clearly missing. Nevertheless, Leeland paced the floor, trying to calm his rage. At eighteen, he stood well over six feet tall, with his father's broad shoulders. Florence would often show him pictures of his father and comment on how much they resembled each other. This time, she would use the specter of his father to calm him and to reach inside his rage.

"Lee, I know you're upset, but you know strikin' out ain't how I raised you and ain't what your father would want for you. If you do anything, you'll just end up in jail or worse. And that's not what we planned for the two of you," she implored. She stroked the anger out of his brow and stood before him, challenging his rage with her love. She met him head on, reached out, and held him tight. "We're a family, and we have to stick together and look out for what's best for each other. Promise me, Lee, that you won't try to do anything to Mr. Dunning."

"You don't have to worry," Ashley proudly told the twins. "I promise I'll never let anyone ever hurt Mama again."

Wanting to ease the tension, Leesa sought a distraction and turned on the small black-and-white television Florence kept in the corner. Leesa hoped by seeking an afternoon game show or soap opera, the tension would soon dissipate. She fixed the dial to a local station, only to find the afternoon programming had been preempted by events taking place in Birmingham, Alabama.

A white elected public official of Birmingham directed the use of police dogs and fire hoses on Negro children – children who were peacefully demonstrating for the civil rights of Negroes in the South. And it was all being displayed live on television for the entire nation to witness. Leesa caught a quick look from her mother as she tried to silently tell her have a job. It's ... I don't know ... It seems like a lot of shit is happening all at once and I can't get a handle on it. And losing my job right now is like the straw that broke the camel's back. You know?"

Just what she needs to hear right now – —that her man can't hack it.

Yet Sabrina kept quiet, letting him get it all out.

"Look, baby, I know it sounds like I'm makin' excuses, but I'm not. I just need you to understand that I will do the best I can for you and the baby. Right now, I'm scared shitless that I won't measure up."

"Measure up to what?"

"To what your father wants me to be."

"Why are you so concerned with what he wants? What about what I want? What about what *you* want? What *we* want?"

"He's your dad. He's important to you. I see how he treats you and how you respect him. I know your mom loves him and he's worked hard for his family. As much as I know he's critical of me, I want to be respected as a father. I want my kid, my family, to respect and love me the way you love your dad."

"Sure. But did you notice he didn't do it alone?" Sabrina responded. "My mom was there beside him the whole time. Don't get me wrong, I do love my father, my parents. But we're not them. We're you and me, and when our baby is born he'll have us, together."

Houston frowned. "When I was telling Iz about the baby, he said something that made me realize that I don't know ... Well, I don't have the slightest idea how to be a father. Hell, I just found out that the person I thought was my mother all of my life wasn't even my mother. So I really don't have much experience with parents to refer to with a kid of my own." His composure slowly began to fracture. "And frankly, I'm scared! With you going on maternity leave and me not getting the job extension or being made permanent when I knew I would, that just ... it fucked me up. I'm so sorry I took it out on you. You didn't deserve it."

"Thank you. That's two you owe me," she said with a smile. "Why didn't you just tell me that when I asked earlier?"

"Because I'm a grown-ass man, and I was being a jerk."

"Yes, you are a grown-ass man. And you're mine." She hugged his neck to pull him closer. They kissed passionately. Sabrina stopped to reassure him, taking his face firmly into her grasp to make him look at her. "Houston,. I know you will make a fantastic father."

"Yeah, but ..."

"But nothing. I know you will because you're a good man. You're a very good man, and I am lucky to have you as my husband. I know you will do whatever it takes to provide and be there for us. I know that we will be your first priority. I know that no matter what happens, we will find a way to work together as a family."

Houston beamed at her, broad and warm. "Wow," he whispered. "I don't know what to say, except now I feel like I'm the luckiest man on earth."

"Well, I had more to say, but since you interrupted, I will agree with you. You are the luckiest man on the planet," she admonished with a twinkle in her eye., "But that just means I'm the luckiest woman on the planet. So it's confirmed. We're the luckiest couple on earth. And I'm positive we'll do our best to be the best parents possible."

Houston held her as they leaned back into the pillows supported by the headboard, the back of her head nestled just below his shoulder. Houston felt relief with her support, realizing that the fear he'd had of ridicule from her was just a fear he'd had of himself. He decided to unravel other feelings that ate at his soul.

"That man from the funeral came to my office looking for me today."

Sabrina thought for a moment. "Jackson ... right? Mr. Jackson. Him?"

Houston pulled her closer into him. "Yeah, that's him. He just showed up while I was at lunch. Bev gave me his note, then said something that kinda set me back. I'm not sure if she picked up on it, but it kinda threw me. She said she might've met my father."

"What?" Sabrina sat up again, turning to look into his eyes. "She said he told her he was your father?"

"No, he didn't. But she said he looked like he could be my father."

He pulled her back to his chest, where he thought they were most comfortable continuing the conversation. "She said his ears stuck out like mine. He left a note. Bev was being secretive about it."

"Honey," she said, hiding a little laugh. "Yes, your ears stick out a little;, I think it's cute. But I'm not sure it's a family trait. He left a note? Did you read it? Are you going to call him?"

"I'm not sure. So much shit is happening so fast. Elizabeth told me Phil was dying right before she fired me. Then asked me to come tomorrow to clean out my stuff. I was hoping to be able to sift through all this slowly, but it's all coming so fast. I can't get my head around everything. All of a sudden I have this emotional pull toward Phil, but I'm not sure if it's Phil or leftover feelings from watching my mom die, and ..." He trailed off, overwhelmed.

"Well, why does it have to be one or the other?" Sabrina asked him. "Honey, you haven't finished grieving over your mother, and that might take a long time. What I think is also bothering you is that you've found out you have unexplored feelings about Phil – —but that's okay. I know he's looked out for you in his own way. I knew he was sick. I think he's been sick for a long time."

"Yeah, I guess so," Houston responded. "I mean lately, he's actually kind of distanced himself a little. Like he thought I might reject him or something. Before my mom got really sick, he and I were actually coming to a kind of understanding. It got to the point that even Oscar noticed it. He said it he was because of you. Then it all kinda stopped, like he ... I guess like he realized he wasn't supposed to like anybody."

"Oh, honey. It sounds like you were beginning to have a good relationship with him. I'm sorry."

Houston's energy level had reached a low point and his stamina started to wane. "I don't know," he yawned. "Ugh, I've got to get my head around all of this. I've got to call Iz tomorrow and see if he can find me something quick. I can't be outta work. I just can't."

"Honey, don't worry. I'm sure you'll find something," Sabrina assured him. "To tell you the truth, I'd rather you go back to school and finish your JD so you can take the bar. I think you'd make a marvelous litigator. You have such compassion for people without representation."

Houston's yawns were starting to come in succession, but he laughed between them. "You're such a lawyer."

"Ready to call it a night?"

"No, no, I'm fine. I guess I drank more than I thought."

"Yes, you did!" Sabrina teased earnestly. Then she reflected pensively, "I'm glad you were able to talk to me about what's going on."

"I've got to ask," Houston said suddenly. "You didn't seem too surprised when I told you I got canned."

"Israel told me."

"That sunnova bitch. I knew he couldn't keep a secret. I didn't want you to know until I found something else."

"Don't be mad at him, honey. He was just trying to help me understand. You know how much he really cares for you." Houston grunted an unintelligible response. "By the way, what kind of lawyer would I be if you thought you could keep something like that away from me?" she added. She noticed he was beginning to fall asleep, with a soft, nasally snore. She snuggled up to him, got comfortable, closed her eyes. "Good night, *mi amor*," she whispered.

Chapter 18

Lafayette, Virginia

Friday, May 3, 1963
2.:23 p.m.

Leeland came home from school in the early afternoon to see his mother in tears and Ashley consoling her while brandishing a cutting knife. At first, he didn't know what to take from the picture before him. Then he noticed the blood streaming from Ashley's nose and the tears both Ashley and Florence shared as his mother tenderly kissed him and thanked him. Leeland rushed to their side and could hear his mother telling Ashley, "It's going to be okay. I didn't know you knew. I didn't know anyone knew ..."

Leeland fell onto the kitchen floor beside them to lend his embrace. His inclination was that Mr. Dunning had something to do with it. Leeland was able to discern some of what had occurred from segments of conversation and his knowledge of the characters involved. He seethed in his secret suspicions, waiting for evidence to be revealed.

Leesa then came in from the side door, carrying her school books, to see the three of them clumped together; her mother and Ashley in tears with blood seeping out of Ashley's nose and onto his shirt;. Leeland hovering over them like a lion protecting his pride. She could feel the tension of the moment.

Leeland explained what he knew to her: that Ashley had stood up to Mr. Dunning for their mother again, and this time it got violent. It seemed that as the children grew, Jasper Dunning's piece of the pie only shrank, and he now had to fight to retain his privilege. As he shared this with Leesa, Florence could see Leeland's pent-up rage boiling inside him. She wanted to clear the air of tension to protect her son from lashing out in anger and ultimately endangering his life. He didn't have the same protection that Ashley did.

Several Enough times, Leeland had stood up for Ashley when little white kids hurled insults at him insults like '"nigga lovah."'. Even some of their Negro friends remarked about 'the way the little white boy followed behind Leesa like a puppy dog.' But Leeland had witnessed his fair share of Ashley's bravery, too, in the face of his father's rage. *It's not always about those that share your blood*, he knew, *but those who will shed their blood for you.*

The twins were budding high school graduates and would be off to college the following autumn, yet they all huddled as small children together on the kitchen floor with Ashley in their midst. Florence could feel the anger elevating in her son. She knew her history with Mr. Dunning would hurt them and was afraid of what Leeland would do if he knew the truth. Her son had grown into a strapping young man, the spitting image of his father. Florence said a quick prayer to her husband, asking for his strength to help her guide their son.

Florence spoke up softly. "It was my fault. I was careless with the money Ms. Evelyn leaves for the groceries and little things we need. I went into next week's budget, and Mr. Dunning thought I was takin' the money for myself. He started yellin' about me stealin' money." She knew the explanation was uncharacteristic of her, but kept on. "I tried to tell him it wasn't for me. And I must've yelled back at him, because I was tired and I didn't want Ms. Evelyn or Mr. Dunning to think I would ever steal from them."

Leeland took in a deep breath, looking to his mother and then to Ashley, deducing her story didn't comport with what he could see. He knew she wanted to keep the peace and would live at the mercy of the Dunnings until he could take the mantle of provider.

He questioned Ashley with a discerning eye for detail. "Mama,

Ms. Evelyn knows you wouldn't steal from her. Ash, what happened? What did your dad do to my mama?"

Never before had he made such a distinction ––*his* mama. He usually included Ashley in everything they did as a member of the Jenkins family. Ashley harbored ill feelings for his own father, that much was obvious. He hoped that, now, he could force Ashley to make a choice: defend his mother by telling the truth, or protect his father by adding to the lie. Leeland drew a line in the sand and challenged the boy who called his mother "'mama'" to cross it.

"Ashley was just tryin' to stop Mr. Dunning from getting angry," Florence tried to continue. "He rushed over to try to calm us both down and knocked his father down by accident. Then Mr. Dunning must've thought he did it on purpose, because he got up and slapped him across the face. Then Mr. Dunning called him names;, that was when Ashley grabbed the knife."

Ashley sat patiently listening to Florence distort the facts, going over the scene cemented in his head.

I was sitting at the small kitchen table when Jasper came in, unaware of my presence. He snuck up behind Mama and pressed himself against her while she was doing the dishes. Then he reached his hand around, touching her, and said, "'I know you're tryin' to turn Evelyn against me. I believe you need another lesson on who really runs things here.'" Ashley gingerly rubbed the bridge of his nose as he focused on his anger. Yeah, you made my nose bleed, but only after sucker punching me when Mama pulled me off of you. You son of a bitch. If you ever try to do anything like that to her again, I will cut your dick off while you sleep.

He knew full well why she was hiding it. He knew Leeland was raring to go. He put himself in Leeland's place, knowing the rage building inside him. He knew what Leeland would do if he knew the truth. Ashley looked him in the eyes and said, "Lee, you know I wouldn't ever let anyone hurt Mama. Anyone."

Neither Leeland nor Leesa questioned the validity of the story, even though they knew vital details where clearly missing. Nevertheless, Leeland paced the floor, trying to calm his rage. At eighteen, he stood well over six feet tall, with his father's broad shoulders. Florence would often show him pictures of his father and comment on how much they resembled each other. This time, she would use the specter of his father to calm him and to reach inside his rage.

"Lee, I know you're upset, but you know strikin' out ain't how I raised you and ain't what your father would want for you. If you do anything, you'll just end up in jail or worse. And that's not what we planned for the two of you," she implored. She stroked the anger out of his brow and stood before him, challenging his rage with her love. She met him head on, reached out, and held him tight. "We're a family, and we have to stick together and look out for what's best for each other. Promise me, Lee, that you won't try to do anything to Mr. Dunning."

"You don't have to worry," Ashley proudly told the twins. "I promise I'll never let anyone ever hurt Mama again."

Wanting to ease the tension, Leesa sought a distraction and turned on the small black-and-white television Florence kept in the corner. Leesa hoped by seeking an afternoon game show or soap opera, the tension would soon dissipate. She fixed the dial to a local station, only to find the afternoon programming had been preempted by events taking place in Birmingham, Alabama.

A white elected public official of Birmingham directed the use of police dogs and fire hoses on Negro children – children who were peacefully demonstrating for the civil rights of Negroes in the South. And it was all being displayed live on television for the entire nation to witness. Leesa caught a quick look from her mother as she tried to silently tell her to change the channel, but Ashley caught wind of the news in time and beckoned Leesa to turn the volume up. It was Ashley's sudden attention that drew Leeland's notice as well.

After watching for a few minutes, Leeland found himself struggling to let go of the rage that flared up again. "Look, Mama. They're spraying school kids with fire hoses! Why do white people have to be so mean? We don't want to take anything away from them. We just want to be treated the same as them."

"I know, sweetheart," Florence replied as she reached to hug and comfort her son. "It's not fair."

"It makes me so angry," Leeland responded as he pushed back from his mother's embrace. "It makes me want to ... to hurt white people back."

Talk of him admitting he wanted to actually hurt someone scared Florence. Having lost both of her parents in the struggle long ago, his words rekindled the pain she'd endured at their loss. She knew if anything he said about hurting anyone was overheard by Jasper, he would exact a punishment on the family no one could survive.

"Lee, violence won't settle anything. Those children know that.

Dr. King knows that. They're fighting to show the world what colored folks' lives are like. What good does it do for us to be as bad as them white folks? Hurting people is never an answer."

Leeland tried to absorb his mother's counsel while controlling his anger, but he couldn't turn away from the images of the police going after kids with dogs and billy clubs. He countered, "Dr. King's way can only go so far. Malcolm X says you shouldn't allow anyone to put their hands on you without doing something back. He says Negro men have to stand up to protect what's theirs and their families. And Stokely Carmichael, he says the same thing, too ..." He struggled to present a cogent argument for himself. "I have to protect you and Leesa and Ashley."

"Leeland, please, you can't let your anger make you hate. Your grandparents died because of hate. I don't want hate to take you, too."

Both Leesa and Ashley moved towards Leeland. Leesa was in near

tears, seeing her mother struggle to get through to him. "Lee, please listen to Mama," she said. "If something happened to you, what would we do?"

"Lee, please. Don't scare Mama like this," Ashley added. He felt insurmountable guilt surging through his body. He knew all too well what the family had gone through at the hands of people like his father and the City Council. He started to cry, succumbing to the anguish surrounding him. He felt abandoned by hope and helpless to change anything.

A feeling of hopelessness tangled with the lingering anger, urging Florence to steer the conversation towards a positive outcome. Speaking to all of them, she sought to encourage their hopes. "If you want to make change, the best way is to get your education and leave the South. This whole country is more than the South, and there are opportunities for us elsewhere. Your aunt and uncle want you to go to California and go to school out there. I think that would be the best place for you and Leesa to go. I'm sure they'd welcome Ashley to come when he graduates, too."

"Your father was just a few credits from graduating before he went into the Army. He knew the importance of an education."

"But why would Dad go to fight for a country that hated him?" Leeland demanded.

Florence once again took hold of her son, leading him to the small kitchen table. "Sweetheart – —your father, bless his soul, believed in the promise of this country. And even though he, *we*, had it hard, he believed that with each generation the lives of Negroes would get better. It has to, as long as each generation keeps improving itself."

"Millions of Negroes have given their lives for this country, and for what?" Leeland responded. "To still be hated? To see their children and grandchildren attacked with water hoses, beaten with billy clubs and chased by dogs? White folks are never gonna let us keep improving."

"We don't have to wait for them to let us if we do it ourselves," Florence said. "And not all white people are like that. There are plenty of good white people that don't want to stop you from being better."

Leeland sat in silence. He knew all eyes were on him and that his choices were the choices that would affect the family most. Leeland was beginning to understand what the mantle of "'man of the house' – "—it often meant he would have to put his personal feelings aside for the family. He thought of the father he never met but idolized through his mother's stories. Leeland was becoming a man sooner than he should have. He recognized and welcomed the challenge. He looked at each one of them, seeing their hopes and fears for him in their eyes. He knew what this moment meant for all of them. He gathered them into his embrace, and they all huddled together in collective silence.

***

Jasper Dunning sat in his small office next to the main hall's restrooms in the City Council building. He poured himself a drink from the liquor bottle he kept in his desk drawer and seethed with anger, contemplating his position in his home and with the City Council. The encounter with his son played foremost in his thoughts in bits and pieces. Recognizing the unadulterated hatred in his son's eyes, Jasper's first thought was to attack out in the open. However, he reconsidered his plan, realizing his son was no longer a helpless child. The fact that his teenage son had grown to stand nearly eye to eye with his own five-foot nine-inch frame bade him cause to consider Ashley's pent-up rage. He'd interpreted Florence's look of revulsion as a look of smug superiority while Ashley threatened to unman him. He spat out any remaining thoughts of Ashley as his son and cursed both him and Florence.

He clasped the tumbler, swirling the alcohol before tossing a full swallow into the back of his throat. His fears demanded justice. Thoughts of revenge swirled in this head. He slammed the tumbler into the solid oak of the desk with a smile, realizing the power he sought was just down the hallway. He poured himself another drink, soothing his anger and bathing in his scheme.

Chapter 19

Lafayette, Virginia

Sunday, August 28, 1955
11.:43 a.m.

Jasper laid the first stone on his path to ascension.

"I have a little job for you to do that is suited to your particular ways with coloreds." Courtland gestured for Jasper to have a seat, which he did. "You have some living in your home under your care, isn't that right?"

Courtland did not truly understand the powerless position Jasper held in the home of his wife. But seeing this as an opportunity, Jasper did not correct Mr. Parker nor sway him from direction. He simply nodded.

"Now, I did speak with Sheriff Clayton, and he assured me of your veracity and your ability to understand what accolades can come with trust, and what castigations can come with misuse of that trust."

Courtland leaned in to ensure Jasper understood, and Jasper did so in kind with eye contact. "I most definitely do," Jasper said. And it was at this moment that both men understood what was being asked and what was expected. No description, no detail, was needed – —only a shared confirmation of perversion and a desire for power engulfing both sides.

Jasper picked up on the crumbs Courtland had dropped and suggested a young Negro boy named Cleavon Jackson. A boy, still grieving from the loss of his father and guardian, Cleavon was a frequent visitor to Dunning's home and sought comfort within the Jenkins' embrace. He had grown attached to Leesa and Florence as they allowed him a sense of family. At home, he had been thrust into the mantle of manhood, and the pants handed to him swallowed him whole. Jasper could sense Cleavon's fears and hopelessness, and when he'd perceived it fully, he'd decided he would take the impressionable colored boy under his wing and mold him into the instrument he needed to secure the City Council of Lafayette County.

Jasper went so far as to seek advice from his son, Ashley, using his young son's desire to please a distant father to gain innocent details about Cleavon Jackson's habits. Jasper knew Ashley was fond of Leesa, and he could sense his son's impatience whenever the Jackson boy was around.

Before Lincoln Jackson was murdered, the four children were nearly inseparable. Leeland often teased Leesa for mothering both Ashley and Cleavon. Jasper had once commented under his breath that his son's comfort with the Jenkins family and his affection for Leesa in particular would be the last thing he would ever allow. But he decided that his son's heart would be the perfect tool to exact what he needed.

***

Jasper placed the second stone.

"Now, it looks to me like that little Leesa and the little Jackson boy make quite a couple for a colored pair. What do you think, boy? You think little Leesa knows that boy is fond of her? From what I see, looks like she might even be a little fond of him." Jasper smiled, watching his son try to hide his feelings, seething at his father's suggestion. Then Jasper added, "I know his family needs money and I could help him. I could put in a good word for him at the Council. I'm sure there are plenty of things that he could do that would take up a lot of his extra time. Earning money for his family. What do you think, son?"

It wasn't long after this conversation that a young black boy went missing from his home and community in a neighboring county. Jasper's idea to isolate and snatch children from Negro enclaves exposed the lack of interest in the greater community towards missing children of Negro families. Under the guidance of Courtland Parker, Jasper learned how to use the Council's resources to disperse their perversion throughout parts of Southern Virginia and North Carolina. If the stories of missing Negro children were taken seriously and followed, an investigation would have shown enough clues. Sometimes the child had been last seen with an unfamiliar little Negro boy perhaps a few years older, or they had been put into a sheriff's cruiser. One or two of the witnesses would have attested that the cruiser was from a different county or state. As their enterprise continued, Courtland and Jasper extended their reach further into Negro communities to pick their victims with surgical precision.

Courtland didn't always come out of these escapades unscathed.

Visible signs of purple and red bruises would be exposed behind dark glasses not large enough to cover the welts he garnered after encountering a child unafraid to fight for their safety. "I like the fight in you, boy," he would contend with giddy anticipation, "'cause it means I'm going to enjoy it all the more when I break you." He called upon the resources of Weldon Michaels to secure and sedate every frightened child. Jasper, meanwhile, logging was logging an accurate account of all the children that passed through Courtland Parker and the members of the Lafayette County City Council.

***

"Your momma an' me didn't always fight like this."

Beauregard Clayton sat before his father, watching with rapt attention. It was a familiar speech he'd heard a dozen times before, packed with his Virginia drawl, but each time he listened as if it were the first.

"Listen here. We used to be in love," his father said. "I guess it was kinda 'cause of me bein' in love that I didn't much pay attention to some of the things she'd say. I'd tell myself she didn't mean it. Or that, when she goet to know some o' my friends, she'd change her mind. But she didn't want to. Lemme tell ya somethin', boy."

A young Beauregard nodded. He was listening.

"Evil can take control of a heart an' squeeze it till all the love an' respect is gone. An' there ain't no doubt 'bout it, boy – —bein' racist is evil. It's a evil full with bein' ig-rant, selfish, an' a coward. Only cowards cain't admit people that are diff'rent suffer 'cause of that difference. It's selfish an' evil that make you wanna hold on to that. Just 'cause it makes you feel better 'bout you bein' you. It's makin' a deal with the devil, allowin' racist notions into yer heart, boy. An' what's the first thing I teach ya 'bout makin' a deal with the devil?"

Beauregard grinned and said with his father, on cue, "Don't!"

It was in times like this, that challenged his patience, that Bo would think of his father in this way. He paced, anticipating the uncomfortable reality of his history with a man he had come to despise – —Jasper Dunning. In their early years, he barely knew Jasper nor had much experience with him. In the few encounters they'd shared, Beauregard was cautious and observant, regarding Jasper as someone he could control and limit by asserting his will over him. Jasper was a timid man who balked at confrontation and cowered in subservience – —he did not yet know of the cunning and sagacious underbelly within Jasper that slithered beneath his countenance. In hindsight, Beauregard would notice the machinations of Jasper's deceit.

A chance encounter with Jasper one afternoon brought him here now. He'd been leaving the lunch counter of the local drugstore, leaning over the swiveling barstool to take one last swig of his second coffee, hitching up his belted trousers and stretching his back, when someone bumped into his elbow with enough force to knock what little coffee was left out onto his service blouse and badge.

Jasper, the offending elbow, had ranted and raved until he noticed who it was. "Oh, I do beg your pardon, Sheriff," he offered. "I am so very sorry for this intrusion into your afternoon. I do hope you will accept my most contrite apology."

Beauregard realized now that the scene Jasper created was designed to annoy him. He should've known he was up to something.

"I must admit, providence is on my side," Jasper went on. "I don't believe this is a chance encounter. Allow me to pay your tab. And I'll remove that stain ..."

Beauregard's vanity caused him to accept the groveling. It was a rare sight. Yet he caught a glimpse of a smile on Jasper's lips as his apology turned into a plea.

"You must know I mean no harm or ill respect. But since this serendipitous moment has brought us together, would it be unkind of me to ... request a small favor?" He tried to pay Clayton's tab, but Clayton had already paid. Jasper tipped the waitress, then, as if he knew Clayton fancied her. Trying not to allow his affection for her cloud his judgment, Beauregard remained silent. He later regretted not speaking up.

"You see, Sheriff," Jasper said, "Mr. Parker holds your advice in such high esteem that just the slightest word from you would aid me in my attempts to assist him to clean up what remains of our former deeds to redirect the Council. If you catch my drift."

Beauregard felt somewhat uncomfortable discussing Council matters in public, let alone in front of the impressionable and cherubic waitress across the counter, unaware that she had been drawn into a role in Jasper's play. He seethed, knowing he had been unprepared for Jasper's charming offensive. Jasper's obsequiousness was his preferred method of manipulation.

To this day, Clayton didn't know why he agreed to offer his word on Jasper's behalf – —or why he had forgotten one of the few axioms his father had taught him. Vouching for Jasper Dunning, as well as Courtland Parker, was one of Beauregard's biggest regrets.

He'd made a deal with the devil.

***

Sunday, July 27, 1975
1.:14 p.m.

Jasper Dunning had Sheriff Bo Clayton just where he wanted him – —at the end of a leash. As Clayton waited on him, growing more frustrated by the minute as Jasper ordered him around – —"have a seat," "close the door behind you" – —he fought the urge to storm in with both barrels, ready to unload his rage on the court jester that had taken the throne. But the look on the Council secretary's face gave him pause. He knew that if he proceeded, he would once again fall into Jasper's trap: a trap that whittled away his remaining hold of power and influence in the Council.

So he did as he was asked. He then planted his large frame uncomfortably in the decorative chair beneath a painting that commemorated the attack on Fort Sumter.

Beauregard considered the subtle changes Jasper Dunning had made to the Council after he'd taken over from Courtland. The windows were always closed and sunlight never entered the room. He took in a deep breath and could smell and then taste the dank aroma of stale tobacco, hard liquor, and musk, as if it had festered inside an oak barrel. Beauregard had always avoided both the company of Jasper Dunning and the logistics of the Council office as much as he could. He didn't want the stench of the Jasper Dunning whiffling around him and his responsibilities to Lafayette County.

Jasper Dunning looked over a file on his desk with smug satisfaction. Jasper had been riding roughshod over his investigation into three Lafayette murders that had taken place under his watch. The destruction of evidence, keeping the case unsolved, had Clayton, defeated, simmering with anger.

"Now, Sheriff," Jasper said, the words spilling over his lips with

languid authority, "we're not gonna have any disagreements about this at this stage of the game here, are we? You know this is a delicate situation here, and we don't want any federal authorities interferin' with the Council's business. We have prided ourselves on our ability to handle our city's affairs internally without any outside influences or ... *external forces* inquiring into the goings-on of our fair town."

Bo returned the stare with hardened eyes that belied the regret in his heart. He was complicit – —they both knew this. But Bo also knew Jasper just liked the sound of his own voice.

"We both know that involvement from federal authorities would bring unwelcome scrutiny into the daily activities of our peaceful and law-abiding organization," Jasper went on. "Now, I know it seems like I'm repeating myself, but the importance of what I'm saying must be understood. I'd hate to think what they'd do to our law enforcement if they thought there was any undue influence or unjustified preference given to the Council."

"You've made yer point," Clayton responded. "So listen, ya lil'

shee-it. If you think you can threaten me with that shit, you an' that slimy doctor, ya betta think again. I know I have to answer fer some things, but that—"

"So we both agree," Jasper interrupted, picking up on Bo's fatal admission. "You *do* have some things to answer for. Don't we, Sheriff?"

Both men allowed these words to be absorbed by the foul stench that traversed the room. Jasper seemed to wallow in it, taking in a deep breath as he offered a half-cocked smile. He shifted the files on his desk just enough to reveal a second one with the sheriff's name scribbled across it. Bo didn't notice his name on the file at first; his attention was drawn to Jasper's bandaged hand, which he had kept hidden under the desk until now. Jasper then gently patted the file with Bo's name, diverting his attention.

Rumors suggested Jasper kept well-documented files on the proclivities and passions of Council members – —a rumor he himself had started and verified with leaked details used to build alliances and influence the subjects of his treachery. He was once called Bumstead and heckled for his obsequiousness. But he bided his time and plotted his ascension, and now he alone held all the Council's secrets.

Jasper made a demonstrative move, placing both files together on his desk, insinuating they were implicitly connected. He returned Clayton's stare with one of his own. Then he dismissed the sheriff with casual concern. "Well, at least our fair city can get back to business now that this revenge murder case is over. I'm glad we had this time to chat. Now, you go and have a good rest of your day, Sheriff."

He stood to watch Bo Clayton defeatedly leave his office. Jasper followed several paces behind him and closed the heavy door with a smile. He returned to his chair, reached into his drawer, and placed the two folders into a secret and secure lockbox. He cracked open the label from his favorite aged whiskey and poured himself a healthy serving.

Jasper placed the third stone.

***

Driving back to the station, Sheriff Clayton got a call over his police radio that requested his presence at the county morgue. For some reason, he kept playing the last words of his conversation with Jasper over and over again in his head. *Revenge murder case.* He couldn't understand what Jasper knew that he didn't.

He arrived at the morgue and was briefed by the one of the employees about a body that had been brought in a few hours earlier. As he was escorted into the basement where the bodies were kept, he was greeted by the stench of burning flesh. He was told that even though the body had been burned beyond recognition, a request for dental identification was turned down by the family – —the military dog tags found seared into the flesh was all they needed to identify the corpse.

Sheriff Clayton glanced over the body without much recognition, but once he saw the Armed Services-issued ID tags, he knew exactly what had

Jasper had failed to reveal about his interest and what he knew about the killings. He stuffed the tags into a small envelope from the coroner's desk and stowed it in his breast pocket. As he drove back to his office, the humidity began to rise and the clouds threatened rain.

Chapter 20

Los Angeles, California

Wednesday, July 21, 2010
9.:15 a.m.

Houston started the next morning regretfully aware that he'd just been fired. Against Sabrina's groggy protests, he pulled himself together to head out, promising to bring back breakfast for her. Sabrina attempted to come with him, but he just wanted to get this taken care of – —get in and out as soon as he could. He'd return to update his résumé and start looking for other work.

As he headed to his car, two solid car doors slammed closed in quick succession and footsteps approached from behind.

"Excuse me, Mr. Jenkins?" a voice said, polite but firm. "Houston Jenkins?"

Houston turned to see two men dressed similarly in dark but ruffled suits,. one white, one black, standing on separate sides of his aunt's car. Federal ID badges were in their left hands, government-issued firearms in their rights. They blocked any route of escape and seemed to move faster and more efficiently than anyone he knew. His heart spiked with fear.

"Yeah, I'm Houston Jenkins," he replied, trying to remain calm. "Did I, uh, do something wrong?"

"We'll figure that out soon enough," the white one said. He approached from the back of the car and placed a firm grip on Houston's elbow. "Come with us. We have a few questions we need you to answer."

Houston's head spun with questions and confusion. Before he knew what was happening, he was placed in the back seat of a dark blue Crown Victoria in handcuffs. He hated being handcuffed, no matter what law enforcement agency was doing it. *They're obviously FBI*, he thought. *Maybe they have some questions about the ... the what? What the fuck am I in here for?* Panic crept into his thoughts.

"Can you tell me what you're arresting me for?" Houston asked.

The black fed took turns between looking at the road ahead and glancing back at him in the rearview mirror as he drove. "You're not under arrest," he said. "We just convinced you to accept our invitation to come talk to us, and you graciously accepted."

"Then why did you 'cuff me?"

"Because it's procedure," the white one answered. "We can't have you sitting back there with free hands. You might have a weapon and taken an opportunity."

They both smirked and snickered to themselves. Houston figured they were not going to be helpful nor sympathetic, so he decided not to state the obvious – —that they had frisked him.

They arrived at the Bureau office in Westwood and deposited Houston into a small, cold room on the twelfth floor. Left alone, he took assessment of his surroundings. The walls bore the color of charcoaled glass. There was only a small table with one chair on each side and two additional chairs against the wall facing the door. No windows, mirrors, or other doors – — just blinking red lights on the two cameras placed in opposite ceiling corners, staring down at the table. A long chain sat anchored to the floor; Houston could only be relieved his handcuffs weren't attached to them. Whenever he touched the chain with his foot, he was chilled by the sound it made of metal clinking against cold concrete.

Houston couldn't be sure how much time had passed, but it felt like hours, left to himself with a dozen questions and no answers. No one had come for him.

"Hey!" he yelled finally. "Ain't I supposed to get a phone call?"

" Didn't they tell you you're not under arrest?" a voice asked.

Houston didn't expect a response, but he got one when a new man stepped into the room. Houston felt that he had seen him before, but couldn't place where or how. He had the look of every graying Caucasian federal agent portrayed on any number of the late-night cop- and-robber shows he'd watched. There was an honest but hard demeanor about him, and a look of sheer determination that an actor just couldn't emulate. This was real life – —the real deal. The man moved deliberately across the room to him and gently placed a manilla folder on the table between them.

The man held out his hand. "I'm Assistant Director Abel Grimes of the East Coast division of the FBI," he said, then gestured to another man who had entered behind him. "This is Special Agent Amir Nooryani."

Nooryani freed Houston's hands from the 'cuffs in time for Houston to meet Grimes's handshake.

"Let's get Mr. Jenkins some ... water? Coffee?" Grimes ventured.

"Nooryani, send someone to bring up some coffee, juice and bagels."

Nooryani was gone and back in what seemed like only a moment, as if someone else wasere waiting outside. Houston began to feel that this whole thing was staged, and he had no desire to play into it.

"Director Grimes," Houston spoke up,. "I'm not interested in any coffee. You obviously have the wrong guy. I've got no idea why I'm here, and I'd like for your agents to return my wallet, my money, and my phone so I can call my wife to come get me. I'm sure this is a mistake we can clear up right away."

"Let's see here," Director Grimes mused, almost as if ignoring him. He opened the folder, rifled through the pages, and flattened it out on the table. "Arrested for not submitting to a field sobriety test ... Released at request and into the recognizance of Attorney Roberto Sanchez. Now, why would the Beverly Hills PD give up a good arrest like that?" Houston attempted to offer a response, but Grimes continued. "We have a CODIS report that shows a biological connection to a suspect wanted for crimes committed in Lafayette County, Virginia, in the summer of 1975. Could it be there's something you or Attorney Sanchez wanted to hide?"

"Excuse me," Houston said, "*what?*" Houston glanced over the photos in the file, which meant nothing to him.

"Or a favor for his son-in-law?" Grimes went on. "Or perhaps for his daughter, your wife Sabrina. Both great attorneys, though she's not quite on Roberto's level."

"I have no idea what you're talking about. My— *Sanchez* isn't the kind of man to hide anything."

Grimes appeared to relish in the moment as he pulled a report from the file and laid it in front of Houston. The header read, '*OFFICIAL FBI CODIS REPORT*'.

"I don't know what this is," Houston said. "All I know is, I haven't done anything wrong. So if you don't mind, *again*—"

"Please explain, then," Grimes interrupted, "why a federal lab determined that *you*, Houston Jenkins, have a mitochondrial connection to a string of brutal murders committed in 1975 in Lafayette County!"

"Wait, whoa, whoa, hold up," Houston protested. "A connection to murders?" Now he was *certain* they had the wrong guy. "Murders where? When? I was five years old in 1975, and I ain't never been anywhere close to Virginia!" You've got the wrong dude;, now *please* let me call my wife!"

The coffee and bagels entered, but Houston was anything but hungry. He didn't want this. He wanted to go home. Grimes took one of the coffees and added way too much sugar, then gestured for Houston to help himself. He also took a full bite of a bagel.

"Where's your father?" Grimes asked with his mouth full, gnashing through boiled dough. "Are you in contact with him? What's your relationship with him?"

"My father?" Houston blurted. "Man, I don't know who the fuck my father is. Just found out my mom ..." He then fell silent and just reaffirmed,

"I don't know who my father is. I don't know where he comes from or anything you claim happened in Lafayette or wherever. I grew up without a father, in California!"

Houston was becoming increasingly emotional and hostile as he spoke on a subject that had frustrated him his entire life. It was only a devastating reminder that he knew absolutely nothing about his parents nor about where they'd come from. All he'd ever known was the woman he'd believed until recently was his mother. Now she was gone, and the truth about him had gone with her. This had to be his fault somehow — by not being curious enough to want to know more about himself. He felt like a hollow tree as the director's words blew through him with a cold wind. He fought off the tears welling in his eyes.

"I don't know what you're talking about," Houston continued, firm as he met the director's gaze. "Sir."

He wasn't certain whether it was his definitive denial or his approach to respect of authority, but he noticed Grimes change to a calmer tone. Grimes seemed to study him.

"Okay, perhaps you don't know your father or who he is," Grimes said. "Do you recall growing up with any man around your home or your mother? A man who might have helped your mother out with groceries, who might have been around a lot when you were a kid? No friend or supposed distant relative that might have stopped by from time to time? No one showed up at your mother's funeral unannounced?"

Houston immediately thought of the man, the one with the gravelly voice, who had come to give his name and phone number at his previous office. He thought about what to say next, the potential gravity of it. But he wanted a chance to speak with him personally first.

"No," he finally said. "There was only my Uncle Milton and his wife, Ethel. My mother never talked about a father. She only ever talked about my grandfather, who died in the war. I can't remember any one man hanging around or tryin' to act like anything."

"Listen, Mr. Jenkins," Grimes said, leaning forward on the table. "Perhaps we got off on the wrong foot. Now that you've calmed down a bit, why don't you eat something?"

Houston felt as though every move wasere being watched, scrutinized, and would eventually be played back in another room to study him for signs of lying. In his state, he could hear the red lights in the cameras buzzing, clicking, whizzing. Thinking it would be a better approach to remain calm and cooperative, he helped himself to a bottle of juice and a bagel.

"You said something about a 'code,', and mitochondria," Houston said. "What do you mean?"

Grimes chose his words. "CODIS is the acronym for Combined DNA Index System. It's a tool we use that allows us to track down criminals through the DNA of family members. And we were able to connect you to serial killings that occurred in Lafayette, Virginia, in one week late July 1975. There's no doubt you're a mitochondrial match for the blood evidence found at one of the scenes. The CODIS doesn't lie."

Houston ventured, "So, a mitochondrial match means ... ?"

"The killer was your father," Grimes answered. He pulled out two pieces of paper from the file. One bore symbols, the other bore a combination of words and symbols. Houston, puzzled, looked over the items.

"I have no idea what this is, or what it means," Houston said. Even so, the numbers and words brought a chill to his spine and made him afraid of whoever the author was – father or not. It hit him, then: the seriousness of the crimes, the murders of real people. "I don't know anyone who'd be capable of crazy shit like this."

"This is Dingir, the Sumerian symbol for God," Grimes said, pointing. "And Ka, the Egyptian symbol for your life force, which separates from your body after death."

Houston buried his head in his hands, fighting back feelings of anguish and guilt. Such vile crimes of murder committed by a psychopath who had somehow planted his seed in his unsuspecting mother. *Could they have been in it together?* "No, no, this can't be," he mumbled.

The director placed a sympathetic hand on Houston's shoulder. "Why don't you give your wife a call? I'm sure she's concerned and would like to hear from you. I'm sure this is a lot to process." He looked past Houston. "Agent Nooryani here will see that you get your phone and personal effects back right away."

Nooryani returned shortly with a large manilla envelope that contained his phone, wallet, keys, an open pack of gum, and a small wad of cash.

Houston didn't expect to see a myriad of distressing phone messages his wife and others had left for him. He skipped the messages – –all sixteen of them – –and called the one person that would make him feel whole again.

"Houston!" Sabrina said immediately into the phone. "Oh my god, Houston, is that you? Oh, *mi amor*, where have you been? I've been going crazy! I've been calling everyone I know;, I called the police, I called Israel, I called Aunt Ethel, my father, your office. Where are you?"

"I need you, baby," Houston responded solemnly.

"Of course," Sabrina said, her concern bleeding through the phone. "I thought something terrible had happened to you. Please tell me you're all right."

"I'm okay," Houston said, defeated. "I got taken in by the FBI, so I'm—"

"The FBI? For what? *Me estas jodiendo?*" she rambled. "Why are you with the FBI? Let me talk to— —I can't believe this. Let me talk to the agent in charge." Houston heard her scrambling in the background with keys and the door.

"It's about my father. Or so they say," Houston said. He explained what he could remember about CODIS and the evidence Grimes had presented. "I'm not sure I've got it all. I'm sure you know what questions to ask when you get here."

"I'm on my way, sweetheart," Sabrina said. "Do you want me to stay on the phone?"

"No, I'll be all right. Take your time, don't rush. I'm just ... a little shocked, is all. I don't know what to say. I'm sure the director will explain it to you."

"Oh, he will!" she said defiantly.

Houston loved her lawyering, but didn't like her being too confrontational on his behalf lest she present herself as a "'mama bear' – "— which he felt was emasculating.

By the time noon approached, Houston's stomach was past grumbling – —his hunger had competed with nausea for most of the morning. Grimes had sandwiches and more coffee sent up from the cafeteria. Houston gorged himself on a tuna salad sandwich, somewhat amazed by the caliber of the federally issued food here. As he waited for Sabrina, he enjoyed a relatively easy conversation with Agent Amir Nooryani.

When he heard, "This way, Mrs. Jenkins. He's in here," followed by the door opening and Sabrina pushing her way past the unnamed agent at the door, bringing her intensity into the room, Houston looked up and smiled. She was his normalcy. He stood to embrace her, knowing she would be able to see the frustration and fear he had tried to hide. He knew that no matter how many times he covered up his emotions, she could somehow feel them all the same, no matter how hard he resisted. She embraced him wholly and placed both of her hands on his face, pulling him in and gently reassuring him with one kiss that he would be all right. Houston exhaled a sigh from deep within his chest as he held back tears. No endorsement of feelings was needed and no additional words were spoken. Their embrace was solemn and cathartic, and whatever tension she may have brought into the room dissipated as the two took a deep breath in unison.

After they sat down, the door swung open and the assistant director stepped into the room with such authority that Agent Nooryani's professionalism returned in a flash. Houston watched him as he quickly surveyed the seating arrangement, grabbed a chair, and pulled it up next to

Sabrina, introducing himself. "Hello, Mrs. Jenkins! I'm Assistant Director Abel Grimes, and we—"

"Assistant Director?" Sabrina interrupted politely. "Now why would an assistant director of the FBI be interested in my husband's family tree?" She gave Houston a reassuring look – that she wasn't there to cause trouble.

The question to hung in the air for a moment as the director unbuttoned his dark blue suit jacket and adjusted his posture so he could address them comfortably. "Yes, ma'am," he said with a smile. "I'm here investigating a cold case that occurred over thirty years ago in a small town in Virginia. We believe—"; he corrected himself, "—we have *evidence* that your husband is related to a person who may have significant knowledge of these crimes. Therefore, we requested your husband's assistance to determine what he may know about the crimes, and/or the person of interest."

"You didn't request shit," Houston protested. "You arrested me!"

Abel Grimes ignored Houston's comment and spoke directly to Sabrina, treating her as Houston's attorney. "As you know, the FBI is allowed some leeway when pursuing an ongoing investigation. And due to the age of the case, there was a bit of urgency required. I can assure you none of your husband's civil rights were violated."

"Tell me, then," Sabrina responded,. "How exactly did you get to my husband? What was the impetus?"

Abel Grimes opened up his file and offered it to Sabrina. He spoke in the tone of an unsympathetic officer. "Your husband was arrested for refusing a field sobriety test and for suspicion of DUI. As you know, once arrested, law enforcement's duty is to test blood alcohol level. We got our connection from here. I'm sure you've heard of CODIS. We have a mitochondrial result that's a definitive and conclusive DNA match to the person who murdered four people in the state of Virginia during a one- to two-week period in July 1975. This person is the biological father of your husband. Furthermore —"

Sabrina interrupted again as she still perused the report. "Yes, I am quite familiar with CODIS and its DNA and racial applications."

"CODIS has proven effective in our efforts to track down criminals and felons who have eluded law enforcement," the director countered.

"What it has done is given law enforcement a tool to track down men of color through innocent family members, who likely have *no* connection to the crime or to the individual. It is a clear violation of privacy and, ast it's used, is a fishing expedition used to circumvent due process and discovery."

Grimes interrupted, "What it *is*, is a useful tool to reopen cold cases and bring justice to victims and their families. Look, Mrs. Jenkins, we are not in a court of law and your husband is not under arrest. We have the right to question him about what he knows of the whereabouts of his biological father. Now, that being said, we now understand that he has no knowledge about his father."

Houston sat in awe of his wife. He glanced at the director, then at Agent Nooryani, with pride. *See? This is what it's like when you fuck with me.*

Grimes seemed a little less comfortable than he was when it had been just Houston in the room. Now, as he loosened his tie and unbuttoned his collar, he looked like he wanted to be anywhere but right there in Sabrina's crosshairs.

Finally, he composed himself and leaned in, as if he were going to unveil a secret. He gave a nod to Agent Nooryani, who then excused himself from the room without making a sound. The director laid both of his hands on the table and let out a soft sigh, then he spoke in a calm and measured tone.

"I understand that the news and evidence we shared today can be difficult to accept. I want you to know that I understand hearing about your father in this way is earth- shattering and discombobulating. Mr. Jenkins, I want to apologize for the way we brought you in here. I'm sure with what you're going through, being brought in like that can be pretty harrowing." He paused to allow Houston time to accept his apology. Houston nodded. Grimes gathered up the CODIS documents.

A moment later, Agent Nooryani returned with new folders and handed them to the director. Grimes opened one up to a collection of crime- scene photographs, police reports, worn newspaper clippings, and a description of the symbols used in the scribbled messages.

He spread the photos and reports out in front of the Jenkins and continued his plea. "Mr. and Mrs. Jenkins, when these murders occurred, I was a rookie on the Lafayette police force – —well, to tell you the truth, it wasn't really a force, more like a police shop;, just a sheriff and a handful of deputies. Are either of you familiar with Virgil Tibbs and Chief Gillespie?"

The Jenkins shook their heads.

"Well, I was new to the county, and new to law enforcement," Grimes continued. "I had big ideas and dreams of making a real difference. I was not prepared for the cronyism and racism that ruled most Southern cities and townships. And I am certain the overt racism the African American community had endured at the time in that county drove people to do things they wouldn't have done, if things had been more ... fair. You see, my first exposure to this began here."

He slid the picture of Don Stiles's prone corpse towards them. Houston quickly turned the picture over and Sabrina pushed it back at Abel as she squeezed Houston's hand.

"Actually, it was my idea to have them take pictures. To keep a record," Grimes went on. "I thought I was bringing modern enforcement tactics to a place that frankly didn't want to modernize. It was a town run by a select group of men who called themselves the City Council and kept the African American community afraid and disenfranchised. It was a town in 1975 that felt more like 1953. They didn't want my ideas or my federal connections once they realized they were dealing with a serial killer. A killer, I believe, that knew the town's secrets."

Grimes's tone grew more impassioned. "I believe the person who committed these murders did so with a motive of revenge, and he taunted the town because he knew that if they exposed him, he could do more damage to them than they could to him. I think that's ultimately why they shut the investigation down once the Council members' doctor was murdered in Virginia Beach. I think your ..." He caught himself. "The murderer was making the town and the City Council pay a price. What that price was, I don't know for sure, but I have a theory."

Grimes paused and gave a look Houston thought was sympathetic.

"You see, when we learned of your connection, we did some research, looking for details about your birth, when and where, hospital records, baptismal records. We scoured the Internet, LexisNexis, city and state records, everything. We couldn't find a thing. No one on my team was able to find anything about when or where you were born. But, eventually, we were able to find that at around the time we estimate you were born, three African American women gave birth in Lafayette. Two gave birth to little girls and one to a boy."

As the director hesitated, Sabrina squeezed Houston's hand for comfort. Houston held on to hers, the only thing keeping him afloat now as all this new information assaulted him. He looked up to see tears welling up in her eyes. He wiped one away.

"Are you okay?" the director asked.

Sabrina's voice stayed only somewhat level as she said, "We're fine. Please continue."

"Well, like I said, we found one male," Grimes continued. "We tracked him down and he lives in Philadelphia."

"So how do you know it's not him?" Houston asked. "How do you know the killer wasn't *his* father?"

"Because the DNA matched *you.*"

"But that doesn't mean it wasn't *his* father," Houston argued, grasping at straws.

"We know it wasn't his father, because CODIS matched us with a mixed-race individual."

"Wait a minute, what?" Houston rocketed straight up out of his seat in anger. Sabrina stood as well, attempting to commandeer the room.

"Houston's father may be *white*? Is that what you want to say, Director?" Sabrina demanded. "I *told* you this CODIS was completely biased and race-based." She took Houston's arm. "Come on, honey, let's go. We don't have to stay here and listen to this. I *knew* there was an angle to all of this."

"Yes! Yes! You are correct, Ms. Jenkins!" Grimes responded, attempting to keep them from leaving. "In most cases, CODIS is race-based. But that's only because most of the DNA stored is from people of color. But that doesn't discount the fact that the DNA showed a connection to your husband. A mitochondrial connection that can only lead to a male perpetrator. I take it Mr. Jenkins is an only child, leaving us to conclude it has to be his father. I'm sorry for the inconvenience of all this, but he remains, in this case, our main suspect." The director held up his hands in surrender. "Now, I know I'm not very eloquent, but I'm asking for your help – —to bring justice for these four people."

"But you're asking me to turn in my father?"

"I'm asking for you to help me find a man you never knew was your father. A man who may well have harmed your mother as well."

"Now, hold on," Sabrina interjected. "That's not fair or warranted."

"You're right. I apologize. I'm just asking for your help. Please take a seat and hear me out."

Houston slowly sat while Sabrina remained standing until Houston pulled her down next to him. The director nodded his head in appreciation, seeming to sigh with relief, and continued.

"This case started when I did. And for thirty-five years, this case has haunted me. Deep in my gut, I know that at the heart of this lies a case of revenge. I know the township of Lafayette and the City Council allowed bad things to happen to the African American community. Solving this case will help shed some light on what happened during that time. It may even help bring closure. You see, I believe there is an underlying case that's connected to the deaths of these four people. A case that went ignored for almost twenty years before that July in '75. A case that links crimes throughout Virginia and North Carolina."

The director took a seat in the available chair and got closer to the couple. He reached into the folder and pulled out what appeared to be newspaper clippings from an extant Negro publication, *The Hertford Courier*. He laid them next to three black-and-white photographs. One photo showed a smiling little girl with pigtails; the other displayed two young black boys holding fishing sticks, standing at the edge of a creek; the third was a family portrait of four. Houston and Sabrina perused the articles while Abel looked on silently.

Houston pored over one article until he saw a name he recognized. At first he thought it was just a coincidence – —until he read the names of the surviving family members. "'Cleavon Jackson'" rang in his mind like a three-alarm fire bell. He gasped when he saw it and tried to cover it up by taking a deep breath. He hoped the director didn't notice. Any indication of recognition might open doors he wasn't ready to walk through. He passed the article to Sabrina with his thumb under Cleavon's name to be certain she picked up on his drift. He looked over the other ragged pictures of children forever frozen in their preadolescent years.

"What's this all have to do with my father and the murders in '75?" Houston asked.

"I'm sure you noticed the date of Mr. Jackson's death," Grimes explained. "It's no coincidence it occurred on the same day the decision came down on *Brown v. Board of Education*. That article predates this second one, by the same paper only a few years later, telling the story of missing African American children that went ignored by every major paper in their respective white communities. Now, the paper doesn't make a connection between the two, but from what I learned about Lafayette and the City Council, I believe all three cases are connected somehow."

"Wait a minute, you didn't say anything about black children," Houston stated, questioning the director's change in emphasis. "You said it was about four white people. Now you're saying it's ..."

"No, I'm saying there is a link to the crimes committed in and around Lafayette County. By my hunch, the deaths of these four people hold the key. I need to find your father to solve one mystery before I can open up the can of worms to settle the others. Houston, I believe you when you say you don't know who your father is. I don't think you could've faked your reaction. But I do think if you take the time to consider everything, you may have a clue. I just need that clue."

"Are you saying the killer – —the man, —the individual, who killed those four white folks –, did it for revenge? For all of that?"

"Yes. I believe there is something there. I know it seems a bit farfetched, but having worked in the Lafayette environment, I can't say it's not probable, let alone possible. You see, no one, *no one*, ever did anything about it. *I* did nothing about it. Not when I heard about it in Lafayette, not when I joined the FBI. I know it doesn't appear to be connected to your father's case, but I can't shake this feeling that these four murders are at the heart of it. And I need your assistance to find justice for everyone."

"That's fairly detailed for a theory. Do you have any evidence to back this up?" Sabrina chimed in.

"You mean other than the thirty-five years this case has haunted me? I put together all the bits and pieces of information I could gather. I was kicked off this case and out of Lafayette because I tried to get an old classmate of mine at the FBI to get involved. I believe, without knowing exactly the who and the why, I've got everything else matched up. And now, with the connection of your husband, I've got the who," Abel Grimes said more in relief than anything. "I need cooperation from you and Houston to complete the theory and help me close these cases, for all of them. To set the record straight."

Houston sat back in his chair. He had fallen into a malaise of acceptance; now, exhausted, Houston wanted no more of the conversation about his murderous father he'd never known. He wanted to go home and crawl into bed next to his wife and sleep until he could make sense of what was piled in front of him. He was tired of Assistant Director Abel Grimes and Special Agent Amir Nooryani and everyone and everything that had anything to do with the FBI and Lafayette County, Virginia. He was so withdrawn mentally that it was Sabrina who asked to take copies of the file home. Abel Grimes made one more plea, asking Houston if he could remember where he'd grown up, or if he could perhaps think of neighbors who might remember his father being around when he was a toddler, or if he could check for old photographs that might contain his father. Houston gave a tired answer and left with Sabrina.

***

"This. Is. *Huge*."

At four o'clock in the afternoon, Percy Hawkins went over his notes on the corner of Pico Boulevard, just outside Century City. He'd just finished a segment meeting with the Cavalier Cable News channel's biggest on-air personality.

Over a year after the Lafayette murder spree had ended, Percy Hawkins had filed his story with the *Lafayette Gazette* in August 1976. It never saw the light of day. His theory, which happened to be close to Abel Grimes's personal conclusions, had not been the story the City Council wanted in the presses. As Jasper Dunning had explained back then, "Your involvement with one of the victims has clearly clouded your judgment." The rest Percy knew by memory.

But here it was at last: vindication. Percy had received a reliable tip that the FBI had found a DNA match to the Lafayette killer. After promising his wife he'd be home before the end of the night, Percy ran to his segment producer and begged to pitch the story to the on-air talent. With approval, he got a one-camera crew to assist him as he headed straight for the Jenkins's home address.

Chapter 21

Los Angeles, California

Wednesday, July 21, 2010
8.:11 p.m.

Arriving at Aunt Ethel and Uncle Milton's home, Houston felt strangely apprehensive. The questions he had on his mind were ones he'd never thought to ask. Why had she kept these things secret all this time? Would it have been so difficult to explain? Now that he thought about it, he'd always suspected Florence was too old to be his mother, but even then she'd always looked great for her age. Houston remembered the men, young and old, who would pursue her, and though to his knowledge she dated none of them, he was now left wondering if it was possible that one of them was his real father. He didn't want to believe Florence had malicious reasons for keeping Houston from his past, but in any case, he had to get to the bottom of this – the truth needed to come to light. Sitting in front of the FBI director as he'd watched hidden parts of his past unfold before him, Houston had felt the sense he was merely playing a small part in his own life. That had to change. He had to take control.

Houston glanced at himself in the sun visor mirror before going in. Perhaps it was only the light, but he thought he looked older. He turned his head from side to side, up and down, examining himself for any resemblance to Cleavon Jackson. Cleavon was a potential direction, and he'd decided to speak to Cleavon personally before going to the FBI with the connection;, but he couldn't help but feel there was something off about that conclusion. From what he recalled, Cleavon's father,

Lincoln Jackson, had been lynched; yet Florence had always told Houston that his grandfather's name was Dillard. But Florence herself claimed she was not truly his mother – could her earlier stories be trusted now?

When the front door finally opened, Houston put on a smile. "Aunt Ethel!" he and Sabrina said in unison. Houston added, "I got you both a mincemeat pie."

"Then why's she holding it?" Uncle Milton laughed from behind Ethel. He gave a conspiratorial wink and planted a kiss on Sabrina's cheek. "We know who likes to take the credit. Come in, come in."

Aunt Ethel rolled her eyes, but took the pie and led them both to the kitchen, where a teapot was just short of whistling. "Want coffee with that pie?" She took coffee confirmations all around, settling on an herbal tea for Sabrina instead.

After small talk, and before anyone left for seconds, Ethel got to the chase. "Houston," she offered, "have you had a chance to look into the box Florence left for you?"

"Oh – no," Houston said. "I haven't had the time yet."

"Well, why not?" Ethel responded, slightly irritated. "What are you waiting for? I thought you came by because you had questions about—"

"Ethel," Milton interrupted. "Let him speak. He's ..." He gestured to Houston, whose eyes had begun to well up.

"I'm sorry," Houston offered. "We didn't get a chance. It's not like we didn't mean to, it's just been ... one hell of a week. And it's only Wednesday." He looked to Sabrina for solidarity. She rubbed at his back to soothe. "I only buried her less than a week ago, right after learning she'd never been my mother at all. I'd actually been on my way here to ask about it all when I got arrested." Houston took a deep breath. "I probably should have come to talk sooner, but ... I was scared. Scared Mama was just losing her mind at the end. Sometimes she'd say crazy things while I sat there with her. Thought she was sleep-talkin', you know? Stuff about her own parents, that they'd been murdered, and someone named ... Denning. Dunning. I don't remember it all."

"You didn't tell me about this," Sabrina said softly, surprised.

"Then I got fired," Houston went on, "and today I got picked up by the FBI and questioned about a string of murders in the seventies in Virginia. So, to be honest, the things Mama left me haven't exactly been on my mind."

The room went deathly silent, so Sabrina chimed in. "Murders his biological father, supposedly, committed," she explained. "Sorry, Ethel, Milton, that was a lot. We don't have to discuss that right now."

Houston could see, by the stunned looks on their faces, that the news about his biological father was a shock to them. He wasn't sure exactly what they knew or would tell him. He went to explain further, but his Aunt Ethel finally spoke up.

"Houston, honey, we had no idea of any of this," she said. "When you and Florence came here so long ago, she was so frightened, we didn't press her into talking about it. We figured she would open up after a while." She spoke with a certain fondness. "You were a newborn back then, and everyone pitched in to take care of you. Your cousin Vivian was at the age that she wanted to help care for you. I know you probably don't remember."

"I can't imagine how tough this must be for you," Uncle Milton added. "To get news about your father like that." After a long pause, he looked to Ethel. "Tell him what you know."

Houston felt Sabrina squeeze his hand, and in that moment he needed it more than ever.

"You must have been a week old when Florence came to us with you," Ethel began. "September, 1975. You were so frail and helpless, and Florence was simply a mess. And then it wasn't for another nine months that Florence was ready to talk about it.

"We had always wondered why we hadn't heard from Leeland or Leesa – Florence's children, her *true* children. Leeland had joined the Navy, gone with hopes of becoming a pilot, right before graduating from Morehouse. He wanted to be like Jesse Brown – —the Navy's first Negro pilot. Leesa was about ready to graduate from Spellman. Florence said Leesa had been dating this young man ..." She paused, trying to recall. "Jackson. Cleavon Jackson. He was a boy they'd grown up with."

The name rang more bells between Houston and Sabrina. But they kept any revelations and conclusions to themselves, choosing instead to absorb all this new information.

"Cleavon joined the Army," Ethel went on. "I remember us talkin' about it like it was yesterday. Florence was shakin' so, she could barely get through it all. She said Leesa was dating this Jackson boy, but she'd fallen in love with someone else. Florence was happy when Leesa broke it off, because she never trusted Jackson, on account of hearing his name from that awful man, Jasper Dunning. Leesa actually broke up with Jackson because she'd gotten pregnant from the other man."

"Did she say what his name was?" Houston asked.

"No, baby, she didn't," Ethel answered. "I'm sorry if I'm not remembering everything as clearly as I thought I might. I guess those yesterdays were long, long ago." Milton lightly nudged her when she became lost in thought.

"And what about Dillard?" Houston implored. "Mama —— Florence— she always told me my grandfather's name was Dillard."

"Yes," Ethel said. "Dillard was your grandfather, and Florence's husband. In fact, the very day Leeland and Leesa were born, Florence received a telegram informing her that Dillard had been killed in the war." She recalled this somberly, albeit with frustration. "They didn't even send over a soldier. Only a telegram. Shameful ..."

Milton left and returned with a box of tissues, from which Ethel grabbed one. "I think we're going to get good use out of those tonight," he whispered.

"On the night you were born," Ethel continued. "a white nurse came to Florence's door. She didn't know her name, and she'd never seen her before. She was covered in blood. She brought you to Florence in tears, saying that Leesa ... Leesa had died in childbirth."

Houston's heart plummeted into his stomach. His birth mother, Leesa ... dead, after giving birth to him. Even if he had remembered as a boy, he never would have had the chance to remember her. He felt a great emptiness for what could have been.

"Florence always thought it was strange," Ethel added. "Why the hospital didn't call, why the baby wasn't in the hospital, why a nurse was delivering you to her in this manner. All the nurse could tell Florence was that a group of powerful men was responsible, and they would kill the baby, too, if they knew it was alive. That if their doctor found out, they'd kill everyone involved – her, Florence, and the baby. The nurse ... Dolores Peters, I think it was. She gave your grandmother some money and helped her pack a bag to get out of Lafayette."

Ethel, having held back tears all this time, finally let a few go. Milton consoled her with a reassuring hug around her shoulders. Sabrina rubbed Houston's back in circles as she watched him absorb his family history, summarized and condensed before their very eyes.

Sabrina delicately wiped tears from her own eyes. "I can't imagine the pain she endured to simply live her life, or the strength she needed just to survive."

Ethel nodded emphatically. "To think of the things that woman had to deal with in her life," she mused tearfully. "So much loss and grief. Losing Dillard was the hardest for her. Because she had the twins to live for, she never had the time to deal with it. Then, enduring the deaths of her children, having to travel over two thousand miles on a bus with a newborn ... I would pray to the Lord to have mercy on her."

Houston, having been unaware of the extent of Florence's suffering, embraced her once more as his true mother. Leesa may have birthed him, but Florence raised him as her own and had taught him everything he knew. Now, he couldn't help but feel ashamed by his mixed feelings towards Florence and her deathbed revelation to him.

"I know Florence was a special angel in the Lord's eyes," Ethel said softly and with reverence, taking Houston's hand. "And Florence would say you were God's gift to her – —her personal angel. God sent you to look over and care for her ... give her a reason to live. Houston, you were a blessing to her every day of your life. I just know it made her so happy to see you and Sabrina married. Sabrina coming into your life was proof to her that she'd done the right thing by you and God."

Sabrina gave her a whispered "thank you,", doing her best to hold back the emotion she felt in that moment.

Now invigorated, Ethel grinned and clapped her hands. "I've got something to show you." She stood with the power of an old woman rediscovering a long-buried energy. In a moment, she returned with a set of black-and-white photographs and placed them on the coffee table in front of Houston and Sabrina.

"This is Florence with your grandfather, Dillard. Taken before he left for the Army. Look how handsome and strong he was ..."

Houston plucked the photos from the coffee table and examined them closely, not sure whether he should feel pride or guilt. Finally seeing where he had come from, a history that had been hidden from him, made him feel as though his life had more purpose: to carry on this legacy.

"He looks just like you, Hou," Sabrina said softly at his side.

Ethel nodded. "I think that's why Florence knew you were a gift. You reminded her of Dillard. Sometimes, she'd call me to tell me things you did or said that made her think of him."

Timidly, Houston asked, "Did she ever regret it or complain about me?"

"Oh, never, not once!" Ethel replied.

Sabrina picked up the other photograph from the table and studied it. "Oh my God, Ethel, is this Leesa? Houston's mother?" She showed the photo to Houston and pointed to her. "She was so beautiful and young, and look. Your mom – —your grandmother –, she's hardly aged at all."

A scrawled caption on the bottom read *Easter 1968*. In the photograph, five smiling people, Florence and Leesa among them, leaned on the side of a tailgate. Florence sat on the banana-colored wheel well of a pickup truck, wearing a yolk-yellow sundress with powder-blue piping. Leesa wore her hair up in a ponytail tied up with a blue ribbon that matched her blue-and-white striped dress. The boy next to them, who looked just like Leesa, must have been Leeland, who wore his hair in a medium Afro and wore a blue blazer over a pressed button- down white shirt and russet slacks. Then another boy – —it took a moment, but finally Houston recognized a much younger Cleavon Jackson standing behind Leesa in his dress uniform, his hand placed awkwardly on her forearm. The only non-black person in the photograph, however, caught Houston's attention. The boy wore faded dungarees and a red-and-black flannel shirt, and his arm lay draped around Leeland's shoulder.

"Aunt Ethel, who's the white dude?" he asked finally.

"Oh, that's Jasper Dunning's boy, Ashley," Ethel replied, peering over to look. "When Florence was working for the Dunning family, she took good care of their son, and he took care of them. She always said he was her third child. She loved that little boy." She chuckled to herself. "Well, I guess he's not such a little boy in the photo. Florence would say he'd grown up into a fine young man." She pointed to Cleavon and she suddenly spoke as if she had a bitter taste in her mouth. "And the one in the Army uniform is Jackson."

Houston couldn't figure why she seemed to despise Cleavon; he could only assume it was from what Florence had told her.

"Did he ever come around when I was little?" he asked Ethel. "Do you ever remember seeing him out here?"

"I can't say I ever did," Ethel said. "I only know he kind of gave Florence the creeps. I suppose he was a little like what kids would call a stalker."

Sabrina jumped in. "Do you know if he was—?"

She stopped mid-sentence as Houston squeezed her hand tight. He softly shook his head at her. No need.

"Houston," Uncle Milton offered, "if there's something else you want to know, just ask. Florence had some secrets, but they were only to protect you."

"Honey, I'm sure Florence answered all your questions in the box she left you," Ethel added. "Why don't you take a look, and tell us what you find?."

Houston could only nod, lowering his head as if he were ashamed. "I will."

The rest of the evening moved along somberly as they shared laughter and old stories of Houston's youth. Milton teased Houston about his first crush and how hard he worked to earn enough money for flowers and candy for the young lady six years his senior when he was only nine years old. Sabrina was delighted to learn the way Houston mispronounced common words. She soaked it all in and held Houston in his embarrassment. She would kiss him quite a bit before they finally made their way home. Having stayed a lot longer than they'd anticipated, they felt exhausted by the time they set off for home.

***

"Yes, I know we were expecting me to have the interview for you live, Sin, but he hasn't gotten home yet!" Percy barked into the phone. "I know, I know ... but I wasn't able to get a meeting with you until ... Yes, yes, I got a promise of a twenty-four-hour advance before anyone else hears about it.

I promise, Sin, we can still be first on the air. We got a copy of his driver's license so we know what he looks like. He just hasn't come home yet.... No, we came right over and have been camped out here since four.... No, we're not leaving until we get something. Even if we have to stay here all night!"

The one-sided conversation was met with groans of disappointment and muffled guffaws. Witnessing Percy Hawkins get chewed out was an immense pleasure to the crew, even if they dreaded the results. Silently, each and every member promised themselves if Percy ever got his own show, they would avoid working on any segment of it at all costs.

"Well, gang, we're here for the night," Percy said, turning to face them all. "If you've got to pee, you can either go in the bushes or go find a gas station or something. But you'd better be here when this ... son of a murderer gets here!"

Percy believed he was exemplifying the headstrong attitude of the executives and producers of Cavalier Cable News. The crew members thought of him as exemplifying another part of the human anatomy.

The cameraman and boom operator were sharing a smoke outside when a late-model Lexus pulled slowly into the driveway. The two pairs of eyes followed closely, until the cameraman finally slammed his hand on the door of the van. "That's him! He's here!"

"Are you sure this time?" Percy groused.

The whole crew watched carefully for several long moments until, finally, Houston Jenkins and his wife walked down the driveway to the front steps and apartment mailbox.

"Hey, Houston!" the sound engineer called out.

Houston and Sabrina both turned towards the unrecognizable voice for a moment. That was all it took.

"It's him! Move!" Percy shouted. The crew all raced over to the confused couple with mics, camera, and blinding lights. Houston quickly shielded Sabrina as Percy made his way forward with his microphone, turning it on the bewildered husband and wife. "Aren't you Houston Jenkins, son of Cleavon Jackson, the first reported black serial killer of Lafayette, Virginia?"

"*What?*" Houston demanded in shock. "I've got no idea what you're talking about – —get the camera out of my face!"

"Are you denying any relationship to the serial killer who murdered four people in Lafayette in the summer of 1975?" Percy insisted. "Didn't the FBI arrest you in connection withto these horrible crimes?"

Houston squared up at Percy. "First of all, you better get the *fu*—"

"No comment!" Sabrina jumped in, stepping around him. "Mr. Jenkins has not been arrested and we are not commenting on an ongoing investigation."

Percy continued on, pushing past her to get to Houston. "Hasn't DNA evidence revealed a family connection? A father-and-son link to the murders?"

Houston jammed his hand over the camera lens. "Back the fuck up off my wife!" he yelled – —a comment that would later be censored.

"Don't touch the camera!"

"Then don't get up in my face! I don't even know who you are!"

"Percy Hawkins from Cavalier Cable News," Percy answered almost sweetly. "And I know firsthand the trauma inflicted on the loved ones of the people your father, Cleavon Jackson, brutally slew! I was a reporter for the *Lafayette Gazette* at the time, *and* my fiancée at the time was one of your father's victims! Dolores Peters! Remember her name?"

Houston went quiet, stunned. He *did* know the name. The same nurse who had helped Florence get out of Lafayette? Was it true?

Sabrina grabbed Houston's arm and quickly pulled him up the stairs to get them to the safety of their apartment, even as Percy continued to ramble about his close involvement. Once the two were gone, the film crew threw up their hands.

"Good going."

"Nice one."

"Way to make the interview about yourself, Hawkins."

Percy Hawkins gave the slash-throat signal to the cameraman, who cut the tape. The irony of the gesture was missed by all but the girl holding Percy's notes, who had only just heard him describing the way his fiancée's throat had been slashed by the Lafayette Killer. As the insanity finally died down and the crew ambled back to the van, Percy propped his hands on his hips.

"That went better than expected!"

***

Inside their apartment, Houston and Sabrina waited quietly, as if someone would hear them, until the news van pulled away. They kept the lights off and moved around in darkness, using only their cell phone flashlights to navigate their own home. Once the van was out of sight, Houston turned on the hallway light as Sabrina checked the bathroom. Once they were certain their place was free from any intruders, they both collapsed into bed, completely uncertain of what to make of their day. Houston broke the silence.

"What the fuck was that?"

Sabrina laughed out loud. Houston couldn't help it and laughed, too, mostly out of exhaustion. As they calmed down, Sabrina suggested they look through the memory box Florence had left for him. Houston refused – —too exhausted to be able to make any sense of it at the moment. He remembered leaving food from Milton and Ethel's in the car, but before he could go down to grab it, Sabrina caught him and pulled him into her.

"Honey," she said with a soft sigh. "Why don't you want to look in the box, huh? Are you afraid of what's in there?"

"I'm just tired."

"I know you well enough to know when you're avoiding something," Sabrina offered. "Please, sweetheart, just be honest with me and yourself. It's okay if you're afraid. Tell me what you feel."

Houston took a deep breath and finally sat back down with her, allaying the rising concern of his heartbeat. "You know, on our way here, I felt a little hesitant about it. The box. Because I don't know what's in there. Hell, I didn't know what was in my past until today, and I still don't know all of it. And I was thinking, maybe I should finally open it. But when that reporter said the name Dolores Peters, it scared me. It made me think – — what if I was him, and it had happened to you? What if Jackson really *is* my father? What if ...?" He trembled. "What if my mom had something to do with it? Even Milton said she had secrets. What if this is the one she hid for so long? What if that's what I find in the box?"

Sabrina held his face and kissed his brow, holding him in tight

until his body seemed to settle. She could only do so much, but her calming presence, at this moment, seemed to be the one thing Houston needed.

"Whatever's in the box," she murmured, "we'll face it together."

Chapter 22

Lafayette, Virginia

Sunday, April 14, 1968
10.:38 a.m.

Cleavon Jackson had only spent a minute in Jasper Dunning's City Council office before he began scanning the place for exits. He was unsure but fairly secure in the notion that they were alone – —yet he wasn't certain that was a good thing.

"Thank you, Sheriff, for convincing Private Jackson here to volunteer a visit," Jasper drawled. "I'm sure he'll be comfortable here with me." He walked around his desk, indicating to the sheriff that his presence was no longer welcome. Jasper whispered something in his ear for good measure, keeping his eyes on Cleavon, and let the sheriff leave. Jasper left the door ajar. Cleavon felt a sweat on the back of his neck as the room went quiet, save for Jasper's slow footsteps as he circled back.

"I guess you were under the impression that you could just waltz back into town unnoticed," Jasper said finally. "I'm curious. Your family no longer wants anything to do with you. You talk too much, boy, and you nearly put your sweet mama in danger."

Cleavon had no response. He'd believed he had a good relationship with Jasper Dunning – —one that would avoid suspicion – —and hoped he could leverage his past relationship with him to get close. He should have known that Jasper would know if he spilled any secrets.

"Well, sir," Cleavon started, a slight break in his voice,. "I'm being shipped off to Vietnam in a few weeks, so I wanted to stop by and visit the Jenkins family before I leave." As the words tumbled out, he remembered Jasper's disdain for the Jenkins family. He saw the way Jasper smiled at his response, a smile that sent chills down his spine.

"If I recall, you and the Jenkins girl were somewhat of an item," Jasper said. "In an on-and-off kind of way."

Cleavon nodded. "We promised each other, when we were younger, that we would run away together." It was a lie – —running away had been Cleavon's hope alone. He'd fantasized that Leesa would go with him, would help him clear away the haunting memories of his adolescence under Jasper Dunning's influence. "I'm just, uh ... letting her know that I will be back after my deployment. I've put in a request for a home on base, and ... I wanted to let her know—"

"That's all fine and done," Jasper interrupted with a dismissive wave of his hand. "But I do recall your words of revenge when you so callously left the Council's employ to join service for my country. Now, although, I'm sure you may have an idea of what revenge is,. I am certain you've no call for revenge on anyone."

Incredulity and shame shaped Cleavon's expression, which made Jasper grin with a sick kind of glee.

"After all," Jasper went on, "if it weren't for your timely help, Mr. Parker might have never been able to enjoy his later years in the manner he so desired. With your ability to handpick selfless participants, who knows what ... *havoc* you saved the community?" He leaned in closer to Cleavon. "Private Jackson, you were invaluable to the City Council. You and your family were given every opportunity to deny the rewards you received. But you didn't, did you? Your mama was *so* glad for the financial compensation, wasn't she?"

"I was a *child*," Cleavon protested. "I didn't know any better. You *used* me!" He matched Jasper's advance with his own, readying his hand at his side pocket where he kept his Army-issued knife.

"I beg to differ," Jasper said, slow and firm. "You were a young man who, in earnest desire to help his family, pointed out where special volunteers could be found." He made a gesture, and two deputies who had been waiting outside stepped forward. One drew Cleavon's revolver; the other put a firm grasp on his readied hand. Unfazed, Jasper continued, "You should serve my country as well as you served the City Council."

Cleavon fell silent as the accusation struck him directly in the heart. He had only been attempting to win the favor of the City Council and the privilege that came with their favor. But he'd never imagined it would have come to this.

"Run along, soldier boy," Jasper said finally. "To your fine young lady friend. Make sure she's safe. Ugly rumors can cost more than the reputations they ruin."

Jasper glad-handed Cleavon, who reluctantly conceded, and disingenuously expressed his approval of Cleavon's military service. He patted the boy on the back and had him escorted out of the office. Once outside, Cleavon wandered the perimeter of the City Council building.

As he walked back into town, Cleavon came upon his father's old business, still as boarded- up as it had been after Lincoln Jackson died. Cleavon sat on the lonely doorstep and stared at nothing. All he wanted to do was run into Leesa's arms and convince her to leave with him. He could never tell her of his relationship with Jasper Dunning. In her presence, he knew, he could never mention that name.

***

Florence was enjoying a cup of coffee and a conversation with Andrew Walker, who had stopped by on his way to testify before the Senate War Commission, when the twins and Ashley showed up in the driveway with a new pale yellow pickup truck. For the past month, she'd thought it strange they'd all been asking her about cars, what she liked, what kind she would get if she ever could. When Florence stepped outside to see the three of them standing before it, she almost went to tears as she shared grateful hugs with them and tucked them in close. They then informed her the pickup had been purchased thanks to Evelyn's good graces. Florence quickly ran up to thank Evelyn for the gift.

Florence rejoined the group outside to see that the mood had changed in the time she'd been gone. Leesa's estranged boyfriend, Cleavon Jackson, had come by. From talks with Leesa, she knew the two were in a transitional period: Leesa had expressed the relationship wasn't working out, and Cleavon was doing everything in his power to convince her otherwise.

Unaware of the tension, Andrew Walker introduced himself to a fellow man in uniform. It was his idea to take photos with his new camera, so he gathered them together in front of the new truck. They offered somewhat strained smiles to the camera, with Leesa attempting to quietly distance herself from Cleavon.

While Florence ran inside to put the finishing touches on the Easter dinner ham, Leesa quickly pulled Leeland and Ashley aside.

"I don't know why he's here," she whispered to them. "I made it clear that we're through. I hope he's not here because he thinks I still want to see him. What do I do?"

"Let me talk to him," Leeland offered. "I'll find out what he's trippin' about."

"Are you sure?" Leesa pressed. "Can't we just go inside and leave him out there? Hope he gets the message?"

"No, I'll rap with him," Leeland said. "Better I do it than sending Ashley to take care of him. He's coming – —don't worry, I've got this." He ribbed Ashley and gave him a knowing wink. Cleavon finally approached the three, and Leeland left them to stop him halfway. "Hey, Clee. Let's take a walk, brotha."

Cleavon didn't complain or hesitate, complying with Leeland on a walk. Leesa and Ashley watched in silence, waiting for them to get out of earshot, before she suggested they watch from inside the truck.

"You could've told me sooner that he was bothering you," Ashley said once inside. "I woulda had a talk with him."

"I know you would have," Leesa sighed. "But I know you, and I know Clee, and I didn't want anyone gettin' hurt on my account. Besides, Clee's still scared of Lee. I'm sure Lee will make him understand." She winced uncomfortably. "I hope Mama doesn't catch on. She's kind of suspicious of Clee, says she's done some work for Jasper he won't talk about."

They sat together in the truck before Leeland finally returned, Cleavon a short distance behind him, kicking the grass. Leesa put the window down so Leeland could fold his arms over the sill.

"He says he stopped by to see his mom before he reports," Leeland explained. "Then he had some business in town. Just wanted to check up on you – —us, rather. He's being kind of cryptic about it. And sad." He stole a glance over his shoulder. "I told him I'd ask Mama if he could stay for Easter dinner with us. Before you say anything, Lees, he's got nowhere else to go. After basic, he's headed off to war. But ... I told him it would be completely up to you. If you don't want him here, he'll have to go."

"Why can't he eat with his mother?" Leesa asked, reserving her sympathy.

"Apparently, she wouldn't see him. Told him not to come back. Probably something to do with how he ran off the way he did."

Leesa took pity on the forlorn figure just beyond her brother. She looked to Ashley, squeezing his hand in hopes of reassurance. After a moment of thought and a deep breath, she said, "Okay, he can stay. Ash will protect me. Right?" She gave him a peck on the cheek.

"Right on," Leeland laughed. "If it's cool with you, Ash, it's cool with me."

Ashley only nodded, rubbing the cheek Leesa had just kissed as if he wasere trying to rub it permanently into his face.

Easter dinner was both joyous and uneventful. The family was graced with the presence of Evelyn Dunning, who, as of late, had been feeling better; despite remaining in a wheelchair, her color and spirits were almost back to normal, even showing off a rosiness to her cheeks. Her face bloomed when all the children plied her with kisses and well wishes.

Ashley and Leesa started a verbal game of word association that had everyone laughing and playing along – —except Cleavon, who silently stewed on his side of the table. Only Ashley seemed to pick up on his demeanor as he kept a watchful eye throughout the night.

After dinner, Florence requested help from Leeland and Ashley to carry Evelyn up the stairs to her room, and Mr. Walker also volunteered. This left Leesa and Cleavon alone at the table. Cleavon attempted small talk, but Leesa, uncomfortable, began to pick up the dishes and clean the table.

Cleavon then grabbed her hand and tried to pull her into him for a kiss on her lips. She struggled to get away from him, fighting his strong grip, turning her cheek away from his wanting mouth.

"You're meant for me and nobody else," Cleavon told her up close.

A firm force pushed her aside as Ashley threw all his might into a right cross that landed solidly on Cleavon's jaw and knocked him back. Cleavon, regaining his footing, grabbed the carving knife. Leeland and Mr. Walker returned to witness the scene. Cleavon, breathing heavily and staring dead at Ashley, appeared to be quietly telling him that this was not over. He dropped the knife and left through the servants' entrance at the back of the kitchen.

When Florence rejoined the family, Leeland insisted in a hushed tone that they keep all this from her. Though Florence didn't ask, she could see that Cleavon was gone, Leesa seemed unnerved, and Ashley stuck close by her side for the rest of the evening. As dessert was denied and cleaning continued, Leesa volunteered herself and Ashley to finishing up the rest and making coffee, while the others took advantage of Jasper's absence to soak up the luxury of the leather furniture.

"Thank you," Leesa said finally, once they were alone in the kitchen. She gave him another innocent peck on the cheek for good measure, which had Ashley attempting to hide his face and the blush that had formed there.

As they cleaned, Leesa snuck looks at Ashley out of the corner of her eye. Ashley's face glowed warm and pink, but he kept to task. Ashley had always been kind to her especially, looking out for her as Leeland did, a knight in shining armor. He'd never once complained about her dating or about having to listen to her complaints of dating. But she wondered, suddenly ... Had he harbored feelings for her all this time? Had he always wanted her happiness even if it cost him his own?

Ashley handed her a clean wet plate to dry. Leesa touched his hand as she took it and let her touch linger, squeezing as he tried to pull back. She gave him a shy smile when he looked up at her. When Leesa planted a soft kiss right on his mouth, Ashley's face glowed beet red.

"Oh," he said.

"It's about damn time," Leeland said from the kitchen door. The two lovebirds jumped out of their skins and separated a few degrees. Leeland only grinned and held out his palm to shake Ashley's with great approval, slapping him on the shoulder with his other hand as he pulled him close.

"You break my sister's heart, and brother or no brother, I'll slice your dick off," he told Ashley with a smile. "Does Mama know?" he asked them both.

"I just found out myself," Leesa admitted.

"You know Mama," Ashley offered. "She knows everything. If she doesn't know, I bet she won't be as surprised as I am."

Leeland left the two to finish up, giving them some time alone. Ashley's head and heart spun at ninety miles an hour, both from Leeland's warning and Leesa's daring move. Despite fighting for her, supporting her, he hadn't the courage to do what he'd wanted to do for years.

"I love you," he told her quietly when they were finally alone. "I've always loved you."

Chapter 23

Baltimore, Maryland

Saturday, March 21, 1970
8.:45 a.m.

On a brisk Saturday morning, at a diner near the corner of Howard and Centerre, a soldier waited for an appointed date. A big blue municipal bus passed by the large windows, reflecting the image of a couple clutching each other in the cold morning air as they hurriedly entered through the glass doors. The smell of bacon, eggs, grits, hot cakes, grease, and coffee permeated the diner. Soon enough, voices went from murmuring to shouting across the counter and the Formica tabletops in the booths, the orders for coffee, waiters and waitresses telling new patrons to wait or take a seat at the counter, short-order cooks clanging utensils alongside the deafening sizzle of the grill. Few of the midmorning patrons noticed the couple approaching the man in uniform, as he gave them a look of both surprise and disappointment.

The couple noticed the soldier's grimace immediately and took it in their stride. Leesa Jenkins wore her hair in a large Afro, big gold hoop earrings in her ears, and a black leather jacket over a white turtleneck sweater, blue bellbottom jeans, and black boots – —looking like she'd stepped out of the pages of *Jet Magazine*. Her flawless skin glistened like the dark chocolate dripping over an ice cream sundae. Ashley Dunning stood tall in a blue denim jacket over a black long-sleeve T- shirt, blue denim jeans with rolled cuffs, black dockers, and a brown apple cap over dark sunglasses. His sandy blond hair fell in streams just above his shoulders. Leesa sat and scooted across the booth bench to the window, leaving plenty of room for Ashley to sit byjoin her side. There was a residue of frost on the window and a chill in the air, but Leesa removed her jacket, revealing the curves her tight turtleneck refused to hide. They barely drew notice from the waitress, who left the booth after refilling Cleavon Jackson's half-empty coffee cup.

"What the fuck is he doing here?" Cleavon hissed.

Ashley leaned his head down to peer over his small round sunglasses, which Cleavon now noticed held a green tint. Ashley ignored him and called for the waitress to come back, a move that only made Cleavon bristle. Ashley's presence here was an affront to what he thought he'd meant to Leesa and what they'd once shared – —what he'd believed they were on their way to rekindling.

"Look, baby," Cleavon started.

"'Your 'baby' is the last thing I will ever be, Cleavon," Leesa snapped quietly. "The *only* reason I'm here is because Ashley – —my *husband* – — wanted to see what you had to say, and why 'leave me alone' isn't enough for you."

"C'mon now, Leesa," Cleavon implored, emphasizing his words with his fingers on the tabletop. "You know I've always been good to you. I am the man for you. I always will be." He leaned forward over the table between them. "This cracker will never be able to take care of you the way I can!"

Cleavon now realized he was drawing unwanted attention. A military uniform approached, which made him stiffen. His own uniform bore smudges and wrinkles, as if it had been worn and slept in for several days. But it took him a while to recognize the familiar face and figure wearing the military uniform of a newly minted ensign. Standing six fooeet tall and tipping the scale at 175one hundred and seventy-five pounds, Leeland's sinewy build served him well in hand-to-hand combat exercises. No one in special training took him lightly.

Leeland removed his naval cap and sat down next to Cleavon, urging him to scoot over. "What's going on here? Is everyone all right?" he asked them, turning to Cleavon. "What happened to you, man?" When the waitress finally returned, Leeland quickly ordered rye toast with butter and honey and a round of coffees, despite the waitress's attempt at flirting.

Cleavon had always carried ample respect for Leeland and his ability to seem threatening without resorting to true threats – —a quality he'd never been able to emulate himself. He shrank. Cleavon explained that he'd been absent without leave and missed his call to rejoin his unit after his last stateside relief. He had attended a party before he needed to report back to base, but got lost in a six-day recovery from smoking a cigarette laced with acid supplied by a white stranger, and the next thing he knew, he'd woken up in a fleabag motel downtown. He'd taken a long trip, never leaving the Baltimore area. Now, he had to get back to base before the military police got ahold of him, but he'd desperately wanted to see Leesa first.

"Well, I'm headed to Annapolis. I can drop you off at your base in DC on my way," Leeland said, hoping to take control of things. "But I just want to make sure you'red clear on one thing: Leesa is done with you. Any hopes you had or have of being with her are through. You get it?" His gaze bored into Cleavon's. "Look at me and tell me you get it."

Cleavon sheepishly acknowledged – —the point was made. He'd lost the battle. But in his mind, the war wasn't over.

"Good!" Leeland said cheerily. "Why don't you all finish eating and drinking. I'm going to get a pack of smokes. Leesa?" He urged his sister to extricate herself from the booth and join him. With that, he departed from the table just as quickly as he'd come, leaving Cleavon and Ashley alone and face to face.

The two of them stewed in silence, staring at each other from across the booth, neither willing to break contact first. When Leeland and Leesa had gone far enough away, Cleavon leaned in close. "You have no idea who you're fuckin' with," he whispered. "Leesa is mine, forever will be. She's havin' *my* baby. That's right – —we've been seeing each other on the side."

Ashley, calm as could be, leaned in to meet him halfway. He removed his sunglasses. "I know who you are."

"The fuck does that mean?"

"I know who you are."

"You don't know shit!"

"I know exactly who you are," Ashley said once more, coolly venomous. "I know that respect for the military ain't gonna wash the stink off you, Cleavon. I know what you did to get those kids to go with you. I know what you did for Jasper and the City Council. I know you had a chance to get out, but didn't take it."

"You mean, what I did for *your father*!" Cleavon snarled, growing heated as his voice broke. "*Your* father!" He said it again, as if it would clear him of blame. "You don't know shit about me or what I had to do to survive in *your* father's fucked-up city. Don't point your finger at me, Dunning, point it at *him*! Your father and that sadistic bastard took *my* life, too!"

Ashley watched Cleavon gather himself and wrestle to get out of the booth. Before he could leave, Ashley snatched Cleavon's arm and pulled him down. When Cleavon attempted to resist, Ashley stood to meet him halfway and gripped him tighter.

"You stay away from my wife."

Cleavon ripped his arm away and stormed quickly out of the diner, fearing that just by looking at him, the entire diner and its patrons would know what he'd done.

***

The trip back to their home in Lafayette was a quiet one. Leesa and Ashley took in the view as they hoped to make good time on the road. Ashley figured Leesa had guessed what had happened while she'd been gone, judging by Cleavon's absence when she'd returned and the subdued atmosphere of the diner after his outburst.

Ashley finally broke the silence. "Husband, huh? You really owned up to that one," he teased. "I thought we were keeping that quiet until we got our own place."

"I know," Leesa sighed. "I guess I just wanted to make it clear to him that he had no chance in hell. We only had a couple of dates in the first place. I had already told him to leave me alone, that I had moved on, and everything else a woman says to a man to get him to bug out. He just wouldn't take no for an answer. Even returning his letters unopened didn't do the trick. Honestly, baby, I just didn't know what else to say. Even saying that and you being there ..." She trailed off.

"Well, I don't think we have to worry about him anymore. I think we got an understanding now."

"You think?" Leesa asked, daring to hope. "Well, I'm glad Lee was able to show up. Cleavon was always afraid of Lee since Lee kicked his ass when we were little." She laughed to herself at the memory, then yawned. As Ashley drove, she dropped her head into his lap. "I sincerely hope he got it this time. I can't handle any more of him."

Ashley noticed a patrol car coming up behind them in the rearview mirror. He checked his speedometer and made sure he was staying in his lane. *The last thing we need is to be stopped way out here*, he thought. Interracial marriage had only just been legalized in Virginia, but there were certain pockets of the Old Dominion state where it would always be illegal, lawful or not. Ashley switched the radio to a classical music station and lowered the volume as he passed.

His father had been livid about his marriage to Leesa and was determined to do whatever was possible to separate them. Concerned about Jasper using his connections to move up Ashley's draft status, Ashley had taken it upon himself to enlist, giving him the opportunity to select his service. Further, with Leeland's track to become an aviator, Ashley hoped that by picking the Navy, they'd both be assigned under the same commander.

Leesa sleepily shifted her head in his lap, and he couldn't help but fondly smile. The life he had felt like a dream – a realization of his personal fantasy?

"How did I get to be so lucky?" he murmured to himself.

"We're both lucky, baby," Leesa answered. She eventually fell asleep there, and Ashley drove with one hand on the wheel (two around police) and one hand on Leesa.

They had just crossed over the Roanoke County line when Ashley decided to head straight to their apartment instead of their planned stop at the Dunning home. He'd wanted to see his mother, but he didn't want to risk an encounter with his father – —determined to keep Leesa as far away from him as she could. As his report date was closing in, Ashley hoped to avoid contention between himself and Leesa. All he wanted was to enjoy what time they had left.

At home, Ashley took care of dinner and let Leesa relax and shower off the day. When he finally entered the bedroom to invite her to eat, he paused. Leesa had fallen asleep curled up on the mattress, bath towels strewn across her body. Her chocolate skin glistened in the soft bedroom light. He flicked the light off and pulled a blanket from the hall closet to drape across her while he removed the damp towels.

Ashley stopped for a moment to caress the small, plump round of Leesa's belly, imagining the small child inside. The pregnancy had been kept a secret so far, shared only with their mothers and Leeland, yet he'd never given Cleavon's remark a second thought. But Ashley had no intention of entertaining any such notion.

Deep in thought, Ashley lingered a little longer than he'd intended. As he withdrew his hand, Leesa took hold of it and pulled him closer to her. Surprised but welcoming the chance to get close to her in her current state of disrobe, he caressed her and held her supple skin, still warm and soft from the shower. He kissed along her neck and down her shoulder, massaging her breast in one hand. Her nipple grew firm under his palm.

Soon enough, Leesa touched the rise in his jeans.

"Take them off."

***

In his dorm at the Naval Academy in Annapolis, Maryland, Leeland Jenkins finished up a phone call to his friend at Fort McNair in DC regarding Cleavon Jackson. Leeland, who stated his intent to speak on Cleavon's behalf, was told a hearing would take place, and they would be in touch.

After Ashley and Leesa left, Leeland had found Cleavon on the nearby street corner, leaning against a lamppost, muttering to himself around a smoking cigarette. He wasn't sure Cleavon was fully aware of the situation he had put himself in by going AWOL, and his state of mind stood on unstable ground. On the drive to McNair, Cleavon slept intermittently between bouts of muttering to himself, wiping his eyes dry, and shouting at the sun through the window.

Leeland wasn't sure there was anything more he could do.

Cleavon's fate rested in the hands of military justice. Had he failed their friendship?

A knock on the door jolted Leeland out of his thoughts. He jumped out of his chair and went to answer the door, only to find his commanding officer on the other side of it.

"Lt. Jenkins, I'm glad you're available," Captain Maynard Spencer greeted him. "May I come in?"

Leeland straightened his back like a rod and saluted. "Sir, yes, sir!"

"At ease," Spencer said, as he entered Leeland's room. "I'm not here to bust your chops, Lieutenant. Let's keep this as informal as possible."

Captain Spencer was a base favorite for his ability to bring out the best in the men who served under him. He'd been given the nickname "'Captain May I'" because he wasn't afraid to allow his men to take chances – —as long as they respected the uniform. Furthermore, he had a strong regard for the way the Armed Forces, and the Navy in general, had treated Negro sailors in the past. Captain Spencer felt the service never gave the Negro sailor the right opportunity to prove himself, and he wanted to change that. Having been brought up through the ranks under an extremely racist admiral in his time in Korea, he vowed that if he were ever given a battleship under his own command, he would allow his sailors' talent and dedication to be his guide.

The captain took Leeland's desk chair, while Leeland took a seat on his bed. Leeland must have had a confused look on his face, because Spencer quickly said, "I know this visit is a bit unusual. So let me get straight to the point."

Spencer pulled a folder from under his arm and laid it in his lap. Leeland took a quick glance at it, seeing his name across the front.

"Jenkins, your test results and flying technique have both proven exemplary," the captain said, patting the folder. "I've been granted the opportunity to establish a special squadron, and I am here to personally recruit you to my team." Capt. Spencer paused, letting it sink in as he tried to get a read on Jenkins's reaction. When he didn't receive one, he continued. "You're not a hotshot. Your ability to maintain control of your emotions is one of your greatest advantages. I've seen you restrain yourself from the comments by those Southern boys. You and I both know it was nonsense – —hell, you showed all of us what you were when you got into the cockpit. But that was high intensity." He paused again, to no answer. "You'll be flying special sorties and recon missions...."

The captain paused, watching Jenkins. Finally, he sighed.

"You've gotta give me something here, son. I've just personally invited you to join a special team and praised your flying skills. You didn't flinch. You've got blood flowing through your veins, right? Don't tell me you're like this even when you're at ease."

Leeland chose his words before he spoke. "Sir, let me be clear. I am ecstatic and overwhelmed that you made the personal visit here to give me the news. My excitement might not come across outwardly, but believe me, I'm thrilled."

"Then let yourself go, man!" the captain encouraged him. "Let me hear you yell, or scream, or show something!" When Leeland only smiled, Capt. Spencer poured a flask of scotch into Leeland's small naval-issue coffee mugs and handed him one. "Here's to your health, son. I'm sure you'll make me proud."

Leeland nodded. "To your health, sir." He waited until his superior officer took a sip before he drained his cup in one swallow.

The captain poured more drink for them both as he elaborated on the special squadron's mission of special sorties and reconnaissance. There was a particular need for secrecy – —Leeland was not to tell his family, friends, or even fellow naval pilots what he was doing. The captain reminded Leeland that he'd earned this. His hard work had paid off. As soon as Spencer was gone, Leeland finally allowed himself to relax and quietly celebrate alone in his dorm room. The scotch burned hot in his chest.

***

Cleavon Jackson, Private First Class, sat erect on the floor next to the bed in his holding cell. He hadn't slept since his arrival, afraid to sleep. When the medic looked him over, he asked for some kind of sleep aid that would let him sleep without dreaming. On the drive to McNair, Cleavon's attempt at resting had been interrupted as his mind seemed to avoid falling into REM sleep.

Cleavon's dreams were plagued by the children who had never made it home; who could no longer enjoy their family's embrace; who would never celebrate another holiday or graduate from elementary school; who Cleavon had convinced he could help. Every time a child had trusted Cleavon's word, they disappeared. He'd never questioned his actions nor his orders from the Council – —it was only years later that he discovered what he'd been a part of. Why would he have questioned it? Adults he'd trusted had told him he was helping, that he alone had become invaluable to them. Until he wasn't. Ashley Dunning's accusations haunted him at every turn out of Maryland and into DC. They would haunt him for the rest of his life.

Finally, Cleavon forced himself into the bunk and wrapped himself up with the coarse wool blanket that covered the bare mattress. He shut his eyes and begged for slumber to swiftly rescue him from his mind.

"I shoulda killed him. I had the chance. I shoulda killed him," he mumbled to himself. "I'm gonna kill him."

Slumber eventually obliged, but his dreams reneged on the agreement.

***

It was nearly midnight, and Leesa couldn't sleep. She sat herself up in bed and took to gazing at her husband, in deep restful slumber. She loved the way he looked when he slept – —his peace seemed to soothe her own. For the last few months, their life together had been nearly perfect, but Leesa's mind continually reminded her of Ashley's looming departure.

Leesa nudged him awake – —too hard. Ashley bolted upright.

"What?" he managed. "Are you okay?"

"I'm sorry, honey," she offered. "I just ... I couldn't sleep."

"Bad dream?"

Leesa shook her head. "Just thinking about you leaving."

Ashley softened. "I know, baby. But I promise you." He gently embraced her. "I *promise*, everything will be all right. I'll only be in for eighteen months. Time will go by fast. Mama will be here with you and the baby."

"But you'll be gone in just two months," Leesa murmured. "You could miss the birth."

"I won't be far away," Ashley reassured her. "And I got the okay from the Quartermaster to a forty-eighty-hour leave as soon as I hear you're going into labor."

Five months earlier, Ashley and Leesa had both walked into the naval recruitment office on an unusually cold, late October morning. In her heart, she agreed that enlisting was far better than waiting for an unpredictable draft notice. But, as most things with time, you never realize how quickly you run out of it until it's nearly gone.

"You're going to be gone in less than a month," Leesa sighed. "I'm gonna spend the entire summer fat, hot, miserable, and alone, till you come back next September."

"You said *two* months."

"I'm pregnant," she said, pouting. "It's going to *feel* like three weeks."

Ashley kissed her to stifle his own laugh. But he could see, beneath her impetuous demeanor, there was true fear in her words.

"Sweetheart, I promise, I will be back for a few days after I graduate basic," he said. "That should be right around the end of July. And I'll write every day, call you constantly. You'll be so tired of me, you'll be glad to have a rest away from me."

"Really?"

"Really. I promise."

Ashley kissed her cheek and held her close. She nestled herself into his arms, feeling her anxieties slightly recede.

"I'm sorry I woke you up," Leesa said softly. I know I'm being emotional, but ... I want to spend all the time we have left as much as we can."

"You don't have to apologize," Ashley responded. "Actually, I'm kind of glad you woke me up. I was having a strange dream. We were chasing our son through a tobacco field. We kept calling out his name. Dillard. Wait, we *are* naming him Dillard, right? After your father?" Leesa nodded. "Have you told Mama yet?"

"No, not yet," she said. "I'm sure she'll be okay with it. But with you, and Lee, both going away while I'm pregnant, I wanted to wait. I'll tell her when the time is right."

"I won't say anything about it, then," Ashley replied. "But I can tell you, I'm sure she'll be proud you did."

Her melancholy made her pause, but then she perked up. "I'm sure little Dillard will bring us lots of happiness while his dad and uncle are away."

"I promise," Ashley said again, "I *will* write you every day."

Leesa smiled. "You better."

Chapter 25

Lafayette, Virginia

Thursday, August 20, 1970
3.:47 p.m.

Jasper Dunning cheerfully pushed open his office door, only to be greeted by the uneasy sight of Dr. Weldon Michaels sitting comfortably in the high-backed throne behind Jasper's desk. Jasper was not one to hold back his displeasure of Dr. Michaels, no matter how much he used him; the next words spewed out of him on instinct, and he wouldn't take them back.

"Just what in the fuck do you think you're doin' here? In *my* chair?" he demanded. "Tell me why I shouldn't just have the deputy outside run you outta here on your ass?"

Weldon's silence and lack of movement unnerved him. The fact that he didn't even seem affected by Jasper's tone made him wonder if the doctor had found the small-caliber revolver hidden in the top drawer of his desk, and the thought dampened his mood.

"I presume ... you have somethin' important to discuss that must concern me," Jasper added with a slight stammer. "Explicitly, for you to break protocol,. Dr. Michaels."

Weldon relaxed as a greasy Cheshire grin engulfed his expression.

He shifted himself in Jasper's chair as if he owned it and tossed an envelope across the desk, then stood to pour himself a glass of bourbon from Jasper's private collection.

Keeping his eyes on the good doctor all the while, Jasper opened the envelope and only tore his gaze away to read through the contents. He gave it only a cursory glance before he read more deeply, darting madly across the page. Reclaiming ownership of his seat, Jasper clutched the envelope's contents until they crumpled. His hand clenched it tight as if it wasere on fire, shaking with his fury. He sat in silence and stared into nothing, only aware of the ghastly noise of Weldon gurgling down the last of Jasper's bourbon. Somehow, the sound and sight of the doctor provided him with a strange sense of calm.

When Weldon finally turned back to look at Jasper, his blood ran cold. Jasper Dunning's eyes held no life in them. Then Jasper's lips morphed into a haunting grin.

"You're gonna take care of this for me, Weldon," Jasper said slowly. "You're gonna take that *thing* outta that nigger bitch and kill it. You hear me?" He looked up at Dr. Michaels without moving the rest of his body. "You're gonna make sure she cain't have any more. You understand?"

Dr. Michaels quickly nodded and opened his mouth to speak. "How—?"

"I don't care how you do it," Jasper said. "Just get it done."

***

The night after her visit to Dr. Michaels, Dolores relived the encounter with tears in her eyes. She regretted having anything to do with such a vile man and wondered how she'd ever come to respect him, how she could ever respect or trust anyone else after this. It made her consider leaving Lafayette altogether. She could leave the whole county behind her and start afresh.

A knock on the door finally pulled her off the sofa. Standing before her was the unabashed face of her nightmares, Weldon Michaels. In the midst of her frozen shock, he invited himself in, kissing her cheek along the way, and took a seat. The rage inside her couldn't find its way out; all she could do was dumbly watch. He patted the seat next to him, then reached into his pocket. Fear struck Dolores's heart, until she saw it was only a piece of paper. Then she realized what it was, what she had left behind, and her fear returned. She would pay for her thoughtlessness.

"Nurse Peters," Michaels said to her. "Your assistance is required."

The doctor laid out his instructions. Dolores mentally considered a way out, but as if he could read her mind, he brought up her own malfeasance and complicit role in the activities she'd performed for him all these years. Were they to come to light, the end of her medical career would be the least of her worries. The sheriff and his deputies would be watching her in case she decided to flee Lafayette.

Dolores's stomach convulsed as he left her as he'd found her, and once more gave her a peck on the cheek.

Chapter 26

Yankee Station, Vietnam / Lafayette, Virginia

Tuesday, September 15, 1970
6.:37 p.m.

As Vietnam's wet season continued, the heat and humidity took their toll on the sailors at Yankee Station. Shore leave was always a welcomed respite for the men in uniform. The sailors, the men who worked the deck of the USS *America*, spent long hours in the port cities in the Philippines, just north of Subic Bay. While many of the aviators would release their pent-up frustration at the officers' clubs across the bay, Leeland never felt comfortable around his fellows when alcohol and women were involved, even though his looks and reputation as a pilot drew in the women serving the clubs. His celebrity would usually lead to jealousy and fights among some of the aviators from the other carriers at Yankee Station. His shipmates were at first hesitant to stand up for him – until they realized the benefit of having him on their side in a fist fight and when seeking the company of the local women. They felt pulled in by his smooth complexion. Some of the waitresses would even ask to lick his face, expecting his skin to taste like chocolate.

    Leeland had been awarded a Silver Star for taking down a Russian MIG during a night raid. But he had become more contemplative as the months drew on. What was at stake for him was something the white pilots would never have to consider. How would his actions affect the black pilots that came after him? He had only been in Vietnam for a few months and was already starting to question the mission.

He struck up some friendships with some of the boatswain's mates, reaching out to the men who loaded the armaments onto his aircraft. It was an immensely dangerous and thankless job they did, and Leeland wanted to make sure they knew he appreciated them. He would get chewed out if the captain knew just how much time he spent with the enlisted men. The few black sailors formed a union to protect and guard each other from pranks often pulled by the white sailors who outnumbered them.

While abroad, Leeland read about Muhammad Ali and his stance against the war and, furthermore, the killing of people of color. The collective vitriol from all corners of the United States press and armed services gave him pause. He'd even been called into the captain's quarters to have a heart-to-heart about Ali's "'unpatriotic'" stance. How ironic, he thought, that a captain who fought so hard for the acceptance of black aviators would be so tone-deaf towards what black civilians faced at home.

While sitting in the officers' galley, Leeland noticed a lively conversation had taken over the room. Some of the pilots had been granted liberty to go to shore. The others would remain for their shift in the cockpit. Leeland, scheduled for the midnight-to-dawn run, chastised a few pilots in good nature and quickly made his way to his cabin to rest. Life on the USS *America* was routine, and many of the daily activities would be taken for granted. But Leeland knew that each time he strapped himself into the cockpit, someone who didn't look like him, or speak the same language, or pray to the same god as he did, would die that night. Leeland said a prayer for that person. *May your God and mine keep you and your family close to his heart tonight.*

Later that night, strapped in his A-7E Corsair II, Leeland checked the time on his wristwatch. He was just minutes away from his midnight launch. He looked over his instrument panel and glanced out into the midnight sky. Gathering clouds suggested rain would fall before the morning arrived. A blend of high humidity and his own anticipation brought on sweat that he wiped from his forehead.

He tapped on his instrument panel, placed a firm hand on the joystick, and flipped the ignition switch on. He sat in the cockpit, ready for the catapult to send him on his mission for the night.

***

Florence put aside the lunch dishes and ran the faucet to wash them, while Evelyn and Leesa sat quietly at the small kitchen table. It was the very same table Florence had used in her time in service to the Dunning family, drinking coffee and listening to the radio with her neighbor Gladys. Her fears and anxieties had ebbed and flowed at that table throughout the years, but she remembered the good times, too: the companionship of others she invited into her space.

In the middle of dishes, Florence suddenly paused to look at her daughter, as if some uncontrollable urge had directed her to think of Leesa.

Evelyn was leaning over to rub Leesa's belly, and the sight immediately calmed her.

Florence was so happy for Evelyn, who had been ecstatic to learn they were expecting a grandchild. Florence had a feeling that Evelyn hoped she would play a bigger part of her grandchild's life than she had for her own son.

A cool afternoon breeze sailed through the opaque white shades over the kitchen windows. Summer was coming to an end, and the leaves on the dogwood trees had begun to change color from vibrant green to burnt orange. As Florence joined them and the ladies relaxed, sharing stories of motherhood, talk turned to Leesa's expected due date – —two weeks away. Evelyn pushed for her plan to have Leesa move back into the manor, sooner rather than later. After carefully considering Evelyn's and her mother's point of view, Leesa agreed the coming weekend would be a good time to move her belongings, and she would spend the night tonight. Evelyn promised to get available men to move and store the furniture and clothing, and even pledged to provide a new wardrobe for the mother and child.

Down the street from the Dunning home, sitting, waiting, and watching, Gary Pierce and Don Stiles traded stories to pass the time. Eventually, Gary lit a cigarette and changed the subject.

"The last fuckin' thing I wanna be doin' is followin' some fuckin' pregnant nigger 'round. I cain't stand sittin' and waitin'. How in the fuck did I get drug into this shit?"

"I told you," Don replied. "The doc wants to have a talk wit her, and I need you here in case her brother tries to start some shit." Don knew Gary didn't sweat the details; he just wanted to feel like his presence was essential.

Gary nodded, considering that. Then, after a pause, he said, "Well, I don't wanna fuck wit no voodoo babies puttin' spells on ya for spittin' on their momma."

"The fuck are you talkin' about?" Don said. "I told you that bitch was lyin'. You gotta stop believin' everything ya hear, Gary. I'm startin' to worry 'bout you."

Gary held up his hand, requesting silence. Don, for once in his life, shut up. He then looked when Gary pointed to the two black ladies leaving the Dunning residence. He spat out his cigarette as Don followed behind the slow-moving Ford pickup.

As they arrived at Leesa's apartment, Florence and her daughter sat in the cab of the truck. "It's nice to see Ms. Evelyn so excited about the baby," Leesa mused. "I've been on Ash's case a bit about calling her."

"It would mean so much to her if he could give her that," Florence said. "She feels so bad for ... well, you know."

"I know, Mama," Leesa replied. "I was just hoping for the baby's sake that Ash would try to be nicer to her. She's really trying so hard. She's so excited about decorating the room. I just couldn't tell her no."

Florence smiled. "I know, and that was so sweet of you to accept her offer. So, then, why don't we just leave these packages in the truck and I'll come in to help you pack a few things for tonight?"

"I don't know, Mama. I just want to lie down for a couple of hours to get some rest. And I really need to take a shower," Leesa responded. "Why don't I just call you later and you can come back and get me?"

Florence shook her head. "You stay here," she offered. "I'll run in and pick out a few things to get you through the night. We can come back tomorrow for anything else."

"That's okay. I want to sleep in my own bed one last time before I move back," Leesa said. "It'll just be for a couple of hours. I promise I'll call and you can come back and get me before dinner."

"I'll come back by four o'clock, then," Florence insisted. "I can help you pack some things and you can come keep me company while I cook."

Leesa absentmindedly agreed as she had already begun to maneuver herself out of the truck. She slid across the seat and opened the door just in time to be assisted by her mother, who had somehow quickly made her way around to help.

"Mama, I'm fine," Leesa grumbled. "I'm not a baby, I'm *having* a baby."

Florence fought back the distant fear in her heart. She couldn't allow her alarm to scare Leesa away, or make her feel as though she wasere losing her autonomy. She had never been the kind of parent to hover, but she felt an urge to do so now more than ever.

"Just wanted to walk you to the door and give you a hug," Florence deflected.

"I can make it to the door on my own. Are you okay?"

"Okay, okay," her mother said. "I just want to make sure *you're* okay."

"You'll have the baby to coddle and pamper all you want in a couple of weeks," Leesa assured her. She hugged her mother and kissed her cheek. "Sorry I'm tired and a bit cranky, Mama. Promise – —I'll call you later."

***

Having only just convinced her mother that she needed to rest, Leesa now found it difficult to sleep. She sat up in bed as her mind kept her awake with thoughts of the drive home. It had been a quick and pleasant jaunt through Lafayette to the west; but as they passed the high schools that were still segregated, she wondered what kind of life her child would have if they'd decided to stay in Lafayette. What advantages, if any, would benefit her mixed baby with the Cartwright name?

None, she concluded. Her baby would have nothing if they stayed in any part of Virginia where Jasper had control.

She'd managed to persuade her mother to move out west to California with her and Ashley. Virginia, she felt, was no place for her baby. Jasper would never leave them alone if they stayed. Her mother had seemed reluctant, and it plagued Leesa with worry over whether she was doing the right thing.

A knock on the front door pulled Leesa out of bed. She had no idea how long she'd been failing to sleep, and by now she figured her mother had arrived to spend the rest of the afternoon with her. Just as she went to open the door, the lock snapped and someone shoved the door into her with such a violent force that it smashed into her mouth and rattled her teeth. A gasp split her lip up to her nostril and sent blood straight into her mouth and onto the floor.

Leesa stumbled and fell backwards, her head woozy from the hit. She held a hand to her mouth, hoping to stem the blood flow, but now the door moved again, and this time struck her in the head. A throbbing pain burst above her right eye and continued down the side of her face, where warm blood now flowed freely. The taste of copper coated her tongue and the smell of it filled the air. She glanced down at her belly as red flowed through her fingers and dropped to her clothes.

As the door opened once more, softer now as the attackers let themselves in, Leesa looked up to see the face of a man she didn't recognize. He felled her with one punch, and her head slammed against the coffee table as she crumpled to the floor.

Outside, a rusting red-and-white ambulance waited against the curb. Dolores Peters had given instructions to the two men to wait for her, but they acted as if they had separate orders. By the time she caught up to them, Don Stiles had cold-cocked Leesa into oblivion, and now there was blood all over her and the floor.

"What the hell?" Dolores exclaimed, pushing past Don and Gary to pick up Leesa's dangling head. A gash had opened across the back of her head, her Afro having padded it only so much against the blunt force. Warm blood dripped through the tight black curls. Dolores quickly got to wrapping Leesa's head and face in bandages. "I thought you were going to let me talk to her."

"About what?" Don asked casually. "You think Doc Weldon gonna let this nigger live?"

"Shut up, Don!" Gary responded, smacking him. "She not supposed to know nuthin'. Let's get her on the tray and git, 'fore anybody see us."

Dolores's mouth dropped open. "What about the blood?"

"Don't know, don't care!" Don said. "Doc will see it gets taken care of. Let's go!"

Before Dolores could do much about Leesa's head trauma, Don and Gary quickly loaded Leesa's unconscious body onto the gurney they'd parked on the street, just out of the ambulance. Don threw a white sheet over her, as if covering an unconscious, full-term pregnant woman with a bleeding wound would be inconspicuous. They loaded her into the ambulance.

"You two dumbfucks are gonna be the death of me," Dr. Michaels said, watching them lift in the gurney from the inside of the ambulance. He lifted the sheet by her head and cursed at the boys. "Didn't I tell you to—?"

"To what, kill her?" Dolores demanded from the back door.

"Get in, Nurse Peters. *Now!*" Dr. Michaels barked.

Dolores, stained with her own tears and Leesa's blood, angrily held the door open to expose the world to what lay inside. "How could I have let you get me to do something like this?"

Weldon, exasperated, motioned at Don. "Get that bitch in the bus." He didn't have to say it twice – —Don was already getting out of the ambulance, grabbing the still sobbing nurse and tossing her inside. He shut the doors, locked them, and banged them with his fist to let Gary know he could drive. Don jumped into the front passenger's seat. The ambulance pulled away into the street.

In all the violence, commotion, and talk of death, life began to take place. As she lay on the gurney, Leesa's waters broke, spilling over her limp legs, soaking the gurney, and dripping onto the ambulance floor.

***

The Liberty Hawks squadron had made it well into the North Vietnamese Army's territory. Their mission: destroy the Viet Cong's supply routes, better known as the Ho Chi Minh Trail, leading through the jungle along the Cambodian, Laotian, and Vietnamese borders. Under heavy cover from canopies of trees and foliage, the trails had been providing the Viet Cong with all the rations and armaments they needed.

The light of a full moon provided the sky above the clouds with an eerie glow. The Liberty Hawks followed the path laid out by the Hueys, which had dispersed defoliants just a few days before. Radar picked up their target upon approach, and the squadron began their descent below the clouds.

As all twelve pilots checked in over the shared communications system, the commander reaffirmed their mission. "Let's take care of business; and remember, we have families to go home to," he told his squadron. "Do not, I repeat, do not, fly off on a hunch. A successful mission is predicated by all of us, all of us, returning to the *America* together."

In humidity, the A-7E Corsair was known to be a little sluggish while reaching top speeds. They were no match for the three MiGs piloted by the North Vietnamese that swept past them as they reached the clear sky. For some of the Liberty Hawks, it was their first encounter with the supersonic Russian Mikoyan-Gurevich MiG-25. The commander ordered his squadron to stay in formation and continue their flight pattern home. The Viet Cong pilots, it seemed, were only trying to bait them and had no intention of taking on an entire squadron.

But sometimes instincts take over training. As they flew, four of the Liberty Hawks peeled off after the MiGs. One of those four pilots was Leeland Jenkins.

"Return to formation!" the commander shouted into his radio.

"These jets don't want a fight, and neither do we. Don't give it to them. Return to formation!"

Just as the four errant pilots turned their jets around and headed back to the rest of the squadron, one of the MiGs peeled off from the other two and swerved toward the retreating pilots. Leeland took the helm as the other three strays watched the MiG catch up with and then pass them by.

"Listen to command," Leeland urged them over the radio. "They might be trying to lure us into a trap. Ignore further pursuit and hightail it back to USS *America*. We're in enough trouble as it is."

Two of the pilots didn't seem to take kindly to being buzzed. They followed the MiG below the clouds. The noise generated by the aircraft was deafening. As the Corsairs drifted down without caution, they came under fire in a ground-to-air skirmish. Vietnamese villagers under siege had been powerless to do anything about a war that it seemed would never end – — until now.

Leeland took charge, diving underneath the stalled pilots towards the enemy fire and strafing the ground with his own. It allowed the pilots to get back up above the clouds. He joined them back into formation and said nothing of the ground-fire he'd taken to afford them safety.

***

The ambulance pulled over to a predetermined site alongside a deserted road at the edge of the county line. Two getaway cars were parked close by, and a shovel stood in the ground. Weldon Michaels had already sedated Leesa, but as he dug into the birth canal with forceps, Dolores stopped him.

"She's in full labor," she said. "The baby is on its way."

It was too late to perform any kind of abortion, even if he wanted to. Dr. Michaels had committed several horrors and atrocities in his career, but killing a newborn child was something he had never anticipated nor was willing to consider. Even for him, that was beyond the pale. Discarding the forceps, he attempted to birth the baby by C- section as his impatience got the better of him.

"Let me take the child," Dolores pleaded to Dr. Michaels as he worked. Her tears flowed automatically now. She'd gone too far, buried herself too deep into this crime. At least this one act would offer her some sliver of redemption.

As Dr. Michaels cut through Leesa's dress and bra, Don shrieked and grinned at Gary. "Look at them titties!" Gary joined in the petulant laughter and sophomoric gestures, the two of them both gleefully ogling her with no regard for her fading life.

Leesa wavered in and out of consciousness. She reached for

Dolores's hand as the nurse attempted to cover Leesa's breast, hoping to offer the slightest amount of decency.

Through the bandages on her face, Leesa spoke in muffled, weak words.

"Please," she begged. "Please don't kill my baby ..."

As her eyes rolled back into her head, she gave an instinctive last push. The child's head emerged from her body, and the baby began to writhe in its struggle for life. Dolores pushed the doctor aside and caught the child with a blanket as it arrived into a violent world. She wrapped up the child and held it close to her bosom, then placed the baby on Leesa's chest and moved Leesa's hand to the baby's back. Leesa, hemorrhaging, remained in a semiconscious state as her baby boy sought the familiar sound of his mother's heartbeat and strained for her milk.

When Leesa had faded, Dolores took up the newborn and rushed out of the ambulance. Covered in blood and barely keeping her wits about her, she ran to one of the getaway cars. Gary ran out after her. Dolores, knowing Gary fancied her, pleaded for help to save the baby's life. He agreed to drive them. "But you owe me," he said with tortured delight.

Dolores never agreed. "Let's go!"

Dr. Michaels and Don sat in the ambulance, offering no assistance as Leesa bled out and her heartbeat stilled. As if they were watching a movie, they watched her life expire before their eyes. When the sound of screeching tires pulled them out of their daze, Weldon slammed his fist into the ambulance door. "Shit!"

He had a change of clothes in one of the cars, and he prayed Dolores had taken the other one. Head to toe in blood evidence, he'd taken no precautions for safety or sanitation, and now he hoped he wouldn't have to pay for it.

At 8.:02 p.m., in Lafayette, Virginia, Leesa was pronounced dead.

***

Black smoke sputtered from the Corsair's exhaust. Leeland maneuvered the plane into the safety net aboard the USS *America*. Hospital corpsmen, boatswain's mates, and pilots rushed to his plane to give him aid. The jolt of the plane's landing knocked Leeland's air mask off, and his head bobbed forward as he faded in and out. He'd taken on more fire than he himself had realized. The ground attack had strewn him with high-caliber armaments — —it was a miracle he'd been able to survive the flight back to the carrier.

Leeland had coughed up blood the last twenty miles of flight, but
even still fought to retain control and guide his airship safely home. His fellow pilots, at a loss with the smoke and lack of communication, could only fly near his plane to guide him. His speech, over the radio, had been unintelligible, and his voice wasn't strong enough to compete with the howling air blowing through the two-inch hole in his windshield where a bullet had broken through. That bullet, they discovered, had pierced the fuselage of his aircraft, up through the back of his seat, and into his lung.

It took the crewmen less than a minute to pull Leeland out of the plane and onto a gurney. Medics took over to supply him with oxygen and locate any other injuries. They rolled him into the medical galley as the surgeon prepared for an emergency procedure.

He never made it into the sick bay. At 7.:02 a.m., on Yankee Station in Vietnam, Leeland was pronounced dead.

***

Florence paced the kitchen floor. Deputy Reynolds had assured her they would check all nearby hospitals to see if Leesa had turned up there. It had only been an hour since Reynolds escorted her back to the Cartwright-Dunning residence and left her with empty assurances, but to Florence it felt like days. No one had answered the door when Florence returned to Leesa's apartment, preparing to bring her over for dinner, and she let herself in to discover the bloody scene.

Her worst fears were confirmed when someone pounded on her front door. On the other side, she found Nurse Peters, her clothing streaked with blood, a newborn baby crying in her arms.

***

After completing SEAL combat training for the day, Ashley Dunning, seaman, was escorted to the commander's office by the Master at Arms. He waited patiently in the outer office, before the secretary directed him in. Ashley saluted. The commander, finishing up a phone call, acknowledged it and gestured for Ashley to take a seat. When he hung up the phone, he tapped the file on his desk and gave Ashley a once- over.

"Sailor, you're listed as the brother-in-law to a Negro Naval Pilot serving on the USS *America*, one Leeland Jenkins. Correct?" He paused as Ashley nodded. The commander let out a sigh. "Look, son, I'm not going to pussyfoot around this. We just received word that Leeland Jenkins was KIA over Laos. I don't have a lot of information, but there is an investigation in process. What I've been told so far is that his death was a direct result of insubordination. Violating a direct order."

He looked for a reaction from Dunning. Ashley showed no emotion.

"Unofficially, I understand he saved the lives of two of his fellow pilots," the commander continued. "I imagine you'll want to accompany the body home. He's going to be buried at Annapolis. I also see you're also expecting a new addition to your family, yes?"

A tear rolled down Ashley's cheek as his body betrayed him. He raised his head to meet the commander's gaze. "Yes, sir."

The commander let Ashley's response hang in the air for a moment before proceeding. "The body is expected to arrive in Annapolis at four thirty tomorrow morning. I'm giving you until Sunday night to get your family affairs in order. I'm expecting you to be back on base by nine Monday morning. Is that clear?" Ashley nodded quietly. The commander couldn't be certain he was reaching Ashley, so he emphasized, "We're at war, son. Casualties are a part of that effort. I need every available hand on deck. Do I make myself clear?"

With that, Ashley Dunning was dismissed. He walked briskly out of the commander's office and found his way alongside his quarters. He hesitated before entering, consumed in the loss of his brother and hero. The world spun around him as he leaned against the wall, allowing his weight to create a small thud of despair against it. A pinprick of fear nicked a small hole into his heart. He fought the urge to release it as his eyes swelled with tears. In that moment, finally alone, he was overcome with memories of

Leeland's smile, warmth, and bravery. He knew, right then and there, that he had to be the one to tell Leesa and Florence. He had to assume the mantle of his brother's role. Ashley let out a deep sob, anticipating their devastation over the news. In the back of his mind, he could see Evelyn sharing in their grief – —while the specter of the satisfying smirk of Jasper sunk into the pinhole, only further expanding his fear.

***

In the early morning hours of Friday, September 18, Ashley sat in the back of a cab in a state of flux. In the midst of his sorrow, he was glad to have a chance to see his wife, mother-in-law, and mother. Part of him desperately wanted to be the one to tell them about Leeland's death. It was as if delivering the news was his familial duty, another way of protecting them as he always had.

Ashley stared blankly out of the window of the plane and thought he would close his eyes for a moment's rest during takeoff. He awoke more than two and a half hours later, when the stewardess lightly tapped his arm to let him know they had landed.

In the cab ride home, Ashley directed the driver to drop him off at the Dunning home. The driver brought them through the gate and up to the servants' entrance, following Ashley's detailed instructions. He gave the cab driver a gracious tip and jumped out, anxious to see friendly faces.

Instead, Ashley was welcomed home to the sight of the sheriff's deputy talking to two of the land hands. Jasper appeared to look on in disbelief. Ashley ignored the rising dread in his heart and burst through the servants' kitchen entrance, calling for Leesa, then Florence. He quickly surveyed the kitchen and could tell no one had been there. When he thought he saw smeared dried blood on Florence's table, he dropped his duffle bag and raced upstairs to his mother's room.

Evelyn sat in her chair beside the window, peering through it as she strained to hear the conversations between Jasper, the deputy, and the maintenance men. When she noticed Ashley had come home, she nonchalantly waved.

"Hello," she said, as if he had just returned from an early morning errand.

"I'm only here for a few days," Ashley said, almost out of breath. "Evelyn, what's going on? Where's Florence and Leesa? Why are they outside harassing Horace and Jacob?"

"Oh, no, he's not ..." Evelyn trailed off. She looked up to see him, and a blend of amazement, gratitude, and fear washed over her. "Oh, Ashley, it's you! My word, I can't believe you're here." She rose up from her chair to greet him with a hug and planted kisses on his brow. Her uncharacteristic affection made Ashley pause, and he pulled away from her for an answer.

"Where are Florence and Leesa?"

"We don't ... I don't know," Evelyn said. "That's why the deputy is here with Jasper. They both ran off without a trace. You don't think something ..." She dared not finish the thought.

Ashley kissed her forehead and quickly excused himself, then bolted down the stairs and back out the door. He found Jasper still talking to the deputy. Jasper welcomed Ashley home and introduced him to the deputy.

"Where are they?" he said, ignoring the deputy.

"That's what we're trying to find out," Jasper answered. "We don't rightly know what's happened. Florence and her daughter are gone. Must've taken off in the middle of the night. No one's seen them in two days." He gestured to the land hands. "These boys here say they think they saw Florence get into a car with a woman in white. But they don't know for sure."

"Well, Mr. Dunning," one of the men interjected,. "I said I seen Ms. Florence leavin' with a white woman and a cryin' baby. They got in a car and that was the last time I seen 'em."

Jasper frowned. "Thank you for clarifyin', Jacob," he said with a slight look of embarrassment. "Sheriff Clayton is already on top of this, and he's got his entire department out lookin' for them. Now, we're not exactly sure there *was* a white woman, or a car, or a baby—"

"What the fuck does that mean, Jasper?" Ashley snapped.

"Now hold on, son," Jasper pleaded. "We don't know if   Florence—"

"Don't call me son!"

Jasper tried in vain to save face. "I know you're upset," he said, "but gettin' angry with me ain't gonna help the situation. All we know is that they're gone. Where, how, and who are questions still bein' asked. For all we know, they might be on some kinda vacation."

The deputy added, "Well, there *is* the matter of blood and broken glass at her apartment."

Jasper cut him a look that revealed his irritation for only a moment, then he innocently corrected himself. "I don't want you getting riled up any more than you already are, Ashley," he clarified. "What we need is to remain calm and allow the authorities to do their job."

Anger rose up into Ashley's body. He turned on his heel and ran back into the kitchen. Once inside, he located the keys to Florence's pickup, grabbed his duffle bag, and headed back outside. He tossed his bag into the truck bed, all the while staring at Jasper and the deputy.

"Something's not adding up," he said to them. "I don't need your authorities. I'm going to find out what it is myself."

Chapter 27

Lafayette, Virginia

Tuesday, July 15, 1975
2.:47 a.m.

Jasper awoke in the middle of the night to the sound of rustling and clattering – what he could only assume was someone loudly rummaging through the personal effects in his home office. With his loaded .22 in hand, he crept down the stairs. His eyes scanned about in the darkness, looking for signs of a break-in, and for only a moment he regretted that the Jenkins family was no longer present to take care of this for him.

As he approached his office, Jasper clocked the broken lock, which left the oak door wide open. The office light had been turned on. Whoever was in there wasn't trying to hide, and not only that – —they knew him intimately. The hairs on the back of his neck stood tall. It was one thing to deal with a simple burglar; another thing entirely to encounter someone looking into his life, his work, his secrets. But he would not allow himself to be the victim here.

"Come in, Jasper," a calm voice said inside his office. "Have a seat. We have a few things to discuss."

Hesitant, Jasper tried to recall the voice. The tone, calm and patient; the accent, not a hint of Southern in it.

Jasper entered his office, revolver raised, to see files strewn across the desk and drawers pulled out far out enough to buckle their hinges. Among them, comfortable in Jasper's chair, pointing with a mere screwdriver that had been used to break in, sat Ashley Dunning.

Jasper pointed the gun directly at his son's head. "You ungrateful nigga lover!" he spat. "How dare you break into *my* home and destroy *my* office. I should shoot you right here and now. Ain't nobody left to care if I did!" He gestured with the gun. "Get the fuck outta my chair, before I blow your fuckin' head off!"

Ashley casually left the chair while Jasper shuffled through the file folders, categorizing what had been exposed. He kept the revolver pointed at his son.

"The Navy was here lookin' for you a few years ago," Jasper said.

"You went AWOL and ruined your career. Over what? That black bitch? You stupid bastard!" He waved the gun at Ashley, who didn't move. "You're a deserter and a coward. They'll throw you in jail."

The quiet disgust and pure hatred in Ashley's gaze almost made Jasper freeze. He stared into Jasper's eyes past the gun and calmly said, "I am going to kill you for what you did to her."

"For what I did?" Jasper responded. "You should be thanking me, boy! I saved you the trouble of killing the bitch yourself." He grinned widely. "She wasn't pregnant with your child, you fool! She was having that no-account nigger Jackson's baby! He told me so himself – —how he'd gone over there while you were away and—"

Ashley leapt over the desk, knocking Jasper down before he could finish and wrestling the gun out of his hand. He straddled Jasper and unveiled a large serrated blade. When Jasper used his one free hand to cover his face and throat, Ashley sliced across the meat of his open palm. Jasper screamed as blood splattered and poured freely from the wound. Ashley snatched his father's wrist and turned it, covering Jasper's mouth with his own palm so that blood flowed into his throat.

As Jasper began to choke, Ashley leaned forward to whisper into his father's ear. "Your time has come."

"Jasper?" a frail voice called out from the hallway. "What's going on in there?"

Just in time, Ashley managed to hide his face from his mother.

Taking advantage of the distraction, Jasper pushed his legs against the desk and raised his hips to free himself from his son, who had already shifted his weight to make an escape. Jasper found his gun and fired two shots, one whizzing by right past Evelyn's head, the other embedding itself into the wall, narrowly missing Ashley as he pushed past his mother and bolted through the back door.

Less than half an hour later, Sheriff Clayton arrived to take a statement. Jasper had bandaged up his hand and Evelyn had taken medication for her headache and returned to her bedroom to rest. Clayton tried to get a peek at the files Jasper was still in the midst of reorganizing.

"As I said, it was probably some hobo," Jasper said. "Scared him away when I shot at him. Those are the bullet holes in the hall. You'd have better luck questioning the usual suspects in alleyways and the taverns near the railroad station, instead of looking over my shoulder."

"And Mrs. Dunning—"

"Mrs. Dunning didn't see what happened," Jasper said. "Nonetheless, it greatly disturbed her. She's resting now. It would be of no help to question her."

With that, Sheriff Clayton closed his notebook and stepped out to do as he was told, leaving Jasper Dunning to stew in the scene of his own victimization.

***

Sunday, July 27, 1975
4.:23 p.m.

The humidity, not one to take a Sunday break in a Virginia July, had only risen to its peak in the late afternoon. Sheriff Clayton sat in his office with the fan turned up to its highest as he waved a file near his face. The heat only irritated him beyond his frustration with the case.

This revenge murder case is over. That's what Jasper Dunning had said to him indifferently just a few hours ago. Several days had passed since the Dunning home was robbed, and just ten days since the murder of Don Stiles had marked the first of a series of brutal killings. Jasper had claimed nothing was missing from his home. Even so, Clayton had managed to spy a few papers bearing Weldon Michaels's name.

The pace of these crimes, along with the unusual interference from the City Council, made the sheriff question his own ability to police this small town. There was a connection missing here, he knew it – —and it had to be right in front of his face. He pulled out evidence packets and laid them out on his desk, before finally bringing out the envelope from his pocket. He turned it over to shake out and release the tags from a body recently burned in a horrific car fire.

DUNNING ASHLEY

The tags made a dull clanking sound as they hit the desk. A few small, black metal flakes spilled around them. The charred tags felt brittle in Clayton's rough hands. He gingerly rubbed the edges, not wanting to rub off any more of the seared metal. Placing everything onto a white handkerchief, he considered the rounded rectangular corners, the raised stamped letters. Somehow, they still felt warm. He took a whiff. Clayton had no formal training in forensic science, but he thought he smelled gasoline. Which wasn't a surprise, considering the cause of death. He just couldn't fight the feeling that Jasper Dunning had more to do with this fire than he would admit. This time, he knew, he'd gone too far.

A soft knock jolted Clayton out of his thoughts. "Excuse me, Sheriff," a deputy said, stepping in. "We got a call from the hospital about the burnt body over there. They want to know if they can go ahead and release it to the funeral house. Seems Mr. Dunning is a bit upset you put a hold on his son's body."

"Oh, go ahead and let the body go," Clayton said with a wave of his hand. He carefully folded the handkerchief over the blackened tags and returned them to the envelope. As an afterthought, before the deputy left, he raised his head and called him back. "And while you're at it, get an APB out on that Cleavon Jackson!"

Chapter 28

Los Angeles, California

Thursday, July 22, 2010
2.:47 a.m.

Waking from a fitful dream, Sabrina was startled by the sounds of rustling papers. Without giving it much thought or turning on any lights, she quickly grabbed Houston's baseball bat from its strategic spot in the corner behind the bedroom door. She crept through the hallway with the stem of the bat securely in her grasp. The apartment was shrouded in darkness save for a glow in the kitchen. She heard the refrigerator door close, and with that, she turned on the lights to reveal her husband sitting down to eat a bowl of cereal in the dark.

Houston coughed, trying to swallow down a spoonful of milk and cereal that traveled down the wrong pipe. When he fixed Sabrina with a guilty stare, she laughed, and then he laughed.

"What are you doing eating in the dark?" she said, kissing him as he wiped off.

"What are *you* gonna do with that bat?" Houston retorted. "Are you going to beat me in the dark?"

"No!" Sabrina put the bat down. "I was having a bad dream, that's all. The noise woke me up." She peered at him. "I heard some papers and file drawers. What was that all about?"

"I didn't realize I was being so loud," Houston said. "Sorry. I was just looking for my birth certificate and any records about my ... well, you know. Couldn't find anything."

"It's almost three. Were you able to get any sleep at all?"

Houston shook his head and pointed to the small, unopened shoebox on the table. "I guess I just wanted to have proof of my birth before I opened it. I'm still kind of ... you know ..." He sighed, staring into his cereal. "Those people died because of me, when you look at it. The ones in Lafayette. The children who went missing. My mom in childbirth, dying to have me."

Sabrina embraced her husband. "Honey, you know it wasn't your fault," she said softly. "You were a newborn baby. You were the most innocent of anyone in this. You, your mom, and perhaps even your dad were victims. Poor Florence – —who knows what she had to go through, escaping in the middle of the night with a newborn after learning her daughter had passed? I can't imagine having to deal with anything like that. I don't want to ..." Sabrina allowed her words and the subsequent quiet moment to linger as she continued to hold her husband. She then directed him to sit down. "I think you – —we – —owe it to your mother, Florence, and those lost children, to open the box and read what she left for you."

"You really believe there's a connection to those kids?"

"I'll just reserve my opinion on that until we see what evidence or connection we actually find. But we won't know until we look, *mi amor*."

"You're right," Houston agreed with a sigh. "It's just a box."

"I understand your hesitation," Sabrina said, as she sat next to him, massaging his shoulder. "It's not just a box. It's your family. It's you. It's seeing everything you don't know about whom you are. I know you've acted like it doesn't matter, but it could also hold the answers about your father. You've always wanted to know."

Houston nodded. "This little box could change everything."

"It doesn't have to change anything. It's just, you know ... answering questions. It won't change who you are. Who *we* are." She gave him a smile. "I'll still be here with you. We're still going to have this baby. It's just going to maybe be answer the questions you've always wanted to know."

Houston took a few deep breaths. Then, as if ripping off the bandage, he quickly removed the lid. Inside sat neatly placed photographs, cards, a baptismal record, graduation diplomas with small notes and letters, and more. His first reaction was to release the breath he'd been holding. His eyes stung with tears. He gathered himself.

"It looks like she kept everything," he said finally. He laughed to contain his emotions.

Sabrina kissed him and left his side to make tea, giving him a moment alone with the shoebox's contents. Houston, oblivious to Sabrina's movements through the kitchen, leafed through the pictures and letters of the life of Florence Jenkins. Eventually, Sabrina guided Houston to the couch and brought over two cups of tea and a blanket for herself to sleep while keeping him company, even as Houston stayed engrossed inwith the letter in his hands. He almost felt embarrassed reading it, as if he wasere watching a couple through a window. Several minutes passed before he put the letter down and noticed his wife's stare and registered the warmth of her body close to him. "I really, really appreciate you being here with me," he finally admitted. "It's not that I couldn't do this alone, I'm just glad I don't have to. You mean the world to me."

Sabrina smiled and settled in next to him, watching over his shoulder as he pored over Florence's keepsakes. As he thumbed through photographs, something caught Sabrina's eye. She pulled it out of the box. It was a photo of Leeland, Leesa, and Ashley standing together on what must have been a cold day. They wore long coats, ear muffs, and gloves. All of them appeared to be enjoying the caught moment, especially Ashley, who was all smiles with his arms wrapped around the two of them.

"What is it?"

"I'm not sure," Sabrina said. "But this just seems like one of those moments when you can see they all really loved each other and thought they'd be together forever. You know?"

"Not really."

"I'm not sure either, to tell the truth," she admitted. "It just looks like they wanted this moment to last forever. But for some reason, I find it eerie."

"You mean because they're all dead?"

"I guess so." She frowned. "Your aunt and uncle didn't say anything about what happened to Leeland."

Houston nodded. "My guess is, if Leeland was still alive, he would have found his mother or aunt, and I would have had him in my life." He pulled out a slip of paper from the box. "But I found his Naval death notice. Shot down in Vietnam."

"How did she get the notice?" Sabrina asked. "This looks like an original ship-to-ship communiqué."

"You know, that's been bugging me, too. The FBI was asking about him. You'd think they would have checked his naval records, right?"

"You'd be surprised at what things the FBI misses sometimes."

"But still, I wonder how she got it."

His questions hung in the air as Houston continued to sift through the borrowed memories of the woman who raised him. The handful of pictures of his family – —his grandfather and uncle in military uniform, Florence with the twins in childhood, a grown-up Leesa and Ashley together – — provided solace. He felt a kinship in the photos of family he never knew.

Before long, he noticed his right arm had fallen asleep, and he shrugged his shoulder to bring back the blood flow. He tried not to wake up his wife, who had fallen fast asleep with her head comfortably nestled between his chest and shoulder. It was now 4.:23 a.m. and he was starting to feel fatigued. Before, his mind hadn't allowed him to sleep, his world having been turned upside down and sideways. Now, the shoebox had calmed his anxiety and given him a sense of self.

Houston gingerly pulled his arm out from under Sabrina and wrapped it around her to draw her closer to him. She issued a sound of approval as Houston repositioned himself on the sofa so she could lay on his chest. He laid his head on the armrest and closed his eyes.

***

Later in the morning, Sabrina and Houston awoke to find a van outside on the curb. A satellite pole stood straight up on the roof of the van, but no one wasstood waiting around it. Sabrina snuck down the back steps to her car, though she wasn't all too worried – —it was Houston they were looking for. Houston, after she left, managed to escape in the car to pick up the rest of his things from the office.

Beverly greeted him at the front desk with a smile. "Good morning, Mr. Jenkins," she said, deferring from her usual first-name basis to a frosty reception. "Who are you here to see?"

Startled, Houston did a double-take. "I'm here ..." He trailed off, now noticing that the morning buzz of the lobby had lowered to a whisper. His former coworkers stopped, stared, and even gestured towards him to their colleagues. It was as if he had never worked there. Houston swallowed. "I'm just here to pick up the rest of my things. Can I go to my desk for it?"

"Your belongings are here," Beverly said. From behind the desk, she pulled up a milk crate containing his personal effects.

"Wow," he murmured. "I guess that's it, then."

Beverly glanced about before she leaned in. "I'm sorry, Houston. You never know when *you-know-who* could be listening."

Houston thought she meant Elizabeth Taylor-Barrings, until he realized it was Neil Watson she was nervous about – —the lead partner and the reason Houston was now unemployed.

"Oh," he returned with a whisper,. "I thought they were gone until Wednesday afternoon."

Beverly smiled, sympathetic. "Today is Thursday, honey. Are you sure you're all right?"

Houston slowly nodded. "Yeah ... That's right. I was occupied yesterday ..."

"It's easy to lose track of time when you're in FBI custody all day," she said.

"Wait—" Houston stammered. "How'd you know?"

"The FBI went through your desk. They had a warrant. That's why we've got all your stuff together – —Oscar gathered it all there for you."

"If it wasn't for me, Old Man Watson would've tossed it out," Oscar said from over Houston's shoulder. Houston nearly jumped out of his skin. "I *really* don't think he liked that Jefferson remark."

Houston turned to give Oscar a proper greeting – —they grasped hands and bumped chests. To get away from their colleagues' stares, Oscar led Houston into the office they once shared.

"So, what's the deal? What did you do to piss off the FBI?" Oscar asked him. "They were asking me about your dad, or if I'd ever seen you around some older black dude you were keeping secret."

Houston decided it was best to just get it out. He explained it all: the drunk driving charge, the FBI interrogation, the photos Ethel had shown him, the box Florence had left behind, even Florence's deathbed confession; everything but his potential links to the Lafayette Killer. Though the news could soon catch wind of it, if yesterday's news crew spread the information around, he felt it best to keep that part under wraps. When Houston got it all out, he realized just how much it was, and how much he had gone through in only one week. As Oscar listened and chimed in with his own comments and questions, Houston felt out of breath when it was all over.

"So you think this black dude you met at the funeral is your real father?" Oscar asked.

"That's what they think," Houston said. "Thing is, it might be someone else. There were photos of this white guy who grew up with my family. They all seemed so close. And the DNA connection labelled me as mixed race."

"Damn, homes!" Oscar exclaimed. "That's some crazy shit. You mean all this time I thought you were a hundred percent Mandingo and you turn out to be *man-gringo*!" He laughed until Houston seemed exasperated.

"Is that all you got out of my story?"

"C'mon. I was just tryin' to make you laugh. You look so sad, and this shit is fuckin' heavy." He grinned at Houston. "Now, I'll have to take your brother card."

Houston finally chuckled and rolled his eyes. Being upset in front of Oscar was useless.

"Too bad that old gringo is gone," Oscar added. "He'd have a field day with this shit. I didn't like the old bastard, but you have to admit, he was funny. If he heard you were let go after your sobriety test, Phil would've said it was white privilege – —they let your white half go, but they turned the blood in on your black half!"

"God, you're just like him!" Houston laughed.

They agreed to have lunch together in a couple weeks, once things settled down. As Houston headed back to the lobof weeks, once things settled down. As Houston headed back to the lobby, ready to grab his things and go, he was stopped by a few more colleagues who had questions about his situation. Michelle, a shy and attractive coworker, congratulated him on Sabrina's pregnancy. Oliver Cole, one of the firm's partners, managed to cut in and wrangle Houston towards his office. Houston was starting to get the feeling he was in a play about his life that was being written as he lived it.

"Just the man I wanted to see. Houston, why don't you come in and have a seat?" Oliver said. "Let's chew the fat. I don't think we've had an opportunity to talk much before."

Oliver was the kind of attorney most idealistic young law students hoped to become. He was an extraordinary litigator, supremely confident, remarkably fair, and generous with his time and advice. He also thought he was somewhat of a comedian. Although he adored his wife, he would always make jokes and comments about their relationship. His devotion to his wife and family were never questioned, but his sense of humor was somewhat sophomoric.

Oliver watched Houston glance at Michelle as she walked away. "You know, in another life, I think she could have been a siren and you would be Jason. Minus the Argonauts, of course," he said.

"Huh?"

Oliver didn't explain the reference as he ushered Houston into his office and told his secretary to hold all calls.

"So, congratulations, Sabrina's pregnant," he went on. "This is your first, right? Wow, I remember my first child. He's an attorney of some status in Sacramento now. He works in a corporate lobbying firm for the oil industry. I must've gone wrong somewhere. Anyway! How are you? How's Sabrina?"

"I'm fine. She's fine. We're fine," Houston responded, feeling a little defensive, his embarrassment lingering.

"Good. Good. And I see you've come to collect your things," Oliver said. "I think it's a shame they're letting you go. I understand you did good work bringing our system into the twenty-first century. I'm not sure you're going to be easy to replace. For god's sake, I hope he's not bringing in his nephew," he added as an afterthought. "You're, what ... almost forty? I suppose that makes you a late bloomer, eh?"

The barrage of questions left Houston with no time to answer any of them. Perhaps this was a lawyerly habit. He glanced about the office, looking for an excuse to leave, when his eyes landed on his own employment file, sitting on Oliver's large glass desk.

Oliver glanced at it, too, and opened it up. "I hope you don't mind, but I took the liberty of vouching for you to a few law offices I know could benefit from your work," he said. "I made some notes and wrote you a reference letter." He clipped the papers together and handed them over.

Houston immediately relaxed, and the dread dissolved from his chest. "Wow," he said. "I don't know what to say. Thank you, Mr. Cole." He leafed through the documents, grateful for Oliver's help. This would get him back on his feet in no time, he hoped. Things were looking up.

They exchanged more small pleasantries, accompanied by Oliver's rambling tangents and references Houston didn't grasp. Still, he felt much better having received a glowing recommendation from the firm's partner, even if Neil Watson had left a sour taste in his mouth. Houston was just about to dismiss himself when Oliver added, "Have you talked to Phil Cantoni?"

Houston paused. "Phil? No. Why?" he asked, taken aback. "I heard he's very ill, but ... I did want to check up on him. He just doesn't seem like he'd be receptive. Know what I mean?"

"As you know, Phil and I are friends," Oliver said. "And as you may not know, I'm also his attorney."

"I didn't think he needed one."

Oliver took a breath. "There's a lot more to Phil than meets the eye.

He comes off as a cranky old bastard, but he's very guarded. He prefers to keep his distance."

Houston nodded. "So how did you two become friends?"

"It has more to do with Elizabeth, actually."

"I always wondered why she put up with him," Houston laughed. "What happened?"

Oliver launched into the story. "Without going into too many details, there was a time when – —well, as you can see, Elizabeth is an attractive woman even now, but thirty years ago she would have made your head spin right off your shoulders. One night, she was working late – —not an attorney then, just a paralegal – —on a case for Neil, when his partner, Wilton Creed, took it upon himself to make ... let's say, *aggressive* unwanted advances. It just so happened that Phil was also working late and waiting on Elizabeth. They'd ride the bus home together. He checked up on her, and it's a good thing he did. Wilton was a large man, and Elizabeth's not a petite woman, but she's no match for a man his size. Now look at Phil, he's maybe five-ten, five-eleven, a hundred and nothin', but, man, was he wiry and fast. Liz said it was like he did some kind of jiujitsu and got himself on top of Wilton and put a knife to his throat."

"Oh my god," Houston breathed.

"To make a long story short, they called in security. Watson negotiated a deal with Liz and Phil to keep it all quiet. To protect the firm. Creed relinquished his position and retired to Idaho. He collects a percentage of his clientele that remained with the firm, but he doesn't practice law anymore."

"I would never imagine Phil would have the balls to do some shit like that," Houston said, incredulous. "Not to mention the ability. I mean, he can be an ornery cuss, but ready to throw down someone bigger than him?"

"Like I said, there's more to him than you think," Oliver said.

"So what about the two of you?"

"Let's see," he mused. "It was right around that incident with Creed. Liz brought Phil to me, back when I was in the DA's office for a couple of years and wanting something else. First thing Phil does is he sits down, stares at me, and says, 'You know, Jewish people are white until it serves their purpose to be Jewish.'"

Houston choked. "What? Really?"

"Yes!" Oliver laughed. "Then, I'll never forget it, he says, 'At the heart of every injustice is the preservation of privilege and hypocrisy.' Like some kind of poet."

"I can't even comprehend," Houston said. "So what did you say?"

"I asked him if he wanted me to be a Jewish lawyer or a white lawyer."

"And you still took him on as a client?"

"Of course I did," Oliver said. "Look, I could tell he was trying to measure me. You don't stick up for someone like he did for Liz and harbor those types of feelings."

Houston shook his head. "I must say, I never would have thought something like that would come out of Phil. I mean, his insights about injustice – —not the other thing."

"What can I say? We've been friends ever since," Oliver said. "I wouldn't say it was a conventional start, but after that, we always respected each other. But that actually brings me to why I called you in here."

Houston sat up straight in his chair, curious. He hadn't thought there was a point beyond Oliver's recommendation, so this came as news to him.

"You know, Phil was always fond of Sabrina," he went on. "And though he wouldn't tell you this in person, he was especially fond of you."

"I'm sorry, *what*?" Houston responded. "I knew he liked Sabrina, but I never would have guessed ..." He conceded. "Well, he was cool with me sometimes. Extra cool when it was just me and him. Sometimes, I'd catch him staring at me. He'd tell me to mind my business if I asked about it."

Oliver laughed, until he put on an air of seriousness. "Houston, I need to tell you – —Phil's condition is serious. He considered you a friend, and he didn't have many of those. I'm sure a visit from you would make his time much more tolerable." He scribbled down the address of a hospice residence.

"Damn, Mr. Cole," Houston remarked. "You can lay down a serious guilt trip. All right. I'll go see him."

Oliver patted Houston on the back as he left and told him to stop by next week. He let Houston go with the recommendation folder so he could collect his things from the front desk. Houston left Watson, Creed, Johnson & Cole assuming there would never be a need for him to return. He squeezed the milk crate of his belongings as his own way of saying goodbye.

Chapter 29

Los Angeles, California

Thursday, July 22, 2010
2.:25 p.m.

Pulling into his driveway, Houston noticed a different news van parked across the street from his apartment building. It wasn't from Cavalier Cable News – —it was from a local station and it had moved farther down the street in an attempt to seem inconspicuous. He assumed they weren't there for him. He parked his car at the curb and hurriedly carried the milk crate up the back stairs to his apartment. As he filled the teapot to make coffee, he looked out the kitchen window over the sink just in time to see the news van pull away. He sat down and put his feet up on the ottoman, shutting his eyes for a minute, as his coffee brewed.

"Houston, come here! Come on, Houston, Mama and I are waiting for you."

"Dad? Daddy! I'm coming!"

He runs with all his might to catch his parents as they walk ahead, just out of his reach. They are young and vibrant, holding each other's hands, smiling, madly in love.

"Come on, baby," his mother calls, holding her arms open, now waiting to take him up and smother him in loving kisses. Oh, how he longs to be held by his parents. His heart pounds as he picks up the pace, faster, faster, through trees and over bushes. They evade his grasp.

"Mama! Daddy! Please! Wait for me!"

"Come on, Houston," his father calls. "I need you to come see me. I've got something for you. It's something Mama wants me to give you. Hurry up now!"

Houston's father turns the corner and vanishes from sight. A crowd fills the spaces between the trees, and Houston desperately tries to push past them. His head spins. He runs through a park in the middle of town. He can see his mother's Afro and the outline of his father's shoulders as they turn the next corner. He cries out one more time.

A school bell rings and his pathway is clogged by teenagers in long skirts, belted slacks, dress shirts, cardigans. He makes one last attempt to reach his father, placing his hand on his shirt. The school bell never stops ringing. Houston's grip on the shirt is lost as a crowd of children of all ages cuts him off. His parents disappear from view.

Houston's heart sinks heavy and his breath grows ragged. He stops to catch it. The school bell keeps ringing. Tears stream down his face, blurring his vision. He keeps running.

In a graveyard, he sees his father's shirt, stuck on an unmarked gravestone, blowing in the wind. The school bell's ring rises, deafening, but he can hear a door opening. He reaches once more.

"Hello, you've reached the Jenkins residence." It's his own voice. Houston stops.

"You've caught us at a bad time. Leave a message and we'll think about calling you back."

"Hello, Mr. Jenkins. My name is Justin Glass;, I'm a reporter with the *Times*. I'd like to speak with you regarding information about—" The end of the voicemail cut off. Forced into consciousness,

Houston parsed his reality from his dream, but he could still feel the longing in his heart and knew the tears he dreamt were real. He wiped his face dry just as Sabrina entered the front door with the mail. He must have been staring at her like he'd seen a ghost, because she paused.

"Honey, are you all right?"

Sabrina comforted him, wrapping her arms around him. He pulled her close and nestled his face into her neck, breathing deeply and taking all of her in. He tried to explain the dream, but it faded from memory before he could tell her everything. The joy he'd felt, seeing and hearing his parents call out to him, yet moving farther and farther away no matter how hard he tried to catch up.

"A reporter," he said finally. "A reporter called. Left a message."

Sabrina nodded. "There's a news van parked out front. They've been knocking on doors trying to find you."

Houston's cell phone vibrated in his pocket, startling him. He answered it as Sabrina gave him space. Israel's name and face lit up Houston's phone screen.

"What's up, Iz?"

"Are you home?"

"Yeah, why?"

"Turn the TV on! Cavalier! Sanity's on. I'll call you back!"

"What?" Houston rubbed his eyes. "You know I don't like watchin' that stuff."

"You'll want to watch this! Just do it!"

Houston sighed and hung up the phone just as Israel did. As reluctant as he was to turn on a TV personality like Sin Sanity, he did as he was told when Sabrina reminded him that Cavalier was the news crew that had ambushed them. Sabrina returned to watch with him as the puffy, heavily made-up face of Sin Sanity filled the TV screen.

SIN SANITY: You're watching the Sin Sanity News Hour on Cavalier Cable News. I'm here with a special guest. The only name you need to know for conservative talk radio, Tush!

TUSH: Your conservative radio host from coast to coast!
The voice of conservative America!

SIN SANITY: Now, before we went to commercial, I mentioned a story about a string of murders committed in a small town in Virginia back in the summer of '75. All the victims were white: a nurse, two ambulance drivers, and a doctor. All pillars in the community. They were brutally hacked to death by what we now know is a black man, who has avoided detection for thirty-five years!

TUSH: Let me state for the record, it wouldn't surprise me to find out the FBI had this information and held onto it. Due to some fear of offending the *black* community by naming a *black* serial killer! It wasn't believed at the time that *blacks* were capable of such heinous crimes!

UNKNOWN: That's not exactly true, Mr. Tush. Actually, the FBI wasn't allowed to investigate, and one of the original deputies—

SIN SANITY: Hold it! Hold it right there. Let me introduce my next guest. A beat reporter in Virginia who was working at the time of these murders, and was actually the *fiancé* of the lone female victim, Dolores Peters. *Percy Hawkins!*

Hearing the name sent a chill up Houston's spine. Dolores Peters, yet again. "That was the nurse who brought the baby, *me*, to my grandmother. Isn't it? That's the name Aunt Ethel mentioned."

"I think it was the only name she could remember. Are you okay?" Sabrina asked, staring at him while he sat up straight, intensely watching the program.

"Yeah, I'm okay," he responded, not exactly sure he was. He frowned upon recognizing the guest as the reporter who had shoved microphones in his face. "That's that asshole from last night. That piece of shit."

"Honey ...," Sabrina chided.

SIN SANITY: So, tell us, Percy, what happened back then? Uh, oh, before I let Percy speak, I want to remind our viewers that Percy has been an employee of

Cavalier Cable News for, what, eight years now?

PERCY: Actually, Sin, I've been here for eleven."

SIN SANITY: Eleven years! Anyhow, go ahead. So there was your fiancée, Dolores Peters. She was the nurse. Correct?

PERCY: Yes, Sin. The victims were Dolores, Dr. Weldon Michaels, and, as you mentioned, two ambulance drivers, Gary Pierce and Don Stiles. Each of them were ... *sliced* across the femoral artery in their legs, then sliced from ear to ear across their throats. All except Dr. Michaels, who appeared to have been especially brutalized.

SIN SANITY: Mr. Hawkins, do we know the motive for the killings?

PERCY: From what I've recalled from the notes I took at the time, and from corroboration with the FBI, there doesn't appear to be a clear motive. It could be revenge, but they're not exactly sure what for. Back in '75, there were rumors of the death of a little black girl, too. But nothing ever came of it.

SIN SANITY: Do we know who the alleged murderer is? I mean, how was the FBI able to find out or track down this guy after all these years?

PERCY: Abel Grimes, who is now an assistant director of the FBI, was one of the original deputies on the first murder. He contacted me a few days ago and told me his findings. Apparently, Dr. Michaels was actually murdered in Virginia Beach, and there was some blood evidence found at the crime scene. No evidence was found at any of the other scenes. Deputy Grimes was able to keep that evidence and send it to the FBI. It was entered into a database that matches blood samples to possible family members.

TUSH: So the connection to the crime was not the actual murderer, but a blood relative?

PERCY: Yes. A local man, Houston Jenkins, was questioned by the FBI yesterday in connection with the crimes. Apparently, he was identified through mitochondrial DNA. That shows a definite connection to a male relative, most likely his father.

Houston and Sabrina sat motionless on the sofa. They stole looks at each other from time to time to gauge how the other was absorbing the news. Percy Hawkins continued to give a scattered background of the crimes and a brief history of the Lafayette City Council. Eventually, Tush interjected with a question.

TUSH: Mr. Hawkins, how do we know that Mr. Jenkins's father was a *black* man? Is it possible he could have been white or Hispanic? What evidence is there other than a *black* son?

SIN SANITY: Who were the suspects at the time? Any white suspects?

PERCY: You have to remember, this was 1975 – —roughly eight years since the landmark *Loving v. Virginia* case allowed legal marriage between a Negro and a white person in Virginia. This wasn't New York City.

SIN SANITY: So, you're saying that even though the court approved racial intermingling in 1967 in Virginia, there's still clear evidence that the races stuck to themselves, or their own kind?

PERCY: Exactly! There were few cases in Virginia that would prove otherwise.

SIN SANITY: So this case is significant. The usual profiling of serial killers shows they generally stick to their own race. And this is a *black* serial killer of *white* people. Isn't that correct?

PERCY: Look, there were two suspects: both of them black.
One was the father of a young girl who claimed that Stiles and Pierce molested his daughter. But there was never any arrest or evidence to prove that. And then there was, and I think the most likely suspect, a man named Cleavon Jackson, who was dating a young woman before he disappeared in 1970 after he went to fight in Vietnam. The young woman, Leesa Jenkins, actually worked in the house of the head of the City Council, Jasper Dunning. And he, Mr. Dunning, told me at the time that she was pregnant and Mr. Jackson was the father. Now, I don't know what may have transpired and why the woman disappeared, or if she was indeed the impetus for the crime. We can date her disappearance to 1970 – —right about the time Mr. Jackson left for Vietnam. Perhaps – —and this is just a theory – —perhaps, she left her son Houston Jenkins in a home or with relatives. When Cleavon Jackson returned from Vietnam, he couldn't find her, so he blamed these victims and senselessly murdered them. I know this may sound a little farfetched, but these murders occurred thirty-five years ago. The FBI is working on this as an active investigation. From what we're told, Mr. Houston Jenkins has no knowledge, or rather no admitted knowledge, of his father.

SIN SANITY: You have some tape from an interview you tried to conduct with Mr. Jenkins after his release yesterday. Is that cued up?

PERCY: I believe we have a snippet. But I must warn you, it was rather late at night, and Mr. Jenkins and his wife were both non-responsive.

The grainy video showed Houston and Sabrina walking towards their building, then cutting to their surprised expressions, then finally to them walking up the stairs to their unit with the sound of the door closing. In the vocals played over the tape, they could hear Percy Hawkins's questions about Cleavon Jackson and the murders, all of which went unanswered. The questions were obviously dubbed over the tape. Sin and Tush shot each other a look.

SIN SANITY: With that and more details to come about a *black* serial murderer discovered after thirty-five years,. wWill the dead ever get justice? Mr. Hawkins, you'll keep us informed on the investigation, won't you? More to come ... later.

The segment ended and cut to commercial. Sabrina turned the television off as Houston's cell phone started to ring. As he answered his cell, the home phone rang as well.

"No comment!" he heard Sabrina yell into the phone, before hanging up.

Houston put his cell phone to his ear. "How did you hear about this shit, Iz?"

"I'm at homegirl's place and she had it on."

"Well, what in the fuck am I supposed to do? Sabrina and I are trying to figure that out."

"Look dude, I'm sure you two will figure out something. You know I'm here for you for whatever you need."

"Yeah, I know. Thanks."

"Okay. You're gonna be all right. All right?"

Houston sighed. "Yeah. I've got no choice but to be."

"Cool. We'll talk later."

"You know what I think?" Sabrina said as Houston hung up the phone. "I think we should go through the rest of Florence's belongings."

Houston nodded. "I don't like seeing my life fucked over on the news. Let's do this."

As they ate dinner, Houston laid out everything in Florence's shoebox across the dining table. There were almost too many photographs to sort through: pictures of what he could only assume was himself as a toddler, with Florence, his aunt and uncle, and his cousins.

A mere two photographs, however, stood out to him. He set the rest aside and took a closer look. He recognized the home he'd grown up in. As a baby, he sat in the arms of a bearded young white man. He smiled into Houston's eyes. In the second photo, the same white man stood against a tree and held hands with baby Houston, who eyed the ice cream cone in his hand.

In every other photograph, Florence had diligently written the details.

Christmas with the cousins, 1973.
July 4 '82 with Mr. Walker, Houston,
and me. At the fair, September '79.

Yet for these two photos with the white man, no words were written on the back or sides; no indication of who they were of, or what year they were taken.

"Houston, your food's getting cold," Sabrina offered.

Houston glanced up at her. "Sorry. I know. I just want to make sure I go over everything. I can't let them continue to pull apart and attack my family history when I don't even know it myself. My mom is gone. I owe her this much."

Sabrina nodded. "We have the contact info for Cleavon Jackson. In the morning, I'll reach out to my contacts to see what we need to obtain his military history. They probably still have a record of his blood work that we could use for a DNA test."

"Don't you think the FBI would have already done that?"

"I don't put a lot of trust into FBI procedures. They should have pulled his records before they even contacted you;, but, as usual, they wanted to make a splash and have the headlines for tomorrow's paper. I'm sure that's how we got ambushed – —someone at the FBI leaked to that Hawkins guy. I can only guess who I suspect."

Houston grinned. "I love having you on my side," he said. "So, what else we got?"

"We have Florence's photographs and letters, and what Ethel and Milton told us. If it comes down to it, I'm sure they'll testify."

"Testify? You really think it's gonna come to that?"

"I was being premature," Sabrina admitted. "Got myself stuck in the case prep zone. But I can't promise we won't be in a courtroom, in front of a judge. By the way, you'll need a court order to get Mr. Jackson's records, unless you can get them from him directly."

Houston tucked into his cooling dinner. "I'll call him. I just want to have my head on straight before I do." He hung his head. "I don't want to be put in a hole like I was yesterday. Never again."

"Of course," she said. "We'll have to be careful with what we give Grimes. I'm not too convinced of his motives. I'll be doing some research myself on the case of those missing children, too. By the way, I forgot to tell you – —I looked up Lafayette County in Virginia. It doesn't exist anymore."

Houston nodded as he returned his attention to Florence's photographs. His copies of the Lafayette Killer crime-scene photographs and taunting messages sat alongside the shoebox. As he pored over it all, a note sticking out of a file caught his eye.

"How did it go, picking up your stuff?" Sabrina said, jolting him out of his daze. "Did they treat you like you'd never worked there?"

"They did!" Houston sighed. "Seriously funky. Except for Oscar, and Beverly, and Mr. Cole."

"What did Mr. Cole want?"

"He pulled me into his office to - —well, he gave me a recommendation letter, too, which was really nice of him," Houston said with a smile. "But he wanted to talk about Phil. I don't know if I told you, but he's really sick. He might be dying."

"Oh, no!" Sabrina cupped her hands over her mouth. "I'm so sorry to hear it."

Houston shrugged. "Hey, don't get me wrong. I like Phil. Like I was telling Mr. Cole, Phil and I were mostly cool. I think he didn't want people in the office to think he liked me, or something. But I think he mostly favored you."

Sabrina laughed. "Don't be silly. You know Phil likes you, and you like him. No matter how much you try to deny it."

"Yeah, okay. I just don't know why," Houston conceded. "Did Oliver say anything else?"

"I think he wanted to get someone else from the office to go see Phil," he said. "I doubt anyone else from the office has paid him a visit. And I know a few who definitely won't."

"Well, why don't we go see him? Where is he?"

"He's at Soylent Green Hospice. Where old folks go to die and nobody knows what happens to their bodies."

Sabrina wrinkled her nose. "Ew, Houston! Hey, that's not far. We should go."

"But what about the case we're building?" Houston objected.

"We've still got all this stuff to go over."

"Well, this stuff ain't going anywhere," she said. "But Phil is. We're going to go see him. Come on."

"Right now?"

"Yes, right now."

Houston acquiesced, quickly standing up from the dining table. The motion knocked a stack of photos and files onto the floor. They both stooped down to pick them up, though he tried to stop her, insisting she be more careful with her pregnancy. "Don't worry, I've got this."

Sabrina lingered, staring curiously at the mess on the floor. She fell silent, then headed down the hall. Figuring she was getting ready to leave, Houston cleaned up the mess and reorganized it all back to the way it had been before. Sabrina eventually returned with a worn greeting card and placed it on the table in front of him. The front read "'Good luck at your new job'." She opened the card, which contained a bevy of well wishes from Watson, Creed, Johnson & Cole.

"What's this?" Houston asked.

Sabrina only continued to shuffle things around until she found what she was looking for. She tugged out the Lafayette Killer's last taunting message to the FBI and set it next to the card.

"Okay," Houston said warily.

"What, you don't see it?"

She pointed to the message, which read *Death makes life precious*.

She then drew her finger across to the farewell note in her card: *Life is precious. – Phil*. After both messages were drawn the same symbols, the Dingir and the Ka.

Houston shook his head clear. "Couldn't that just be a coincidence?"

"They have the same handwriting," Sabrina insisted. "They're using the same hieroglyphs. The same phrase. I've seen prosecuting attorneys turn less than this into 'reasonable suspicion.'."

"You think ... ?" Houston stared at the two messages until they melded in his mind. He still had no idea what to do with this new information, even if it wasere true.

"I don't know," she said. "But I knew I'd seen those symbols before and couldn't place it at the time."

"It might be a big stretch," Houston admitted. "I know you've been working hard on your cases lately. And having all of this thrown at us is tough. But to jump to Phil having a connection to this case because of some words on a note he wrote to you is an FBI kind of leap, don't you think?"

Sabrina searched the table until she found two pictures. "How about these photos, then?" she said. "You, and the man under the tree. Doesn't he look a little like Phil? Those eyes, that crooked smile. And that other photo your aunt gave us. Do you see it?"

"Not really," Houston said with a head shake.

"I'm not saying it *is* Phil," Sabrina said. "Just that perhaps Phil may ... you know. He ..." She sighed, not wanting to say it. "Well, at least he can tell us where he got those symbols. Now *that's* too much of a coincidence. We're going to see him anyway. So ... ?"

Houston threw up his hands. "I guess we're going to see Phil," he said, a little exasperated. He grabbed the file and scooped up the two photographs. He placed the card in the file as they made their way down to the car.

It was a short trip to the hospice facility where Phil Cantoni was spending his final days. Houston checked the time to see it was now almost seven thirty7:30 p.m., and he wondered aloud about visiting hours. Sabrina jokingly reassured him., "Don't worry, we can say we're family!"

"Maybe you could pass as his family," Houston said. "There's no way they're going to look at me and think Phil and I are related."

Sabrina shrugged off his remark. On the drive, she brought up Lafayette County again. "As I said earlier, I did some research. Lafayette County doesn't exist anymore. It used to be between Norfolk and Virginia Beach. But it was divided, and Norfolk and Virginia Beach each absorbed half of it. If you went there now, there'd be no way to tell it ever existed. Even the graveyard was relocated."

"Any idea what happened to it?" he asked.

"The file didn't say too much, other than how it was divided. The report only said 'it was a benefit for the people of the county to be absorbed.'. There was little mention of anything else. Most likely the town was never incorporated."

"What year was it divided?"

Sabrina paused and went quiet. "1976," she said. A year after the murders.

As they approached the glass doors of the hospice care facility, Houston began to feel queasy, unsure if this was the right time to make this visit. Sabrina could sense the change in his demeanor and took his arm into hers. She pointed at the visiting schedule detailed on the pane:

Visiting hours
9.:00 a.m. to 8.:00 p.m.

"See? We made it just in time."

At the front desk, Sabrina asked for Phil Cantoni's room. Houston hung back, taking in the residence. He immediately thought of Florence. It had been less than a week since her funeral, and almost two weeks since her death. He remembered the smell of the antiseptic used in the hospital Florence had died in. He fought back a small regurgitation. He was so wrapped up in his thoughts that he didn't hear his wife's beckoning. He was a little out ofr sorts until Sabrina walked back to him.

"Are you all right?" she asked him. "Look. We can just turn around and go home if you aren't up to this."

He soldiered on. "No. I'm okay. I can do this."

Approaching the room, Sabrina knocked softly before she opened the door. A nurse was finishing her visit, adjusting the pillow under Phil's head for comfort. She turned and smiled as they walked into the dimly lit room, then to Phil as she announced, "Mr. Cantoni, you have more visitors. Such a pretty couple. Are you family?"

"No, no, we're coworkers. We used to work with him," Houston responded as if he wasere speaking to someone who didn't understand the words coming out of his mouth. The nurse nodded and removed herself from the room.

It was then that they could see how gaunt and gray Phil had become. Phil Cantoni presented a skeleton smile, despite wincing in pain. IV lines looped down from two bags of solution, plugged into withered, pale, spotted skin. Visible blue-green veins covered his delicate, bony arms that appeared as if they would break if you applied the slightest amount of pressure. A breathing tube surrounded his mouth, forcing oxygen into his nostrils.

"Oh, my god, Phil ...," Sabrina murmured, covering her mouth as she stepped closer to his side.

Phil looked to Sabrina and his face lit up. He reached out to hold her hand and spoke in soft whispers between labored breaths. "I didn't think

..." Hhe paused as he tried to summon up his strength. The head of the bed had been raised, but the nurse had reattached his morphine drip. She would come back into the room later and lay his bed flat. "Didn't think you'd come," he rushed out.

"Of course we'd come," Sabrina started to say, not really understanding the statement. "Phil, as soon as we learned ..."

"That's not what he means," Houston cut her off. "The nurse said more company, so that must mean someone else was here earlier. Was it Mr. Cole?" Houston asked, detached and distant. He did not want so much familiarity of death. Even now, he could relive Florence's last moments and the helplessness he'd felt in his inability to help her.

Phil nodded his head. They could all see that Houston kept his distance from Phil and held the FBI file close to his chest, in plain sight. He focused on Phil, looking for something. His head down, Houston held the stern demeanor of a man looking for answers.

Phil attempted to reposition himself in bed, an act that triggered another memory of Florence in Houston. Houston immediately softened and reached out to assist him. The look in Phil's eyes held something Houston had seen before: appreciation, love. Houston recognized the soft blue eyes that had given him that same look over thirty-five years ago.

"I asked Oliver to speak with you," Phil said. He was so tired and his speech came out labored. He seemed nervous and timid, not at all like the Phil that Houston was used to. "I don't know what he's told you."

Houston's recognition stopped time in his view. Memories he had convinced himself he'd forgotten now began to flood his head. The dream of the beach teetered between recollection and reality. He saw the wrinkles under Phil's eyes, and he recognized the years that had not been kind to him. He knew who Phil Cantoni was. What he didn't know was why. Houston wiped at a tear that had seeped from the corner of his eye and tried to keep a stern visage.

"He just mentioned I should visit with you and how fond you were of me. Of me and Sabrina," he added.

"Is that all?"

Houston nodded. "I'm really sorry about your illness."

Phil took a deep breath to gather his strength. Glancing at the FBI file in Houston's hands, then to Sabrina, finally to Houston, he managed to speak. "My real name is Ashley Dunning," he said. "I'm your father."

Tears had already welled up in Houston's eyes. He knew. Seeing him now, it was clear.

Ashley fell back into his pillow, breathing heavily. The morphine was kicking in, and he was struggling to stay conscious. Houston reached into the file and pulled out the photograph of the two of them when he was a child.

"This is you. Isn't it?"

Ashley nodded as he reached for the picture with renewed intent. He looked deep into Houston's eyes, searching for acceptance. Houston watched as Ashley ran his fingers over the images in the photograph, outlining them as if they were raised. Houston could palpably feel the loss his father had dealt with through the years, as if all of Ashley's lifelong emotions, turmoil, fears, and pain now transferred to him as he watched the depleted man relive a life he could never understand. Holding onto the photograph, Ashley squeezed it tight and held it to his chest. His breathing had become heavier and louder.

"I just have to ask ...," Houston began, finding it difficult to finish, as if afraid of what he would find. "Those murders ... Why?"

Ashley looked to his son with tears rolling down his cheeks. "I love you," he whispered, ragged. Houston kissed his forehead, dropping his own tears onto Ashley's furrowed brow. Ashley accepted the soft kiss with closed eyes. "I loved your mother. Leesa. With all my heart ..."

The silent room was suddenly filled with the whine of the flatline. Sabrina began to openly sob and raced to embrace her husband. She cried for his loss and her own. Phil, Ashley, had always been so caring and protective of her in his own way. And for the first time, she realized he knew who she was all along.

Houston held her and stared at the man he now knew to be his father. With a free hand, he adjusted the pillow under his father's head. The lights appeared to dim as the green flatline rolled across the screen, and the glaring beep followed its eerie glow. A nurse finally rushed into the room to mark the time of death, silent as she allowed the couple their time.

He had been unprepared for this moment, but accepted it with grace and strength. The loss of his mother had made him ready for the loss of the father he'd never known;, the father he'd never known had been with him for years, the man he had stared at almost every day. For a moment, it all seemed surreal. Houston wondered if he had dreamt all of this, but the warmth of his wife's tears on his chest confirmed it was real.

After an hour alone in the room, Houston told Sabrina it was time to leave. "We'd better go," he said. "I suppose I'm going to have to make funeral arrangements. And I'll have to see Mr. Cole in the morning —— I'm sure we have a lot to discuss."

They stopped by the nurses' station to leave their information and made an appointment to return the next day. They obtained the name of a funeral home from the facility and promised to make contact in the morning. As they headed out the door, the nurse pointed to a news van parked in front of the building. "They got here shortly after you," she said. "They've been sitting there waiting for you. They asked who you came to see, but we couldn't give them any information."

Houston exhaled, exhaustion catching up to him. After checking herself in the mirror, running her fingers through her hair and wiping away any last tear remnants, Sabrina grabbed Houston's arm. Towing him along, she plunged out the door directly towards the camera. She glared right at the reporter, then into the camera, before a question could be asked. "No comment!" she yelled. Holding Houston's arm, she briskly walked towards their car. They could hear the news team scrambling for frame shots, sound bites, anything. Questions were tossed.

"Mr. Jenkins, who were you here to see?"

"Have you heard from your father?"

"How does it feel to be the son of a serial killer?"

This last question made the hair on the back of Houston's neck rise. He stopped and turned, but Sabrina tightened her grip on him and pulled him towards her. "Honey, don't! Let's keep going."

Once in the car, Houston let his tears flow. Was it for the loss of a father he'd never known, or for the loss of what could have been? Was he feeling sorry for himself or for his father? Was it because he realized that for almost two years he'd shared a room with a somewhat disagreeable man he would develop concern for, despite his best efforts not to care? Was it that he'd ignored his gut feelings and chose not to look for the person underneath, the way his wife had? It could be all of them.

The news crew followed them to the car and filmed as he wept while his wife consoled him. Hearing the commotion of the camera and crew, Houston quickly started the engine and drove away. By the time they made it home, it was nearly eleven o'clock at night.

***

"Are you up to this?"

Houston hesitated before he admitted, "Probably not. But I know you think we should."

Sabrina handed over the open shoebox. They spent the night poring over photographs of Houston's family history. They laughed at haircuts and fashion *faux pas* of the period. They fell silent as they came across pictures of Ashley and Leesa. Sabrina couldn't help but comment on how happy they looked together. Houston's spirits lifted.

Underneath all the various keepsakes, Houston found a small sealed envelope with his name on it in Florence's handwriting. Among everything else, he hadn't seen it before. He showed Sabrina. She put everything else down and nodded to him.

Inside sat a few additional pictures of a young toddler, Houston, and his father. Captions told him what they were.

Houston's 3rd birthday.
Ashley and Houston at the park,
1972. Christmas, 1974.

Sandwiched within the photos was a note. Sabrina read over his shoulder quietly as he wiped away tears and took it all in.

Houston,

There are so many things I wish I had the strength to discuss with you. So many times I tried to start a conversation about your parents. But you would look at me with those big brown hopeful eyes and I knew the truth would hurt you. I am so sorry. I hope you can forgive me.

You are the son of Leesa and Ashley Dunning. Your grandfather, Jasper Dunning, was a vile and racist man, but very powerful in Lafayette County. He is the reason your mother was murdered and why your father decided to face him so long ago. It has been decades since I last heard from Ashley. My fear is that Jasper had him killed, too.

We left Lafayette the day you were born. I don't know how, but your father found us. He was so happy to see you. You filled his heart with such joy. How I wish he had never left to face Jasper. I wanted so badly for him to be a bigger part of your life. But he said he owed Jasper a reckoning for Leesa's sake. Your mother was such a sweet girl. I don't think I ever got over her death, and I am so sorry for those moments you saw me crying and I couldn't tell you why. Your Uncle Leeland is buried in Annapolis Naval Cemetery in Maryland. He, like his father, your grandfather Dillard, served with bravery and distinction, but paid the ultimate price for our country.

Houston, I am so sorry you have to learn about this after I'm gone. I wanted to tell you, I tried to tell you so many times, but I let time run out.

I'm so sorry. I love you so much. You have grown into such a fine and responsible man. I am so glad you have Sabrina in your life. Your parents would have loved her the way I do, and they would be so proud of you. I love you so much.

 Love, Mama

 Houston wept softly and tried to smile through his tears. "I guess in the back of my mind, as far back as I can remember, I always thought it was my fault I didn't have a father," he said. His voice broke. "That I did something wrong to make him go away or that I wasn't good enough. I would feel sorry for my mom, because I thought she was alone because of me. Never in a million years could I have guessed it would be something like this."

"Oh, sweetheart," Sabrina whispered.

"I wanted so bad to have a father, I didn't think about what it was doing to her."

Sabrina started to speak, but Houston kissed her silently. The moment carried their hearts to the future as Sabrina placed Houston's hand on her belly. Houston smiled.

"Now I'm going to be a father," he said. "I know I've said this before, but I promise to be the best father I can possibly be to our baby boy."

"A baby boy!" Sabrina agreed through tears of her own.

Houston pressed his head to her belly. "Did you hear that, little buddy? You're going to have the best daddy anyone's ever had! I promise!"

He leaned back into the pillows and sighed, pulling his wife into him. Sabrina allowed her weight to fall into his arms. Houston kissed the back of her head and closed his eyes, hoping to finally catch up to his parents in his dreams.

Chapter 30

Los Angeles, California

Friday, July 23, 2010
10.:35 a.m.

Houston managed to avoid news vans on his way to the office. As he stood in the cafeteria, regretting his purchase of a stale blueberry muffin and burnt coffee, a familiar voice called out to him from the cashier's line. "Houston!"

Oliver Cole was in the middle of paying for a pre-wrapped sandwich, a bag of chips, and a V-8. By the time Houston saw him, Oliver had already closed the distance between them. "Hope you're here to see me."

"I am," Houston said. "Phil ... I mean, Ashley. I don't know if you're aware, but he died last night. Sabrina and I spent a little time with him before he passed. He said you have some things for me?"

Mr. Cole met him with a pensive look. It appeared he hadn't received the call about Phil's passing, nor had he expected to learn about it in this way. His mind seemed to race as he responded, "I'm sorry for your loss. I have to go through his file now. I know there was something he—Yeah, go ahead and finish your meal and come see me after. I'll let Be-Be know I'm expecting you so you can come right in."

Houston wondered just how much Mr. Cole really knew about Phil's true identity, as well as his connection to Houston and the Lafayette murders. Yet through it all, he could tell there was a fondness Oliver held for Phil. Houston quickly swallowed the last of his coffee to wash down what was left of the muffin, tossed it all, and headed to the office.

Sitting on the small couch behind an antique wooden coffee table,

Houston waited for Oliver Cole to join him. On the coffee table were a few files strewn across the top and a small locked file box. Houston took his time to look around the office, hoping to calm his anxiety. The room had a great view of the city. He had never noticed how much construction was occurring just a few blocks away. His eyes made their way around the room, and he joked to himself that Oliver's wife had to have picked out the decor for this office.

"I know, the room doesn't really suit me. Does it?" Oliver asked, entering the room and startling Houston.

Realizing Mr. Cole had been watching him, Houston sheepishly tried to deny it. "I guess I thought you'd have more of a seventies look because of the way you ..." He stopped mid-sentence, realizing he might be saying something offensive.

"Because I dress like a corporate hippie?" Oliver laughed.

Houston, though embarrassed, was amazed at how effortlessly Mr. Cole had made him feel at ease. *No wonder, Sabrina thought he was such a good lawyer.*

Oliver offered to pour Houston a small drink to ease any lingering anxiety. Even though Houston refused, Oliver poured him one anyway. He brought two small glasses of twelve-year-old scotch to the table and smiled. "I don't like to drink alone," he said, as he handed Houston the glass. Taking a small sip, Houston could feel the warmth of the liquid dive into his body.

"Good! That should make you feel better!" Oliver exclaimed as he unlocked and opened the box. He took out some pictures and legal documents and laid them in front of Houston. Houston quickly perused them and noticed they were recently dated and notarized.

"What's this?"

"So, Phil, I mean Ashley ..." He paused. "Do you mind if we just refer to him as Ashley?"

"Sure. This is just so strange to me."

"I won't say I understand, but I can imagine how you feel. I've got to tell you, I've known him for almost thirty years and I never knew he had a secret identity. We would have philosophical and political conversations and he would blow me away with his insight and knowledge. I have to tell you, your dad was a very bright man." Oliver seemed to realize immediately that referring to Phil as Houston's father may have been shocking. Houston clocked his trepidation.

"I guess that's something I'm going to have to get used to," he said. "Will I have to take a blood test to be sure?"

"We can arrange that. We will need to see what the FBI has and match that up as well."

Houston was surprised that Oliver knew about the FBI, but then realized he and Ashley must have discussed it. "How long did you know that Phil, I mean Ashley, wasn't ... that he was really somebody else and that he could be my father? When did you find out?"

"Believe it or not, I learned at your mother's funeral. Well, your grandmother's, really," Oliver said. "At the gravesite, Phil approached me and asked me to be his attorney. I'm sorry, I said Phil, didn't I? I guess this is going to take some getting used to for the both of us. Anyway, he told me about his disease and that he didn't know how much longer he would last. He wanted to produce a last will and testament, and he had written a couple of letters to be delivered after his death."

Houston looked up. "Wait. He was at my mother's funeral? I know I saw you and some other people from the office there, but I don't remember seeing him," he said. "To tell you the truth, I don't know why, but it did bother me a little. You know, we worked together for almost two years, and I guess I thought it was just common courtesy. But that fit with his character, so I guess I shouldn't have been too surprised."

Silence fell over the room as Oliver allowed Houston to gather his thoughts and go on. "Then why would he go out of his way to aggravate me? It seems like he would get a hard-on, pissing me off sometimes."

"That, I wish I knew. Seems he got a hard-on pissing everybody off when the opportunity arose," Oliver chuckled. "But he took extraordinary pleasure in pissing off Neil. I think to the rest of us he did it just for fun, but I think Neil triggered something in him."

"I guess I wasn't the only one he would piss off," Houston said. "But he was funny about it, most of the time. He really got under Oscar's skin. I guess I could say he got on everyone's case but Sabrina's. He was always nice and reverent to her. Why? Because of me?"

"I have to be honest and admit I don't know the answer to that one.

Though he once admitted to me that she reminded him of someone. Thinking now, knowing what we know, she might have reminded him of his late wife, your mother."

Houston took another small sip of scotch. The warmth soothed and relaxed him. He wasn't used to having alcohol this early in the day, but under these circumstances he was glad to have it. Oliver took the time to get up from the small couch and poured himself another drink, then topped up Houston's glass.

"You know, Ashley wasn't a big drinker," Oliver said. "But he did

like this particular brand of scotch. He actually gave this to me as a Christmas gift a few years ago. It's a rare whiskey. Don't ask me how he came by it. But here it is."

He offered Houston several photographs and papers to look at. Houston immediately recognized a black-and-white picture that he'd seen Ashley looking over on the day he left the office. He could now recognize the people caught forever young on the celluloid paper: Florence, Leeland, Leesa, and Ashley, all smiling, all content to be together. Holding onto the picture and closing his eyes briefly, Houston decided he would go all in and find out everything he could.

"Please, tell me everything you know and even what you might suspect about my father."

Oliver nodded. "When he first started talking to me, I wanted to record him, but he wouldn't allow it. I don't know how much you know or are aware of. The FBI hauled you in and gave you their side of the story. They never suspected him, did they?"

"Not that I know of," Houston answered. "I mean, they said the murders were committed by my father. But they're sold on the idea my father is a black man, Cleavon—"

"Jackson! Cleavon Jackson," Oliver interrupted. "Oddly enough,

Cleavon Jackson was someone who dated your mother once. Ashley wanted me to see what I could find on him. He'd kept tabs. He seemed to pity the guy, because his own father used Cleavon to commit crimes when he was a child. He wanted to make sure that Mr. Jackson's life turned out okay. All I know about Cleavon Jackson is that he was given an honorable discharge from the Army in '74 after serving several years and ranking Sergeant. Then he basically disappeared. No trace of him anywhere. No arrest records or death notices. I guess that's why Ashley wanted to know if I could find him."

"Mr. Jackson came to the funeral," Houston told him. "I have no idea how he found out. But he was there. He even came by the office to see me. Should I give his information to you?"

"Yes, please do. We assumed he'd dropped off the grid. I'm sure the bad press he's receiving won't go unnoticed."

"What do you mean?"

Oliver tapped one of the files on the coffee table. "I have a full confession here from Ashley that he wants to go public. I saw how the press harassed you and Sabrina the other night, and I'm sure you've encountered other organizations calling or trying to get comments from you. I'm sure they're scouring records to find Mr. Jackson as well." He smiled. "But I'm sure he won't have a problem finding representation."

Houston nodded. "It's all pretty crazy. I've never been in the public eye before."

"Well, once one news org gets a special leak or a lead, the rest scramble to play catch-up," Oliver admitted. "They're also inundating the FBI for their lack of transparency. Before we sat down here, I called and spoke to Assistant Director Abel Grimes and told him I had a full confession. They can use their labs to do a handwriting analysis and confirm a DNA match. Grimes is flying back out here soon, and we'll have a press conference to reveal our conclusions. I'm sorry, Houston, but your engagement with the press may last just a little bit longer."

Houston shrugged. "I guess there's nothing I can do about that."

Oliver leaned forward in his chair, taking a more compassionate tack. "How are you taking in all of this?"

Houston sighed deeply. "Honestly, it's discombobulating," he said.

"I've got all these questions running through my head. I've been emotional the last few days – —hell, the last week or so, since my mom died. Pressure from the FBI, the news, and ... learning about my dad. And on top of all that, finding out I'm going to be a father!" He smiled a little. "You know, when we walked into his room yesterday, I had this strange feeling. It was like ... It was hard to explain. But, you know, I was at peace about it. Like I knew who he was. In those photos, the way he looked at me – —I've seen Phil, Ashley, look at me like that before."

"So you weren't completely shocked?"

"I wouldn't say I was shocked. Don't get me wrong, I wasn't sure, but ... I guess, with what you were saying about him, and the way he really felt about me, it seemed like I was in a movie, or *The Twilight Zone*."

Houston reached for his glass and took a deeper swallow of scotch as Oliver went into further detail of what Ashley had explained in his letter and intended to happen after his death. The letter explained that Ashley's motive was retaliation for the brutal death of his wife Leesa. Ashley had intended to kill his own father, Jasper, but once he came across a confession letter from Dr. Weldon Michaels, he believed justice would be better served if he used the confession to ruin his father and the City Council. It worked better than he had hoped. He sent an anonymous letter to the governor of Virginia and to the *Virginia Union Free Press*, the local newspaper in the state's capital of Richmond. It was at this time that the governor was considering a run for the Senate, but later it was revealed he had a small connection to the Lafayette City Council. The governor was forced to distance himself from the scandal and allow the attorney general, also mounting a run for governor, to use it, posing himself as a champion of the great state of Virginia. He set out on a campaign as a fair and civic-minded politician cleaning the state of the vestiges of the Klan and like organizations. Virginia disbanded Lafayette County and split it in two, distributing a half each to Virginia Beach and Norfolk.

Oliver patiently detailed Ashley's last will and testament. Hoping to be close to Houston as he was growing up, he'd purchased a small home near Ladera Park in the Ladera Heights part of Los Angeles. He left the house in a trust, naming Houston as the beneficiary, and left all assets and bank accounts to the same trust. Oliver then explained that there was a Cartwright living trust and that Houston was now the sole beneficiary. It had remained untouched for the last thirty-plus years without a beneficiary to claim it since Houston's grandmother, Evelyn Cartwright-Dunning, died of heart failure in 1976. Records showed that Jasper Dunning was never arrested nor indicted for any of his crimes, but he died penniless and in disgrace in the 1980s long after Elizabeth had kicked him out for good.

Houston sat motionless, allowing the history, the alcohol, and the room to swirl around him. He imagined this was what an out-of-body experience felt like. He could see himself with drink in hand as Oliver Cole laid out photographs and documents. Houston pictured his parents' faces in his dreams. He was finally catching up to them.

Eventually, Houston explained that he needed some air. Oliver agreed and suggested he call Sabrina to let her know what was going on. "If Sabrina is anything like my wife," he said, "she'll be in the lobby waiting for you."

Outside, Houston ordered a coffee and lunch. He called Sabrina to give her a rundown of everything Oliver had told him. He finished by telling her he wanted to ask Oliver to be his attorney.

"One day you'll admit I'm right about everything," she said with a chuckle. "I think it's a good idea to have him settle things for you. A natural fit. You won't find a better attorney."

"Not even you?"

"Don't be silly," she said. "I'll see you when you get home, all right?"

"Just as soon as I finish with Oliver. I promise," he said.

He returned to Oliver's office with a renewed determination to get through this and past it. He started to understand this would be an ongoing process that would probably take a while to undergo, but he knew he couldn't put it off. Now, as he processed all the new information, something was bugging him.

"There's one thing I don't understand," Houston said, sitting down. "You said my father faked his own death. Do you know how? I mean, did he use someone else's body or did he kill someone who had nothing to do with Leesa?"

"No, and I'm glad you asked," Oliver said. "This was one of the things Ashley regretted nearly as much as not being a complete part of your life."

"What do you mean? Why didn't he just make up an identity?"

"In the letter, he writes about how he became Phil Cantoni. I apologize, this gets ... difficult. After he finished off the doctor, his plan was to commit suicide. He knew his father would know he was behind it all, and he knew that his father would turn him in or, at the very least, use the information to control him. He didn't want to have to answer to his father. The rest is purely tragic happenstance."

"I don't understand," Houston responded, somewhat perturbed.

"He stopped at a bar just outside of Lafayette. He bought himself a bottle of scotch. He already had some pills. His plan was to get drunk and overdose, then drive his truck into Lafayette and crash it into the City Council Hall. He'd stashed a can of gasoline behind the passenger's seat to ignite a fire. So there he was, sitting in his truck, drinking. He'd already taken some pills. Then he started driving towards Lafayette. Thing is, he'd been training to be a Navy SEAL when he went AWOL looking for your mother. His training served him well. His body rejected everything he'd put in it, and he pulled over to throw up. It must have sobered him up enough to make him realize he needed another way."

"Okay. But, how did he get to be Phil Cantoni?" Houston asked.

"He gunned the car down a dark dirt road. At some point, he became distracted and swerved trying to pick something up from the floor of the car. The real Phil Cantoni, unfortunately, had been out walking his dog. Ashley accidentally killed him."

"Are you serious?"

"According to Ashley's statement."

"Did he kill the dog, too?"

"Unfortunately, yes," Oliver admitted. "Now, don't forget, he was
still somewhat inebriated, and he hit his own head on the steering wheel, so it seems he wasn't thinking clearly. He was only going to bury the bodies, but he decided to use them to fake his own death instead."

Houston ran a hand over his face. "That's fucked up. I can't believe he could do that. Use the death of an innocent person, that he caused, for his own benefit. Fuck."

"Look, Houston, I'm not here to justify what your father did. There's a reason he lived in secrecy all this time. And you're going to have to find a way to deal with it," Oliver said. "But allow me to present you with another perspective. Yes, he accidentally killed a man, and then used the corpse to escape his own life. And let's be frank, he did indeed murder four people. Heinously. Whether they deserved it or not will be a part of his final judgment. But what I can say is that he did those things to protect you and Florence. He believed, if Jasper knew you were still alive and living with Florence, he would have killed you. He knew that if he wasere caught, they would have found you and Florence and killed the two of you. No matter how you want to look at it, the potential deaths of you and Florence were key factors in his actions. However heinous and wrong they were. In his state of mind, he was protecting you."

Houston didn't know how to respond. He sat pensively, contemplating a response. "I don't know, Oliver. I know you're a good lawyer, and perhaps in a court of law—"

"Houston, his guilt or innocence is not in question here," Oliver interrupted. "We know for a fact that he is guilty. We have a signed confession. No one – —at least I'm not – —is condoning what he did, and I take it neither are you. But what you must do is clarify within yourself what you would have done – —if someone brutally murdered Sabrina and ripped your child out of her stomach, then threatened to kill the baby and anyone connected to it." He met Houston's eyes. "I don't think you or I could say, in that circumstance, and with the life he led up to that time, that we wouldn't have made a similar decision. Now, regretfully, the real Phil Cantoni suffered from a tragic accident. And let's not forget it was an accident. But we can't do anything about that now. All we can do is move forward with your family and preserve the Jenkins family legacy."

Houston remained silent, staring at the photographs and papers on the coffee table as he listened, and his stomach turned. "I see why you're such a good lawyer. Was that what you call a closing argument?"

Oliver smiled. "Thank you," he said. "In any case, regarding the Cantoni family, Ashley kept a copy of Phil's identification. We may have tracked down a family member. Phil's sister. It's a place to start."

Houston left his glass of scotch alone and attempted to wrap his head around what he was hearing. "I guess it is what it is," he eventually resolved. He took a deep breath. "One last thing. Are you able to be my lawyer through all of this? I don't want Sabrina going through anything like this while she's pregnant."

Oliver reached out to shake Houston's hand. "I would be glad to have you as a client. It's what your father would want. I'll just have to clear it with the partners, including Elizabeth. Avoiding conflict of interest. By the way, are you interested in being at the presser with Grimes?"

"Not really," Houston admitted. "He bugged me. I won't mind not seeing him or having anything to do with the FBI again."

"I understand," Oliver said. They stood, and he led Houston out of his office and into the lobby. "Take care of yourself, and we'll catch up in a few days."

Houston felt eyes on the back of his head, but this time he was fully aware and ignoring their whispers. He wasn't certain whether they were for the news about Ashley or the FBI intrusion. Either way, one or the other would be the result of Ashley.

***

Houston hurried home, glancing for lurking news vans before he ran up the back stairs and entered through the kitchen. Sabrina seemed to be feeling better since their call, having fixed herself something to eat and left the kitchen a mess. He heard the television in the bedroom and knocked before going in.

Sabrina lay sound asleep in bed. He smiled to himself and gingerly removed the remote from her grasp to turn the television off. She awoke almost instantly, excited to see him.

"You're home," she yawned. "I cooked. Ate almost all of it. But there should be enough for you, too."

Before she could get out of bed, Houston was upon her, kissing her and stroking her hair. Sabrina wrapped her arms around him, delighted, and Houston placed his hands on her belly. A moment later, he brightened.

"He moved!" he said with awe and pride. "He can sense me!"

"Of course he can," Sabrina sang. "He knows I'm happy. We both love you so much."

Houston basked in her presence for a long while, holding her, grateful for everything she provided for him. A life, a family, a home, a child. He could not have dreamt of something like this.

"Do you want to talk about it?" Sabrina asked finally, hesitant to spoil the mood.

Houston buried his head into her neck. "He wrote me a letter," he said, muffled. "I want to read it, but I don't think I'm ready yet. I'm not sure I'll ever be."

Sabrina kissed the top of his head. Houston slid himself down onto the floor, kneeling and placing his head in her lap. She stroked his neck.

"I'm sorry for pushing you to read Florence's letter," she said. "I shouldn't have done that. You'll know when it's time, and I'll be here when you're ready to talk about it."

Houston smiled and kissed her. "I know. I have no one better to go through this with. I love you."

Sabrina beamed. "I love you, too, *mi amor*."

Time passed fluidly, and before long it was dark. As Sabrina slept through the night, Houston wasn't ready for sleep. He cleaned the kitchen of the mess Sabrina had left. He ate some leftovers. He perused some photos of his family. He tried returning to bed, but could only lie in darkness, staring at the ceiling. Part of him felt so alone with his thoughts. So he stood, went to the dining room, and laid his father's letter open on the table.

He stared at it, unable and unwilling to move or start reading. He had learned so much about his family and his life in the last thirty-six hours – —so much that had been kept from him. He was still working on recalling memories he had long forgotten. How many times had he seen Florence crying in the middle of the day? At the time, he'd thought he had done something wrong or disappointed her. He tried to put together a profile of the man he knew his father was, the relationship he'd had with him.

Considering what he now knew, Houston didn't want to call up the name his father had stolen, in fear of aggravating the universe. He considered Ashley at most times an ornery man who actively pushed people away as if he had deadly secrets to hide. As it turned out, he did.

Houston knew it was time.

Dear Houston, my son,

It's strange for me to say that out loud as I'm writing this. I've wanted so badly to talk to you like a father. I miss every moment I wasn't able to spend with you.

I'm sure that, by now, you've learned more about me than you may have wanted. I did some very bad – —no, terrible – things in order to make myself feel better about the promise I broke to your mother. I killed people. Even though they deserved it, I shouldn't have been their judge and jury, let alone executioner. I didn't have that right. Even though I know this, I have no regrets for metering out the punishment they deserved for taking you and your mother away from me. I do regret the circumstances that led to the death of Mr. Cantoni, and me taking his identity. I became Phil Cantoni so no one would think to look for you and Florence. I know it probably doesn't make sense to you, but I did it so that I could somehow, some way, stay in your life. Even if it was just a small way. I began to realize how selfish a choice that was, but by then it was too late.

I made a promise to your mother, and I broke it. I promised her I would return in time to get her out of Lafayette before you were born. And I failed to keep that promise. I've relived my failure over and over in my mind. How different everything would have been. I was a fool, thinking I could make up a promise I had broken. I was a fool to think my father had any shred of decency. I failed Florence, Leeland, Leesa, and especially you. If you learn anything about the tragedy of my own making, please learn that promises should never be broken.

Houston, I do love you. I always have, and I am so very sorry, my son.

Your dad, Ashley Dunning

Houston pulled a tea light candle out of the cabinet. He placed it on the table, lit the candle, and turned off all of the lights. He arranged the photographs around the tea light and the letter in front of it. He sat in silence, watching the flame flicker and illuminate the room with a small glow. He watched the shadows dance along the walls. A tear rolled down his cheek. Houston closed his eyes and opened his heart, placing his spirit into the hands of the universe.

Chapter 31

Los Angeles, California

Sunday, August 8, 2010
2.:46 p.m.

At a small diner on Third and Gale, just outside of Beverly Hills, Houston calmly took a small sip from his cup of coffee. Across from him sat Cleavon Jackson. Cleavon had expressed the desire to meet, and Houston had somewhat reluctantly agreed – —before he would make the decision to reveal his whereabouts to the FBI. Learning about the relationship Cleavon shared with his family had given Houston pause, but it also gave him reason to bestow some faith and trust, albeit reluctantly.

"Thanks for coming, son," Cleavon said in his gravelly voice. "I wasn't sure you'd show up."

Houston allowed the errant remark to slide, but showed mild irritation. He remained quiet, letting Cleavon continue.

"I know you probably got a lotta questions 'bout me and your mama. I don't know everything you heard. But what I'mma tell you is God's honest truth." He fidgeted in his seat. "First, lemme say what I didn't get a chance to say at the funeral. Ms. Jenkins was always nice to me. She treated me like I was one o' her own when we was little. 'Specially after my dad died. I would cry in her arms and she would just hold and console me. My own mama had my lil' brothers and sisters to deal with. Ms. Jenkins helped me be strong for my family." He hesitated so Houston could absorb his story.

"I fell in love with your mama when we was lil" kids. I guess I was drawn to her. I honestly think she and I was meant to be. But I fucked that up. I got jealous of the way she was nice to everybody ... especially Ashley. Looking at it now, I know it was all my fault."

"What do you mean, all your fault?" Houston asked.

"I been readin' 'bout what's been goin' on with you in the paper, and from what I seen on the news, DNA testing showed Ashley was your daddy. But I shoulda been your daddy." Cleavon stared into Houston's eyes to see if his words had any effect. Houston returned Cleavon's visual inquiry with a pensive stare, picking up his mug to take a sip.

"What I mean is," Cleavon went on, "if I hadn't been so jealous of Ashley, I coulda taken Leesa away from Jasper and she would be alive today. I fucked things up with my jealousy. I know we coulda worked things out if I coulda had any patience."

Cleavon's admission prodded at Houston's heart. For a brief moment, he considered an alternate universe where he had grown up as a Jackson. As sudden empathy for Cleavon's loss found space in his heart, he softened his defensiveness towards Mr. Jackson.

"I'm sorry things didn't work out for you and my mom," Houston said. "But things didn't work out too good for anyone. All I've got now is a past I don't recognize and a future I need to embrace. Mr. Jackson, I know a little about what happened in Lafayette and I know about what happened to you. In some ways, we share connected tragedies. I'm not blaming you, and I don't think you should blame yourself. From what I can tell, Jasper Dunning and the institutions of that town were the catalyst for everything that happened. My only regret is that he didn't live to see me as a grown man. A testament to my family."

Cleavon stared deeper into Houston's eyes, as if he were measuring him. Then he looked around to see if anyone could be paying them any attention. He leaned closer to Houston over the counter.

"I killed him," he said.

Houston was unsure of what he'd just heard. So he let it slide until Cleavon said it again.

"I killed that sonnuva bitch myself." Cleavon admitted it with guarded pride. "I found him and I killed him. I put a pillow ova his head and didn't let go until he stopped kickin'."

"Wait a minute. The FBI said ..." Houston took a breath to return to calm. He quickly checked his periphery to see if he had caused any heads to turn. "The FBI said it was suicide, but ... *you* killed him?"

"You can't believe everything the FBI says," Cleavon responded.

"After I left the Army, I moved back to Lafayette into my daddy's house. My family had moved out a long time ago and it was all boarded up. But I was fixin' it. I was there when them murders was happening. I wasn't sure about why, until Sheriff Clayton arrested me. Oh, he lemme go after Jasper closed the 'vestigation. And he was pissed! He was yellin' and stompin' all around. He told me Jasper was up to somethin'. I didn't know what he meant until almost a year later, when I read the story in the paper. A state purveyor came tellin' me my home was being redistricted to Roanoke, and I'd hafta go over to the Roanoke courthouse to file ownership papers for taxes. Otherwise they was gonna take my home away from me."

He paused, feeling the frustration of nearly losing his childhood home. Houston read the anguish written across the man's forehead. "After reading 'bout the connections to the City Council and what they printed 'bout Dr. Michaels, I looked and looked to see if they ever had anything 'bout them poor little black kids. It didn't surprise me – —the paper acted like it didn't happen. Not one word was eva mentioned 'bout it. So I sent some letters to the FBI with some details. I neva heard anything back. So I went lookin' for Jasper myself." Cleavon paused to drink some of the coffee he had ignored. "I guess this musta been around 1979 or so. Your grandmama had already kicked him out a while before she died. That was another life Jasper Dunning ruined.

"It took me a couple o' years, because all his friends acted like they neva knew him. I don't blame 'em. They was scared. I don't think they got ova the killings being so close to 'em.

"I found him livin' in secret in a small black part of Hertford. I couldn't believe it. This sunnova bitch was hidin' amongst black folk —— the people he hated the most. So I take my time and plan everythin'. I creep ova there late one night. He try to act like he didn't recognize me at first. I almost bought it 'til I saw the gun in his hand."

"A gun?. Did he shoot at you?" Houston asked.

"No. He was a pitiful old man, just fulla piss, a coward. Just holdin' the gun for show. I don't think he even knew how to use it. Afta I took it from him, he started beggin' and tryin' to convince me he'd saved me from a childhood of misery. I was thinkin' 'bout jus' walkin' away, 'til he started talkin' 'bout Leesa. He started lyin' 'bout her, claimin' she got pregnant to get Ashley's money. I knew he was just sayin' stuff to piss me off and weasel outta me doin' anythin' to him.

"But, I wasn't there for Leesa. Ashley took care of that." Cleavon raised his head, staring blankly at Houston. "I was there for them kids. I know Jasper keeps files. I forced him to show me, if he wanted to live. Once I got 'em, he tried to tell me I knew what I was doin' all along. That I was to blame for them children. Can you believe that? Here's this old racist white bastard, who probably had somethin' to do with my daddy dyin', who *definitely* had somethin' to do with Ms. Evelyn dyin'. Who had your mama killed and tried to kill you!" Cleavon paused, abating his anger. "He was still tryin' to convince me it was my fault them kids was never goin' home. I got so angry. I hit him as hard as I could. He just lay there on the ground, not movin'. So I took one of his pillows and held it ova his face. He kicked just a bit. Then it was over."

Cleavon looked away from Houston, through the window and out into the street, as if he didn't want to see the look of shame Houston might give him. Houston remained silent, absorbing a lifetime of leftover frustration and pain Mr. Jackson had just shared. After an uncomfortable silence, Cleavon spoke again.

"I know he was your grandaddy, by blood," he said. "But he was no good. He was no good to anybody 'cept himself. I don't think anybody missed him. It took almost two weeks before they found his body. It was a cold snap in North Carolina, jus before summer hit that year. I guess the cold kept him from stinkin'."

Cleavon drained the last mouthful of his cold coffee. He got up to purchase another cup. "You want one?"

"Uh, no. No, thank you. Go ahead," Houston responded, his head spinning. He gazed out of the window into the slow late-afternoon traffic, pushing away the evil that was his grandfather. He thought about the missing children and what was left to do to bring their souls peace. It felt like so much pressure.

Cleavon returned to the table, and Houston immediately started to speak. "You know, the FBI is probably still looking for you. Director Grimes said he was trying to make you a priority when we talked. But that was when they thought you were my father. Since then ..."

Houston's words were interrupted by a sullen thud as Cleavon placed a large manilla envelope in the center of their table.

"What? What's this?"

"Look, Houston,. I know you coulda gave me up to the FBI when they had you or afta you got my information. I appreciate, like you said, you wantin' to talk to me first," Cleavon said. "Personally, I don't think the FBI was really lookin' all that hard for me. And to tell you the truth, I'd ratha they still not find me. Take this."

"What is it?"

"It's the information Jasper had on them kids. I can't remember all the names, or exactly how many. I didn't look through it, 'cause ..." Mr. Jackson's gravelly voice appeared to falter as he wiped his eyes with the back of his hand. "I don't wanna have no more nightmares. I finally got free of them dreams, until just before Ms. Jenkins died. It was why I went lookin' for her. I got there too late. I wanted to see her again, afta all these years. I wanted to tell her I was sorry. I wanted to tell her I killed Jasper. I wasn't gonna say nothin' to you, but I knew I had to. But I thought I saw a ghost. I thought it was Jasper, coming to get me, take me down the grave with Florence and Leesa. But I realize now –—it was Ashley. I didn't know he was still alive. He looked just like his daddy."

Houston pushed the envelope aside as if he wasere afraid to touch it. "What do you want me to do with this?"

"I was hopin' you'd give it to the newspaper," he said. "So they can bring closure to those kids' families, clear their names. I wouldn't give it to the FBI. They'd probably just keep it quiet."

"Why don't you do it? You can send it to them as easily as I could. Anonymously, if you have to."

"I figured, since you been in the news, and the way the FBI messed up lookin' to blame me ... if you gave 'em the information, they'd do somethin' 'bout it. Besides, the longer I can't be found by the FBI, the betta." He pushed the envelope closer to Houston." "I know what kind of man Ms. Jenkins raised. I know you want to help them kids' souls get peace. I hate to put this on you, but I got no one else I know who would understan'. Just you."

Houston forlornly took hold of the envelope. He'd begun to accept Mr. Jackson's reasoning. After everything he'd been through in discovering his family's history, this was yet one more thing to do to reconcile the past. He knew that it was his final duty to make things right – —to clear the sins of the Dunning family and the county of Lafayette from his blood. It had to be him.

Epilogue

Los Angeles, California

Saturday, May 19, 2012
10.:13 a.m.

It's a beautiful Spring morning. It's also moving day for the Jenkins household. Paid workers gather up boxes of clothes, dishes, and knick-knacks while padding plastic bubble wrap around furniture. Houston Jenkins bounces his baby boy Dillard on his knee in the last unpacked chair. He stares out of the window as Sabrina directs the movers, before she hurries back into the apartment.

Dillard is vibrant and curious, playing with his father's cell phone. He's a healthy boy, gurgling slobber as he gnaws at the plastic casing. His curly black hair contrasts beautifully with his light cinnamon-brown eyes, long eyelashes, and warm cherubic cheeks. Houston wrangles the phone away from him and snaps a selfie, then confides, "Don't tell your mom or sister. This is a secret between just the men in the family." He hands the phone back to his eager son. The moment he places the phone back into those chubby grasping fingers, it rings with a jazz melody and Houston has to take it away again.

"What up, Iz? I thought you and Patricia were coming to help."

"Don't worry. I'm waiting for her to get back from the store so we
can leave. Can you believe she wants to buy two car seats?"

"Well, yeah, man. I've got two kids. What, you think you can just take one?"

"How about none?" Israel remarks. "She can put the seats in *her* car. I can't be ridin' round with two kids in my car. I don't care how adorable they are. And for the record, they are adorable. Are you sure they're yours, nigga?'

"Tell me again why I should have them call you uncle."

"Because I'll be the best thing that'll happen to them. Besides Sabrina."

"No doubt," Houston laughs. "What time is she coming back? We need you guys to take the twins so I can help Sabrina with the movers."

"We'll be there in a bit. Don't worry. I know you're just sittin' there with Dillard. Doris must be with Sabrina gettin' boob time. And before you comment, I can hear *only* Dillard in the background."

"Yeah, she likes to feed them separately. She'll be out to get him in a bit. Then I get to take some father-daughter selfies with my little angel."

"Damn, you sound pathetic."

"Never thought I could be this happy," Houston says warmly. "My kids are great. Doris will be the bossy one between the two. She likes to take toys away from him. Dillard has a real gentle spirit, and boy, does he love to laugh. It's a trip watching how curious they are. It makes me wonder what I was like as a child."

"You were a little pain in the ass. And it's a good thing they look like their mother," Israel chuckles. "So, you're finished now with the court shit? That was yesterday, right?"

"Yeah, we settled with the Cantoni family," Houston responds.

"They're getting the house in Ladera and all of my dad's direct assets as Phil Cantoni. I think they're gonna put the house up for sale."

"Yeah, I would, too. Who wants to own a house a serial killer lived in? Sorry, dude."

"Nah, I know what you mean. I wouldn't want it, either."

"So yesterday's judgment said what?"

"That they couldn't touch the Cartwright trust," Houston explains. "It was separate. Plus, Ashley hadn't benefitted from it at the time."

"How much is in the trust?"

"Jasper nearly drained it, but since it's been growing over the last thirty-five years or so, it's got close to twelve million."

"And this is after the crash in '08? Fuck, what would it have been if the crash didn't happen?"

"I don't know, and I'm not worried about it."

"I bet old man Dunning had no idea that a black man would be benefitting from it."

Houston laughs. ""Right ..." When Dillard grabs at the phone,

Houston coos at him, offering to let him say hello to Izzy. In a few moments, Sabrina comes bounding into the room, adjusting her top and reaching for Dillard.

"Hi, sweetheart! How's *mi hijo*?" she purrs. "Do you mind, sweetheart?"

"Wait, where's my angel?" Houston responds in earnest. "I thought we were doing a fair exchange."

"She fell asleep, so I just laid her down. I know Patricia will be here in a little bit and I want to spend some time with him before she tries to *kidnap them*! You hear that, Israel? I'm on to you two!" she yells into the phone.

Houston stays on the line as Sabrina takes Dillard and asks Houston to oversee the movers.

"Hey, what ever happened with the families of those kids?" Izzy asks.

"I don't know," Houston answers. "It took them a long time to verify the information I gave them. But once they checked it out, they did a good job with the story. It put pressure on the FBI to tell the truth."

"So the FBI's helping?"

"As far as I know. I got a call from that FBI director, saying he could charge me for lying about Mr. Jackson. But Mr. Cole tore into his ass and they dropped it. I got invited to attend some of the funerals, but I turned them down. I don't think I deserve to be there – —since it was my father's father who did all that shit."

"Damn! You got some fucked-up family history."

"But what can I do about it?" Houston sighs. "You know, I'll just let the universe decide what to do about that."

"Fuck the universe. The devil chooses your relatives."

"Then God's a sonnuva bitch."

"Are you two still on the phone?" Sabrina interrupts. "Honey, did you check on the movers yet? Please, sweetheart."

"I'll head outside in a minute. I'm checking on them from here."

"So, after all this shit, your black-and-white ass comes out smellin'?" Izzy comments.

"Maybe it's because I'm actually Saint Malo."

"Hah! You are a lotta shit, but Saint Malo ain't one of them."

"Yeah, but I could be!"

"No! Not you. Sabrina might be after all of this. But I'll be damned if your swirl-ass is Saint Malo!"

"Yeah, fuck you," Houston responds.

"Houston! What are the movers doing? Are you watching them?" Sabrina calls out from the hallway.

"White-ish! You better run, son."

Houston peers out the window and watches his sofa and television being lifted onto the moving truck with care. He sits for a moment in pensive thought, recalling the week that changed his life forever – —two years ago now. He reaches into his wallet and pulls out an old picture that was in Ashley's keepsake lockbox. It's a small black-and-white photograph of his mother Leesa and her twin brother Leeland. He sets it down next to the picture of his own twins, Dillard and Doris. He combs over both photos, looking for similarities. He recognizes the large oval eyes, the curves of their cheeks highlighting the deep dimples tucked into all four of their chubby smiles.

A soft breeze blows through the window. Houston closes his eyes and concentrates on the sounds of the movers. He can discern two languages calling back and forth and boots climbing the stairs. Houston breathes a sigh of relief and embraces the two photographs: two generations of the Jenkins family, worlds apart, together again.

I promise to do the best I can for my family, for my y beautiful wife Sabrina, my adorable children Dillard and Doris, for Aunt Ethel and Uncle Milton, Inez and Roberto, even Izzy and Patricia. I promise to do my best for those who expect and deserve the best of me.

THE END